MW00534008

MISSING YOU,
MISSING ME

Tylor Paige

Copyright © 2018 by Tylor Paige

Missing You, Missing Me

ISBN: 978-1-7329108-1-2

All rights reserved.

No part of this book may be reproduced in any form or by any electronic or mechanical means, including information storage and retrieval systems, without written permission from the author, except for the use of brief quotations in a book review.

Nickolas, I followed my dreams because of you. I can't wait to spend a lifetime helping you follow yours.

Chapter One

ATTENTION

*T*he van pulled up containing our rival band, Cruel Distraction. Once the van parked, three men filed out the back. I didn't see him. Where was he? The anticipation was killing me. I heard another door shut and he appeared from the other side, tossing keys to one of his bandmates. My heart began to race.

Ethan Andrews; twenty-two years old, tall, slender but toned, and drop-dead gorgeous. His dark hair was buzzed on the sides, while the top was left longer, leaving it to flop to the side. He was about twenty feet away, but I could clearly see the bright blue of his eyes. His face was still as perfect as I remembered. I watched him pull out a cigarette, light it quickly and inhale. He didn't even look my way. I wasn't sure why, but it felt like a slap in my face. He was still angry. Couldn't really blame him.

We haven't seen each other in almost three years. The last time we were this close, he was begging me to stay with him, and instead I ran. Literally.

I stood next to the tour bus they would be sharing for the

summer with my band. I took a deep breathe and repeated in my head, "You are the loud and proud frontman of the alternative rock group Maria Maria." I had to keep reminding myself. I needed the courage to get through today. "You are confident, sexy, and successful," I repeated over and over. I was so nervous about today I was becoming self-conscious. I promised myself I would be cool. I hadn't seen or spoken to him in almost three years,, since that night.

Reflexively I rubbed my neck. I could trace the exact lines of the beautiful script there. I glanced back at him and my nerves went haywire. There, right on his own neck, was the tattoo that matched mine. I had his name, and he had mine.

"Cleo! You coming? I want a drink." I turned towards Derek, our bassist. He was the goofball of the group. His soft blue eyes paired well with his scruffy blond hair. He, along with Mark and Adrian, were my best friends since elementary school. We grew up in the same neighborhood our whole lives. We had seen each other through everything, and now we were standing here, back in Chicago, co-headlining a tour with one of the biggest bands right now. Once again, we would be competing for top billing.

That was the whole theme for the tour. We would be "battling it out" every night for the crown and title. Many of the posters and merchandise for the tour had mine and Ethan's faces blown up and glaring at each other while our bands played in the background. It actually looked kind of cool. All of it was really cheesy, but it sold tickets.

That's actually how our bands met. However, both of our groups had achieved success, so our fights would now be a lot more friendlier, or were supposed to be anyway. Ethan's apparent cold shoulder made me start to regret agreeing to the tour.

I glanced back at the band who was hugging my friends and

unloading their equipment. All the bands touring were meeting here and, of course, Ethan and his crew had to be the last to arrive. He always had to make a show of things. I turned away, quickly following Derek inside the club to start getting ready.

Many of the stage crew smiled and greeted me kindly. I remembered a few of them from the last time we had been here. I signed a woman's crew shirt for her son. We walked over to the back of the club and ordered a few beers to take the edge off. I was nervous about this show. We chatted with the bartender, patiently waiting our soundcheck. Cruel Distraction got to go first.

I heard their drummer fiddling with his drums just as Adrian said "Dude, we need to see this."

Mark and Derek sat down, and Adrian pulled up a seat. I smiled and scurried onto his lap.

When we were seventeen Adrian and I dated for about a year. With his mess of curly hair, he kept bleach blond, smooth caramel skin, and soft brown eyes, he wasn't bad on the eyes. Unfortunately, it didn't work out.

One weekend when we didn't have a show, he came over unexpectedly, looking guilty. I was sitting at my grandmother's old piano when he took a seat next to me and abruptly dumped me, for a guy.

He was the first boy to break my heart. My first love. Looking back now, he was the best boy to do it. He did it gently and so lovingly that we were still best friends even now, four years later.

It was odd. I had seen hundreds of other groups play over the years. Seen countless hot guys around, either on stage or in the crowd. I even went on dates with a few of them. But even after all this time, Ethan Andrews was still one of the sexiest men I had ever seen.

Ethan was someone else on stage. I watched as he adjusted

his jacket and then his tight jeans. I moved my gaze to his arms and then his chest. He had nothing under the jacket, leaving plenty of skin exposed. He was covered with tattoos. I noticed that he was more toned than he had been before. Although his body was still slim, he was rocking a solid six-pack. His forearms were thicker than I remembered too. I forced my attention back to his tattoos. I tried to ignore the ink on his neck. The one that matched mine. My stomach fluttered. His pale skin contrasted with his jet black hair and dark clothes. Memories washed over me with such force; it was hard to think about anything else.

To this day I still wondered why he never covered the tattoo up or tried to hide it. We had always told each other we'd keep our relationship private. No one had to know. However, once he started his tour, which included interviews and photoshoots, the rumor mills began turning. I can't tell you how many times I was asked to move my hair or if we were secretly dating. I had to laugh. I was so stupid, I thought to myself for the millionth time.

Ethan took the microphone off the stand and began pacing around the stage as his band fiddled with their instruments. I glanced at the other members. They were all attractive, but nothing close to Ethan. Finally, their drummer counted down and, with a scream, they started their sound check.

Cruel Distraction was good. No, not good. Great. I was honored to be co-headlining with them. Granted at first, I was hesitant in joining the tour, for obvious reasons, but we couldn't exactly say no. We were both under contract with the same label. They tell us what to do. Plus, if I did fight the decision, then I would be overruled, and all of the guys would think I was ridiculous and tease me relentlessly. This tour was big for us. It was selfish of me not to want to do this.

I cringed remembering the last night Ethan and I had seen each other. It was not my finest hour. I had dreaded going back to the real world, but I couldn't stay there. I felt smothered. He wanted more than I was willing to give. At the time, leaving was the simpler choice. I couldn't admit to myself what I felt for Ethan.

When I got back to my band, I tried to sneak in and lay down with the guys, but I woke them up. Derek noticed my neck first. Mostly because I usually had my hair tied up, so it was weird that it was down. I had covered it back up after seeing it the first time with Ethan. I was too afraid to look at it. I knew it was permanent, but I was still hoping it would disappear. Hell, I didn't even remember getting it done. We were doing shots in his hotel room, I wanted to end things. I had met someone, and he had proposed. The last thing I could recall is Ethan pulling me out into the hallway, promising me just one last night of fun. Well, he sure delivered.

Despite trying my hardest not to cry, I couldn't help it. I broke down and told them some of what had happened that night; I didn't remember much. They were shocked, considering I was openly dating someone else. They never judged me though.

After much resistance, the four of us crowded into the little motel bathroom to get a good look at it. The room fell deathly silent when they saw the fancy scrawl under my right ear. Ethan.

"Holy shit," Adrian whispered. The tears that I had managed to put on pause erupted again and there was no consoling me. All I could think was how much of an idiot I was. I cried all day and almost all night. I thought about calling him, but I couldn't. I was too embarrassed. He was probably pissed. I was such a train wreck. Everything I did just made things worse. I should have just left, instead of sneaking off one last time.

I told my friends I never wanted to talk about it again after that night. So, with that in mind, I sucked it up and signed the contracts to do this tour.

My mind went back to the stage, and I watched in awe as Ethan took on an entirely different persona. Offstage he was always very serious, always moody. From what I had remembered, anyway. On stage he was still dark, but the way he moved his hips and had that sexy smile made me feel things I had no name for. When Ethan Andrews walked onto that stage he morphed from the shy boy with the adorable smile to the sexy, fearless flirt who could do things the offstage Ethan would never do.

The music started, and he began to sing. His voice was deep and smooth. I recognized the song immediately. It was a song about having sex with strangers. I raised my eyebrows, shocked and irritated. I knew he picked it on purpose. We made eye contact a few times. I didn't smile back. When he put his mic stand between his legs and rode it slowly, looking dead at me, I could feel myself blush all over. I didn't even hear the words he was singing anymore, all I could focus on was his eyes.

The first song ended and the second was a slower one I was also familiar with. He dragged a stool from the side and sat down, one leg on the floor the other on one of the pegs. His face morphed from the seductive bad boy to a deeply sexy, brooding man. He looked up, right at us again. Seconds later our eyes locked. I gasped and squirmed in Adrian's lap.

He leaned down and nipped my ear with his teeth. "He's watching you," he whispered. I ignored him, keeping my eyes on Ethan. He squinted and shook his head as he continued singing. When the song ended, he stood up and kicked his stool back swiftly, it flew back with a clunk. Turning to face his band, he was back to the original Ethan Andrews stage personality from before. Only now he was purposely not looking our way. He looked angry. His jaw was tense and his eyes hard.

They ended their sound check a few minutes later. We all stood up and hurried to the stage. There were lots of pats on the back, handshakes, and small talk. Spencer, Christian, and Seth all looked just as I remembered. I looked around for Ethan, but he was already gone.

I chatted with Christian for a bit. He leaned in and whispered, "So are you going to go talk to him?" I followed his gaze to where Ethan had hurried off to.

"I don't know what to say," I shrugged, giving him a half-hearted smile. So, they did know. I figured as much but the confirmation stung a little. I was always an ostrich with my head in the sand. I pushed the dark thoughts away as we moved to start our own soundcheck. I went to the microphone stand and fiddled with it. I looked out into the empty room. It was huge. Tonight was a sold-out show. I closed my eyes and relished in the feeling. This is what we have been waiting for since we picked up instruments so long ago. I started to warm up my voice before we got our cues.

I heard heavy steps behind me. The rest of the band had followed me into position. I grinned wide at Adrian, Derek, and Mark. Mark was an awesome drummer. Even when he wasn't behind his instrument, he was pounding on things with his hands, pencils, or chopsticks. It drove us nuts, but we would no doubt miss it if it were gone. Mark was tall and scrawny. He kept his blond hair dyed jet black usually, with it short in the back and longer in the front. His eyes were gray behind thick glasses. Light freckles covered his face, but you couldn't see them unless you were close.

He moved to sit at the drum kit. "Are we playing?" He shouted out, picking up a pair of sticks and clicking them together impatiently. Suddenly the lights started flashing, and I saw a spotlight move to me. Adrian grabbed his guitar while Derek picked up his bass to start warming up.

After a minute I turned to face the invisible crowd. The crew gave us our cue and Mark banged his sticks together to count down and at three we came to life. I let my thick hair fall in front of my face as I banged my head back and forth. I smiled, and my entire mood changed. I went from feeling a little stiff from the drive to energized and ready for the summer ahead of us.

I leaned down and danced across the stage, singing the lyrics to our biggest hit 'Broken Record'. We sounded amazing. Seamlessly we moved into our second song, 'Not Me'. It was a slower song, but that's what they wanted for sound checks. One fast-paced and then a slower song. I was growing excited just being on the stage, even with no audience.

It had always been easy for me to perform in front of people. I didn't have the shy gene. It never bothered me. There wasn't much time to be shy when you had a family as big as mine. I was the youngest of six kids. My siblings were all significantly older than me. My brother Ben was the second youngest, and he was 15 when I was born. Living in a small house with seven other people, it was never quiet. I think it helped me to deal with a life like this, constant chaos with never a private moment.

Finally, I dropped to the floor and threw my hands up in exasperation. I was in blue jeans and a black hoodie. My massive mess of hair falling everywhere was not helping. The guys finished and then erupted into fits of laughter. I ripped my sweater off and threw it as far away from me as I could. Leaving me in one of the guys' undershirts and my jeans. We thanked the crew and took off quickly to let the other bands do their sound checks. The hall was filled with laughter and happy chatter of things to come. The energy was palpable.

I paused in my walk when I noticed Ethan staring hard at me from across the room, arms crossed over his chest, and one of his legs was raised, leaning against a beam. He was standing behind some amps. The rest of his group was around him staring at their phones and talking to crew members. His hard gaze made my mood falter. His face looked made of stone, making me unable to judge any emotion.

I looked away quickly and grabbed onto Adrian's shoulders to jump onto his back. He grabbed my legs, and I directed him forward to the tables where a few boxes of pizza were waiting for us. I took a slice of mushroom and pepperoni while we discussed our set list. Our conversation was light. I forced myself not to look his way. I refused to give him a second look if he was going to keep glaring at me.

We moved the party back towards our bus so the other bands could have some space and finish getting ready for tonight. I overheard Mark and Derek talking to our bus mates about a pre-party on the bus until the show. The three members that were around heartedly agreed and hurried inside with us.

After finishing my makeup and putting on my clothes for the show, I went back out to the common area. It was a wild mess. I saw both bands that would inhabit the bus this summer and members from some of the openers. Why weren't they trashing their own bus?

Mark turned the stereo up and then began passing around shot glasses. He grabbed my bottle of tequila and I lunged over Christian to snatch it back. "Hey, that's mine!" I shouted and took a swig before passing it around. We all laughed as I sunk down onto the couch next to Derek to relax. Looking around, I realized that one person was missing.

It was killing me to know, but Adrian finally asked "Hey where's your buddy? He too good for us?" He was practically lying on Seth. I tried not to be interested, but I instantly perked up to hear the answer.

Spencer shrugged. "He was pouting today. I don't know. He gets like this sometimes." I wondered how much Ethan had told them about us.

They probably thought I was a horrible person. Even I could admit that I did Ethan wrong. Every time I thought back to that night instant guilt would wash over me. Why hadn't I stayed or tried to talk to him and figure out what had happened? I slammed the door on that idea when I ran. I was awful for what I did. Glancing at his bandmates told me that they had similar opinions about me. I couldn't help but notice the dirty looks they gave me when they didn't think I was looking.

The group started to move on to talk about some movie that was coming out. Drunk Adrian wasn't finished speaking. He leaned over Derek. "I saw him looking at you, Cleo. Go find him. Cheer him up before the show!" He winked at me. My friends started hooting and hollering. I threw the closest pillow at him, and that just made them laugh more. I felt my face get hot.

"Oh, come on! It's not like this is the first time you have to work with someone you've…" he started, but Derek punched him in the gut, making him double over and shut up. I felt my entire body blush. The bus got much quieter in an instant. I quickly stood up and started towards the front. I didn't want to wait to hear one of them say anything else.

This only excited the men more. I flipped them my middle finger as I reached the door, but paused when I heard Adrian's voice again. "We used to be together. Cleo and I. She was good, real good. But I told her, 'Babe, this horse, me, I'm a horse. I can't be tied down at seventeen, you see,' So I had to let her go." I turned around, my anger rising. That was not how it went down.

"Really Adrian? So, you guys breaking up had nothing to do with you being gay?" Derek said. The room was dead silent waiting for Adrian's drunken response.

"Well yeah, that too," he laughed and the room roared. I sighed and headed out the door as Adrian tried to explain that he wasn't entirely gay, but bisexual. He liked everyone, and everyone liked him.

When the cold night air hit me, only then did I remember how cold Chicago could get. I was wearing black shorts and a tight black tank top. I completed the look with white suspenders, fishnet tights, and my black converse. On stage it gets hot, I would be sweating within minutes, but out here it was pretty chilly. I shivered. His voice came out of the darkness causing me to jump.

"Cold?" I paused and looked around. His voice sounded close. I heard the rustle of his vest before I saw him. My eyes were still adjusting to the dark.

A moment later I was looking straight into Ethan Andrews deep blue eyes. Now I was never into blue eyes, but man did he make me into them. Even before we had gotten together, I had always found him cute. We played shows together for almost two years before we... I shook my head, pushing the memories away.

Up close his face was even more gorgeous than I remembered. His nose was perfectly straight, his jaw and chin strong. I noticed that he had pierced his nose and lip. There was a thin, silver hoop over his nostril. Moving lower I paused at his perfect, kissable lips, and that hair. I loved his hair. He took off his black jean jacket and handed it to me. I noticed he had put a black shirt on under it.

I took it and put it on quickly. It was surprisingly warm. "Thanks. I forgot how windy Chicago is." He smirked and raised his eyebrow. We stood in uncomfortable silence.

"You ready for the show?" He asked me. It sounded so forced.

"Yeah, I guess. Ready to get it started. The waiting is the worst. There's nothing to do," I shrugged and pointed back to the bus that was almost rocking. I groaned, praying that nothing of mine was getting broken. He looked at the bus and extended his hand. I took it. He was already leading me away before he closed his hand on mine.

My stomach was a wreck. This could go either good or bad. We didn't walk far. We stopped in front his bands' van, and he dropped my hand. Pulling the keys out he unlocked it and opened the back. He motioned for me to get in. I hesitated, not feeling entirely comfortable with this.

He sighed, rolling his eyes. "I won't bite. I just want to talk and there's nowhere to go where people won't be eavesdropping," he said. That made sense. I climbed inside.

The inside of their van looked similar to ours, heavily lived in. They had been playing almost as long as we had. He got in after me and closed the door. I sat down on the first bench, my back on the wall. He sat down next to me but scooted over towards the door. The tension was palpable. Neither of us wanted to be here, but I think we both knew we had to talk. Might as well get it out of the way.

Along with the shirt he threw on, he was also wearing thick black eyeliner now, which only made him hotter. I pulled my legs up onto the seat and wrapped my arms around them. I would wait for him to speak first. His body was stiff, he glanced at me and realized I wasn't going to talk.

"So, how have you been?" he finally asked, his voice heavy with pep and sarcasm.

"Fine. You?" I said tightly.

He scoffed. "Just dandy." Silence followed. Honestly, I didn't know where to start. I jumped when he suddenly slapped his palms on his thighs and gave me the fakest smile I have ever seen. "Well, now that we have finally talked we can enjoy the rest of this summer together without everyone asking about it," he said and put his hand on the door handle.

In a panic I opened my mouth and said, "Wait," He turned back to me, eyebrows raised. "Do you hate me?" I blurted out. It took him by surprise; his jaw tightened again.

"I don't know. Kind of. Why? Do you hate me?" He asked, his eyes curious.

"No. I just, I'm sorry. It was a dick move," I said lamely. His eyes rolled.

"That's the understatement of the year," he smirked. I glared at him. He relaxed into his seat, stretching his legs. Silence returned.

"You didn't want to do this," I finally said. His hands were resting behind his head. He turned and looked at me.

"No, no I didn't." With a sigh, I shifted my body, putting my legs on the floor. I wasn't sure what I had been expecting. He sat up straight and turned towards me. He looked irritated.

"Don't make me the bad guy. I know you didn't want to either," he accused, his eyes turning icy.

"Because I knew you'd act like this!" I protested.

"Like what? You dumped me! You broke my heart and left me with this!" His finger jutted to his tattoo. I noticed the muscles in his neck were tense. I flinched. He saw it and calmed himself down. His body was tense and he turned to look forward, refusing to look my way.

"Did you expect me to forget? I couldn't move on as fast as you could," he spat.

"You have no idea what you're talking about," I said, crossing my arms. I could feel my eyes beginning to water.

"You're right. I have no clue. Because you left. You left me sitting in a hotel broken, alone and with a permanent reminder of you." I stood up and took a step closer to him.

"I was scared!" I shouted back at him. He pulled back and looked up at me in surprise. His anger slipped off his face and turned into pain. I sat back down and glared at him.

"And you think I wasn't? Cleo, I had never felt like that. I was in love with you," he said, no longer yelling. My stomach flipped again. I stared at him, his eyes were torturous. I had to look away. I caused that look on his face. Guilt flooded me.

"I'm sorry Ethan," I said lamely. He shook his head and turned his back to me.

"Nothing to be sorry for. I had my chance; you made your choice," he told me. I clenched my jaw to keep my mouth shut. It wasn't what he thought. Not anymore anyway.

"I don't want to spend the entire summer fighting. We have to share a bus and stage. I screwed you. Big time. I get it. I remember it every single day," I told him, moving my hair to show him my matching tattoo. His eyes flicked briefly to it then back to my face. "We need to be professional. I'm not saying we have to be best friends, but we can't be like this," I motioned to the air between us. I stopped talking, and he nodded.

"You're right. I just needed to get it out of my system," he said, giving me a half-hearted smile. I smiled back and put my hand on his. He looked down at it as I squeezed it. He squeezed it back.

"We should probably head out there," he murmured pulling away and opening the door quickly. We stepped out and he locked up before turning back to me. I offered my hand and he took it. We walked back together. His hand was warm and calloused from playing guitar. A spark of memory flashed across my mind. The first time I saw him play.

Back then he also played the guitar for shows along with vocals. I was backstage waiting for my bands turn on the stage. He happened to turn his head and saw me watching him. He smiled as he sang into his microphone. I was sixteen.

Memories flooded over me. Fighting, flirting, our first kiss, the first time we…

"Was it bad? After the magazine cover?" I asked suddenly. He looked down at me and raised an eyebrow. God, he was so cute.

My mind quickly shot to the painful event right after our break up. It had all started with Polygraph Magazine's February issue. He had mentioned he was going to be in it and surprise surprise, Ethan had made the cover. He had his face to the side, with my name written very clearly on him. I got a phone call from our manager before I could open to the page where his interview was on. Sam was furious that I hadn't told him. He wanted to know everything and figure out if we needed to do damage control. I figured if Ethan had said anything bad about me, I probably deserved it. But he hadn't. I had memorized the words. He only said:

"She broke my heart, and I'm still working through things. I wish her the best."

Within hours everyone was calling Sam trying to get information. Some offered large amounts of money for just a statement or photos. It was nuts.

Since we were signed to the same label, the bigwigs had wanted us to cash in on this, make some music together, do a video or something. But Sam talked them out of it, for the time being. That didn't stop them from trying. Hence the current tour. But I think everyone thought enough time had passed that we'd be okay seeing each other.

Ethan squeezed my hand tighter, bringing me back to him. "Yeah, it was. It sucked." My heart sank. I knew the answer but hearing it from his mouth made it real. He dropped my hand, and I felt his body tense next to mine.

"So, you really married him," he said solemnly. My eyes started to fill with tears. I nodded.

"Yeah. I did."

The media painted me as a slut who had moved on too quickly. Ethan was the miserable, lovesick fool, while I was the whore who got married to some stranger. People told me that I was a life ruiner and that both men were way out of my league. I received hate mail and photos of me with nasty words painted over my face. It was awful, but I couldn't help but feel like I deserved it.

"How did he react, by the way? I mean, he still married you, so he must not have been that mad," Ethan asked. I frowned, I didn't like to think about it.

"He was confused and a little upset. He doesn't often get emotional." I had to give him credit. He took it all pretty well, swearing a few times. Then he asked me if it was over, which I told him it was. Eventually, he calmed down and asked me to get it removed. I said I would, but I kept putting it off. I just wore my hair down most of the time.

"I told him that I understood if he wanted to break up, but he said he still wanted to marry me. So, we went to one of those 24-hour chapels in Vegas and did it," I said. He raised his eyebrows slightly but then frowned.

"I remember seeing the picture. What's his name?" His voice was cold and distant.

"Christopher," I said, barely above a whisper. The pain returned thinking about the last time I saw him.

"He sounds like he really loves you," he replied flatly. I didn't say anything else. Maybe, once upon a time. Somewhere along the line things changed. He wasn't the man I thought I had married.

"So where do we go from here?" He asked.

"I don't know. Can we be friends?" I asked him, and he turned to look at me. We were almost to the bus.

"I'd like that," he smiled down at me. That smile was beautiful. My stomach flipped. Why, after all this time, did he still do this to me?

"I like the hair, by the way. Pink suits you," he added. I tugged self-consciously at my long cotton candy locks.

"Thanks. I brought enough dye with me to last the entire tour." He laughed and I couldn't help but relax again.

I dyed my hair a week or so before the tour. I had been moping around Derek's apartment for weeks. They finally got me up and forced me to shower and go outside.

"Enough of this sad girl shit. This is not the Cleo we remember. You're in a rock band! Act like it!" Derek said. Adrian and Mark agreed.

While we were at the drug store picking up black hair dye for Mark and other various toiletries we would need for the tour, Adrian picked up a box of hair dye. He waved it at me playfully. He raised his eyebrows up and down. "What do you say? You wanna go full beauty school dropout?" I thought about it and decided, screw it. Why not? We spent the rest of the afternoon in Derek's bathroom dying my dark head pink. Oddly enough, it did make me feel like the old Cleo.

I looked back at Ethan who was smiling softly. His shoulders loosened. He was finally relaxing. The bus door swung open and the group of loud men fell out laughing and yelling at each other. Damn them. I guarantee my tequila is gone. Sure enough as I moved aside to let them climb out, Adrian let out a high pitched Mexican grito, "AYE AYE AYE!" and then hurled the empty bottle across the parking lot, shattering it.

"Oh, come on!" I groaned. I had just gotten that bottle.

"Show's gonna start soon," Ethan whispered. I looked up at him. He leaned down and kissed me quickly on my neck. Right on his name. I almost leaped out of my skin it was so unexpected. I looked around, and thankfully everyone was too excited and drunk to have seen us. I stood there with my mouth open. He turned back to me and winked. He was grinning ear to ear. I shivered and I wasn't cold. I placed my fingers on the skin his lips had briefly touched. What was that?

I followed everyone, my arms around myself, inhaling his scent off his vest. Oh, he smelled so good. I realized that it was the same scent from when we dated. It only took a few seconds for me to catch up with them and just a slight push to get Adrian on the ground. I remembered my bottle of tequila. I stepped over him while he pretended to be hurt. "Aw man, help! Guys help!" He called, but my fellow band mates had been through this routine, so they just kept on with their conversation.

"Where's the little girl?" I demanded as I dropped my body onto him. His eyes widened with realization of what I was doing. It was a long-standing joke. We've all been trapped once or twice over the years. I do believe he was the last one to get me, so this was definitely owed to him.

The air rushed out of him, but he just kept calling for help. "Where's the little girl Adrian?" I asked again as I began to tickle him mercilessly.

"Oh, come on! No, stop, please!" He struggled to say as he wiggled under me and tried to breathe.

"What do you owe me, Adrian?" I continued, pausing to hear him. He groaned and mumbled. "What was that? I didn't hear you. Do you know where the little girl is?" His eyes widened, and he shook his head furiously.

"No, no. I owe you a new bottle. I'll get some tonight, swear!" I smiled and called to the other guys.

"Hey, have you guys seen the little girl?"

Mark and Derek with grins, said in unison "No, where is she?" I plunged my hands into Adrian's sides, tickling him until he cried, tears streaming down his cheeks. "There she is!" We all shouted as everyone erupted in laughter.

I stood up, letting Adrian breathe. He moved slowly but got onto his feet grumbling about losing his buzz while holding his sides. I shook the dirt off of me and smiled at the group. My eyes found Ethan's briefly, but he hurried inside ahead of everyone. The rest of his band followed him into the building.

We could hear one of the opening bands playing already, so we knew it was almost our time. The wind passed through me making me shiver. I wrapped Ethan's jacket tighter around me catching another whiff of him. I couldn't get enough of it.

We stopped at the doors. Mark and Derek wanted one more cigarette. It was just the four of us. We made small talk about the tour while they smoked. Adrian asked if I was nervous. I smirked and Derek wrapped an arm around my shoulders.

"We are going to rock this joint!" Derek shouted, squeezing me tightly. One by one they flicked their cigarettes onto the ground and stomped them out. We all cheered and fist bumped.

That was the closest we would get to a sappy moment, and we all knew it, so we went inside before it got weird.

The last opening band was on stage now. I felt someone behind me. Turning, I saw Ethan grinning at me. "Have you been brushing up on your acting skills?"

Chapter Two

PUNKS DON'T DANCE

*W*hen we were signaled to head to the stage, I
turned to him. "Let's get this over with so we can
crush you," I said in a growl. He tried to stay angry, but we both
burst into laughter. We gave each other one last look before
walking onto the stage together.

The crowd began to cheer and scream when they saw us. I
stalked over to the microphone. I went to grab it when Ethan
came up and took it right from my hands. I gasped but then
quickly crossed my arms, glaring daggers at him. He smirked at
me. He was good at this.

"Hello everyone! We want to play fair at this battle of the
bands. We were nominated to come out and flip to see who gets
to play last. So, get over here Barbie," he said to me. I almost
lost it, breaking character when he leaned over and pulled on
one of my ponytails. I ripped the microphone from his hands.
He looked taken back.

"Alright, alright. Ethan can make his jokes, but let's see if he
can really perform," I looked him up and down slowly, starting
from his feet. When I reached his eyes, he was blushing. Ha, I
got him back. It took everything in me not to start laughing. He

took the mic back and rolled his eyes big enough for them to see.

"Okay. Let's flip this coin so we can get this party started. Plus someone might need some extra time to practice," Ethan said and flipped the coin. He pointed the mic at me so I could shout out, "Tails!" It fell to the stage. Of course it was heads, which we both knew it would be. He had a double-sided coin. The crew would be irritated if we changed the schedule every night. It was all for show.

I glared at his smug face. Finally, we ended our little intro with doing the faceoff pose that was on all the posters. Our fists were in the air as we stared each other down. The crowd went berserk. Hurrying backstage, everyone hooted and congratulated us. The crew moved past us to get the stage set up.

"That was freaking awesome," Seth said.

"Yeah, the crowd is loving this whole thing," Mark added excitedly.

"Wait until we start playing," I told them. They agreed, and the other band wafted away. While we waited for our cue, I sang a few notes. There was a tap on my shoulder.

"Hmm?" I turned, irritated to see Mark. I was ready to get in front of that crowd. The anticipation was the worst. Once I was on the stage with the mic in my hand it was no big deal. He shrugged and looked towards the stage again.

"I was just wondering where you got that jacket. It looks familiar," he smirked. I shot him a look but said nothing.

"Hey, I know how it is, being on the road all the time; with a perfect husband like yours." He wasn't even trying to hold in his sarcasm.

"It's just a jacket," I said quietly. Adrian ran up behind me, grabbed my shoulders, and whipped me around. I silently thanked Adrian for his perfect timing.

"You ready babe? This is already an epic night! If you're good, I have a present for you," he winked. Laughing, he turned to talk to Mark. A crew member came up and signaled us. I reached out to grab their hands and squeezed them tight.

All at once we announced ourselves by bounding to the stage, running towards the screams. I grabbed the mic, and the music began pounding in my ears. The cheers from the fans energized me. My long hair hung in front of my face as I put the microphone up to the crowd to sing along with us.

As I headbanged to the music, I made my way towards Adrian. I was crooning the second stanza when he leaned over and bit my neck. The bare side. I jumped, pretending to be shocked and appalled. I could hear the crowd enjoying the show.

When the band began playing a calmer tune I called to our fans. "Alright Chicago, I think we could all use a round. So, who's buying me a shot?" Fans greeted me with various screams and shouts, and after a moment I was reaching out to the crowd to grab four shot glasses. We cheered as we all met in the back where Mark was standing behind his drums to toast to a great opening show. I thanked the kind gentleman who bought us the drinks and asked him if he had a request. He shouted back for us to play 'End It With A Love Song', which was one of my favorites. I wrote it for our first album.

The rest of our set went smoothly. I told the crowd goodnight and hurried off the stage. As I ran behind the curtain towards some fresh air, I ran straight into a hard, warm chest. I looked up and felt the heat rise to my face. Ethan was amused. I bet he was; I felt gross covered in sweat. I hated being hot and sticky like this. He smiled and stepped back. I could tell something in his mood had shifted from before our performance. My smile faded slowly. His pupils were huge. Was he high? He opened his mouth to say something but was interrupted by Sam, our band's manager. The thin man in the gray suit and ridiculously thick blond hair came up, inserting himself between us.

"Cleo! Great set, as usual. Can we talk?" He asked, already pushing me forward. Sam was nice, but stern. He was very no-nonsense. Directing us towards an office, Sam quickly closed the door behind him and turned to face me. I stood there uncomfortably before he grinned his smooth, conniving smile.

"I have a proposition for you," he said, shutting the door.

"No. No way." It was out of the question. I glared at Sam who rolled his eyes and leaned on the big desk behind him.

"Come on Cleo. The label has been hounding me for years. This is the perfect time to do it. All in one go. Then when the tour is over you don't even have to think about it ever again," he argued.

"Sam, I can't. Chris would…" I started, but he blew me off.

"Come on, that guy's a piece of work I tell ya. This has potential. For everyone involved! This could be big, Cleo. Please, just think about it," he pleaded, pressing his hands together to mimic praying. I put my hand to my forehead. This is all too much in one night. I sighed deeply again and glared up at Sam.

"I'll think about it. Let me talk to the guys. What about him? Did Ethan already say he'd do it?" Sam shrugged. He didn't look worried. He never did. Sam was always one step ahead of us.

"Their manager is going to discuss it with him. Honestly, we don't really need the bands on board. The label only cares about getting you two," he told me bluntly. Of course. I crossed my arms. In their eyes they could always replace the band behind the singer.

"So, what would this entail exactly?" I asked, and he lit up like a kid on Christmas.

"Okay, so first, record a duet. Either a love song or a

breakup ballad. Your choice. If you guys can write one, good. If not, we can get something for you guys to perform. We have endless amounts of songwriters at our disposal." I waved my hand at him to continue. We write our own stuff. Plain and simple.

"Okay, then you do some hype about it. Perform it live a few times. Get the word out. Then we'll shoot and release the music video. Perform it a few more times, and then you're good to go back home to Mr. Senator," he said, sarcasm dripping at the end of his pitch.

"I don't know. This is too weird," I said, hesitant. Sam sighed again and crossed his arms.

"Cleo, I'm not telling you to screw the guy. Just a few pecks for the video and sing with him. Jesus. You musicians are so difficult sometimes," he joked, but I could see irritation behind that smile.

"Fine, but I'll write the song. I'm not singing some crap you pulled out of a folder full of pop songs for wannabe divas," I told him. He straightened his posture and slapped his hands together.

"Hot dog! Finally, something to give them! They were starting to really get on me. Now to get Andrews on board and we'll start getting everything around."

"Why didn't you approach me before the tour about this?" I asked him as we left the room, returning to the chaos backstage.

"You didn't even want to do the tour with him. I figured get you here, let you guys talk some stuff out and then convince you," he grinned devilishly at me. I couldn't keep from smiling, but I lightly shoved him. I glared at him but couldn't stop a smile from peeking out. I could never stay mad at him. As stern as he was, he was a good manager and friend.

By the time we came out of the office, Cruel Distraction was already on stage. That gave me a minute to find my bandmates and tell them what Sam had proposed. Of course, they were excited.

"I want to help with the music," Adrian said, which helped me get on board further. I couldn't do anything without my best friends. I told them that, and we drank to it. We sat around backstage hanging out with some of the other bands while Cruel Distraction played their set. When they finished, we were signaled to join them on stage. I forced a smug smile and stormed onto the stage with my band. The crowd cheered. The singer from one of our openers came out with us. He reintroduced himself and reminded the fans to buy his cd.

"Anyways, we're gonna try to be fair, so I'll be the judge. Who won the battle of the bands tonight?" He asked. A stagehand walked out with a ridiculously sparkly crown on a little red pillow.

Judd, the singer, took the crown and went over to Ethan. He held it over his head and pointed the mic towards the crowd. Ethan smiled wide and bowed to the fans. They went wild with screams of adoration. He waited until it died down to walk over to me. Ethan was sticking his tongue out at me, while I remained cross-armed and impatient. When he came over and waved the crown over me, I moved forward and started jumping around, waving my hands, hyping the crowd up. They went berserk, and the winner became obvious.

"Well, I think we have an answer. Sorry Cruel Distraction. Maria Maria, you are the winners of the battle of the bands tonight!" He shouted, and the crowd erupted. I thanked him and took the microphone. Derek and Adrian grabbed guitars quickly, while Mark ran to the drums. We played one more song as an encore. I thanked the crowd, motioning to my new crown, and bound off the stage.

I sighed with relief that the concert was officially over. Phew, what a night. I looked back for my friends. They followed behind me, covered in sweat and grinning ear to ear. I laughed, knowing the feeling. The rush of adrenaline from performing, it was like nothing else. I looked for Ethan. Scanning backstage, I spotted him. He was shirtless. A flash memory of his shirtless body pressed against mine came to me. I quickly pushed it away. He had more tattoos than I remembered.

I saw a man with a ponytail and long brown beard pass us and walk up to Ethan. He said something to him that made Ethan turn his head to look my way. My heart began beating furiously. Placing his hand on his back, the man led him away. I didn't hear a word of what anyone said around me. My attention was focused on the door they had gone through.

After what felt like an eternity, they came out. Ethan was smiling weakly while the man looked quite excited. Ethan's body was tense. Turning away quickly, I pretended to be engaged in what Spencer was telling us. We all laughed at his joke and then I felt a light tap on my shoulder. I turned around to see a grim-faced Ethan. My smile faltered.

"Can we talk?" He asked quietly. I nodded, and we left out through the exit doors to the parking lot. People were all around. Stagehands, band members, bar staff, fans. There was no real privacy. He looked around and quickly grabbed my hand, pulling me towards the busses. My other hand went to my crown to keep it from falling. There were two actual tour buses, while everyone else would be providing their own transportation. He found a spot that wasn't super busy and stopped. We stood in between our buses. Surprisingly no one was near. He dropped my hand and fell back, leaning against the cold metal of the bus. His head tilted down.

Neither of us spoke for a moment. I stared at Ethan, but he refused to look at me. Finally lifting his head, his hard eyes softened and grew melancholy. "I kept it," he said softly, his voice dripping with sorrow. I was on the verge of tears myself. I felt like such a jerk. I had agreed to make money on our pain… on his pain. I knew this was a bad idea.

"I kept my tattoo because I thought that one day you would come back. And you had to have felt something for me because you kept yours too," he accused. He was angry and hurt, and I was to blame. He was right; although I'd never say it. Reflexively I pushed my hair over my neck, covering it. He pushed off the bus and moved towards me.

"I waited. For months. Every time my phone went off, I would hurry to pick it up hoping that it was you. That I finally got your attention!" My eyes widened, but I didn't say anything. His face contorted with emotion and pent-up pain. He had been waiting years for this. "I just wanted you to notice me," he said with a finality that brought me to tears. I was so sorry for what I had done to him. He wiped away some makeup, sweat, and tears from his face. His eyes swung back to mine and a chill went up my spine.

I stepped back and hit the other bus. Ethan continued moving closer to me, pinning me against it. I heard the clink when the metal crown hit the metal bus. His icy blue eyes bore into me. He put his hand on my hip. I saw his eyes fall down to my lips. I felt his breath on my skin. My blood raced in my ears. He leaned down and just as our mouths were going to touch, he pulled away.

"Is this something you're comfortable with?" He whispered.

"What do you mean?" I asked, confused. He looked at me with exasperation.

"We'll be on screen, kissing, touching. Cleo, memories are going to resurface, and that might not be a good thing," he warned me. He was right again. I gulped and crossed my arms over my chest. The hand on my hip started creeping higher, teasing me. He played with the bottom of my shirt, his fingers slipping under, but remaining low. My skin burned from his touch. My body reacted before my brain. My back arched, my leg moved to let him between my legs. I gulped, seeing what he meant. But I still didn't move away.

"And what about your husband? You think he's going to be okay with you pretending to be in love with your ex on camera? What's he going to say?" He asked, his voice low, his lips under my chin. Suddenly he pulled entirely away from me. I straightened, pulling my shirt back down.

"You said he was pretty understanding, but a guy can only take so much, Cleo. This isn't as simple as just pretending. We have history and everyone knows that. There will be rumors, and the label is going to add fuel to the fire. They aren't thinking of us. We're just money tickets." I turned my face away. I wasn't going to cry in front of him. He was saying everything I had been thinking.

"I'm not saying we shouldn't. This would be great for both of our careers, but you need to know what we are getting ourselves into. If you don't want to, that's fine. They asked me, and I was on the fence already. I would understand. Our history is too much."

"Ethan, I can't think about this right now." I closed my eyes. My mind flooded with images of my husband. The last time I saw him. It was a rush of emotions I couldn't, no, didn't want to deal with right now. When a tear slipped, I put my hands to my face. I felt the crown slip off my head and hit the pavement with a tiny clink. I didn't look towards it or make any movement to pick it up. Speechless, he stood there, letting me cry.

"Cleo, I didn't mean to upset you. I'm just unsure of all this," he tried to explain.

"He's cheating on me!" I blurted. I burst into tears and slipped down to the pavement. He instantly dropped down to crouch next to me. I cried into my knees not looking up.

I heard a door open and people talking. I pulled my head up and stood up quickly. Ethan tried to touch my back, but I pulled away.

"I don't need your pity. I bet you're happy. It's what I get, right?" I spat at him. He sighed and looked at me one last time

28

with those damn blue eyes. His makeup was smeared all down his face. He opened and shut his mouth quickly like he was fighting with himself over whether or not to say something.

Wiping the tears from my eyes and cheeks, I brushed past him and stormed onto the bus. I laid down on my bunk and closed the curtain. I didn't want anyone to see me crying. I grabbed my phone and saw that I had two messages. One from Sam and one from Chris. I opened the one from my husband first.

Cleo talk to me. I miss you. I don't like being away from you for so long. I'm lonely.

I felt a twinge of guilt. It was hard being in a relationship with someone who travels for work. Did I throw Christopher into the arms of a stranger? Was it my fault he found company in someone else? I didn't reply to his message. I couldn't right now. The memory of his naked body entangled in hers was still too fresh.

It was a few weeks before the tour. I had been at Derek's getting our set list hammered out. We went out for food and I wanted to stop by my house to pick up my songbook. I had something I wanted to show the band.

We stopped by and I hurried inside. I realized that Christopher's black BMW was here. He worked long hours at his law firm, so I was excited to catch him home. I called his name as I walked around, but the house was quiet. I climbed the stairs and went to our bedroom for my book. Pushing the door open I froze.

In an instant my life as I knew it completely shattered. There he was, his bare ass in the air. They didn't see me at first, but then she opened her eyes and screamed. Chris whipped around and tried to cover them, but it was too late. There was no denying what they were doing.

I grabbed my songbook from the table right next to the door and left, tossing my ring on the kitchen table. I hadn't been home since.

I closed my eyes and tried to calm myself. I wiped my face off and took a few deep breaths. You know what? Screw it. Apparently he didn't care about my feelings. I pulled the curtain open and stood up. Moving to the front, I saw that my friends were back on the bus now. Smoke was clouding the room.

I saw all of my guys were sprawled on the couches drinking and passing a joint around. No sooner had I come into the lounge area the door swung open and Spencer, Christian, and Seth came in holding liquor bottles. They quickly joined the rest of the guys. The bus was packed. This was going to be my summer. This was where I was most comfortable. I didn't want to go home to Christopher. It was too late.

"How's it going?" Derek asked Christian. The other band was grinning and covered in sweat and grime. I scanned the room but didn't see Ethan in the mess of men. Adrian grabbed me, pulling me down onto his lap. I let out a yelp, as he kissed me.

"Oh I love ya Darlin'," he said with a hiccup. I wiped my mouth with the back of my hand and wiggled to get up. He tasted like dark beer.

"Hey, I have something for ya," he said.

I heard another voice I couldn't identify say "I have something for you too!" Followed by more hoots and hollers.

Adrian stood up and pulled out a brand new bottle of tequila from under him. I snatched it out of his hands and thanked him. I left the party and went back to the sleeping quarters. Taking clothes out of my trunk, I went to wash up as best I could in the bathroom. Pulling on some pajama pants and a tank top, I went back to the front to see how long we had left before we started driving. Less than an hour and we'd be off the driver, Bill, told me. He was about to start counting heads, so I better stay close.

I thanked him and decided to go look for Ethan. Mark was the closest to me. He asked if I was going outside. I told him I was and, without hesitation, he pulled off his black hoodie and gave it to me. I loved my guys. I blew him a kiss and he rolled his eyes. I saw a tiny smile cross his face as I bounced down the stairs.

The party on the other bus was just as loud, but there were some stragglers outside. I ignored some catcalls and focused on the task at hand. Looking around, I saw some of the crew finishing up. This was the first tour where we didn't have to load out our equipment, so I took a walk around. It was nice not having to carry all the heavy instruments and amps and stuff it into a trailer. It was even sweeter having my own bunk and not sleeping either in the passenger seat or leaning on Derek or Adrian and praying no one had gas. This bus was already trashed, but it was so much better than before. I would never complain again.

I wasn't going to admit I was looking for him, but sure enough, he startled me when he stepped out from behind the building. He sauntered over with one hand in his pocket and the other behind his back. I noticed he had put his shirt back on, but I was cold even with Mark's hoodie. He had to be freezing.

"You look lost," he said, an amused look on his face. His lips curved into a goofy smile and his eyes were dark and slightly bloodshot. The thought crossed my mind that he was high again, but I tossed it away. I had to focus.

"I'm in if you're in," I said, as confidently as I could. Ethan paused, letting it sink in before smiling wide. He took a drag of the cigarette I hadn't noticed before.

"I guess I'm in."

The bus door flew open and the driver called out. Ethan

pulled the hand out from behind him to reveal the crown I had dropped earlier. He dropped his cigarette and stomped it out, while he put the crown gently back on my head.

He pulled a fresh cigarette out of his pocket, lit it and took a long drag. When he saw that I was watching him, he winked at me. I cracked a smile and thanked him. Smoking never bothered me. My first two real boyfriends, Steven and Austin, both smoked. Ethan shrugged and put on a sloppy grin as we headed towards the bus.

Once inside, he took my hand and pulled me past everyone to the sleeping area. All of my bus mates cheered and made comments like "Queen Cleo" as we walked through. I smiled and waved as we passed. Closing the curtains and turning to face the bunks I saw we were alone. My heart began to beat a little louder. We continued, quickly moving past the beds to go to the way back.

The third section of the bus was a smaller lounge area. Moving the curtains aside, we saw that it was merely two long couches set together in an "L" shape. There was a TV hanging near the ceiling and a small table coming from the wall. This is the only place people will give you any kind of privacy.

Ethan plopped down on one side of the couch, and I laid down on the other, resting our heads in the middle so we could talk but not look at each other. I took the crown off, placing it on the table. Ethan grabbed the remote and turned the TV on. He clicked through the channels until he found one that only played music. I closed my eyes and enjoyed the peaceful moment.

One of my favorite bands began to play through the speakers. I sighed with contentment and started singing the lyrics softly. This was nice. No shouting or arguing. No one was passing gas or trying to punch me because they saw a bug or some car. Not that I didn't love them. I did. I wouldn't trade them for the world. But this was nice too.

"You have a beautiful voice," Ethan's soft words pulled me out of my thoughts. I opened one eye and smiled as I finished the song. Sitting back up, I looked at him in the light. I had forgotten how handsome he was.

I was born with dark hair that had a very slight wave to it. My eyes were a soft brown, and my face was what my mother called "doll-like." I was born with a button nose and the pouty lips to tie it all together. My skin had just a tint of a permanent tan. I was the palest in my family. Everyone used to tease me that my father was the mailman, especially since I never learned to speak Spanish like my siblings.

The only thing I was self-conscious of was my smile. I had a very noticeable gap in between my two front teeth. My parents couldn't afford braces so over the years I have learned to embrace it. In fact, Sam and many of the other reps at the record label encourage me to show off my smile. They say it makes me stand out, which in this world is a good thing. But it wasn't always that way back home.

I was teased mercilessly by kids when I was in school. Girls could be so cruel. They would ask if I was wearing joke teeth, or if I had food stuck in between them. It got to the point where I didn't like to talk. But that mostly stopped when I met the guys. They became my protectors. I couldn't even count how many times they beat up a guy for calling me a "gap-toothed bitch," or managed to get revenge on a girl for teasing me to tears. They saw something in me that I didn't. I was their unofficial sister, and they were my brothers for life.

My parents, although cold and lacking in affection most of the time, agreed with Sam and the label. They loved my gap. Every once in a while, I'd see my mom pausing in the kitchen to look at me and smile. Her eyes would grow distant like she recalled something pleasant. One time I asked her about it and she revealed that I was the spitting image of her mother. Although I never had the chance to meet her, everyone swore I was her incarnate. All five feet tall and slender frame. The only difference my mother would tell the family was my breasts. "Her boobies are way bigger than Ma's ever were. Ain't that right Teresa?" I recalled her nasally, lightly accented voice as she would repeat those words over and over at any family function I attended. I didn't make it a habit to visit. I didn't think anyone really missed me. I was more of a nuisance than anything. Just the kid no one wanted, but they got anyway.

I sat up and turned to look down at Ethan. He looked up from where he was lying and just smiled. As I stared into Ethan's bright blue eyes, all I could think about were his lips. I wanted him to kiss me. Would it be wrong to practice for the video? I forced myself to look away. Yes, it would be wrong.

"That whole thing was a mess, wasn't it?" He said suddenly. "I still see stuff about our "secret romance" every once in a while," he tried to joke. It made me crack a genuine smile.

"Yeah, there were so many theories and stories about us, how we'd been dating for years. People saw us getting hotels under different names and wearing wigs so we could see each other," I laughed. I shook my head at it. People were crazy. We were never that clever.

"It was fun though, while it lasted."

I frowned. Yeah, it was. But then I panicked and fled. I ran right into Chris' arms, thinking he was the only one who understood me. What a ridiculous notion that was.

"I'm sorry about your husband. That sucks. How'd you find out?" I gulped.

"I saw them. In bed." I said. He sat up quickly and stared at me, his jaw dropped.

"What? Cleo…" he started, but I put my hand up to stop him.

"What about you? You don't have a girl waiting at home for you that's going to kill me for kissing you on stage?" I asked. I tried to keep my voice light, but I was still hurting inside. There was a pause, and then he said,

"Nope. Just me, myself and I." I tried not to smile, but it peaked out.

"So, are we cool now? Or is this going to be a very awkward and uncomfortable tour?" I asked after I pondered his response. I decided to get it out in the open. He rubbed his nose a bit and stared off into the distance. I noticed he was very twitchy like he had drunk an entire pot of espresso and chased it with a pound of sugar and an energy drink. He slid closer to me. Leaning over he kissed my neck where his name was. I gasped as his hand fell onto my thigh.

"I think we'll be fine," he said laughing. He had to stop kissing me there. I moved away reflexively, and he respected my distance. "I'll stop with the jabs about the past. If we plan to work together, I can be professional. I promise," he swore, moving his fingers across his chest. "Cross my heart."

I let out a huge breath I hadn't realized I was holding. Watching me, Ethan started to chuckle, which naturally made me start to giggle and soon we were both bent over in laughter. I began to fall off the couch, but he quickly grabbed me and laid me flat on my back. He moved over me, our bodies parallel. I felt his body throb against my hip. We locked eyes for a moment, but he suddenly jerked away. I looked to see the curtain had opened. Seth and Spencer were grinning at us with drunken smiles. Ethan sighed and we moved apart. Glancing at each other again both of us burst into smiles. Oops. Ethan's band mates started laughing and gave each other a knowing look. I threw a pillow at them. Seth finally pulled the curtain back, leaving us alone. Although I had a feeling they were still watching.

I waited until I was sure they went back to the party before returning to my bunk I grabbed Ethan's jacket from my bed and returned to Ethan lying on the couch with his eyes closed. I tossed it gently to him. He looked up at me with confusion. "I gave this to you," he said quietly.

"You don't want it back?" I asked, and he looked hurt.

"No, you keep it. You looked good in it. Wear it for the video or something," he grinned wickedly. My heart sped up. Quickly I snatched it back before one of us changed our minds.

I went to lay back down on the couch with him, but he got up and went to his bunk. He pulled out his large duffel bag and began rummaging through it. I watched him purely out of boredom. That was until he winked at me as he unbuttoned his jeans slowly. I blushed when I saw his thin, dark trail of hair leading into his boxers. He raised one eyebrow at me and turned around to bare his ass. I couldn't help but let out a small giggle. Quickly he changed into lounge pants, leaving his shirt off.

He sprawled out on the couch. Knowing that other people might come back, I chose to stay on the opposite side of the room.

"Do you like movies?" He asked.

"Yeah, turn it to something funny," I told him as he reached for the remote again. He scrolled through the channels until he found an old comedy I'd seen a million times. I laid down and tried to get comfortable.

I tried to focus on the movie, but I couldn't stop thinking about Ethan's reaction to my confession about Chris. He wasn't happy or vindictive. I couldn't put my finger on what he was thinking. I turned my head to look at him only to find his blue eyes staring back at me. So many words between us were still left unsaid. I had a feeling that in time it would all come out. But did I really want that? Or would it be more heartbreak?

Chapter Three

STILL INTO YOU

The next day we were more cordial with each other than the night before. We were scheduled to play a show in Indianapolis that afternoon, and then we'd be right back on the bus traveling to the next city. It was a crazy schedule, but sometimes I felt like I was just going through the motions. I smiled and joked with all the guys, but there were some days I just wanted to lay down and tune out the world. I was still hurting from the truth about Chris.

Despite my tragic home life, touring with the guys was a blast. We would play our shows, sign autographs, take some pictures and do a few interviews. Then the rest of the time was ours. Every night we acted out the whole old rivals thing. Some nights our band wore the crown, other nights Cruel Distraction took the win. It was just for fun after all. It was the best job in the world. It helped take my mind off my problems at home.

As much fun as we were having, we were also being hounded by Sam to get him a song. So most of my free time was spent in the back of the bus with Ethan while we tried to figure out lyrics, melodies, and what we wanted to tell. After much discussion and arguing, Ethan and I decided on a power ballad.

It would start out with us angry, upset and demanding to be heard by the other person. It would then turn slowly into us apologizing to each other and making up.

It was hard at first, trying to write lyrics about something so intimate. There were more than a few jabs at each other about this or that. However, once we finally got into a groove, working with Ethan was going great. I was impressed with how he knew what notes would sound perfect with what line in the song. I thought we had something with great potential.

After that first night when we almost kissed, it never happened again. There wasn't any long stolen looks or kisses on the neck. He treated me like one of the guys, which was good, kind of. Sometimes I would catch him staring at me. He would quickly turn away when our eyes met. I couldn't help but wonder if he still had any lingering feelings.

A bunch of us were chilling at a skatepark outside Detroit that the guys insisted we visit while we had some downtime. Both of our bands came from Michigan, so we knew these cities like the back of our hands, literally. Maria Maria lived closer to the wrist, near Indiana. Cruel Distraction was slightly higher up, towards the middle of your palm. They came from the capitol; Lansing, Michigan.

Ethan and I sat on a picnic table outside the gates while the guys skated and tried to pick up girls. Today was one of the rare times we weren't working on the new music. It was a nice break.

Ethan grabbed my hand and raised it to look at the tattoo on my wrist. It was a simple block of script.

"All for one, one for all."

He read the words aloud then looked at me, amused. "Is that from The Three Musketeers?" I laughed and took my hand back, rubbing the spot where the words lay forever.

"We all got it done when we left home. We swore to each

other that we would never regret leaving everything behind. It's a reminder that even when this sucks, we are all in it together. Always," I explained, looking towards my friends. Derek had pulled out his hacky sack, and a few people joined him in a circle playing.

"It's crazy to think back to the days when we were sitting in Derek's garage playing our hand me down instruments. We were all so stupid. I was dating Adrian at the time. I swore we'd be together forever," I laughed at the memories.

"That's a love song I'd like to hear," he joked, and I shoved him with my shoulder playfully. After a moment it grew quiet again. Ethan sat with me listening intently to me. No one did that. Ever.

"Tell me another story," he told me, his face sincere. I thought about it and then laughed.

"For the first summer we toured, Mark had a dog. It was this pug he named Fart. He took it with us in Derek's small van we bought off of his mom," I smiled at the memories. "I hated that dog, but now that he's gone I almost miss him."

"What happened to him?" I snorted when I laughed, which made Ethan crack up. I smacked him to stop. When I caught my breath, I continued.

"We were at a festival, and he got stolen! We found him weeks later with this band where Mark had screwed their bassist. She was so pissed at him for avoiding her that when he was in the bathroom she snuck in and took him."

"Did you get him back?" I shook my head, laughing at the memory of the little guy.

"Nah, Mark felt guilty for what he did, so he let her keep poor little Fart. She renamed him Sammy." I said as we laughed.

"What about you? Tell me about your tattoos. I see you've got some new ones," I said, glancing at his neck.

"But I only got to ask you about one of yours. I wanted to

ask about the one on your neck," he teased. I shook my head and poked one on his arm.

"This one? She's my newest one. I got it a few months ago in Germany. We were opening for Accepted Perversion, and they were hanging out with this chick who turned out to be some award-winning artist specializing in pin-up work. She's from California, but was doing some work there and offered me a deal if she could test some stuff out. So, she gave me this mari-onette. It's pretty cool huh?" I nodded. It was a stunning piece. It was a girl with pigtails, her face painted like a cute clown. She wore a corset, tutu and striped socks while she posed provoca-tively. It was bad-ass.

"Did any of the other guys get anything from her?" I asked. Her work was smooth. I almost wanted something done. I had some room on my back left. He shook his head.

"No, it got kind of weird. Emile, their vocals, I think they hooked up or something. Have you ever met him? He parties hard and, when he's high, he can be a huge dick. Right after that night he made us leave," he said.

"I've seen him at festivals, but never met any of the band," I commented. Accepted Perversion was huge right now. Every-where you looked Emile Dahl's face was plastered on every magazine and every music channel on TV was playing their videos. They were calling him "rock royalty."

"Yeah they're cool, but Emile is sort of nuts." He looked like he was thinking about something, a memory maybe. He turned back to me with an evil grin. "Alright, let's see the tattoo all your friends keep telling us about," he teased and raised his eyebrow daring me to show him. I blushed, fully aware of which one he was talking about.

"I swear I'm going to kill them all one day," I swore.

"Let's see it!" He urged. Sighing, I jumped up on the table and unbuttoned my shorts and lowered them to bare my ass cheek. I heard the hoots and calls from the guys around the park. I was wearing black lacy boy shorts, so you were able to see the massive rose with a skull in the middle of it. Not my wisest decision but it was a nicely done piece. I did it on a dare. Plus, I had at least one tattoo that was a worse decision than this one.

Ethan reached up and smacked my bare bottom hard! I yelped and grabbed my shorts. Hopping back down, I punched him in the shoulder. He feigned pain, and I scooted closer to him, resting my head on his shoulder. He took my hand in his and squeezed.

"Why didn't I stay?" I asked him, sadness dripping in my voice. He didn't say anything for a long time. My words having more power than intended.

"It's not all sunshine and rainbows with me, Doll. I was in a bad place when we were together. I still have trouble with stuff sometimes," he told me. I understood him without having to push it.

No one talked about it, but Ethan was doing harder drugs than the rest of us. Before shows he would lock himself in a bathroom, taking this little box with him. When he came out, he was higher than a kite. Then, after the shows, he'd disappear again. It was obvious what was going on, but he didn't seem to let it affect his work. Maybe it was what made him so fantastic on stage. For the most part, he was pretty easy to be around afterward. I had toured with some people who were downright awful. Mostly he was just jumpy and hyper. I tried not to think about it.

He never offered me anything and kept whatever was in that box to himself. Although I didn't partake in smoking, I still couldn't judge anyone's life choices. I was almost always a little drunk, and they passed weed around the bus like candy. We all had problems. I squeezed his hand and kissed his shoulder.

"No one should be all sunshine and rainbows. You know how annoying that would be?" I replied, trying to pull him from the darkness he was trying to escape to. I smiled at him, but he just stared blankly at me. After a long moment, his face relaxed. I snuggled my head closer, inhaling the scent of his cologne. It was familiar and comforting.

I felt a twinge of guilt when I realized I hadn't even thought about Christopher in a day or two. It was easy to forget my home life when I was with Ethan.

As the summer went on and we moved from city to city, I was able to be happy again. People noticed my drastic mood change pretty quickly. Three weeks in, when it was only me and my bandmates having dinner, Mark spoke up.

"You guys act weird around each other. You already have inside jokes. All you do is flirt. You're trying to tell us that you're just old friends?" His tone was skeptical. I blushed just thinking about Ethan. "It's not like that. We've been working on our song," I replied.

"But you inked his name permanently on your skin," Derek reminded me. I pursed my lips.

"We were drunk. I don't even remember doing it. You are making it into a much bigger deal than it is," I said, shutting it down before this conversation got out of hand. Mark glared at me but moved on to discuss which waitress he wanted to bang. That next night though, Mark decided he wasn't ready to let it go.

We finished our show and had just stepped onto the bus to travel through the night to the next state over. I had worn a skirt and long sleeve shirt with long tights on stage. They weren't exactly lounging around clothes, so as soon as I could get to my bunk, I grabbed some pajamas and changed quickly.

When I returned to the front of the bus I saw Christian was pulling out three large bottles of tequila from his guitar case. "Who's up for a little game?" He asked. People cheered their various agreements. Seth, their drummer, was getting shot glasses down from a cabinet. "How many people? Seven, that's it? Where's Ethan?" He sounded tipsy already. Nobody answered. Ethan had gone to the back of the bus. He had taken his little wooden box with him.

"Make it six. I'm out," I yawned, and everyone either groaned or called me something crude. I ignored them all and went back to my bunk to listen to my iPod. Pushing play, I laid down and closed my eyes, making sure to have it loud enough to drown out the idiocy going on in the front of the bus.

I must have fallen asleep because I was rudely awakened by Derek shaking me. My headphones fell out of my ears, and I screamed for him to stop. Focusing my eyes on him I saw that his curly blonde locks were gone. He now had a very badly cut mohawk. His eyes were huge and bloodshot. He was utterly wasted.

"Cleo. I need your help. Adrian won't let me have his guitar. Help me. I need to play," he begged. I groaned and tried to lay back down, but he grabbed my arm again.

"Go away!" I put a pillow over my head and with an obnoxious moan he left me to find Adrian's guitar. He must have found it because only a few minutes later I heard him screaming out the lyrics to "La Bamba." I tried to go back to sleep, but the party was so loud I couldn't take it anymore. I got up and went back up front. Out of habit, I looked for Ethan.

"He's not up here," Mark called over Derek's song. I glanced over and instantly noticed he was close to blackout drunk. La Bamba always came right before the blackout.

"I wasn't looking for him," I lied and of course Mark saw right through it.

"Sure, and you two aren't hooking up either," he quipped, making the rest of the group chuckle.

"Whatever," I mumbled, too tired to argue.

"So, it's true," he accused. I glared at him. He glared right back.

"Nothing's going on. Will you leave it?" I asked, and then Adrian piped in.

"Then why haven't you told Chris about the song. Or the video," he demanded. All eyes were on me. I could feel my face getting hot.

"It just hasn't come up," I muttered.

Mark stood up and walked over to me slowly. "So, what? You're gonna go back to his cheating ass?" He said, his eyes incredulous. I looked away guiltily, then glared at Adrian. He was too drunk to care that he spilled my secret.

"No, I didn't say that. Can we drop it?" He backed up and plopped down on the couch. The room grew quiet, everyone's eyes were on us.

"Does he even know you went on tour with him? That you're sharing a bus?" Mark pushed, and the tears started to pool. He didn't. Mark grabbed his shot of tequila Christian had poured him. He looked me dead in the eye and said in a low voice

"Ethan's a good guy. He may be high all the time, but at least he cares about you. You made the wrong choice." He tipped his head back, taking the shot. The glass slammed down on the table. No one moved. Things had gotten intense fast. I was about to break.

Finally, Christian raised his glass and coughed. "All hail the King!" He said, tipping the crown he had won earlier. Everyone followed with forced, awkward cheers and took swigs of their drinks. The party started to settle down after that. The only person still fully wound up was Derek.

"Cleo, I love you. Your hair looks like cotton candy. Can I touch it?" Derek asked. He didn't wait for me to answer him before he was pulling me off the couch and into his lap to pull lightly on my hair.

"Adrian. Please. Please, Adrian. I need it. I need your guitar. Please Adrian, please," he begged him. He dropped to his knees. Adrian kept telling him no, but the second he went to the bathroom, Derek jumped up and ran to where Adrian had returned the guitar to its case. He pulled it out and hurried back to us to play the only song he knew. We groaned as he started shouting the words out to "La Bamba" again.

He played the song over and over, singing the words. He ignored our shouting. We threw things at him, but we couldn't crush his spirit. He closed his eyes, leaned back, and played his drunken heart out.

Adrian tried to take the guitar out of Derek's hands, but he snapped his eyes open and glared at him. The only way Adrian was getting that guitar tonight was if he tore it from his hands, most likely in two pieces. I couldn't take it anymore and told everyone goodnight. I went to my bunk and grabbed my headphones. Just as I was putting them on Mark came and sat on the bed across from me. I turned away. The last person I wanted to talk to was him.

"Go away," I said, but he ignored me.

"Cleo, I'm sorry. I'm drunk. I didn't mean it," he said, but I wasn't in the mood for his half-assed apology. "He doesn't deserve you. Chris. He's a piece of shit. Always was. He uses you," he continued. Geez, thanks. I turned back to look at him.

"For what? I don't have anything to offer him. He's..." my words trailed off thinking about him. He really was quite a catch. Smart and handsome, he had a good career and was already creating a buzz around the political circuit as the next potential state senator.

I was nothing. Nothing like Holly. She was more his type. Beautiful and smart. She was his assistant. I was just a girl he picked up at a party one night. He could have picked any girl, and he chose me. I was the lucky one. Or so I had thought up until recently. Now I wasn't so sure.

"He's a liar. I don't trust the guy. Never have. You should be with Ethan," Mark said. I sat up to look at him face to face.

"Well, I'm not. I married Chris. You don't have to remind

me every chance you get. Sometimes you don't know when to stop," I told him. He looked away. Guilt in his gray eyes.

"You know I'm not trying to hurt you," he tried to explain, but I didn't want to hear it. I was over it. I couldn't hear him apologize one more time. "Things aren't the same," he said flatly.

I hated to admit it, but things had changed since I married Christopher. There was a rift in my relationship with the band. It had never been this tense before. I had always put my friends first, and they did the same, but Christopher didn't like that. In fact, he hated all of them. He wanted me to quit the band and stay home. I didn't want to have to choose between my best friends and my husband. I knew they felt it too, and that's why they were pushing me so hard to leave him.

In the beginning of our relationship, Christopher had made it seem like he fully supported my career choice. But once we moved in together and he started his job at the firm things changed. Sometimes it felt like he didn't like anything about me. It made me wonder why he wanted to marry me in the first place.

"I know," I said. There wasn't much else to say. I looked back at Mark. His eyes were heavy. He suddenly looked exhausted. "I know you guys mean well, but Mark, you have to let me figure this out on my own," I told him. He sighed and rubbed his face.

"Yeah I guess," he mumbled.

"You know I love you right." I reached for his hand and squeezed it. He gave a half smile and stood up.

"Alright. I'll drop it. Love you too," he said and left me alone with my thoughts. I needed to go to sleep before I drove myself crazy.

The next afternoon, while still on the road to the next venue the four of us were in the bunks by ourselves. After my talk with Mark, things were a little weird. Slowly we began chatting again about regular tour stuff. I wasn't angry. He meant well. They all did.

"Look, we just want to see you back to the old Cleo. With Ethan, you're... you," Derek, now sober and not happy with his new haircut told me. "Plus, we've read your journal. That new stuff you've been writing is killer. If whatever you two are is making you write like that, then by all means, keep being friends," Adrian said while making quotations in the air. I whipped my head around. His big brown eyes grew even bigger with guilt.

"Where is my notebook?" I demanded suddenly.

"Adrian has it," Derek accused. Adrian slugged him in his shoulder from the bunk under him. Derek yelped and glared at us.

"Screw you! You guys cut my hair last night!" He shot back when Adrian glared at him.

"Yeah and we listened to La Bamba for three hours. Get over it. Adrian give her the book back." Mark snapped. He was hungover and tired of listening to us argue. Adrian pulled out my black notebook from under his blanket. He handed it to me and I snatched it, holding it tightly to my chest.

"Is it too much to ask to have one thing to myself?" I said.

"Yeah, you have Ethan," Derek replied. The other two started laughing, and I glared at them all.

"Oh, shut up," I said and left the bunks to go find something else better to do than be berated by them.

Everyone was still feeling the effects of last night's party. The bus was pretty quiet. Spencer, Seth, and Christian were hanging out on the couches. Ethan was the only one who looked alive. He glanced up from the magazine he was reading when I came in. "Hey you. What's up?" He asked, setting it down. I instantly relaxed and went to sit with him.

"The guys are extra annoying today," I told him.

We settled in to a movie on the TV, resting while we could. It was a short drive today. As soon as the bus stopped, Cruel Distraction wanted to eat. They invited us, but none of us were interested. Derek was still pissed at Christian for shaving his head, Mark hungover, and Adrian wanted to bleach his hair and retouch mine for tonight's show.

While Derek and Mark slept, Adrian squeezed us into the bathroom and began working on our hair. I did his and then he did mine. Since we were only touching stuff up, it didn't take long. Once the chemicals were all rinsed, I went to rest in my bunk before I had to get up for the show.

I must have fallen asleep because I stirred when the other band returned. Most of them went to rest in their bunks. I noticed Ethan was missing. I stood up and went to join the gang in front. They had turned the TV on to play another racing game. No one turned when I walked in. My phone went off. I had left it on the couch, next to Adrian. I leaned over to grab it. There was a text from Christopher.

Talk to me love. I miss you. I need to talk to you. When is your break again?

My stomach turned. I felt nauseous. This always happened for a few minutes after Chris' texts or calls. I wasn't ready to see him. I didn't want to hear his bogus explanation. It was all lies anyway. I just wanted the whole situation to go away, but I was still legally married to this man. I was so confused about what to do. I set my phone aside and laid down, setting my head in Adrian's lap.

"Psychiatrist?" I asked him. It was a thing we had been doing for years. A little game that helped us deal with being on the road so much. It helped us not go crazy. He moved his arms to give me more space.

"Yes, patient?" Adrian changed his voice. He was now British. A tipsy British to be specific.

"What do you think about everything?" I asked him, begging him to decide for me.

"I think that we were less than an hour away from home and Chris chose not to come visit you," he said. I stared blankly up at him. He shrugged.

"What? Did he ask you for a pass to get in?" He asked, accusation in his tone. I looked away. No, no he didn't. Chris never came to my shows. "If anything, he probably expected you to catch a cab after the show and run home. Confessing how miserable you are without him and that you'll quit the band right this moment and you're ready to have dozens of his babies," he said with such sarcasm in his voice it practically dripped onto my face.

"Oh stop. No, he didn't come. But that doesn't mean anything," I defended. Adrian rolled his eyes.

"Why do you want to be with Chris? Like seriously. He's a jerk, and Ethan is… " he started, but I cut him off.

"Ethan is my friend. He said so himself. Just friends. That part of our lives is over. We are doing the song together, but that's it," I recited for the millionth time. Adrian sighed deeply.

"If you don't make a move on old blue eyes soon, I'm going to," he warned. I sighed but couldn't help a smile from creeping up.

"You honestly think he doesn't like you?" Adrian said, his eyes skeptical. I shook my head. Not like that. Not anymore. "He follows you everywhere. You guys are always flirting. How many nights have you guys spent alone in the back hanging out while we partied? Don't give me that 'We're writing' excuse, because otherwise you'd have a whole freaking album to show us. Cleo, he got your name tattooed on him! Drunk or not, he chose to do that. You can't tell me you don't feel anything." I chose not to respond. "He's perfect for you," he whispered, playing with my hair.

"I used to think you were perfect for me too," I reminded him. His face softened, and he smiled the same smile he gave me that day he hugged me and confessed that he loved me too much to stay with me just to appease me.

"It may not seem like it right now, but this will make sure we still stay close. If I waited, then it would end up ruining this."

It was hard to hate him for being right. "Yes, let's imagine what that would have been like, shall we? I think I would have knocked you up because I don't think we ever were smart enough to use condoms. Do you even use birth control now?" He asked me. I shrugged.

"Yeah, I get a shot every few months. Not that I need it now. I haven't had sex in forever," I complained. He raised his eyebrows and grinned evilly.

"Well, you know as your Doctor I am always here to help with some stress relief. Get rid of all that hysteria." I grabbed a pillow and swatted him in the face with it. I giggled as he tossed it across the bus.

"Alright, back to me being pregnant with your child," I said and snuggled closer to my best friend. He wrapped his arm around my middle. I was so comfy; I didn't want to move. "Well, I then take a job at my brother's shop, changing people's oil, replacing windshield wipers. You know, real hard labor. I would insist you stay home with Adrian Junior, little Marky, and baby Derek. We would…" I cut him off, putting my hand up.

"Whoa, we have three kids? And I let you name them Adrian, Mark, and Derek?" We looked at each other a moment and then burst into laughter. "My time is up for today Doc," I sat up and grabbed my phone, pushing the button to turn it off. I didn't need to stress about Chris right now. Maybe Adrian was right. Standing up to go back to my bed Adrian snapped his fingers.

"Bring me a beer, wife," he demanded. I looked up and glared at him. He winked, and I moved to the fridge, grabbing two bottles. I handed him his, and he took the top off. I let him take a sip before quickly tapping the opening with my bottle. The beer rushed out of the top, spilling all over his shirt and lap. He swore at me, and I ran to the bunks before he could stand. I pulled my bag out and started to get ready for the show.

After my clothes were on and my makeup and hair finished, I stepped out of the bathroom. I could hear that the other band was awake and in the front with my guys. I decided to go to the back where Ethan most likely was. He used the lounge area more than the rest of us. It was another one of those unspoken things. I stepped in and saw him lying there, eyes closed on the couch. He had his little brown box with stickers all over it sitting next to him. Whatever he was taking was in it. I was curious, but knew the value of privacy in this world, so I let it be. I think a part of me was afraid to know what he was doing. I wanted to stay blindly innocent to it.

He heard me come in and opened one eye, smiling softly then frowning when he saw my face. He pointed to his eye and raised an eyebrow. I must not have covered the bruise up well enough. I explained what happened with a shrug and he just laughed and sat up, itching his nose.

"I've got some makeup you can use to cover it up," he joked as he moved to get his clothes and eyeliner on. "You ready for tonight? I heard you changed your set," he said while taking off his shirt. I admired his toned body while he moved around the tiny space. I loved that he took my music seriously and liked our songs. Chris always told his friends and family that it was a nice hobby I had. Artists were so low in his mind. They were worthless.

"Yeah, nothing special. We just added some songs we've been practicing. Some covers," I said nonchalantly. I was super excited for tonight. I loved trying out new songs. It was nerve-racking and thrilling at the same time. You never knew how the crowd would react.

"When are we gonna do our song?" He asked. I pondered that for a moment.

"I can ask Sam if he cares or if he wants us to wait until we record it," I replied. He came back towards me.

"You should stick around. Watch my set." I almost always did, but I told him I would anyways. I helped him paint his face thick with eyeliner. He played with my pigtails while I held his chin.

"You're the best," he said when I finished. My stomach fluttered. I knew he was just being nice, but it still did something to me. We shared a long look before I moved away. What was I doing? I was a married woman. I shouldn't be sitting here with Ethan. Just because my husband cheated doesn't mean that I was allowed to do the same. Was it cheating? I mean, we didn't kiss or even hug. Sure, we flirted, but I flirted with everyone. What was crossing the line? I wasn't sure of anything anymore. Neither did my husband apparently. Why did I marry him anyway?

He was impressive right from the start. At his graduation party, after we performed, he came right over to me and introduced himself. Christopher Thomas, attorney at law. He was dashing and exciting. I loved how confident he was, and even now, I still couldn't deny he was gorgeous. He had an air about him. He was the complete opposite of any guy I had dated before. I think that's why I liked him. He was different. We could go off and do things without the band. We never talked about music. It was a nice reprieve from everything. At the time, I loved it.

Now, looking back I should have seen the signs. He hated my friends. Christopher had me meet his family right away. His mother wasn't exactly pleased with our sudden wedding, but after we got to know each other, she came around to me. In fact, the last time I saw her she practically begged me to settle down and have his babies. That's all he wanted me for, to have someone to bring home. Holly apparently wasn't good enough. I was just the stand in wife, to use when it was necessary. He didn't love me. I shook the thoughts out of my head. I didn't want to think about my cheating husband while I was around Ethan. It confused me.

Our show that night went awesome. I didn't hiccup once on the lyrics to any of the new songs or stumble on any cords on the stage. The rush from the show was flowing through me. I pushed the guys out into the lobby where the bar was. We sat down, and I ordered rounds of vodka and energy drinks for everyone.

We were only there about a minute before someone noticed and people wanting autographs surrounded us. I agreed to take pictures with anybody that bought us drinks. I would have done it anyway, but being a musician meant that I was always pretty broke. I did have Chris' credit card, but I hated using it. It just made me feel that more dependent on him.

Cruel Distraction was announced and I jumped up. "Crap! I was supposed to watch the show tonight. Come on. We need to go back," I said. Derek and Mark ignored me.

"I don't think I can make it back up the stairs Cleo," Adrian mumbled that he wanted to stay at the bar. He had drunk at least double the drinks I had. I pulled him off the stool.

"No, I can't miss this. Let's go to the floor," I urged, holding on to him. The room was full. We had to squeeze through the crowd before people started to recognize us. Only then did they back up and let us move. I wasn't trying to be close to the stage. I didn't want to be pushed around and groped. I just needed to see him. I needed him to see me.

He came onto the stage looking gorgeous as usual. The screams were deafening. I felt someone grab my waist and I jumped, startled. I looked back and saw Adrian struggling to hold us both up. I looked at him, and we both erupted into laughter. He was wasted.

They started their set. I had heard it a dozen times now but being in the crowd was different. Closing my eyes, I let myself enjoy the show. I danced along to the music. I hadn't been in the audience at a concert in years. I had almost forgotten the feeling. Everybody dancing and singing along to every line. All of us sweating and screaming, hoping that one of the people on stage would see us and smile. Maybe give us a shout out or toss a drumstick.

After a few songs, I heard a very familiar melody. I stopped dancing and looked up to the stage. Ethan was standing in the middle holding on to the microphone stand. The baseline pounded in my ears. No freaking way.

"So I have a story kids, gather around," he said, which made everyone clammer in closer. I took the opportunity to step back and breathe. What was he doing? I asked myself, quickly sobering up with each note the guitars played softly. Only a handful of people knew that song.

"There's this boy. He fell hard for this girl, and she tore his heart out. Stomped on it, ripped it to shreds. It took time, but he finally decided he was over her," Ethan tipped his mic stand over and caught it with his leg, kicking it back into his hand.

"But then she just showed up, just to stir up old memories that he was trying pretty fuckin' hard to forget. And now she's moved on but turns out he still can't. He wants to tell her, but he doesn't know how. So, from me to you, babe. If you're out there, this is for you. This is for what should have been said years ago," he told the crowd as the band launched full force into the song. Our song. Our duet.

I watched in shock as he started singing. He sang about the first time we met. The first time we kissed. Then the first time we…

"I screwed her, but I didn't realize until it was too late that she had screwed me,"

I gasped, hearing it for the first time performed was odd. I panicked when I realized that my part was coming up. I started pushing past people to get to the stage. Ethan stormed across the stage as we had rehearsed. He was playing his part well. His anger was very convincing. A little too convincing. I felt a twinge of pain when I realized that some of that anger was real. His first verse ended, so he paused and the band played on.

The crowd erupted in cheers and screams. Some people let me through quickly, but others glared at me and swore. Suddenly I felt a tap on my shoulder. I turned to see two big guys motioning for me to let them lift me up. I nodded and before I could thank them I was crowd surfing. People were screaming about getting me to the stage, and a few girls boo'd. I just had to laugh. The security made sure it was me before helping me grab Ethan's hand. He pulled me up and his mouth locked onto mine in front of everyone. My eyes flew open. This kiss wasn't planned.

The screams were deafening. I pulled away, and he kissed me again, harder. His lips were soft and tender, while his mouth was hard as I kissed him back. Finally, remembering that we had an audience, I pushed him forcefully away. He stumbled back in surprise. I bit my lip, trying to look apologetic without breaking character. He understood and straightened back up. Glaring at each other, I never took my eyes off him as I was handed a microphone. I pulled the hair ties out of my hair and shook my head, letting my hair fly all over. His eyes shone with excitement while the rest of his face stayed hard. They dared me to fight back. As soon as I heard my cue, I launched into my part of the song. My verse was filled with just as much hate and pain as his was.

"You wanted everything that I couldn't give you. I wanted time, and your solution was a tattoo!" I sang into the mic.

We walked in a semi-circle, never breaking eye contact. I could feel the heat between us, and I felt like the crowd could too.

Then we met up in the middle for the chorus. We pressed our backs against each other and sang out to the crowd. As if we just couldn't bear to look at each other anymore. The fans went ballistic.

We kicked off each other and sang our parts again, when we returned to the chorus again we went to each other. Although this time our hands found each other's. We interlocked our fingers still pressed against each other's backs. So that even though we said we were through with each other, our body language revealed we were lying. All part of the act of course. We had been planning this for weeks now, and it was going perfectly.

The next part of the song was sadder, more about the heartbreak and pain. It was about missing each other. Me regretting not staying. Him wishing he ran after me. We finished the last few lines together, our arms around each other, looking deeply into each other's eyes.

The song ended, and we stopped singing, but he didn't let me go. I could feel his chest rising heavily from the excitement of our performance. Looking up at his face, I saw pain. I let my mouth hang open just a bit so I could breathe better. My hair and clothes clung to my skin.

Ethan moved one hand off my hip and raised it to brush my hair away from my neck, revealing our matching tattoos to the fans. Still, he never took his eyes off me. I hadn't realized how much the song drained me until I felt a tear slide down my cheek. Before I could wipe it away, Ethan moved to brush it away with his thumb gently.

I saw him gulp and open his mouth just a fraction. I was still in shock over what had just happened, I couldn't speak. That was a fantastic performance. He was extraordinary. Suddenly he pulled away, and we moved to stand next to each other on the stage. He gripped my hand still and pulled me into a bow. I looked at the screaming fans, but my mind was elsewhere. Did we just… what was that?

He put the mic to his mouth again. "Alright, that's it for us. Good night folks!" He said and, still holding my hand, he pulled me off the stage. When we were behind the curtain, he let go of me, and we turned to face each other. We were both drenched in sweat and grinning ear to ear at each other.

I hurled myself at him, hugging him. "That was crazy! It went perfect! They loved it!" I screamed. He laughed, and when I let go, he was beaming.

"I thought it would be better to surprise you," his eyes sparkled with mischief.

"That was one hell of a surprise. I need to go find the guys," I told him, hurrying off to find my friends. They were rushing backstage when I saw them. All of us were jumping up and down in excitement.

"You were amazing Cleo! That was insane!" Derek shouted. Adrian picked me up and spun me around.

"That's our girl!" He said.

"We should call Sam. That song is fire!" Mark said.

We caught up with Cruel Distraction, and they were all just as excited as we were. I found myself gravitating to Ethan's side. His beautiful blue eyes shone with happiness. I could only assume my brown pair matched his because I was riding a high like no other.

He took my hand and squeezed. I leaned into him. I felt him lean down and kiss the top of my head. I didn't care if people saw us. Chris never once came to a show. God forbid he support me in any way. I think people assumed that we had separated. Granted that wasn't exactly the truth, it also wasn't far off. I didn't know where Chris and I were at anymore. Let people think what they wanted.

We held on to each other until we heard someone clear their throat. I moved away to look towards the sound. I felt Ethan's body tense next to mine and drop my hand as we looked at a woman dressed in a tiny green dress that barely covered her naughty bits. She was gorgeous with her fuchsia hair, big eyes, and full, pink lips to match her shiny locks.

"Ethan?" She asked, her face contorting into a look of confusion, and then pure hatred when she looked from me to him. I looked back at him, but his eyes were wide and focused on the very famous pop star in front of us. He gulped, and I saw the blood drain from his face.

"Dixie?"

Chapter Four

MIGHT TELL YOU TONIGHT

$\mathcal{I}$ couldn't decide what made me more uncomfortable. Was it that the first thing Ethan did when he realized who was there was pull away from me or that I felt like we had been caught doing something wrong? Was this what Holly felt like? No, because I felt guilty. When I slammed the door shut on my husband and his bare-assed assistant, entangled in each other, I heard laughter. She had thought it was hilarious. I, however, did not enjoy feeling like I had destroyed someone's relationship. Even if it was just for show.

They left through a door moments later leaving me standing there like an idiot. Mark strode over and took my hand. I tried to let go, but he wasn't going to let me get upset here. He let go and moved in front of me. Bending over, he let me climb onto his back. Without taking my eyes off the door they had left out of. Wrapping my arms tightly around my friend he carried me away. I was so confused.

I had seen her face before on TV, and on every magazine at the gas stations. To the world, she was Duchess, the newest pop princess. He called her Dixie. Was that her real name? Must be. Of course her legal name wasn't Duchess. No one in Hollywood kept their real name. But why was she here at our show, of all places? Deep inside I knew. It was obvious.

Mark took the long way out of the building to make sure we didn't run into them outside. The rest of the guys followed us out. When Mark put me down I looked at my bandmates. They had looks of pity on their faces. I would not cry. Screw him. I was furious. Why didn't he tell me?

"What do you want to do?" Adrian asked. I shrugged and stormed onto the bus. They joined me shortly and we sat together in cold silence. Finally, Mark turned the stereo on so it played softly. He couldn't sit in silence. I leaned back against Derek who was sipping on a beer.

"Why do I do this? I'm married. I don't care about it. Him or her. God, I'm so stupid!" I said, more of to myself than them.

"Well screw your marriage for one," Mark said. "And Ethan, in his defense, probably wasn't expecting her to show up to a show."

"What do you mean?" I turned to look at him. Derek thoughtlessly started playing with my hair. We were all too close, I thought to myself. It was like we were all one person. None of us had any sense of personal space. I pushed him away. He frowned. I wasn't in the mood.

"He didn't tell you? They dated for a few years." I leaned back into Derek's chest. "Seth mentioned it, but he said they broke up," Mark added as an explanation. It didn't matter. Ethan lied.

He knew she could show up. Why wouldn't he warn me? I told him about Christopher. Why didn't he tell me about his girlfriend? Ex-girlfriend? I doubted it since she looked crushed when she saw us holding hands. I asked him directly if he was seeing someone and he lied to me. Why did I even think this would work? Was he using me to make her jealous?

Duchess was one of the most recognizable celebrities right now. She was a huge popstar. How could I compete with her?

Why didn't he mention her? I kept repeating the questions over and over in my head. None of this made any sense. Adrian went to the fridge and brought us all another round of beer.

"I'm just gonna chill for a while. Pretend my life doesn't suck for a bit. You guys go ahead and party, or whatever. Don't worry about me," I told them, but no one moved to get up.

Derek spoke from behind me. "I think we all need a night in." With that, Mark turned the TV on and got a movie started. I snuggled deeper into Derek's chest. I heard him sigh and ask Mark to hand him another beer. I started to relax, but tensed when I heard voices outside.

I looked out the window and saw we were still in the parking lot of the venue. Glancing around I saw my friends looking at me, wondering what I was going to do. I got up quickly and left them on the bus. I didn't want to argue with them. I knew if I paused to say something, we would.

I climbed down the steps, catching Cruel Distraction right outside the bus. They were yelling and cursing, but stopped when I came out. They glanced at me, then moved past me to get on the bus. Only Ethan stayed. Standing in front of me, eyes red and puffy, looking so sad. I could tell he was tweaking. He looked rough. I wanted to be angry, but I instantly wanted to go and soothe him. See why he was so upset. I looked around to see if anybody else was around. Other than the guys on the bus, we were alone.

"We need to talk," he said, his voice hoarse. I just glared at him. I didn't want to just run back to him. I needed him to know I was angry. He screwed up. He lied to me for no reason. I folded my arms across my chest, flinching a bit. My muscles were sore from the show.

He crumpled to the ground. "Cleo, you don't know. I need to explain. Dixie. It's not easy. She had some free time and wanted to see me. She came to bring some things that I had left at her place," he stood up, opening and closing his mouth. He looked uncomfortable, as if he wanted to say more, but didn't know how. I decided just to let it be. Not make him explain anything. Honestly, I didn't want to hear about it. Just thinking about him with someone else was weird. I'm sure he felt the same way.

"We're not together. Not anymore. I mean, we were. I broke it off before the tour. I think she's having some trouble with it," he rushed, trying to explain. I shook my head.

"Ethan, it's cool. Don't worry about it. I guess I deserved it. Look, I need some time to think," I said lamely. Hurt flashed on his face, but quickly disappeared and turned into a look of determination. He grabbed my hand and pulled me forward. I wanted to fight, but I also wanted to go with him. Wherever that was.

We walked away from the bus. I didn't realize how exhausted I was until he stopped and turned to me. He asked me if I was alright. We were on a busy sidewalk. People were entering and leaving the bars; passing by, not recognizing us.

"Sorry, I've had a long night. Give me a minute." I told him, but he shook his head slightly as if to say, "This will certainly not do." I grinned, imagining him saying that in one of his funny voices.

Ethan turned around and bent over, slapping his back to indicate for me to climb on. This was becoming a popular mode of transportation for me lately. It probably helped that I was short and light. I moved forward and practically fell onto him. With a slight groan, he stood up, straightened, and grabbed my thighs while I wrapped my arms around his neck. He started walking. Leaning my head against his, I inhaled his scent. Cologne and sweat. I adored it.

I closed my eyes and may have fallen asleep because soon enough he was calling my name and shaking me around lightly. "Cleo, did you fall asleep? Cleo, wake up." I groaned and hugged him tighter. I wasn't ready to walk.

"We're here, I'm setting you down," he warned me as I climbed off of him. I stumbled, looking around.

Grinding the sleep out of my eyes, I see we are at a low-key club. There were no windows or advertisements. Just a tiny sign at the top of the door. It said WHAT'S THE PASSWORD in neon pink letters.

"What is this?" I asked him, and he smiled as he opened the door for me to go in. A large man in a black suit greeted us at a second door. He had a clipboard in his hand. He looked up and smiled warmly at us. He opened his arms and Ethan embraced him in a hug.

"Ethan! Long time no see! How've you been?" The music from the next room was blaring, and there were cheers just as loud. It was exciting and made me stand at attention. Suddenly I wasn't tired anymore. The energy was contagious.

"Great. It's been too long. Look, Marshall, I'd love to stay and chat, but my girlfriend has never seen the show," he told him. Marshall nodded and smiled kindly at me. I blushed a little behind Ethan. He called me his girlfriend. My stomach flipped. "Well, you are in for a treat then, Miss…"

"Cleo!" I shouted at him, trying to be heard above the music.

"Cleo. For you two, no cover. Enjoy the show." He winked at me and opened the door for us. Ethan pushed me in front of him and I gasped.

The DJ was blaring some cheesy 80's song about sex. It reeked of cigarettes and cheap perfume. Lights were all over the stage where two performers were dressed in extravagant dresses singing to each other. The rest of the club was dark. I had to squint to look around. There were small, intimate round tables covered in maroon tablecloths. The rest of the large room matched the tables. Dark and sexy.

Screaming, whistling, and laughter filled the room as the people performed. Some people close to the stage had their arms outstretched with dollar bills in their hands. I looked closer at the stage, at the performers, and that's when it hit me. We were at a drag show. I was in shock and awe at the same time.

I turned back to Ethan who was grinning ear to ear. He held up his hands. "Hear me out. We need a night free of all the stress. Come in with me and have fun. I promise you won't be disappointed. We can talk after this."

His innocent big blue eyes made him hard to turn down. I didn't have time to decide because the song ended and the MC took the performers place.

"You two, at the door, are you in or out? Don't be shy now. Come and join us at a table before we make you join us on the stage," she, or well he, said. Embarrassed, I took his hand as he led me down to a table in the front. The MC wasn't done with us.

"Well, well. Who do we have here? What's your name honey?" She asked me. Ethan left me at the table to go to the bar, so I was the main focus. Why did he just leave me like that? I was suddenly terribly nervous.

"Cleo." I told her shyly. Suddenly, and for the first time ever, I didn't want the spotlight on me.

"Cleo, Cleopatra? It looks like we have another Queen in the house tonight!" She purred. I sat with my mouth open in awe. She was fascinating.

"Well, for those who are just arriving, my name is Chelsea Sometimes, and I am your Mistress of Ceremonies tonight. Now can we give another round of applause for our last Queens, Amber Mist and her lovely partner in crime Porsa Lynn, and their rendition of 'Opposites Attract'."

The crowd and I cheered and clapped. Chelsea Sometimes talked some more and gave a little introduction for the next performer. I didn't hear her words. I was too entranced in everything. Her, the music, the atmosphere was electric.

Chelsea looked amazing. She wore a purple sequin thigh-high dress. It had to be from the eighties from the look of the neckline and the various giant bows all over. She had shoes to match that looked to be at least six-inch stilettos. Her face was gorgeous. She had Tina Turner blond hair, her dark skin making her look the part perfectly; that and the over exaggerated makeup looked awesome. I was a little jealous; I didn't have that kind of skill. I usually just slapped some eyeliner and lipstick on and called it good. Just watching her walking around the stage proudly, and confident was inspiring. I wanted that.

Ethan returned with two long islands, and just as he was about to sit down, Chelsea saw him. "Ethan Andrews, is that you honey?" He grinned, stood up and waved to the crowd. I had to laugh; we looked so out of place here. Everyone was in bright club clothing, and we looked like two goth kids leaving the mall.

"Ethan and Cleo, well, well, well. She has no idea, does she?" She asked him. He just laughed and lifted his shoulders apologetically. "Well sweet cheeks, there's no hiding here. Cleopatra, dear Cleopatra, what your date hasn't told you is that we here at 'What's the Password' helped make this boy famous." She began to walk around the stage lazily, eyeing the crowd. She was sizing us all up. That's when I realized where I had seen those moves before. Ethan used them every night. Holy crap. I turned to stare at him open-mouthed, and he cracked a sheepish smile.

"This boy would come in with his brother and watch the show every Friday night. They would stay after and talk to us, wanting to know how we do what we do. He had a voice like no other but was shyer than shit. At first, we thought we had a future Queen on our hands, but sadly this ridiculously sexy boy only likes chicks without dicks." She made an exaggerated frown and encouraged the crowd to say "Aww". Someone pointed a light at our table so people could see who she was talking about. I cringed at the harsh light.

"We told this boy that if he wanted our help, he would have to get up on stage himself. He was a hit. Do we have a picture anybody?" She asked the DJ and some of the other workers around. Someone shouted for her to wait a moment.

Soon enough she pointed to the wall and the spotlight shown on a white curtain. A moment later a picture of Ethan in thick makeup, wrapped in a red feather boa was projected onto it. His hair was longer, but he was still in his ripped shirt and skinny jeans.

The crowd cheered like crazy. Ethan stood up and bowed, a grin on his face. He looked at me and winked. I was in awe; my mouth was open. I don't know why but this made him way sexier than before. Confidence is everything.

The projector cut out and was replaced with soft pink lighting from before. Chelsea and the spotlight returned to her position front and center. "So dear Ethan, you have been missed while you have been traveling the world. However, you made a mistake slipping back into the lion's den tonight. I am going to have to push back some acts, and you are going to show us what you have learned. C'mon now, let's get you backstage."

A drag queen came up behind us and tapped him on the shoulder. She was gorgeous as well, dressed in a sexy sailor costume. "Come along now." The deep voice threw me off a little bit, but Ethan's perma-smile encouraged me to sip my drink and relax a bit.

I turned to Ethan and couldn't stop smiling. "Is this for real?" I asked him, and he shrugged, he wasn't ashamed. "Where else could I have gotten my moves?" He stood up to follow the sailor through a door to the side, not before kissing my cheek and squeezing my hand.

I watched a few acts in anticipation, waiting for them to announce Ethan's turn. This guy was unbelievable. No one, not even Adrian, would be caught dead doing this. After a solid half hour, Chelsea Sometimes came back and announced him.

He stepped out, and I cupped my hands to my mouth. I couldn't stop laughing. They gave him raccoon eyes and put him in even tighter jeans and took his shirt. I didn't think tighter jeans existed, but there he was, slathered in oil, his hair wet and holding the boa from the picture.

He took one long look at me and blew me a kiss. The crowd squealed and cheered. He took the microphone from Chelsea and looked out into the audience. "Before I do my thing, I'd like to dedicate tonight to my brother, Evan. Or as some of you more seasoned groupies might remember Penelope Felony." He smiled wide, even though I saw his eyes were shining with tears trying not to fall. He bowed his head, and the room fell quiet for a moment of silence.

Suddenly Ethan whipped his head up and pointed to the DJ. The crowd laughed and cheered. I didn't have time to dwell on the fact that his brother was a drag queen before I was entranced with his performance. He jutted his hip out and tapped his boot to a very familiar song. I gasped and then burst into laughter again. Ethan had made me a playlist to listen to on the bus, and this song had been on it. It was Sin with Sebastian's 'Shut up.' I knew all the words. Ethan kept it on his iPod in his warm-up playlist. It had become sort of a thing for us on tour.

I sat back down at my table, making sure I was at a good angle. I didn't want to miss a moment of his act. He lifted up his microphone and sauntered a few steps further onto the stage. The spotlight hit Ethan at the exact right time. He started dancing and singing his song. Actually singing. Some of the Queens' lip-synced while others chose to use their own voices. Ethan made the right choice.

Soon he was getting cheered on. He loved this; I saw it in his eyes. He was so comfortable here, it was amazing. I couldn't stop grinning. He moved to the head of the stage as he danced. My eyes followed his every movement in wonder. I was impressed. Never in a million years would I have guessed that this was his secret to success.

As he sang, the crowd began to react. People stood up and cheered. Some were even thrusting dollar bills in his direction. It was crazy. I felt so exhilarated. I mouthed the words as he sang them. Standing up to clap as the song ended Ethan held out his hand for me. I moved away from the table and walked to the edge of the stage. I let him pull me up. He spun me around and kissed me. He held it way longer than I expected, making me blush. When he finally let go, his eyes were sparkling with laughter.

"Don't worry; I'll be good. It's just for show," he whispered in my ear. Every time he touched me it felt like a jolt of lightning. I felt him lift my hair away from my neck to show the crowd his name on it. They cheered. The way we were facing you could see our tattoos. It was becoming our signature pose. He kissed my neck again, and the crowd went wild. He pulled away, and we both turned towards Chelsea who was crying. Full on bawling; her mascara was running down her face. She pulled a handkerchief out of her ample bosom to wipe her face. She rushed over and embraced us both.

"You are the cutest things I've ever seen! We are so lucky to have had you with us tonight. The best part of my night. Now go get cleaned up to watch the rest of us Queens stumble around this stage." She pushed us towards the curtain, which we gladly went through. The people in the back rushed us and squeezed us just as tight. I had never been more excited and confused. After a slew of compliments and kisses, he was left to wash up and return to our table to watch the other acts.

I held Ethan's hand the rest of the night. There weren't any electric sparks this time, but instead it was a comfortable closeness. I would never forget this night. We listened to renditions of Cher, Madonna, Paula Abdul, even a David Bowie song. It was a great night. I was able to forget about everything for a few hours. I can't remember the last time that had ever happened.

Finally, Chelsea came on and announced the finale where the whole crew came up and performed their last song. It was glorious. I asked Ethan if he wanted to stay and chat but he shook his head. "I would have never known," I told him as we stepped outside. He smiled softly. He kept hold of my hand as we began walking.

"My brother showed me this place when I was in high school. He was a hit," he said quietly, looking a bit sad.

"I had no idea you had a brother," I said.

"Yeah, just the one." His face grew hard.

"Sorry, you've never really talked about him before. Was he sick?" I asked, wanting him to talk to me. He shook his head and sighed.

"Nah. Maybe sick of our mother maybe. Or more specifically, her big shot husband," He smirked. I frowned, feeling sorry for him. Even though I wasn't close to my siblings even a little, I couldn't imagine losing one.

"It must be hard visiting home," I said, not knowing what else to say.

"Well, when your brother kills himself because of them, it's hard to want to come to Thanksgiving," he said in a harsh voice that told me the conversation was over.

"Oh," I said lamely. I felt instantly guilty. I shouldn't have pried so much. The look on his face was of deep pain. I tried to apologize, but he put his empty hand up while keeping his other hand laced through mine. Poor Ethan. Suicide. I couldn't even imagine what going through a loss like that must have done to him.

"It's fine. Come on. We should probably get back," he said with a forced smile. I had almost forgotten we were still in a very public place. Talking about something so personal felt weird now. I was a little sad that we had to go back to the bus.

"What are you thinking?" Ethan asked me. I didn't say anything as we continued to walk.

"I don't want to go back. This was nice. I felt free in there. Thank you."

"You're welcome. I understand the feeling." We walked in pleasant silence for a while. "Could we talk about today now?" He asked. I sighed and stopped.

"If you let me on your back," I told him, and he instantly dropped to his knees allowing me to hop on his back. He picked me up with ease and we continued on.

"I am sorry about Dixie, or er... Duchess. It's weird with her. She used to mess with my head. It was all a game. We broke up, and I moved out. Apparently she didn't take the hint. I took off after the show to break it off for good," he insisted. It was easier to talk to each other when we weren't able to look at the other's face.

"Do you love her?" I asked him, fearing the answer.

"No. I thought I was in love. I proposed, but we didn't announce it or anything. I didn't want to make a big deal out of it. It was good for a while, but I'm glad I broke it off. We are so bad for each other." I didn't respond, unsure of how to feel about it all.

"Did I come up?" I asked tiredly. I didn't realize how exhausted I was from our concert and then the drag show.

"I told her I didn't want to deal with her drama anymore. It was too much," he told me instead of answering my question. There was a long pause before he spoke again.

"Can I confess something?" He asked. My heart began to pound furiously. I was sure he could feel it on his back.

"Sure, I guess," I told him.

"When I found out we were touring with you guys, I broke it off," he revealed. I didn't say anything. What was there to say? It was confusing. Ethan was so hot and cold.

"She went on a little bender. It was bad. She was pissed

when she saw us together backstage. I wanted to make sure she wasn't going to do something stupid," he added, and I lifted my head. Was this girl crazy? I had dealt with a few crazy exes from the guys. I mean, one stole our dog for Pete's sakes.

"Like what?" I asked him, trying not to sound eager to hear about her.

"Well, when she tried to get me to take her back and I refused, she confessed to cheating on me when I was gone. She said it was a big joke between her and her friends. She kept asking me if your husband knew about us." I felt my blood run cold. Duchess was going to tell. I don't know what Christopher would do if he found out what I had been doing these last few weeks. In my defense though, tonight was the first night we kissed, but it was strictly professional. Just on stage. Well, twice now; at our concert and then the drag show, but still, it was all an act. But was it? It didn't feel like it either time.

"Is she going to tell him? He wouldn't understand. I haven't told him yet," I squeaked out. I don't know why I even cared. He apparently didn't care about my feelings. When I caught them together, he didn't run after me. He stayed with Holly. The tears came quickly again. He was such a bastard. I was here with this crazy awesome guy who was carrying me at least a half a mile back to the bus, and all I could think about was the husband who betrayed me.

"I don't know. I explained the situation. Told her we weren't together or planning on it. When we parted, she seemed rational, but who knows. I'm sorry Cleo. I don't want to drag you into my mess," his voice apologetic. I decided to change the topic. I was tired of being sad. I needed to soak up as much happiness as I could before the summer was over.

"So, I was the first girl you ever took there, huh?" I teased him. He snorted.

"Most people wouldn't understand. I didn't at first either,

but my brother was fascinated by it all, so I started to get into it too."

"Well, I can honestly say that was one of the best experiences of my life," I told him. We were silent again. "I thought you were from Michigan," I asked, realizing that we were in Ohio. That was hours away from Lansing.

He nodded, his head bobbing against mine. "I lived in Michigan, yeah. This was the only club that would let us in underage. We would leave right from school on Fridays and drive for hours to get here," he told me.

"Wow. That's crazy."

"We moved from Ohio when she married Bob. That's how Evan knew about the club," he added.

"Oh, so you have family here?" I asked. He never talked much about his family.

"I don't know, probably. My grandparents were never really close to us. My mom got pregnant when she was seventeen. I guess she had a promising future and they thought she threw it down the drain when she had us," he told me.

"What about your dad?" I asked him. I felt like if there was ever a time he was going to open up to me, it was now. I was going to ask everything I wanted to know until we were back on the bus, where I knew the conversation would end.

"He died. My mom didn't even know she was pregnant when it happened, so he never knew." I was speechless. This man's past was one filled with one tragedy after another. Poor, poor Ethan.

"I'm sorry to hear that," I told him.

"Eh, she never really made a huge deal of it. It is what it is. What about you? I think I've sufficiently poured my heart out enough tonight," he said with a dark, humorless laugh.

"Hm, well my parents were old as dirt when I was born. They never really seemed to care what I did. My siblings all treat me like I'm a child still. I feel like a pariah most times. They are all close in age, so they grew up together. I always feel like the odd one out. No one bothers to talk to me long, except for my nieces and nephews. Some are only a few years younger than me."

"My brother never had any kids thank God. I don't think my mother could have handled grandchildren," he laughed dryly.

"Well, what about when you have kids?" I asked with a yawn. This was something me and Adrian played. We talked about a make-believe future with the 2.5 kids, rich husband, or in his case super hot wife whose life was totally dedicated to making him sandwiches and giving blow jobs. That was it though, make-believe. I don't think either of us could live ticky tacky lives. We were dedicated to the road.

"No way. I can barely take care of myself most days. That and I don't want to be the dad who's never around. I can't stay in one place, so it's probably a good idea to not reproduce." I smiled and snuggled tighter into him. We were one in the same.

"Same here. Although everyone else thinks they can decide for me." Christopher returned to the front of my thoughts. Our conversation moved on to lighter things as we finished our trek back.

"Mmm, you rock," I told him as he climbed onto the bus still carrying me. He took me to the back, and I rolled onto the couch still in my shoes and nasty, sweaty stage clothes. He crept around, shutting the light off and left me to go to his bunk. I sighed and pushed back the aching desire to go to him, to squeeze into his bed with him.

Chris flashed in my head for just a millisecond. His smile, memories of us when we were happy sped through like an old film reel. Guilt washed over me. I was married. I had promised to love only him. But did he make the same commitments?

The curtain opened again, and Ethan tossed a blanket in to me and told me good night. I felt confused. Sometimes it was hot, the tension between us almost too much to handle. Then he would be cold, almost as if I was annoying him.

"Thanks again for tonight. I needed this," I said to him. He relaxed and chuckled low.

"I knew it. I could see it in your eyes. They were telling me, take me to a drag show." We locked eyes, and then he quickly, almost as if he was running away, pulled the curtain back into place. Shutting me out again.

Chapter Five

HIMERUS AND EROS

$\mathcal{W}$e were on the road before I woke up. No one asked where we had gone. I let them assume what they wanted. I didn't want anyone ruining a fantastic night. At that club, I had seen a different side to Ethan. I couldn't help but look at him differently now. He showed me he wasn't just some hot bad boy. Ethan Andrews wasn't just the sexy, smoldering rock star with pain in his eyes. He was a regular guy with a heart that had been ripped, cracked and broken many times over.

We spent that summer having the times of our lives. I had never had more fun on tour as I had with this group of guys. My bandmates were happy too. We finally decided to call the song 'Better Off Missing You". Everyone loved the title. It was the last line in the chorus, so it worked well.

The success we had with performing the song had inspired me to write more for my own band. I showed the guys some of it, and they were very enthusiastic about it. I felt on top of the world. Finally, after three long weeks of being non-stop on the road with only truck stop bathrooms to bathe in, we were told that since we had three days in between shows they were going to fly both bands out to California to get the song recorded.

Some bigwigs had flown out to see us perform the song on the road. They were so happy with it that they wanted to get the gears rolling quickly. Sam had even mentioned they wanted to try to film the music video in that time too. I glanced at the schedule on his phone and my excitement deflated. He had us scheduled down to the very hour. It made me nervous. What if we couldn't get the song finished in the time allotted? Would that put a kink in everything?

The label put us all on a plane to California, it would only take a few hours, but it felt like an eternity. I couldn't wait to take a hot shower. While touring, those were rare. Most of the time we were washing up with towels and dousing ourselves with body spray. I remembered to grab my clothes too. Hopefully, they could get washed while we were at the hotel.

I took a nap on the plane to pass the time. Derek had to shake me awake. We took a cab to a hotel and quickly jumped out with our duffel bags to start heading into the building. I wasn't the only one excited for real showers and beds, if only for a few nights.

The energy circling our group was infectious. The Chatter around us grew louder. I saw people taking pictures of us. There was a buzzing wherever we went. Everything was going great until we talked to the clerk at the desk. She had three rooms booked for our stay. Two rooms had two beds, and one room was a mini-suite with only one. That room was reserved under mine and Ethan's names. Our group of eight were silent for a minute, taking the information in. Instantly I felt the heat rise to my face. I knew why they had done that. It seemed like everyone wanted us together. Suddenly I was very uncomfortable.

The woman at the desk held out a handful of cards for room keys, and I backed away, bumping into Adrian. I didn't want anything to do with sharing a room alone with Ethan. The silence was becoming awkward. Thankfully Adrian stepped up.

"I call the single bed! All you guys can split the other rooms!" He said triumphantly, as he plucked a card out from her hands. With a huge sigh of relief, I took a card to a shared room and Christian took the other.

With our luggage in tow, we headed towards the elevators. I walked next to Adrian while everyone else fell behind us. "Here," he said, passing me the key card to the suite. I stared at it. I didn't want this. Ethan and I weren't together. Our so-called romance was strictly for show. He and I both agreed on this.

"No thanks," I said and tried to hand it back, but he refused.

"Just take it. If it gets too weird, Ethan can switch rooms with me and I can share the super comfy suite bed with you. Or him, I don't care," he winked, and I sighed. That was probably the best scenario.

"Fine. We'll see," I told him and stepped into the elevator.

Looking at the cards, I saw that my room was on a higher floor than the others. I watched all of my friends get off on the floor just under mine. Ethan looked just as uncomfortable as I felt. "Should I go with them?" Ethan asked me. I rolled my eyes and gave up.

"We can share the suite. Maybe there's a couch or something," I said. Ethan shrugged and continued up with me to our room. We entered the suite and dropped our stuff. I had to admit, even though I was pretty pissed about it, this room was killer.

It was huge, and more like a mini apartment than a hotel room. There was an actual bedroom, then a small living room area. To the far right was a kitchen, with a regular sized fridge and stove. As I walked around, I went into the bathroom to find that it was bigger than the one at my house! I was in heaven. I couldn't wait to get into a hot, steamy shower. I returned to the living room. Ethan was pulling clothes out of his bag, tossing them onto the couch. Guilt washed over me. If anything, I would take the couch. It was only fair since I was the one upset about the situation.

When he saw me watching him, he straightened and smiled at me. Without really meaning to I took a good look at him. He was looking hot as usual, with the standard ripped t-shirt and tight jeans. I probably looked a mess with my slick, greasy hair and stained shirt. If he noticed, he pretended he didn't. I looked away quickly.

"Hey you. You ready for the first real shower in weeks?" He laughed. The life of musicians wasn't as fun and glamorous as people thought. It involved way more dirt and sweat than people saw. Thank God for deodorant and Febreze.

"Yes! I call first dibs. I need hot water," I told him as I grabbed my bag.

"We could share the shower," Ethan said to my back. I whipped my head around with my eyes wide.

"What did you just say?" I demanded. He pursed his lips before erupting into laughter. He moved to hold his gut as he bent over. I relaxed and hurled a pillow from one of the chairs at him before hurrying to the bathroom.

I tried my hardest to enjoy the hot water, but my thoughts kept going back to the man in the next room. Was he as nervous as I was about sharing a room? Did it bother him? No sooner had Ethan disappeared from my mind did Christopher take his place. No doubt he'll be pissed when he sees the music video, or the stupid tabloids. I was already imagining the ridiculous headlines.

'Cleo And Ethan - Scandalous Love Affair'; 'Cleo: Pregnant with Triplets!' 'Emo Prince Weds Punk Rock Princess In Secret Wedding.' People would eat that garbage up. Anything to make a sale.

I stayed in the shower for almost half an hour. The cascade

of hot water was heaven. When I finally turned the faucets off and grabbed my towel, I already missed it. Wrapping a towel around me, I stepped out of the bathroom. Ethan was in a recliner facing away from me. He was leaning over the coffee table. He must not have heard me open the door because he didn't turn.

It gave me the opportunity to check him out again. Ethan Andrews was so sexy. Toned, covered in tattoos, and his nose and lip were pierced. How he walked, how he talked; everything about him drew me in. Don't get me started on his voice. When he got on stage and sang the songs his band created, I would let him take me right on the stage if he asked. Hypothetically, of course. I respected him, I reminded myself as he stood up and stretched. We were only colleagues. Nothing else. Not anymore.

He turned slightly and jumped when he saw me staring at him. I looked away quickly and hurried to the bedroom as he lunged for the little box on the table. I heard him snap it shut as I closed the door.

I pulled out the brand new clothes Sam had given me courtesy of the record label. When he handed me the bag, I was weary at first. I didn't want anybody to turn me into some bubblegum pop princess. I didn't want to become the next Duchess. However, I was pleasantly surprised to find a black t-shirt, black leather jacket, some black and white striped skinny jeans and a pair of suede booties. It was a little more girly than I usually would wear but still close enough to my style that I would wear it.

I laid the items on the bed and began drying myself off. Pulling the towel off of my head I realized that I had left the hair dryer in the bathroom. Stepping out of my room I saw that Ethan was gone, but I could hear the shower running.

Holding on to my towel tightly with one hand I decided to knock. He didn't answer. Just as I had stepped back, the door was ripped open. I jumped, startled and then I started laughing.

Ethan was standing in the doorway, in a towel, looking impatient. He was wearing a shower cap, and as my eyes lowered, I saw he had also put on the complimentary fluffy white slippers. I laughed as he tried to keep a straight face. He crossed his arms over his heavily tattooed chest.

"Did you need something? I have a routine, and you are breaking it," he said as seriously as he could muster. His lips twitched as he tried so hard not to smile.

"I need the hairdryer," I told him and shook his head.

"No can do. It's my bathroom time. You can have it when I'm done," he said and began closing the door. I lunged forward quickly and snatched the purple cap off of his head. He tried to grab it back, falling out of the doorway. I pulled away and moved deeper into the room. He took chase, and I squealed as I turned and tried to move faster. His fingers touched my towel, but I pulled away quickly and ran into my bedroom giggling. I jumped onto the bed and waved the cap like a little purple flag. One hand was clutching my towel for dear life, while the other holding his cap. I dared him to come get it.

He raised an eyebrow at the door. He wouldn't dare come in. He dove at me, knocking us both down to the mattress. I gasped in shock. Somehow he managed to pin me under him. Out of the corner of my eye, I saw his bright orange towel was falling off the edge of the bed. With a mischievous grin, he moved my hand towards the middle of my body and snatched the shower cap out of my fingers with his teeth. He pressed his body against mine. Our noses touched as we locked eyes.

He was so hot. Hot and naked. Hot, naked, and aroused. On top of me. The only thing between us was my lavender towel. We stared at each other for a moment as we both realized this. Finally, he kissed me quickly on the nose and leaped off of the bed snatching his towel quickly. Not fast enough, because as I sat up, I saw his massive erection. How did I not remember that? Was there anything wrong with this guy? I swear I had yet to find a flaw.

My body was already responding to him. I was this close to joining him in his shower but chickened out in the end. That was not how I wanted our first... well not first, or second. No, not any time. There wasn't a next time. Why did I have to keep reminding myself this?

Once I calmed myself down, I realized he still had the hair dryer. With a sigh, I decided to get ready without it. Pulling on my clothes, I did my hair and makeup and exited the bedroom.

I tried to watch TV to take my mind off of him, but I couldn't stop thinking of him... it... no him. Definitely him. Looking around the living room, I noticed he had already unpacked. His clothes placed neatly on the side table next to the couch. His cell phone lay on the table on the other side next to his little wooden box. Before I could decide whether to pry or not, he came out fully dressed.

He came to relax with me on the couch. We made small talk, but the tension was still there. He was clearly still attracted to me. As was I to him. Maybe one of us should trade rooms with Adrian. This was exactly what the label had wanted, I frowned.

A joke on TV made him laugh. I forced a chuckle, but I had no idea what was going on in the show. I couldn't focus with him here. He nudged my shoulder with his, and it was like a jolt of lightning. I jumped a bit. This was bad. I couldn't go down this road. I wasn't like Christopher.

Suddenly I thought about Duchess. I remembered her face when she saw us holding hands. She had been crushed. Is that how Ethan was when he found out about Chris? That led to me thinking about all the other women who had gotten the pleasure of experiencing all that Ethan offered after me.

"When did you start dating Duchess?" I asked him, trying

to sound casual. I felt him tense up next to me. He turned to eye me carefully.

"Why are you asking?" He asked instead of answering. My eyes narrowed.

"Why aren't you telling me?" His eyes darted away.

"Because it doesn't matter. It's over," he groaned. "We weren't good together."

I turned my body to face him completely. "I thought you said it was a while before you started dating her," I said, not letting it drop. He looked away guiltily. I noticed he had moved away from me. Before we were almost cuddling, now he was a good foot away from me.

"Well, not exactly. After Christmas they flew us back out here to record some stuff. She was at a party. We were introduced. You're getting angry. Why bring this up now?"

The room fell silent. We broke up on Christmas. Ethan wasn't as hurt as he made it sound after all. I don't know why but it bothered me. He wasn't pining for me. He practically jumped into bed with her at his first chance. My insecurities kicked in.

Duchess was the biggest star around these days. Perfect face, flawless body, millions of fans. Sure, most of her songs were auto-tuned, but that didn't mean her fame was any less daunting. I was a nobody compared to her.

"Wow. You gave me so much crap about being with Chris so quickly, but it was okay for you to hook up with Duchess right away?" I said, accusingly.

"That's different," he said flatly, shifting further away. His face soured.

"How is it different? It's no different, Ethan." I glared at him. He stood up and moved to the other couch, laying down to stare at the ceiling.

"She isn't like you see on TV. We never had anything meaningful. That's the difference. You loved Chris. I never loved Dixie," he said.

The room fell silent. He was right. It felt like everything I had been avoiding this summer was finally out. That was why I couldn't call him. Why I was avoiding thinking about Christopher. He broke my heart. I loved him with everything I had, and he didn't love me.

"Is that what you think?" I asked.

"I don't think anything. I know," he snapped. He moved off of the couch and went to the window. Refusing to look my way.

"I liked you for years. Since the first time we saw you play. I was like fifteen. At that battle of the bands. Do you remember?" He paused, giving me time to think about it. I did. It was just a little gig. Five different bands, five hundred dollar prize. We needed the money to pay for some new equipment. In the end, it was us against Cruel Distraction. They won. It was what started our little friendly feud. It was a good memory. I remembered how cute I thought he was, but I was dating Steve at the time.

"You have no idea how much I wished you'd give me the time of day. Just once. Just one extra look or smile. But it was always someone else. Adrian, the guys, or any of the other boyfriends you had. When I finally had your attention, I thought it meant something. Every time we snuck off together I fell more in love with you. I thought you wanted to be with me. But then you took off. You were just in my bed, and you took off to be with another guy. You were so cold. You didn't care about me." He turned back to look at me. I opened my mouth to argue, but he continued.

"It messed me up. Having to look at your name every day, seeing what I screwed up. Not knowing what was wrong with me. So yeah, I found someone who did want me, Cleo. Even if it was just my body and my name. Is that so bad?" He demanded, stepping towards me. I looked down, ashamed of what I had said to him. What I had done to him.

"Ethan, I am so sorry. It wasn't intentional. It just…"

"It just what? Wasn't what you pictured? Was it just me that you didn't like? Why didn't you love me?" He yelled, and I couldn't take it anymore. I stood up and pushed past him to leave. I don't know how this conversation got this far, but I wasn't going to sit here and let him scream at me.

"Oh, just leave again. Sweet. Do exactly what you always do," he said, and I couldn't do it anymore. I turned back.

"Screw you, Ethan. Don't try to pretend you know everything. You have no freaking clue!" I said and stormed out. I slammed the door shut and fell back against it, slinking to the floor. I put my head down between my legs and sobbed.

I don't know how long I was in the hallway before the door opened just a fraction, making me fall back into the room. I looked up to see Ethan with bloodshot eyes. He was staring down at me. I glared at him, and he almost flinched.

"Can we talk?" He said. My chest was heaving; I was trying so hard to calm the urge to kick him in the face. I stood up and let him open the door all the way to let me in. He shut the door behind me, and I glared at him, crossing my arms.

"When I first got to Cali, we stayed in this mansion. Well you know it, you've been there I'm sure." I had been there. We were signed to the same record label. They owned a gigantic mansion that they let all of their clients use. We only stayed a night here or there and never had our paths crossed with Cruel Distraction.

"We were the shiny new toys there. There were parties all the time and one of them Duchess came to. I wasn't big into it all. I was still pretty depressed. She saw me in a hallway and decided right then and there that she wanted me. I needed that. Cleo, after you and my mom and my brother abandoned me, I needed someone to want me," he told me.

"We weren't perfect. Hell, most of the time I didn't even like her. But she was there. She stayed. She called me, and came to visit, and never once insisted our relationship be a secret. That's why I moved on so fast. I deserve to feel wanted!" Tears that had been resting in the corners of his eyes were now falling down his cheeks. His big blue eyes seemed even bigger. He pushed his pointer finger into his chest.

"I deserve to be loved," he said, his voice cracking. I leaned forward quickly to embrace him. He tensed, but after a moment relaxed and let me hold him. He was right. Again. He did deserve all those things. I was awful. How could I have treated him like that? I cried alongside him. I never wanted him to feel unloved again. He didn't do anything wrong. It was always me.

By the time I pulled away, we were only sniffling. Looking up into Ethan's eyes. I wanted so much to kiss him. He pressed his forehead to mine. I loved it when he did that. I knew looking into those gorgeous, bloodshot eyes we were going to be okay.

Sitting there, holding on to him for dear life I thought only of him. For the first time since Ethan came back into my life I wasn't comparing him to Christopher. I lay in his arms, enjoying this stolen moment. Who knows when we would have this time again.

Ethan pulled away. His eyes gazed upon me with such longing I could feel his need for me. I watched his eyes fall to my lips, and then back up at me. His breathing grew heavier. I watched as he slowly lowered his lips to mine.

His kiss was tender and slow. I opened my mouth slightly and felt him open his. His hands were around my waist, his fingers touching the skin that was exposed.

"Cleo," he whispered as his mouth went from my mouth to my neck to my collarbone. I moaned, but only when his lips started moving further down did I snap back to reality. I pushed him away, and he stepped back confused.

"Ethan, we can't. We just can't," I stumbled, trying to figure out what just happened. I didn't have any time to think before there was a pounding on the door.

"Hey, lovebirds! Get out here! We're heading to the studio! They want us there in twenty," Adrian shouted through the door. Ethan mumbled an apology, and I tried to apologize as well but was failing. I was so embarrassed. I hadn't meant for that to happen. Walking around the suite, I grabbed my cell phone and wallet. The whole time not making eye contact with Ethan. He stood with his hands in his pockets, looking troubled.

It felt like the walk of shame coming out of that room. All six of our bandmates were standing on the other side waiting for us. When we opened the door, cheers rang out through the hall. I could feel the heat rise to my face. I looked over at Ethan who was laughing. He ran his fingers through his hair and shrugged at me. As if to say "eh, what can we do?" But I could only scowl and pray the heat left my face quickly. I knew they were only joking but if they only knew what had just happened.

After everyone got their laughs, we continued downstairs and got into a large cab. "Have I told you how much more fun tattooed people are to see naked?" Ethan whispered in my ear once we started moving. I glared at him, afraid that someone could have heard.

"What are you talking about?" I snarled. I had changed in my bedroom. He chuckled.

"Don't act like you didn't take a peek when my towel fell off," he accused. I blushed. He leaned in even closer. His lips grazed my ear. "Your towel didn't cover nearly enough," he whispered. My heart began to race. I glared as he was smiling at me, playing innocent. He laughed. I glared at him and prayed everyone else's loud chatter drowned him out.

"I can't wait until I can get a better count. I only got to four," he said, a little louder than a whisper. Now I was sure people heard. I saw Mark whip his head around and stare at us. I looked away from him back to Ethan. I punched his arm, and he pretended that it hurt, pulling away and holding the spot. "What was that for?"

"Cleo always was weird after sex," Adrian said nonchalantly, not taking his eyes off his phone.

"I don't think they did it," Derek replied.

"How can you tell?" Christian said. I paled. This was another example of my bandmates having no boundaries.

Mark cleared his throat and sat up straight. He took off his glasses and breathed on them, fogging up the lenses. Then he cleaned them on his shirt. He did this all rather slowly, making a show of it. When he finally put them back on, he stretched and then clapped quickly.

"Ethan just whispered to Cleo that he had only counted four tattoos of hers. That means most likely he saw her neck, her ribs, her wrist, and the one right here," He pointed to his right pectoral. He was correct.

"Ding, ding, ding!" Derek shouted. I glared at them to shut up but of course, they wouldn't.

"Just wait until you get to number six," Mark said to Ethan. Mark looked at me and winked. I stared at him with disgust. He bumped fists with Adrian. "We got your back man," he said. Ethan just laughed and pulled me closer to him. Reflex made me want to pull away, but I liked this. I snuggled in closer and pulled my legs up onto the seat.

"So are you ready to record?" He asked me. I put my hand to my chin and rubbed it thoughtfully.

"I suppose. Although, my partner could work on his pitch," I accused. He raised his eyebrows.

"Oh really? Because last night I distinctly heard someone's voice crack at the end of the first chorus." I pulled away from him, mock offense on my face.

"How dare you," I started, and he held up his hands. He

had a silly, amused smile. "I'm just calling it as I hear it," he retorted, and I rolled my eyes. Moving back to relax on him again. He put his arm around me. He was so warm.

We started chatting with the rest of the group then. I tried to put what happened in the hotel room out of my mind. That would only distract me.

When we got to the recording studio, we jumped out and hurried inside. The technicians and both of our managers were there already. Stepping into the booth with my band and Ethan, we started warming up. I grabbed the headphones and microphone. I glanced at Ethan who was doing the same. I looked back at my bandmates as they played quietly in the back, waiting for my cue to start up. He was eying us, looking uncomfortable. He was used to his own band.

The song was played last at shows now, instead of the battle of the bands' thing. We did still use the crown and hype the contest during the show. We just didn't have the winner play an encore. Instead, we sang our song with Cruel Distraction, but Sam insisted we try it with both bands to see what version they liked better. Mark, Adrian, Derek and I volunteered to play first.

"What do you guys warm up to? I can try to do mine with you," Ethan said. Derek snorted which made Adrian, Mark and I crack up. I couldn't hold my smile back. I nodded at them, and they started up our usual song. Ethan listened intently to Derek and Adrian play but only when I started singing did he burst out in laughter. He was clutching his gut in pain. It took everything in me not to join him.

This had been a tradition since we were kids. Derek's mom loved country music, and since we were in her garage, she insisted we learn to play something she liked. It wasn't our thing, and we always hated it when she would try to enter us into county fair competitions, but now it was a fun joke. So today we played Shania Twain's 'Whose Bed Have Your Boots Been Under.' One of my favorites.

I was feeling brave with Ethan there as my audience. I smiled at him and raised my eyebrow as I sang the words directly to him. He didn't blink. I don't think he was breathing. I moved closer to him, swaying and putting my hands on my hips and shuffled over to him I got right up to his face. I was right; he wasn't breathing.

Finally, he turned quickly to his mic and belted out the chorus, falling right into step with us. Smiling at me the whole time, he didn't falter once. I tried not to let it trip me up. We finished the song together, and when the band behind us stopped playing, they started cheering. I think Mark even whistled. Ethan turned red with embarrassment. He glanced at them and then turned back to me with a small smile.

"Well that's a first," he laughed. His eyes turned a little more serious. I pulled away from him and smiled.

"Yeah, little inside joke. Do you need something to warm up to?" Ethan squinted his eyes in thought and then turned to the guys.

"I don't really know any country. We usually do some classic rock. Do you got anything?" Adrian's eyes lit up, and he started strumming a familiar tune. Derek caught it quickly and started the bass. It took Mark half a second more, but quickly they were playing a familiar Blondie song. Ethan considered the song, then grinning he turned back to his microphone to warm up. I joined in, and we sang 'Hanging On The Telephone.'

Maria Maria played our original song and then had us switch out and let Cruel Distraction play. After a long debate between the techs and both Kyle and Sam, they decided that we would record the song with Cruel Distraction. My bandmates were disappointed, as was I, but I understood. The other band knew the song better. However, I insisted that when releasing the song that the credit be given to both groups, and not Cruel Distraction featuring Cleo De La Rosa. It was a collaboration of both bands. Everyone agreed with me.

Once we were warmed up, we started working on recording the single. Overall I felt it went pretty smoothly. We finished it by early evening. My voice was only a little sore. We all left the building in good spirits. Sam informed us that we would have the rest of the evening to relax but first thing in the morning we would be shooting the video.

"There's a party at the house if you guys want to go. But it'd be smart to stay close, in case we need to get going quickly," he said, in almost a warning. Adrian flinched, knowing that Sam was talking directly to him.

All of us agreed that we just wanted to relax at the hotel, so that's what we did. We spent the evening hanging out, having a few drinks. We sat around the pool for a while. Everyone was in swim shorts that the label had provided, but I was sitting in a t-shirt and shorts. They had supplied me with a ridiculously skimpy lace bikini. I tossed it right back in the bag. It didn't bother me though. I was still having a lot of fun with everyone.

Ever since our kiss that morning I couldn't help but notice Ethan hovering around me. I was becoming paranoid. Did anyone else notice? Could they tell something had happened? No, nothing happened. It was just a kiss, I told myself. I was being ridiculous. I shut it down before it could go any further.

We kiss on stage every night. I'm sure they'll make me kiss him for the video tomorrow. It was nothing. It meant nothing.

While everyone else was in the pool, I lounged around in a chair with Ethan next to me. When he finally stepped away for a bit, Adrian came to sit with me. "You are lucky they gave you your own room. Derek already threw up in ours," he told me. I laughed, thrilled I didn't have to deal with that for one night.

"Who got the single bed?"

"Me of course. I threatened to force them to spoon naked with me if they tried to make me share." We laughed. Adrian liked guys, yeah, but he wasn't flamboyant or super horny, like the stereotypes. That and we made a pact. We both agreed that no amount of money could get us in bed with Mark or Derek. We were all way too close to each other to have sex. Adrian was the exception of course, but it was different then.

"So, did you do it?" He asked me. I glared at him, ignoring the question. Finally, I decided to speak.

"Would you have if you shared a room with him?" I asked, looking over at Ethan who had just come back from the bathroom. He scratched his nose and looked our way. Smiling, he chose to leave us be, and jump in the pool with his bandmates.

Our attention turned to the game of Marco Polo. It was harder for them to all play with beers in their hands. I was sure we were about to get kicked out. Ethan glanced over and smiled. He then bumped into a closed-eyed Spencer. Who then grabbed him and shouted, "Got one!" We laughed, and Adrian turned to me again.

"And where does he rank on the scale from best to worst?" Adrian asked me. Normally I would be appalled by anybody asking me that, but it was Adrian.

"Well, since we haven't done it..." I started, but Adrian cut me off.

"You mean done it again," he pursed his lips together and raised his eyebrow. I laughed and slapped his leg.

"Yeah, yeah. Well, all I can judge are his kisses," I said. Adrian raised both of his eyebrows and smiled coyly.

"Off stage kisses?" I couldn't stop the smile from forming. His eyes shone with glee. I instantly felt regret. Why did I reveal that? He would tell the guys.

"Don't tell anyone," I said quickly, and he just waved his hand dismissively.

"So, he's good with his mouth?" I rolled my eyes, relaxing.

"Number one," I laughed. Adrian would keep my secret. "Without a doubt," I added. He looked over, faking a look of hurt and pain.

"Remember I am on that scale somewhere too!"

"Yeah, and where do I rank on your scale of best lays?" I demanded. He softened and turned his face the other way so that I couldn't see him. Adrian always had a hard time looking at someone when he talked about serious things.

"One," he sighed. I swung my head back to him, confused and surprised; but he hurried on. "Not because you were great or anything but because you were the only one I had any sort of real feelings for. Don't worry, when I finally find someone else you will slide down that list. Most definitely." Really? He couldn't be serious for one full minute.

"Well if you keep talking, you are going to drop behind Steve!"

"Oh, come on, sneezy Steve? You're kidding me!" He took offense to that. I laughed, thinking back to the boy I lost my virginity to. A guy in a band from the next town over. He had an odd quirk in the bedroom. When he orgasmed, he would sneeze, and he never covered his nose. It was disgusting. We fizzled pretty quickly.

"Oh yeah, maybe I should call Steve up and see how he's doing," I teased and stood up as we saw a staff member from the hotel came out to kick us out.

Chapter Six

I WANNA

$\mathcal{W}$e fled the pool before we were kicked out of the hotel itself. Everyone got off the elevator on their floor, leaving Ethan and me to go up one level.

Once we were alone, I felt the mood shift. Suddenly I felt very uncomfortable. I wondered if he could feel it too, this awkward tension. Was he replaying our kiss in the room earlier? I was. I didn't want to be, but I was. I didn't know whether to address it or pretend it didn't happen.

After setting my things down on the counter, I went to my bedroom and dug out some pajama pants and a large shirt. Putting my hair in a giant bundle on the top of my head, I stepped out of the room. I decided I would wait for him to bring it up. If he stayed quiet then obviously he wanted to forget it.

Looking around, I saw Ethan already changed into some maroon colored pajama bottoms. When he saw me, he came over and extended his arm for me to take it to head downstairs. It felt more friendly than romantic. I hooked my arm in his, and we left the room.

We stepped into the elevator and, as the doors closed,

Ethan, still holding on to me spoke. "Are we going to talk about it?" He asked. Thankfully we only went one floor down, so it opened quickly. I hurried out, not looking at him.

"Nope," I said and knocked on one of the doors our bands had.

Ethan let go of me. "Are we pretending it didn't happen?" He continued. I focused hard on the peephole. Finally, the door swung open. I sighed with relief when I saw Adrian in his pj's holding a bowl of popcorn.

He glanced at us and lifted his chin. "What's up?" He asked, not moving to let us in.

"I'm trying to talk to Cleo, but she's stubborn," Ethan told him. I looked over at him, my mouth open to protest. Adrian raised his eyebrows, clearly amused.

"Well if that's the case, Cleo, come in. Ethan, sorry. Go play with everyone next door." I ducked under Adrian's arm and hurried into the room.

"Really?"

I turned back to look at him from the safety of the room. Adrian nodded his head. "Really. I'll talk to you later," he said, shutting the door in Ethan's irritated face.

Adrian came into the otherwise empty room and shut the light back off. He had been watching a movie. I got under the blankets with him and moved to steal the warmth from his body. He raised his arm to let me get closer. "Are we going to talk about it?" He asked.

"Nope," I said.

Adrian didn't argue and turned his movie back on. He wanted one night of peace, so he kicked out the guys. We were an hour into the movie when someone knocked. We looked at each other, as I got up. Moving towards the door, I felt for sure it was Ethan. I paused and took a deep breath. My heart was beating furiously. Was he coming to try to talk again? I grasped the handle and opened the door quickly. My heart sank. It was Sam.

He looked up from his phone and frowned when he saw me. "What are you doing down here? Are the guys here?" He peered in past me but frowned again. I stepped aside for him to come in. He sighed when he realized Mark and Derek were gone. He paused a few steps in and stared at the bed Adrian was in. He then turned towards me with bulging eyes.

"What?" I asked, moving further into the room to see. I burst into laughter. Adrian had taken off his shirt and tossed his pants and underwear on the floor right at Sam's feet. He was clutching the blanket over his lap.

"You two? Again?" He almost shrieked. In between gasping for air, I threw Adrian's pants at him. He caught them mid-air and slid out of bed to slip them on. I turned away just in time that I only saw his bare ass and not any of his front.

"Never. Again," we both said in unison. Sam scowled and pulled out his phone.

"Well anyways. I'm glad you're here because I was going to make sure you all were ready for tomorrow. We head out at ten a.m. Everyone be showered. It doesn't matter what you wear. Cleo, no makeup. Same old routine.

I also wanted to tell you guys that I found out what the concept for the video is. It's going to be big," he said excitedly. I sat down cross-legged on the bed and Adrian did the exact same on purpose. Sam eyed us with annoyance before taking a seat on a chair across the room and continuing.

"They hired a bunch of extras. I think they are going to have you guys performing for them," he paused. "Also, I heard that Duchess, the Duchess, is going to be there." My good mood deflated. Why was she going to be there? Did Ethan know?

"Cleo, you'll be kissing Ethan. Maybe another man too. Eh, it's complicated. I'll just let you be surprised," he quickly finished when he saw me open my mouth to protest. I didn't want to keep kissing every man they told me to.

"Who do I get to kiss?" Adrian said, thankfully changing the subject. Sam looked up from his phone.

"Pick an extra. But don't get it on camera. I know both bands were part of this, but let's face it. This is all about Cleo and Ethan. Hate to say it, but it's the truth. We want to see them kissing. Not you. We can see you kissing anytime, anywhere, anyone for that matter," he muttered.

Standing up, Sam reminded us of tomorrow's schedule. He made us promise to get the others there in one piece. I should probably get some rest, I yawned. Sleep meant going back to my suite. That put a pit in my stomach. Had Ethan gone next door, or back upstairs? I toyed with the idea of moving Adrian upstairs with me. On one hand, I didn't want to lose the opportunity to sleep alone. On the other hand, if I was alone with Ethan that could lead to bad things.

"Adrian, let's go get Mark and Derek, and then we'll go upstairs," I finally decided. Adrian put his hands up in innocence.

"Hey, I was just messing with Sam. I don't know what you're thinking but..." I took that moment to push him off the bed. He fell with a thump! Standing up, we went to find the other members of our band.

Thankfully Mark and Derek were still in the room with Cruel Distraction. You could hear the music from in the hallway. I made Adrian go in after them. When they didn't come out, I went in myself to remind both bands that if they didn't sleep off some of their drunkenness that they would look like crap for the biggest video of our careers to date.

The party goers, I assumed old friends or new fans all groaned and booed me. I flipped them off, and Mark and Derek followed me out. Before we shut the door, I heard someone say that I was right and they should probably get the party wrapped up. Told you, I thought. Ethan hadn't been inside.

We got them into their room. Now that Adrian was coming with me they each got their own bed. Once they were asleep, which wasn't long, we headed upstairs. Before I opened the door, I paused to listen. I didn't hear anything. My stomach was in knots. As much as I didn't want to talk to him, I still hoped he was here.

Happiness flooded me when I opened the door and saw him watching TV on the couch. Ethan turned, and his face brightened until he saw Adrian behind me. "Really?" He said, annoyed. I looked at Adrian, who threw his hands up.

"I'm out," he said, and turned right around heading downstairs. I tried to protest, but he was already gone. I trudged inside. Without speaking to Ethan, I went into my room.

Closing my eyes, I tried to force myself to sleep. There was a knock and Ethan opened the door a few inches. I opened my eyes. "Am I really taking the couch? It's cold out there," he said, looking so disappointed.

"Where else would you sleep?" I snapped, harsher than I intended. He flinched and then his face hardened. A second later he strolled over and climbed into the bed. I sat up, my mouth open and I turned to him. "What are you doing?"

He grabbed the blanket and pulled. "The suite was in my name too. You get that side, I'll sleep on this side," he told me. I was dumbfounded. Plopping back onto my side, I pulled the blanket back over to me.

"Fine, but you stay over there," I snapped. He laughed dryly.

"Alright. I don't think I'll be the issue," he said. I rolled over to glare at him.

"What are you saying?"

"Nothing. Go to sleep." He told me and turned away, pulling the blanket back over to him. I let out a frustrated sigh and tried to relax. He fell asleep quickly. I could hear his breathing steady. I was still wide awake. I turned back to him. He looked so comfy. I had taken back the blanket, leaving him half uncovered. I took the time to admire him.

He had toned all those muscles. His once soft, flat belly was now a hard six pack. I noticed his arms were harder, thicker. Nothing a stranger would notice, but someone who knew his body intimately could tell. I wanted to run my fingers up and down his chest, to trace all of his new tattoos. I shivered, a chill running through me. It was freezing in here.

I wrapped myself in the blanket but still couldn't get warm. I glared at Ethan. Warm and peacefully sleeping. I wanted his heat. Hating him for being right, I scooted closer to him and pushed my bare feet against his legs.

He jolted awake. "Wha..." he mumbled and then looked down at me. I smiled apologetically. He smirked and with no hesitation pulled me into his arms. I snuggled close, and in moments I heard his breathing slow again.

Letting the warmth of his body seep into mine, I closed my eyes, finally able to get some rest. I woke up to him stirring. I groaned and squeezed the arm holding me. "I hate you," I moaned, my eyes still shut. Ethan chuckled, and I felt his lips on my neck. A shiver went over me.

"I know," he kissed my shoulder.

"You're a furnace." I wiggled closer to his core.

"I know," his hands moved from my belly upward. His lips began to explore past my neck. I shivered with pleasure.

The alarm that woke us started beeping again. We tried to ignore it, but the sound grew louder. With a sigh, Ethan pulled his lips away from my ear and shut it off. I sat up, embarrassed. Why was I letting this happen? He turned back to me with hooded eyes and that sexy smile. He tried to nudge me back down, but I put my hand up. He frowned.

"Ethan, this is a bad idea. I don't think we should… I have Chris, and you have Duchess."

"I don't have Duchess," he said sharply.

"Really? She's going to be at the shoot today," I accused. He let out a frustrated groan and moved off the bed. I stayed on the bed while he hurried out. I heard the bathroom door slam and the shower start.

We got ready for the day not speaking to each other. It wasn't hard, most of the time he had been on the phone. Whoever was on the other side got an earful. I had a strong feeling it was his manager. "What made you think this was a good idea?" He demanded. "I don't care. I don't care. Kyle you better fix it. No. No! I'm not kidding." He hung up, and the room grew silent. You could hear a pin drop. It felt terrible.

When we got to the studio, we were all separated. Ethan and I got our own dressing rooms, while everyone else shared one. I was disappointed that I didn't have anyone to talk to while we were prepped. After Ethan's phone call rant, word had spread like wildfire. I heard someone whisper that it was me who didn't want her here. I didn't, but I wasn't the one causing a fuss.

As soon as we arrived, Ethan walked in and stormed right into his dressing room, slamming the door. After stepping into my own, I heard someone say that Duchess' room was also ready. Was she given a private dressing room for a music video that wasn't hers?

In my room, I found a rack filled to the brim with clothes. There were four women inside. Tammy and Linda for my hair, Christine for makeup, and Tonya was wardrobe. They all introduced themselves at the same time. They were all super bubbly, making my sour mood quickly disappear.

"I love the concept. So romantic," Tammy said as she brushed my hair.

"What is it?" I asked. The girls all paused to look at each other with conspiratorial smiles.

"Missed connections," Christine said cryptically, causing the women to erupt into giggles.

They dressed me in a white dress shirt and tie, with a red plaid skirt. My lips were ruby red, eyes dark with eyeliner and black eyeshadow. After they freshened up the pink in my hair, they threw a wig cap on me and set a dark brown wig on my head. I was looking at the 16 year old version of me. They covered up Ethan's name with concealer. I protested, but they assured me that Ethan was getting his covered too, just for a small bit of the video.

Finally, they took a step back announcing I was ready. I stood up and went to the set. There was a stage, and our instruments were set up. The black curtain behind everything was spray painted with the words "battle of the bands." All of the extras were dressed like fans. They chatted while waiting for filming to start.

I looked around for my bandmates. I wanted to laugh. It was like stepping through time. We were all teenagers again. Mark had a long blond wig on his head. They gave Derek a beanie and Adrian was wearing baggy pants and armbands. Wow, we were huge dorks.

Moments later Cruel Distraction stepped out. They were dressed similarly. Ethan was wearing tight jeans, a ripped black shirt, and spiked bracelet. They had laid on the eyeliner super heavy and had spiked his hair up. Most of his tattoos had also been covered. The other guys looked similar to him. This was pretty hilarious. Half of us looked amused, while the others looked embarrassed. Ethan was scowling.

The director, a middle-aged man with dirty blond hair and warm eyes, came over and introduced himself. His name was Paul, and he was a big fan he told me. He called both bands over and began explaining what he wanted us to do.

"Okay Cleo, this scene is pretty self-explanatory. We are going to play one of your old songs to perform for the battle of the bands where you and Ethan first meet. He's going to be standing in the wings. Arms crossed checking you out. You see him and kind of pause, smile, flirt a little. Don't stop singing. Then we'll trade bands and have Cruel Distraction play, while you, Cleo, are on the sidelines talking to one of the extras. Ethan, you get determined to win her. She looks over and sees you and eyes you like bring it on. Got all that?" We all agreed more or less and got into place. I stood at the front of the stage and waited for my cue.

They started to play our song. I started jamming and pretending to sing. Seconds later "Cut!" was called and the music stopped. I looked around confused, and then I heard the yelling.

Searching the room, I found the cause of it. Ethan and Duchess. Ethan was screaming at her. Her arms were crossed over her chest, while his hands were clenched into fists at his sides. Everyone turned to watch them.

"Why are you here?" He yelled. She smirked.

"I thought you could use a little help. You throw in a real celebrity, and your video shoots to the top."

"We don't need you. I don't want your help."

"We? Or her? I'm not stupid!" She screamed.

"Me! I do not want you here. Can I make it any clearer?" He shouted.

"I'm staying. Just be glad it's me and not her husband," she said, not caring who heard. The blood drained from my face.

"Someone get them apart!" Paul shouted, and suddenly two giant men came up behind Ethan. He rolled his eyes and stormed off. Duchess looked quite pleased with herself. She turned to look at the crowd that had gathered. She flashed her smile and bounced off to her dressing room.

We waited another five minutes for Ethan to return. He was significantly calmer. Apologizing, he went to his marker and we started shooting again. The music blared, and I started singing again. I relaxed and let myself enjoy the moment. I wasn't going to let her presence ruin today.

I saw one of the crew members motion for me to look to my left, I did so and saw Ethan standing there. He was smiling at me, his eyebrow raised. It felt real for a moment. I returned his smile and turned back to the stage. We did this a few more times before trading spots.

When it was my turn, I locked eyes with Ethan as I rubbed my hand on the cute extras arm. His jaw tightened as he turned away. They loved it. I secretly loved it too. Something inside told me that his jealousy wasn't strictly for the cameras. That was real.

Next, they filmed me taking his hand and leading him away. We had a few quick kisses, then a montage of us doing stuff together. We had to change clothes three times just for this part. Changing the outfits went quickly, but changing wigs was a pain in the ass.

Then they put us in front of a tattoo parlor. It was dark, as if night time. They had me sitting on a short cement wall, lip syncing. I was wearing a wife beater and short mini skirt. Ethan had a leather jacket and jeans, his hair pushed back like an old school greaser. They had removed our makeup on our necks, we would be revealing our tattoos to the world.

"Okay, now I want you to make out. You guys are madly in love with each other. Are you guys good?" Paul asked. Ethan shrugged and turned to me. I gave a thumbs up.

"I'm ready whenever," I said, tired. I felt like we had been at this for hours.

We got into place. Ethan placed his hands on my neck and hips. I grabbed his neck, pulling him between my legs. The director yelled action, and the song began to play. He pressed his forehead to mine, and I smiled up at him. We kissed and then I opened my mouth to make this scene as hot and heavy as they asked. It felt very technical and not even a little sexy. They were continuously shouting at us to move this hand, turn that way.

Suddenly, I felt something hard press against me and without thinking I grabbed him and pulled him closer, almost desperate to kiss him. He went with it. His lips suddenly dipped lower, and he kissed my tattoo. I shuddered. Suddenly the director yelled cut. We both pulled away quickly. That last kiss was real.

Ethan mumbled an apology and turned away from me to adjust himself. There were chuckles, but we quickly moved on. Next, they wanted me to be leaving. I had a duffel bag in hand. We were arguing. He punched a wall and broke down as I turned and left.

Next, we started shooting the "missed connections" my style team had mentioned. I came to visit him and found him flirting with another girl. He surprised me with roses only to see me receiving flowers and kissing some other guy. A model named Andrew. When we tried to make it work, we would argue again. I was told that this would all be on the screen in between shots of both of the bands performing the song.

That was the easiest part of the day. Just performing the song. The rest of the afternoon was spent in and out of wardrobe. It was tiring. With all the craziness, I had all but forgotten about Duchess and her role in the video. Finally, I was told that I had one last outfit change. I sighed with relief and hurried into my room. Tonya was so excited; she was almost bouncing.

When I was ready, she came back with a humongous white gown. It was beautiful. A strapless ball gown with a sweetheart neckline. It wasn't super elaborate, but it was still gorgeous. Once the dress was on, they went to work on my hair and makeup. I got to take the wig cap off, and she brushed and fluffed out my pink locks. Then she went to work shaping it into big, soft curls.

When they slipped my veil on, I gasped. I was beautiful. With the help of my team, I got to the set. This stage was a church. It was small, with all of the extras in formal wear standing in the pews. Black and baby blue flowers covered every available space. It was beautiful and made me a tad bit uncomfortable. I was swallowing hard at the whole scene in front of me until I looked up the aisle and saw Ethan.

Dressed in a tuxedo, they pushed his hair back and took off all his makeup. He cleaned up well. He was so handsome. My heart began to race. He stood there, tall and lean, with his hands folded in front of him, waiting patiently.

Paul walked over and started to talk, but I didn't hear him for a solid minute. I couldn't take my eyes off Ethan. He was striking in that suit. Paul snapped his fingers in front of my face, and I turned my attention to him.

"Cleo, you there? I know it's been a long day, but we're almost done. Okay. This scene is easy. Just walk up the aisle, smile and be happy. You're going to get up to Ethan and then give us a cheesy grin. It's the happiest day of your life. He's going to lift your veil and then frown. So are you. When we get the shot, we're going to replace him with Rich over here, and then we'll replace you with Duchess.

When you realize you're not up here with Ethan, falter in your smile. Maybe look past him, over his shoulder, like you're not really there," he ordered. I nodded and glanced around. That's when I saw Richard, another good looking, dark haired, light eyed man; and next to him stood Duchess.

Duchess also wore a wedding gown. Her hair was dark, like my natural color. Her dress was bigger, more elaborate and I'm sure more expensive than mine. She was wearing gloves and a mini tiara. I instantly felt like I was dressed in rags compared to her. She was breathtaking. She saw me looking and smiled smugly. I was handed a bouquet of black roses, and then the same guy went over and handed her a bouquet of red roses that was easily three sizes bigger than mine. Wow, it really was her show. I was nothing.

I looked away quickly when Derek came and tapped my shoulder. Turning to him, I forced a smile. He and my other bandmates had been cleaned up as well to stand with me as my brides men. I loved it.

I was helped into place, and they flipped my veil over my face. The music started, and Paul yelled "Action!". I started down the aisle, slowly with that forced smile. I couldn't stop thinking about Duchess. Why was she doing this?

I reached the end of the aisle and started up the three small steps to reach Ethan. Paul yelled "Cut!" and repositioned us to get the shot.

The music started back up, and Ethan raised my veil. We both were smiling ear to ear until our eyes met and our faces fell. Paul was ecstatic over our reactions. Quickly we did as Paul had envisioned. Richard took Ethan's place, and I held Richard's hand, mouthing the song. I looked past the model. This was all starting to feel too real.

Suddenly there was a loud boom, and the music stopped short. Everyone looked towards the noise on the other side of the set. Ethan stormed through the doors, his hair wild, his shirt unbuttoned. I pulled away from Richard. Everyone's eyes were on Ethan. He held a hand up to stop us. He was breathing heavily, his determined eyes locked on mine. The room was deafeningly silent. Finally, after what felt like forever Paul yelled cut, and people began clapping. Ethan straightened and smoothed his hair back.

People came over and helped me down, and Ethan took his place back at the altar while Duchess was then filmed walking down the aisle and then meeting Ethan. I was still so confused until Ethan suddenly dropped her hands and rushed out of the room. I realized then that they would edit the scenes all together so that he ran out of his wedding to stop mine. I loved it. I couldn't wait to see the finished product.

Thankfully, the director yelled cut and "That's a wrap everybody!" Chatter began immediately, and people were moving quickly around to start breaking down the set.

I looked around, but Ethan was nowhere to be found. Neither was Duchess. Mark walked towards me. He was already undoing his bow tie. "Finally. I need a cigarette," he said. "You coming?" I shrugged, looking for Ethan as I followed him outside.

It was a nice and quiet when we stepped out. The sun was starting to fade. Filming had taken all day. A few people passed by. I saw one take a picture with their phone, but I didn't care. I was too tired. Mark must have also been because he didn't try to make small talk. We were only outside a few minutes before we heard people step out chattering loudly. Mark pulled me away from the door and behind some large crates.

I turned to him and smiled thoughtfully. "Thanks, but I think I'm going to head in. I should probably change into my clothes. They'll kill me if I get this dress dirty," I told him but froze when I heard an all to familiar voice.

"It's all an act. I feel bad for her," Duchess said. My eyes widened. I glanced over to Mark who had stomped out his cigarette and swore. He grabbed my hand and tried pulling me forward, but I couldn't move.

"Come on. She's just jealous," Mark muttered, but I didn't budge. I had to hear what she had to say.

"Oh, but it's so romantic. They still love each other after all this time. Plus, the tattoos. I saw them in concert two weeks ago. There was definite chemistry," the girl argued. Duchess laughed. "It's all one big story the label came up with. She had that tattoo way before she met Ethan Andrews. The Ethan she was stupid enough to get inked on herself was some loser who took her virginity at fourteen. Both bands were signed at the same time. The label saw an opportunity. They paid Ethan ten grand to get that tattoo. All of this was done for one thing. Money. He can't stand her in real life," she claimed. I stood next to Mark in shock. Why would she say all of these things? Why was she so mean? I knew the truth, but her words still hurt. I blinked the tears away and shook my head. I was not going to let her get to me. I refused to let it bother me.

"Wow, I had no clue. I really thought there was something there."

"Nope. I mean, you've seen her mouth. Who would enjoy kissing that? Has she not heard of veneers?" They burst into laughter. Ouch, I flinched. That stung. It wasn't anything I haven't heard before but coming from her was a little too much to take. My hands reflexively went to my mouth. I felt one lone tear slide down my cheek. I quickly wiped it away.

"Don't believe everything you read in those magazines. Ethan and I are as solid as ever," Duchess told her after they finished laughing at me.

"Oh Duchess, I am so happy for you. I was worried!" The girl exclaimed.

"Don't be. Ethan would never pick her over me," she stated. A few seconds later I smelled cigarette smoke. She must have come out here to smoke too.

Mark stepped out from behind the boxes and pulled me along with a little more force than before. Duchess turned her head slightly and flicked her ash in our direction. She had slipped out of her dress and was standing in just her undergarments. She still looked like she could walk down a runway right now if asked. Looking at us her eyes rolled, but no other part of her face moved. She took a long drag of her cigarette and continued ignoring us.

She knew we were there, I realized in shock. She knew. That's why she said all those awful things. Instead of giving her the satisfaction, I decided to pretend that I hadn't heard her. She didn't acknowledge me. That was her tactic. Intimidation. I strode back inside and hurried to my dressing room to take the dress off.

Changing back into my street clothes, I waited for everyone else. About an hour later everybody was squeezing into one vehicle. Sam got into the packed van with us. I groaned, moving to sit on Derek's lap. "Okay, so we fly out first thing tomorrow morning. So be ready to leave the hotel at four am. We still have to finish this tour. Good job everyone. I think we have something here," he told us.

When we got back to the hotel, all I wanted to do was take a nice long bath, get into some clean pajamas and get a decent night's sleep before we went back to the bittersweet tour bus. I needed to forget about this day.

Maria Maria took a separate elevator than Cruel Distraction. Mark held my hand and squeezed it periodically. I looked up at him and smiled half-heartedly. "I'll be okay," I tried reassuring him. His face looked like he didn't believe me. He asked me out loud if I wanted company before they stepped off onto their floor. Derek turned and gave us a questioning look.

"Hell no. I want one night without all of you. I need one night to myself," I joked, and that seemed to relax him. He let go of my hand, leaving with the others to his room. In all my life, I would never have better friends.

Once in my room, I took a luxuriously hot bath, using the oils and fancy shampoo the hotel provided. I picked out my comfiest pajamas and fell asleep watching a movie, trying to forget about the mess and stress of the last few days. I hadn't seen Ethan since we left the studio lot.

I woke up with a start! Bolting up, I tried to focus. Someone was opening the door to the hallway. I climbed out of bed and went to the edge of the bedroom door, peaking my head out just a bit. Instantly my fears slipped away. Ethan.

I was such an idiot. Stepping out, I glared at him. "You

scared the crap out of me! Do you know what time it is?" I scolded. He stared at me blankly.

"We're sharing a room. How did I scare you?" He said, amused.

"Oh, shut up. I'm going back to bed." I turned back towards the room.

"Today was horrible," he said. Grinding the sleep out of my eyes, I turned.

"Ethan," I started and looked up into his big blue eyes. They were red-rimmed like he had been crying. I stopped talking. He was worn and tired. He must have been up all night.

"That video was a little too real. It's what I should have done," he said. I shook my head. I didn't want to talk about this. We couldn't keep going over what could have been.

"Ethan, we can't change it," I said softly.

"Why not? Do you still want to be with him? After what he did?" He demanded a response. I recoiled away.

"And what are we doing Ethan? I'm no better than him!"

"Yes, yes you are. How do you not see it?" He yelled back at me. His eyes were welling up again. I looked away quickly. He didn't know what he was talking about. "Why are you trying so hard to stay away from me?" He asked, taking a step towards me. He was breathing heavy.

"Ethan, what happened yesterday…"

"What happened is that you kissed me back. Not stage Cleo, real Cleo," he said, his voice hard. He was right, I thought. I wanted him too. I shook my head.

"I shouldn't have. It was…"

"A mistake? Because I don't think it was. Cleo, I have wanted to kiss you, really kiss you, since we started the tour a month ago. Every time I see you I want to be with you. Holding your hand, playing with your hair. I want you to cuddle with me. Not your friends. Not stupid fucking Chris. Me. I know you feel something too. I know you do."

I gulped, not knowing how to respond. I wanted those things too. But we couldn't. We shouldn't. This could all end so badly. I shook my head at him. This wouldn't work, Ethan and I. It never did.

"Tell me. I need to hear you say that you felt nothing," Ethan demanded, stepping towards me again. His eyes blazing. I glared back at him, and my chin began to tremble. I couldn't talk to him when he was like this.

"I don't know what you're talking about," I lied and took a step back, but he matched my steps, keeping himself close. He grabbed my wrist. Lightly, but firm. He placed his other hand on my waist, pulling me into his body. I didn't move away. He pressed me to him.

"Let me remind you," he took one hand off my waist to lift my chin. His kiss was gentle, like a whisper. My heart slowed down. When he pulled back, I paused before returning his kiss with a firmer one of my own. Our kisses became frantic and felt long overdue. It felt like we both knew our time alone was precious. His hand moved off of my wrist to my hip. His fingers toyed with the bottom of my sweater. Slowly they slipped underneath and started creeping higher, teasing me. He stopped at my belly button, pulling his hand out.

He groaned and urged me gently backward, towards the bedroom. I didn't want to stop kissing him. I felt like someone who had been lost in a desert and had finally stumbled upon a well. A well that was always full and had a cold glass waiting for me to take a drink.

Something in me had awakened. I wanted Ethan. I needed him to keep kissing me, touching me. I let him push me closer to the bed. Falling on the fluffy pillows, I quickly darted towards the head of the bed. Ethan climbed on top of me and pressed his body against mine. He kissed me deeply. I opened my mouth, and he moaned my name. His lips moved lower. He kissed my chin, then my neck.

"You're a song I can't get out of my head. A melody I hum in my sleep," he lowered himself to my waist, kissing the skin peeking out. I arched my back letting him remove my sweater. It was happening so fast. Both of us frantic to get the other naked. Almost as if we paused for even a second one of us would realize what a horrible idea this was. I knew it was, but I didn't care. I needed him, and he needed me.

My top was off, and Ethan sat up, quickly removing his shirt. He leaned back down to kiss my collarbone and right as his lips started traveling towards my breasts, we heard someone.

"Oh shit. Sorry! Fuck. Oh shit." It was Derek. I let out a scream, grabbing my sweater. Ethan rolled over and swore. Adjusting my clothes, I hurried out. Derek stood by the door to the hallway looking everywhere but at us. He was holding two coffees in tall paper cups.

"What are you doing here?" I asked him and only then did he look my way. "We got thirty minutes before we have to leave. Adrian sent me to come wake you up. Uh, here," he said, handing me my coffee. I turned to see Ethan going into the bathroom. He shut the door loudly. Mortification flooded my face as he immediately started the shower. He needed a cool down apparently.

I glared at Derek who lifted his shoulders as if to say, "How was I supposed to know you'd be making out with the guy who you kept saying was just a friend?"

"What?" I snapped, and he put his hands up. One hand still holding his coffee.

"Nothing. I'm heading back down. See you in a bit." Turning the door handle, he opened it.

"You're going to go tell the guys," I sighed, not asking.

"Yep," he said, stepping out before I could protest. Taking a long sip of my way too sweet coffee, I got to work packing my things. Ethan came out twenty minutes later fully dressed but hair still wet. He looked at me and gave me a half smile.

"My friends have no boundaries," I told him, and he agreed.

"Yeah, I figured that out a while ago." We chuckled and finished packing up.

A few minutes later there was a loud, obnoxious knock. Mark and Adrian opened the door and kept it open just enough to poke their heads in. They looked around and found us. They had huge grins on their faces. "Are we good to come in?" Adrian asked.

"Is everyone fully dressed?" Mark added. I glared and went to shut the door. They laughed, opening it all the way. They came in with their bags in tow. Soon Cruel Distraction joined us.

As soon as we all had a head count, we headed down to the shuttle bus that took us to the airport. Most of this was done in relative silence. Everyone was exhausted, and we had a concert tonight.

Once we were back on the tour bus, everyone was back in high spirits. By that time everyone had heard Derek's story of catching us. Every time we tried to talk or sit next to each other someone would come interrupt or lie between us. They were all getting a huge kick out of it. Eventually, we gave up and decided to relax with the gang. Someone made a joke about Christian's beard, and Ethan piped in with his own opinion.

"Shut up, cold shower," Christian spit back. The bus erupted into laughter. Ethan flipped him off but then glanced at me across the bus. He smiled, making my chest flutter. With that, I stood up and walked over to where he had been sitting with Mark and Seth, discussing music. Ethan was strumming his acoustic while Mark was tapping his hands on the table, making a beat.

He stopped when I came over, and I took the guitar out of

his hands, setting it down on the floor next to him. He watched me curiously. With everyone looking at us I sat down on his lap. Wrapping my arms around Ethan's neck, I planted a firm kiss on his lips. I didn't care anymore. The room fell deathly quiet.

"I missed you," I whispered. He grinned and kissed me back.

"I missed you too."

Chapter Seven

BACK TO YOU

*I*t didn't take long, but Ethan and I were the topic of conversation once the tour picked back up. We weren't trying to hide our feelings for each other anymore while on the bus. Our bandmates were soon complaining, so we took the back room most of the time.

The music video aired on TV and uploaded to the internet within a week of filming it. Sam called the next day to tell us that thousands had already downloaded the song and the video had over a quarter of a million views in one day. The world loved it. He was already talking about magazine features and guest appearances. I was too excited and frankly too shocked to pay attention to all his ramblings. I was going to go with the flow.

However, each day after the video was released a sense of dread grew in the pit of my stomach.

When I first left for the tour, Christopher would text and call me at least once a day. Since the video, there had been nothing. He was mad. His abrupt silence told me more than any phone call would. I tried to put it out of my mind and enjoy the little time in the spotlight I was getting, but sometimes my guilt would come up and rush over me. I was still married, yet every night after the show I was rushing to be with Ethan. The more time that passed between his last call was making me feel worse and better at the same time. I loved my husband. He was charming, handsome and smart. He still married me after the tattoo and loved me despite my many flaws. I think this was the final straw. Maybe his silence was the message. He didn't call because he didn't care. Finally, after two weeks, I stopped checking my phone. I didn't want to bother anymore. I wanted to be free, to let myself fall for Ethan. So that's what I did.

At a stop in Dallas, all eight of us got buzzed and wandered into a sex shop. We had lots of laughs playing with all the various toys. At different moments each drunk band member wanted me to try on this or that. I rolled my eyes and kept browsing until I found some men's underwear that looked like an elephant. They were gray thongs with eyes, flappy material for ears, and a long pouch in the front to serve as the trunk.

"If all of you guys try these on," I teased. "I will think about it." I didn't expect any of the seven guys to take me up on the offer. I moved on to the stripper shoes, thinking back to Chelsea Sometimes and whether I could rock them like she did when Seth, the one with a slight beer gut and an adorable baby face, grabbed the underwear from the bin.

"Sold!" He went to the register where a cute redhead with a pixie cut was laughing having heard our conversation. The rest of our group looked at each other, shrugged their shoulders, and all grabbed themselves a pair. My chest was thumping. I never thought they would. My guys wouldn't have done it without the other band. Men get brave when around other men.

I stood at the shoes and watched as even sweet, shy Spencer

was rung up. They all stood in line with their arms folded over their chests, looking at me.

I raised my eyebrows and folded my arms in defiance. "I said you had to wear them," I smiled in satisfaction. We walked here.

There was a devilish glint in every one of their eyes. I frowned as I realized where I had messed up. None of these men had any shame. They were used to everyone looking at them. I looked to Ethan to plead for him to save me but he just shook his head with a smirk. Ethan didn't take his eyes off of mine as he went to the counter and in a loud voice asked the girl. "Do you have a dressing room we could use?"

The girl batted her eyes at him, but he didn't see her. He was still holding eye contact with me. It was hot. I bit my bottom lip, and I felt my heart pick up pace.

"Yeah, of course, over there next to the costumes," she replied. He looked away and with a flick of his hand motioned for Christian, the redhead with the lumberjack beard to go to the dressing room. With a grin, he hurried to change into his new bottoms.

One by one, they filed in and came out wearing only the elephant undies and their socks and shoes. The other customers were staring and laughing. Some took pictures. Spencer had bought a cowboy hat earlier to go with his new cowboy boots. The sunglasses completed the look. Mark was pale as paper with a farmer's tan. Seth had been wearing long socks with his keds. Ethan was the last to come out, and even with his dick in an elephants trunk he still looked sexy with his black converses on. My eyes followed down his thin dark happy trail to the underwear. Who knew elephant undies could be sexy?

The cashier stood behind them all, damn near panting. I swear she would have to wipe up her drool when we left. I had to admit, not one of them was ugly. They were all cute in their own ways. Adrian, the only naturally tan one took a step forward and began going through the lingerie racks and held up a few pieces that were almost nothing. The guys cheered or booed as he showed everybody his choices. Finally, he came to me and put his hand on my shoulder.

"I think it's only right that the guy taking it off should be the one to pick what you'll be wearing tonight." What? No.

"Tonight?" I squeaked, my eyes wide. I shook my head, and they all turned their mouths up in evil smiles.

"You're looking at our costumes for tonight's show, baby," Adrian said. "Alright, Ethan step up and pick Cleo something good!" Ethan raised his eyebrows. After a second he got over the surprise and changed his face back to the sexy, confident man from before and started going through the racks. He finally found a black lace teddy. No, I couldn't wear that out in public! It was padded on the breasts so you couldn't see my nipples but still, the rest was lace. He handed it to me, and the guys all cheered.

"You can keep your shorts. That's it. If we're wearing these," he gestured to the elephant, "Then you can wear that," he smirked as I snatched it out of his hand and stormed into the dressing room. I understood a deal was a deal, but I was still married. Chris would kill me if he saw guys picking out lingerie for me. But he would also kill me for fooling around with someone else. Maybe wearing this wouldn't be as bad as I thought as I clipped the tights to the rest of it. Why did I even care about what he thought? We were done. He could have his girlfriend. I eyed myself in the mirror. I looked good. Really good. I was quite comfortable in the lingerie I was shocked at how natural it felt. I didn't feel the need to cover myself up. This could work.

I shimmied back into my jean shorts and came out with my arms raised. I spun around for them and handed the tag to the cashier who kept staring at Ethan's crotch. The guys went outside for cigarettes while I finished up. Before I gave her the cash, I spotted something dark red and fluffy. I grabbed it and finished my purchase.

I had her keep the receipt and hurried out with the other guys. My clothes were in the bag that should have held the underwear I was now wearing on the streets of Dallas.

The guys ran around, lunging, doing cartwheels. People stopped, some honked their horns. They were eating it up. Halfway back to our bus I stopped and grabbed Ethan. He paused, and I pulled the blood red feather boa out of my bag. It was just like the one from the drag show. He took a step back in surprise. Grinning ear to ear he wrapped it around his neck and ran to join the rest of the guys. Tonight's show was going to be crazy. The fans will be in a frenzy once they see us. Suddenly an idea popped into my head. Oh, this was going to be fun.

Adrian pulled back a bit and walked with me. "How does it feel?" He asked. I shrugged, flipping my hair behind my back to expose my bosom.

"I think I'm going to get a weird tan, but there's a nice breeze." He laughed and shook his head.

"I wasn't talking about your teddy. By the way, how come you never wore one of those for me?" I punched his forearm.

"If not my clothes, then what?" I said, ignoring his little quip.

"Being in love." I stopped and looked at him. I wasn't in love. Was I? I'd admit my relationship with Ethan was nice. He was perfect for me.

"I'm not in love," I stated and started walking faster. He kept pace with me. He wasn't letting this go apparently.

"Don't lie to me," Adrian hissed. "Or are you lying to yourself? Cleo, he is crazy about you. Like over the moon. He's doing everything he can to show you. Why don't you see it?" His face was angry. I turned away.

"I have five weeks left before I have to see Christopher. I don't know what to do, Adrian," I said barely above a whisper. I didn't want to think about going home, but I had to face him eventually.

"Screw Chris. Just let him go. We have been best friends since I got caught stealing your newspaper off your porch. That was what, ten years ago now? Have I ever steered you wrong? Don't be stupid Cleo. I love you. Please, for me. Let him in," he begged me. I sighed and reached out to hold his hand.

"I love you, Adrian. Thanks," I told him, and we finished walking to the bus in silence away from the rest of the crew. Adrian's words never left me. I tried to push them out of my mind, but every time I looked at Ethan, I knew he was right.

Ethan pulled me aside when we got back to the bus and thanked me for the boa with a hug and kiss. "You are seriously awesome."

"Keep it to remind yourself of me," I said with a smile. He frowned.

"Five more weeks," he reminded himself, his voice suddenly serious. I nodded looking away guiltily.

"Yeah, I know," I said and dropped his hand. Somethings were better left unsaid. The countdown to the end of this was one of them.

Before the show, someone brought out baby oil, and the guys all insisted someone lather them up. Only Adrian and Ethan had any real muscles, so they all looked kind of ridiculous. What had me in tears was that I refused to help them and they couldn't get anybody else to do it, so we had seven awkward guys in elephant undies and tube socks rubbing oil all over each other. I curled my hair and did my makeup but other than that I didn't have much prep for the show.

I didn't tell any of the guys about my plans. I wanted their reactions to be genuine. I kissed Ethan quickly before our names were called. We decided we were going to march on to the stage in a line. That way we could each show off our costumes. The screams when the audience saw Adrian right behind me were deafening. Earlier I had asked the band to start playing as soon as we could, so we started our set pretty fast.

I enjoyed the rush of wearing next to no clothing on stage. A tiny bit of me felt trashy, but after a few drinks I was kind of okay with it. I needed the courage for sure. I was completely exposed, there was no hiding any flaws tonight. Halfway through, while the guys were playing softly, I took the time to talk to the crowd.

"Alright, Dallas! We have a treat for you tonight. I have right here on this stage three hot, single, men looking for love. They are all oiled up and ready for a nice girl, or guy in Adrian's case, he's not picky, to take home tonight. So, let's do this!" I shouted and jumped over to Derek who had the deer in the headlights look. Which I knew he would since none of them knew about this. I put my arm on his shoulder and moved the mic to my mouth again.

"Derek here tells everyone his favorite movie is The Night-mare on Elm Street, but it's really The Princess Bride," I told the crowd. The fans screamed. "He's looking for a tall drink of water with a thirst for his bass."

Derek's eyes grew huge, and he shook his head. His face was growing red fast. He tried to hide his face behind his blond curls, but his new mohawk make it difficult. "The first girl to buy us a round of Jager bombs gets this sweet ass," I called as I spanked him hard. The crowd began to laugh at us.

Derek jumped and grinned ear to ear as a pretty redhead brought us a tray of his favorite drink. I knew once the shock wore off they'd have fun with it. Security pulled her up, and Derek kissed her on the cheek as she was led backstage.

I moved on to Mark. He was laughing hysterically but stopped short when I moved closer. While he was shaking his head no, I said, "Alright, now we have sweet, sweet Mark. Come on Mark and stand up. Let's see that elephant." He jumped up and sat back down quickly.

"Mark once tried to convince a girl that he was the lead singer of Coldplay." Laughter and screams filled the room. "Now, who's going to buy us a round of fireball?" I asked the crowd and watched as a pretty caramel-colored girl with bright brown eyes was let through with a tray of Mark's drink of choice.

"I hate you!" Mark yelled my way, trying to be heard above the crowd. I winked at him and saw him crack a smile.

Mark's new date for the evening made it onto the stage. He kissed her on the cheek. Finally, I sauntered over to Adrian who was flexing and putting his leg up and asking fans if they wanted him. By this time, my words were becoming slurred. The adrenaline plus the alcohol was a buzz like no other. This was the best feeling ever.

"Alright. I saved the best for last. Now, this hot piece of ass is worth more than just a round of drinks. Adrian, my dearest, most bestest friend," I started, but Adrian grabbed his microphone and grinned.

"Oh, I need no introduction. Ladies, gentlemen. I like tequila," He said low and sultry. I had only heard that voice when he was working his powers of seduction on someone. I gave him a raised eyebrow.

"Thanks, babe, but I got this," he added, and we looked back at the crowd. They were going ballistic. I saw about twenty people running to the bar. Adrian pulled his guitar back around and went swiftly into a solo as we waited for a tall, cute guy who reminded me of Tarzan with his muscles and dreadlocks brought us all tequila shots.

Adrian was so excited, he put his instrument down and hopped into this guys arms. Planting a huge kiss on his lips. It was adorable. Tarzan put him down, exiting the same way the others did. We resumed our show. Someone shouted they wanted to buy me, but I shook my head and winked at them.

We staggered off the stage pretty damn drunk. It was a great show. It took me a minute to catch my bearings, but finally I found Ethan standing off to the side. I smiled at him and took a step to go to him, but his face was severe. He shook his head just ever so slightly it made me halt. He was standing in front of a table with a tray of rum shots and cups of ginger ale to chase it. He was going to buy me, I realized.

"Wow, what a show!" The familiar voice made me freeze. No wonder Ethan was acting strangely. I turned around to be face-to-face with the man I had been dreading to see. The one who I had spent my summer hating. My husband was here.

"Babe, you look smoking!" He grabbed me, squeezing the air out of me. I wanted to throw up. Why was he here? I looked into his face and only felt disgust. I pulled away and just stared at him, dumbfounded. The alcohol in my system was starting to come back up. Did he think I forgot about his naked ass in the air as he plugged that pretty redhead in our bed? He looked concerned. I was feeling sick. Was he upset? Did I hurt his feelings? Was I supposed to feel bad?

"Hey, I rented a room about ten minutes away. Why don't you stay with me tonight?" Chris asked me. "I've missed my wife," he whispered in my ear seductively. Did he forget why we weren't talking? Was he that delusional? I shook my head, but my drunkenness made me dizzy. Christopher grabbed my waist hard to steady me. His fingers dug into my side. I felt like I was going to pass out.

"I have to stay to finish the show," I mumbled. He scoffed, putting his hands up in exasperation.

"You just played. Let's go," he repeated, but I pulled away.

"No, Chris. I have to go back out to sing my new song. That's how we end the show," I told him, eying his reaction carefully. His face revealed nothing.

"Fine. I'll wait here with you," he said. We went to the lounge to join my bandmates. They were hanging with their dates. Mark was flirting with his girl, while Derek's new friend was sitting on his lap. Adrian and Tarzan sat on the other side of the room drinking beer and just talking. They looked like old friends.

When I walked in with Chris, the room grew silent. My husband nodded towards them and went for a bottle of water out of the small fridge. He gave me one, and we stood around, feeling slightly awkward as we waited for the cue to go back to the stage. When it was time I asked him if he wanted to watch and he glared at me.

"I've heard the song," he said coolly. Guilt hit me hard. It was cruel for me to flaunt it right in front of him. I nodded and went to finish the show.

Tonight the chemistry between Ethan and I on stage was terrible. We were both tense and aware of who was behind the curtains. Our kiss at the end was passionless, and we moved away from each other as soon as we could.

I rushed to find Chris as soon as I finished. He was standing right behind the curtain tapping his foot. He looked furious.

"Can we go now?" he asked, irritated. I looked over at my crew. They were preoccupied with their dates.

"Yeah, sure," I said before anyone stopped us.

We started towards the exit, where Ethan happened to be standing. I tried to pull away, but Christopher held my arm tight. He stopped at the table where Ethan, still clad only in his elephant underwear, was holding drinks just watching us. Christopher was in a sharp gray suit like he had just come from a meeting. The stark differences in the two men made my stomach lurch. My husband picked up one of the shots and downed it quickly.

"Thanks, bud," he told Ethan, slamming the glass back down with a clink. He looked Ethan up and down, smirking. I couldn't help but feel embarrassed for him. This was not the greatest time to meet. Ethan looked uncomfortable. He shifted his body and gulped. Oh no, this was not good, I thought. "You're the guy from the video," Chris said to Ethan. Ethan nodded.

"Yeah. Uh, Ethan. You must be Chris," he said eventually. Putting the other glass down Ethan extended his hand. Christopher glanced at it, but refused to shake it. Ethan was beneath him. I knew how he thought.

"You're a good actor. People are eating it up," he said. The words were innocent enough, but the look in his eyes when he looked at Ethan was deadly.

Ethan nodded again, crossing his arms and leaning against the table trying to seem relaxed. "The fans love it," he said. Chris scoffed, raising his eyebrow to Ethan.

"That's who you're doing it for, right? The fans. They dreamed up this whole fantasy romance between you two, and you're just giving them what they want." His voice was losing its control. I opened my mouth, but nothing came out.

"Look, man, I don't know what you…" Ethan started, but Chris put his hand up.

"I don't need to hear your excuse. I feel like I should remind everyone that I'm the man she married. Not you. Do what you need to do to feed that crowd, but remember at the end of the day, she's my wife," Chris said with a finality that said the conversation was over.

Ethan kept his eyes on Chris. After a moment, he nodded and looked away. Chris pulled me out the door before I could argue. I stumbled over my feet to keep up. I looked back, but Ethan was gone. It was Chris and I alone now. The cold air hit my face, helping my stomach. I was able to think for a second. Pulling away from my husband's grasp, I glared at him.

"What are you doing here Chris? I can't deal with you right now!" I started walking away from him, going nowhere in particular. He caught up to me and snatched my arm twisting me around. I gasped in pain. He was using a lot of force.

"Why can't I visit my wife, huh?" he said. "I had business in Dallas and figured you'd want to see me. It's been two months. I know you can't go that long without me." He pulled me close and planted his scorching hot lips on mine, pressing hard on them. I couldn't breathe. I fought his grip and finally got away.

"No, I can't do this Chris. Where's Holly? Why don't you go spend time with her before I come back for my stuff," I snarled as I wiped away his spit.

He looked like I had slapped him. Surprise was in his eyes. A shadow passed over his face.

"I ended it with her the day you saw us. It's only you, Cleo. I can't lose you. Please, I've changed. I swear. Come with me and we can talk," he pleaded.

I couldn't think. There were too many thoughts swimming around in my head. Ethan, Christopher, Holly, Adrian, Duchess. Everyone was screaming at me and telling me what to do. I opened my eyes again and saw my husband's face. He looked like he was telling the truth for once. His gray eyes were soft and seemed genuinely sorry for what he had done.

Despite my anger, I had missed him, I realized. With a giant sigh, I followed him to his rental car. I let him help me in, and I watched out the window as the band came out and looked my way. I shrugged, giving them a weak smile before I turned away quickly. They had their dates with them, so they wouldn't say anything about it until morning. We liked to keep things like this private. I didn't want to read about it on the internet or a magazine later.

Chris drove us to a restaurant. He helped me out and to a table where he ordered for me. Typical Christopher. I didn't like salads. I'd much rather have some nachos or a burger.

"I need you by my side right now," he started, "Don't end our marriage because of something stupid, Cleo."

"What do you consider what you did?" I retorted, ready to leave again.

"An innocent mistake. Men have little affairs all the time. But that's it. They never leave their wives for their mistresses," he smiled. I stared at him blankly. He couldn't be serious right now. Seeing that I wasn't rushing into his arms, his eyes grew small, and his face turned hard.

"I've given you everything. You wouldn't have the house, the car, or your studio without me. You have access to my bank account, and I don't complain. You have it good with me. Don't throw us away because of this. We can make it work if you're willing."

I stared blankly at him. What, was I supposed to be the perfect, doting wife now? Was I supposed to hold my head up high because he decided to stay with me and not her?

"I am going to be a very successful man someday, Cleo. I am going to win this upcoming election for the board. I'm in line for the Senator position in five years. It's almost a sure thing," he told me proudly.

I didn't say anything. Was this really what I wanted for myself? A politician's wife? Would I still be able to travel and play music?

He reached for my hand, and I pulled away. No, this wasn't going to work. I couldn't do this anymore. I didn't want to. Just as I was scooting out of the booth, I heard a very familiar song come on from the speakers. It was a Duchess song. 'Crocodile tears.' He looked up at the ceiling and smirked.

"Isn't that his girlfriend in the video? I heard she's going to do her own song with him."

I blanched. That couldn't be true. He would have told me. Chris saw my confusion, and he enjoyed it.

"He didn't tell you?" He mocked. "It's been all over the news." My mind went blank. Who could I believe anymore?

Christopher took my hand and flashed that perfect smile at

me. Memories of the good times rushed back, making me sit back down and ask him "Have you really changed?"

He relaxed and smiled triumphantly. He knew he had won. My head drooped as I knew it too. Chris was like a deadly drug to me. I hated him so much but seeing him here in front of me, it was impossible to end things. I wanted to give him a chance. I needed to. I didn't want to throw three years down the drain.

"Well, I took a step back and decided to clean up my act. I've spent most of my time with mother. She was the one who told me to come apologize. I can't win the seat without a wife and kids. I need you, Cleo. I can't do this without my girl." He smiled, revealing a perfect set of teeth. He was always the most handsome when smiling. That was also when he was the most dangerous.

When I first met Christopher, I thought he was a model. When I first saw him in just his underwear, I was convinced he had posed for Calvin Klein. He was gorgeous from head to toe. Washboard abs and a tan you only get from being on the beach all day every day. I fell hard for him. I looked at him, across from me. Despite him doing so many ugly things, I still found him attractive. He had excellent bone structure and eyes the color of granite. His nose was straight as were his teeth. He kept his blond hair cut and styled just right. He could walk outside and be ready for a photoshoot right now.

He leaned forward and took my hands. Holding my gaze, he winked at me. The wall I had built around my heart crumbled. The look on my face must have pleased him because his smile had turned into a full grin. He squeezed my hands and then pulled away to use his hands to tell me more about what I had missed while on tour.

"I've been fixing up the house like you always asked. The master bath is completely remodeled. A pool is in the works. When you come home, you'll see. I'm a changed man, Cleo." I looked into his eyes and the face of the handsome man I fell in love with. Like before, all my reasoning went out the window.

We left without getting our food. After driving around the city, I realized that he wasn't taking me to his hotel. He drove us to an empty parking lot, parking us towards the back where there were no streetlights. I felt like a teenager making out in the car. Thoughts of Ethan singing with Duchess sat at the edge of my mind, pushing me towards my husband and I didn't know how to handle it anymore. I just needed to feel wanted and right now, Christopher wanted me.

Christopher was on a mission to get me naked as quickly as possible. "It's like you knew I was coming, wearing that today. You look so hot. I don't even care that you wore that in public. I forgive you," he murmured as he nuzzled my neck. I wanted to laugh. He forgave me. I was worried for a moment, I thought sarcastically.

His kisses suddenly felt disgusting and scalding on my skin. Everything about this felt wrong. I didn't want to be here with him. I don't think he even took his clothes all the way off, but he was almost tearing mine apart. I felt cheap. Like some whore he picked up off the street. I started to move away, but he bit my neck hard where Ethan's name was. I let out a yelp, but he kissed it softly.

"When you get home, we should talk about removing that." I wanted to protest, but then he slipped his hand lower. I shuddered, suddenly remembering the good times. Before Holly, before the tour. I let him trail kisses down my body, giving in to his advances.

Opening his door, he practically pulled me out of the car and onto the warm hood, his lips not breaking from mine. It was rushed, yet for the first time with Christopher I felt like he needed me. I thought he had missed me. He pulled down his pants and ripped my shorts down. They fell to the cement. This was becoming less romantic and more harsh.

He was rushing now. I wasn't ready. I told him that, and he groaned with frustration. His hand moved down to my sex. He slid a finger inside me and slowly moved it in and out. Nibbling on my neck, he continued until I was slick with arousal. I moaned when he pulled out. With almost no pause he replaced his fingers with himself. I cried out in surprise as he thrust into me. "Oh yeah, baby. You really missed me," he murmured as he took me, thrusting in and out quickly.

It had been so long since we had been together I was struggling to fall into sync with him. He took my grunts as those of pleasure. After I adjusted to his rhythm, pleasure began to build. I moaned and moved toward him to let him sink further into me. Just as my orgasm started to grow, I felt him stiffen and let out a loud groan. No! My body screamed as my big finish disappeared leaving me aching.

I was frustrated, sexually and mentally. Why was I surprised? Instant guilt washed over me. It was almost three months since I had caught him with Holly. If he had ended things, then that meant it had been that long since he had sex. No wonder it was short lived. It couldn't be helped.

Removing himself from me, he buttoned his pants quickly. I wanted to hold him under the night sky, but Christopher started complaining about bugs, then the humidity. It didn't bother him when he was pile driving me on top of the car, I thought bitterly. Putting my shorts on, I got back into the car. I waited for him to start driving. I had nothing left to say. My mind was blank. I felt empty inside. Once we were back on the road I asked him if we were going to his hotel, he hesitated before answering.

"I'm going to take an early flight. You know how I don't like being away from home. My business was finished this afternoon. I only stayed to see you." He patted my thigh like he was rewarding a dog for rolling over on command, which hadn't been far off, I realized miserably. He started to talk about the house and the things we were going to do when I got home. I stopped listening. I felt like garbage. He paused in his bragging to roll his eyes at me.

"What is wrong now? I give you the world while you're acting like a whore all over the country and I'm still the bad guy? I saw your video. They made you look like a slut," he told me. I didn't say anything. Was it true? I felt tears starting to come. I didn't stop them when they began to fall.

"Cleo, I've put up with a lot from you. I didn't leave when you got his name tattooed on you. I allowed you to go on tour with him, and this is how you repay me? By screwing him on camera and letting everyone see it? You know how bad this looks for me?" He screamed. His hands were gripping the steering wheel tightly. I looked over at him and could see veins popping in his neck. I still didn't say anything.

Nausea rolled over me and suddenly, without warning, I bolted forward and threw up onto the floor. Chris slammed on the brakes and hurried to pull me out of the car. Letting me drop to the cold ground, he went to my seat trying to assess the damage. Giving up on cleaning it, he started cursing and storming around the car.

"This is a rental, Cleo! An expensive rental! Why do I let you drink, God!" He kicked a nearby tree. Oh no, he probably just ruined his expensive shoes now too, I thought bitterly. I stood up shakily and wiped the vomit off of my mouth. Looking around, I recognized the area. The busses were right around the corner. Stumbling a bit, I started to walk that way, not caring if he came for me. I knew he wouldn't. I left him cursing and screaming about the car and his whore of a wife.

"I'm going to have to call a cab to come get us and take us to the airport," he spat. I turned back around and glared at him.

"I'm not going anywhere with you," I said, and he turned from the car, stalking over to me. He put his hand under my chin and squeezed tightly.

"Fine. Go be the slut everyone already knows you are." I refused to let him see me cry anymore tonight. I pulled away before the tears could fall and started walking again.

Did he even have business here, or did he come here for a booty call? No, I realized. It wasn't even that. He wanted to claim me. To remind me that I was bound to him. He came to berate, belittle, and take me. There was no love there.

I stopped at a fountain in the middle of a little plaza before reaching the busses. I washed my face and hands with the freezing water. I could still taste the bile in my throat. I leaned down and took a few mouthfuls of the liquid, gargling it. I didn't care where it came from. It was better than the taste of vomit.

I stood up and felt the dizziness from alcohol and no food returning. Moving slowly, I finished walking to the busses. Ethan was leaning against ours, fully dressed but shaking. He was high again. I could tell right away, but I didn't care. I went to him and without saying anything kissed him. He pulled me closer and kissed me back eagerly. I wanted him. I needed him. Ethan was my cure. He could make me forget Christopher. I wanted to forget about everything but him.

Even though we risked getting caught, I pulled his shirt off and his hands quickly went to my shorts. He played with the button, teasing me. I groaned and pushed myself against him, urging him to take them. He did as I wanted but then paused.

"Make me forget," I whispered into his ear. I kicked off my shorts. They hit the ground with a thud.

"Cleo, I'm done stopping this. I can't keep resisting this. Tell me to stop," he warned me one last time. His voice barely audible, but still I could hear it cracking.

"I don't want to stop this time," I told him, and that was all he needed to crush his lips to mine and push my back against our bus. I felt his need for me. He was just as desperate to be with me as I was with him. He unzipped his pants quickly and lifted me so I could wrap my legs around him.

Seconds later he was plunging inside me. I gasped at the length of him. He gave me a moment and asked me if I was okay. No one had ever asked me that. I nodded and bit his shoulder lightly as he slowly started to move in and out of me. Pain quickly turned to pleasure. I closed my eyes, leaned back against the bus and let myself enjoy this. I moaned as he bit my neck where his name permanently was. Where Chris had bitten. Only this time it was loving, not full of hate. I opened my eyes and saw that his were locked on my face. He was so ridiculously sexy, concentrating on me. I pushed Chris out of my mind. It was only the two of us here.

His rhythm turned quick and before I even realized my body was exploding around him. I gasped as my orgasm took me by surprise. My muscles clenched around him and he gasped. I clung to him as my body started to go limp. Suddenly he let out a moan, and I felt his body rock with his own orgasm. He let go of me gently to pull his pants up, and we fell to the ground in exhaustion.

We held each other on the cold, hard pavement next to the bus. No one spoke as we caught our breaths. We were both in shock over what just happened. I leaned against him more. We were drenched in sweat.

"I didn't know what to do. I wanted to run after you..." he started, but I held up my fingers and then pressed them to his lips. He clutched me tighter. I couldn't tell if it was the sex or the drugs that had him sweating and shaking, but I didn't let go.

"I knew he was coming. You left your phone in your bunk, and it kept going off. I grabbed it just to shut it off, but then I saw his texts. I deleted the messages," he told me. It was all making sense now. That was why he just showed up out of the blue. Why I had been so confused. I was numb to the whole thing now. I didn't even care that Ethan had invaded my privacy.

I kissed his bare chest, and he scratched his nose like a nervous tick. His eyes were dilated. He was high. My mood fell a bit. I hoped that he wouldn't regret what we did when he was sober.

The reality of what I had done hit me suddenly. I was a slut. Just like Christopher said. I slept with two men in the course of a few hours. How could I judge either man for doing the things they did? I felt disgusting. This was not how this was supposed to be! This wasn't romantic or sweet. I had imagined roses, candles, or at least a bed. I just had sex with Ethan against a tour bus. I was just as trashy as the groupies that came around after the shows. Not only that, I was reckless. I didn't think Chris used a condom. I should have asked. Oh god, what if he was still sleeping around and caught something?

I realized that Ethan and I hadn't used a condom either. Why would I do this? What happened to me?

"We didn't use a condom," I said to him, my voice dead. He sprang his head up. His eyes widened in horror.

"I was kind of in the moment; I wasn't thinking. I am so sorry Cleo. I don't even have one on me," he told me.

I was an awful person. I didn't deserve Ethan Andrews. I deserved men like Christopher Thomas. I said a silent prayer that I didn't just give Ethan some virus or anything else that Christopher could have gotten from his mistress. I sat next to the man I should have married trying to figure out what to do about the one that I did. If I told him the truth, I risked losing him. If I lied to him, I would know. It would always be in the back of my mind. I laughed out loud. It came out cold and harsh. Who did I cheat on? My husband, or my boyfriend?

Chapter Eight

HANDLE THIS

*T*he next few weeks went too fast. Christopher called every day promising he had changed, begging me to come back. At first, I ignored the calls. He couldn't have made me feel any worse about myself that night. I couldn't handle being berated again.

The rest of the shows went great. My time spent with the guys was fun. We stayed so busy it was hard to dwell on my marital problems. With the release of the song came interviews and photoshoots. The video and the single went to number one on the charts. People were chanting the lyrics as we sang them every night. They made signs and t-shirts.

Ethan and I talked about that night in Dallas. Although I didn't necessarily regret what Ethan and I did, I wasn't sure I wanted to keeping doing it. I explained to Ethan that I wanted to take a step back. Seeing Chris in the flesh made me remember the vows we took. I wanted a divorce before Ethan and I had sex again. He understood and agreed when I suggested we tone down the heat when in public. There was no need to make Christopher more angry than he was already.

Chris sent flowers to a few shows with notes that promised

things would get better. He would try counseling. He said if I gave him another chance, he would take anger management. Arguing with him was exhausting. In the end I would just sigh and agree to think about it, hanging up quickly before I could let him suck me back in.

During interviews, Ethan and I sat next to each other. However, we never touched and made sure to bring at least one or more band members with us to remind the fans that this was a collaboration of the bands, not a love reunion.

Of course, people would try to bait us. They asked all sorts of embarrassing questions. They tried to get us to slip up, reveal our true relationship.

In Providence, Rhode Island about 14 weeks into the tour, a man and a woman from a magazine approached us before a show. We had been doing a meet and greet with some fans. The man was holding a giant camera over his shoulder, filming the brunette holding a microphone. She smiled widely and introduced herself.

"Hi, I'm Candace from Bulletproof Magazine. Can we get a few quick candid words from you two?" She asked quickly. I looked at the man behind her who was fiddling with his camera. She waved her hand at him like he didn't really matter. "That's Chase. The camera's not on yet. I just want to ask some stuff about the tour, the song. Just a little something for the fans. Nothing formal," she pushed. I looked at Ethan who smiled and shrugged.

"Sure. We've got a few minutes," he said and just like that Chase was counting down the camera. I took a step away from Ethan, but Candace quickly pushed me back towards him. She threw her arm around me and squeezed herself into the frame. It would have looked better to have her in the middle but having me and Ethan close to each other would make people think things, I thought. I was already regretting this.

"Candace here for Bulletproof Mag, live in Rhode Island

with the two hottest things in rock right now: Ethan Andrews and Cleo De La Rosa. I caught up with them during a meet and greet with the fans and they graciously gave me some time to talk to them. So Ethan, Cleo, what's it like reuniting for the tour after a few years of not speaking?"

I didn't respond at first, so I looked at Ethan with a forced smile. He looked back at me, his eyes twinkling with amusement.

"Well, it was definitely weird at first. I mean, we were eighteen when we were together, just kids really. But I think we both realized that it was years ago and just wanted this awkwardness to be over. So, we talked about it and decided to grow the hell up and be friends again," he finished cheerfully. I smiled, thankful that he answered her. That wasn't what Candace was hoping for. I saw her frown but that didn't stop her.

"Friends? I wish I had a friend like you. We've all seen the video. That is some hot stuff. Some people seem to think that you two have some residual feelings left," she fished. It was my turn to speak. I smiled politely at her and pulled at one of my pink ponytails.

"Yes, the video turned out great. I hate to break it to you guys, but I think when this is all over Ethan and I are just gonna keep being good buds. He's cool, but I think we both know now that it's better to leave stuff in the past." Candace was downright pouting now.

"Aw, don't tell me that! The world is begging for more of you two!" Ethan put his arm around my shoulder and squeezed.

"Don't worry, we still care for each other, but our relationship has changed over the years. I mean, Cleo's married. I'm doing my own thing. Who knows, maybe the bands will do some more collaborating. It's really up to the fans whether we do another collaboration," he said. She flashed another smile and continued.

"Ugh, I hate how cute you guys are. We will forever have to

agree to disagree. You two are my ultimate ship. Congrats to the man that snagged you Cleo, and Ethan, I'll have to get your number after the show." She winked at the camera and Ethan let out a forced laugh.

"Thanks for the time guys, have a great show. I can't wait to see you both perform separately and together. I'm Candace Tucker and this was your exclusive interview with Cleo De La Rosa and Ethan Andrews," she said cheerily and made a motion with her hand for Chase to cut the camera. Once the camera was off she turned towards us and shook her head with a sly smile.

"Cool as cucumbers, huh? You guys aren't going to give us anything," she laughed, but her smile was tight, her eyes showing her annoyance. Ethan forced another smile and I followed suit.

"Sorry!" I said brightly and she rolled her eyes but kept the smile.

"Thanks though, I'll take what I can get. People will hear what they want to hear anyways. We all know that. It was nice meeting you both. I really appreciate you guys taking the time to talk to me," she said. We exchanged a few more pleasantries and then she disappeared back into the crowd.

After that interview, fans became obsessed with trying to catch us touching each other or looking longingly at the other one. It was almost exhausting trying to act aloof when around others, which when on a tour was always. When we did get time alone we made out like teenagers, but those moments were few and far between. I wanted nothing more than to touch him again, to kiss him wherever, whenever. To embrace the rumors and be his. But until I figured out what was going on with my marriage, I couldn't.

It felt like in the blink of an eye the tour was over. The last concert went perfectly, we couldn't have asked for a better performance. I bounded off the stage back to where the man I had fallen for this summer was waiting. I was walking over when suddenly my stomach turned. Hurrying to find a trash I ran off and threw up in a small wastebasket. Oh god, I hadn't even drank that much tonight. My stomach flipped once more and I vomited again. Ethan hurried over to me and grabbed my hair.

When I finally stood, I wished him good luck but told him I needed to lay down before the finale. He understood and let the guys take me to the bus. Closing my eyes, I was aroused only fifteen minutes later when Adrian put something on my pillow. I grabbed it and tried to read it in the dim light. I sat up quickly, realizing what this was. Adrian looked at me with solemn eyes. I stared back at him blankly.

"Go take it," he whispered.

In the tiny bathroom, I wanted to throw up again just waiting for the stick to tell me what I already knew. Sure enough, two minutes later I saw that I was going to be someone's mother.

Unable to stop the tears, I lifted my legs to my chest on the toilet and let myself cry. Adrian squeezed into the tiny room. Looking at the stick then back at me. He leaned down and pulled me into his arms to comfort me. We stayed like that until a knock on the door told me I had ten minutes until I had to be on stage.

I glanced up at Adrian in horror. I had forgotten about the finale. I washed my face and brushed my teeth quickly and hurried back into the building.

I watched Ethan from behind the line, he was so happy. What had I done? This couldn't be real, it was a mistake. Adrian came up behind me and squeezed my hand.

"You can do this," he reassured me. I wasn't sure I could. Cruel Distraction played their final song and the lights went dark. The band ran backstage excited. Spencer came over and told us that for the final performance they want all of us on stage with them. Adrian and the others were so excited they ran on to the stage to take their positions. I looked for Ethan, but he was nowhere to be found.

I waited for him, even though I was being called. Finally he stepped out of a closet, stuffing something in his pocket. Just looking at him I could tell he had just gotten high again. This was a disaster. I was so stupid. Feeling quite empty I took the stage with him one last time. Everything about my performance was forced and fake. Maybe we were better off without each other.

"What are you going to do?" Adrian asked after we stepped back on the bus, quickly moving to the bunks. The music blaring in front covered our voices. Ethan was in the front with everyone else.

I knew what he was asking me. It was quite common for people chasing fame to go have the procedure. Most agents and managers pushed it.

"I can't. I can't, Adrian." I shook my head, tears falling down my cheeks again. I was shaking. He wrapped his arms around me tighter. That's the only reason I was here. My parents were devout Catholics. Pregnant at fifty or not, my mother couldn't have an abortion. I couldn't either, I realized. I refused to even give it a second thought.

"It's okay. Everything will be fine. We will be here. All for one, remember," he reassured me. I leaned back into him and continued crying silently.

"How far along do you think you are?" He whispered. I paled.

"Dallas."

His eyes went wide with realization. "So Chris is..." he started but I shook my head.

"I don't know."

"Once you go to a doctor, you can see how far along you are and that will tell you who did it," Adrian assured me.

They wouldn't be able to tell. I hadn't told anybody, not even Adrian, about what happened that night. I couldn't. It was too embarrassing. I wrapped my arms around myself.

"Yeah, but what if it's the wrong guy?" I said. "God, I don't even know who the wrong guy is anymore. Chris is a jerk, but I know he would love a kid. He wants a family."

"And what about Ethan?"

"Ethan is the best thing to ever happen to me, but he still wants to tour and travel. I can't do this to him. I don't know what I want!" I was on the verge of tears again. Adrian hugged me and calmed me back down.

"Go with Ethan. Chris will be there until he gets bored. Ethan will stay," he told me. I shook my head.

"Ethan does not want kids. He told me this. He is still a kid himself. He doesn't need to be tied down to me or a baby. Plus, he's still doing…" I trailed off. I didn't want to say it. "He isn't ready to be responsible for this. Hell, I'm not even responsible enough to do this," I finished, burying my head in my hands again.

Adrian shook his head. "I can't make the decision for you, love. Figure out who the dad is and take it from there. But don't regret your choice." He gave me a stern look.

He was right. Whatever decision I made, I had to remember why I made it and that I couldn't take it back. This wasn't just about me anymore. I looked down at my flat stomach and it instantly rolled again. There was a little guy in there. It was a bizarre idea to me.

I hurried back to the bathroom just in case my stomach decided to empty itself again. Sitting in the bathroom, in the calm and quiet, I made the decision to tell Ethan. I didn't even have to tell Chris I was pregnant. We could sign divorce papers in our own separate places and be done with each other. He would never have to know.

The loud shouting from the bunks startled me. I strained to hear who was yelling. It was Ethan's voice like I had never heard it. Loud and shrill, like he was dying. I stepped out of the bathroom to see what was going on.

"Where is it, Spencer? I saw you with it! Where the hell is it?" He was screaming at the top of his lungs. There was a loud crash.

"Dude, calm down." One of them started but I heard a loud thump and more Ethan screaming. I moved to the front of the bus, where everyone was standing, yelling, and trying to get out of his way.

I looked to the front and saw Seth talking to Bill, shaking his head. Bill reluctantly opened the door. We must be close to leaving. Seth ran down the stairs, with the rest of Cruel Distraction and my bandmates following fast behind them. I was about to ask what was going on, but they were gone before I could get a word out. When I turned back to Ethan, he was in the bunks now. More smashing sounds came from behind the curtain so I decided to just brave it and see what Ethan was freaking out about. I could probably calm him down.

He didn't see me at first. He was shirtless in just his jeans, searching frantically through everything. His muscles bulged. I could see his veins popping in his neck and arms. The bus had been turned upside down and ripped apart. Everyone's suitcases had been opened and ransacked. Garbage was everywhere, I saw a shirt that had been ripped in half. I stood there in shock, taking in the scene.

Eventually he saw me and turned. His face was contorted in pain and anger. He was breathing heavily and visibly shaking. I was actually frightened. He reminded me of a feral dog, ready to attack for a piece of steak. His eyes were dark, his pupils were huge.

"Where is it? Did you take it?" He accused me.

"Of course, Christian got to you too huh?" He answered himself and went back to digging through someone's suitcase.

"Where's what? Ethan, you're shaking," I stammered, still shocked. He snorted and jumped over all of the mess and came face to face with me. He looked into my eyes and I was terrified. He was a maniac.

"My box. Where is my box, Cleo?" He gritted his teeth as he pressed his forehead to mine. His face was shiny with sweat that covered his entire body. I pulled away, the pressure on my forehead was starting to hurt.

"That wooden box? I don't know. I haven't seen it. Do you really need it? I saw you at the show," I told him, crossing my arms. I tried to stay calm and not show my fear. He started to laugh like a mental patient, moving away quickly to open a cabinet and throw out all the food in it. I flinched when a bag of chips flew past my head.

"Don't tell me what I do or don't need," he said through gritted teeth. I took a step away and he turned.

"Help me find it! Please, baby please. I had a full eight ball for tonight." He moved back to me, pleading with me. His eyes huge and watery. I shook my head and backed away towards the curtain. With a gasp his face brightened and moved around me to open a guitar case, where sure enough the box he wanted was.

As if I wasn't even there he pushed past me to the lounge and plopped onto what was left of the couch and opened the box up. I stood frozen to the spot as I watched him pull out a little clear baggy with white powder inside. He dumped it carefully onto the coffee table and dug back in the box for a credit card. He started to cut the cocaine. I didn't know what to do. I had never actually seen him use before. Only the before and after. He didn't even seem to see me. It was as if I didn't exist. It was just him and the drug.

When he was satisfied, he pulled a twenty-dollar bill from

his wallet and rolled it up. In one quick, smooth motion the white powder disappeared. He snorted two full lines and then sat back relaxed. I didn't move until Christian touched my shoulder. I hadn't even seen him come back in.

"You weren't supposed to see this. I'm so sorry Cleo, go for a walk or something. We have to clean him up," he said gently. I nodded and in silence left the bus. Too stunned to even think. I was pregnant with either my cruel husband or my cocaine addicted boyfriend's child. Where did I go from here?

Leaving the bus, I found the sidewalk and started walking, going nowhere in particular. I walked for almost a hour before Ethan suddenly joined me. I wasn't ready to talk to him. I was still in shock from what happened on the bus. He was panting from trying to catch up. I glanced over and saw he was gleaming with sweat. His eyes told me he was still high as a kite.

"Cleo, can we talk? I never wanted you to see that." I stopped and glared at him.

"See what? You doing cocaine? Destroying everyone's things? I don't want to talk to you right now. I can't handle this." I cupped my hands over my ears and started walking again.

"Handle what? You act like this is all new to you. Did you really not know what I was doing all summer?" He shouted at me. I turned around.

"I didn't…"

"Oh, don't give me that crap. You knew. You just didn't want to see it," he stalked over to me. "You didn't want me to be exactly like him." I blanched and moved away.

"Go to hell," I sneered. He laughed, shaking his head.

"What? Can't admit it? Yeah, I'm not perfect, Cleo. So I do a little blow to make me feel alright. So what? I've never asked you to try it. You don't have to be involved in this. Cleo, stop! Please, don't leave," he cried as I continued walking. I didn't turn back, I was afraid of what I would say. Or what he would do. He was messed up in stuff I had no interest in. I couldn't get involved in this.

When I finally stepped back on the bus everything had been cleaned up. It was as if the whole scene hadn't happened. Ethan was nowhere to be found.

I decided to stay in the front with everyone to avoid getting forced to talk to Ethan again. About twenty minutes after me, he stepped onto the bus and we took off.

He didn't say anything, but his eyes were red rimmed from crying. Every time our eyes met I looked away quickly. I know he wanted to ask me if I'd still go with him to California. His drug habit was getting out of hand. I couldn't handle that. I didn't want to have that argument with him. By the look of him, he didn't either. He kept fidgeting. All I could think about was whether it was the drug or my unspoken decision that had him so jumpy.

This morning my choice was easy, but now I was on the fence. This morning I hadn't known I was pregnant. I only had to worry about myself. I could do whatever I wanted with no consequences. Well not any consequences. This situation was the result of that kind of reckless thinking. I wanted to stay with Ethan, but I couldn't be with him until he got help. Not with a baby on the way.

On the other hand, when Chris finds out I'm pregnant he will assume it's his. I am his wife. Of course it's his baby. He'll fight for me to stay. His mother always used to ask me when we would start our family. With her being sick he will do anything for her to have grandchildren.

If I stayed in my marriage, Ethan would know I had slept with Chris. He wouldn't understand why Chris would take me back, pregnant with another man's child. Ethan would be crushed. I couldn't tell him.

I was so frustrated with myself. I can't believe we didn't use a condom. Ethan would think I had lied to him about everything.

In his eyes, I would be everything Christopher had called me that night.

I could never ask Ethan to drop everything to be a father. Did he even have a solid place to live? He was a traveling musician. I couldn't expect him to give all that up to do this with me.

He was not ready for something like this, we were both still kids. I couldn't force it on him. He had his own issues. I wish I had known the full truth before now. Knew how bad his addiction was. No, I thought back on this summer. I had known, but I wanted to pretend I had no clue. The signs were all there, but I ignored them all for my own selfishness. What would I have done if I had acknowledged it, though? Would I try to save him? Glancing at him I knew the answer. No, that wasn't my place. Ethan's demons were just that. Ethan's. He would have to do that on his own. Nothing I could have said would have helped him.

Suddenly, he stood and came to sit by me. I moved away reflexively. I didn't want to be around him right now. I wanted a beer so bad, just to take the edge off. I argued with myself. I was only a few weeks pregnant, but I was aware that it was in there. I couldn't have a drink in good conscience so I opted for water. Only Adrian noticed. He smiled warmly but moved on quickly.

After the bus was cleaned up, everyone just wanted to relax and party. Just Cruel Distraction and Maria Maria, for the last time. No crew or fans. I doubted anyone had any intentions of going to bed tonight, so I decided to grab my blanket and pillow and move to the very back of the bus to try to relax and think. I left Ethan in the front with the rest of the party.

I remained stressed and restless. I had such dreams for us. We were going to follow each other on tours. We'd collaborate on more music. Maybe even rent a place together.

I wanted that life more than anything. Now I would be changing diapers while writing songs at home. Would I ever tour again? It was doable. I knew women who toured while their children stayed home. Who would I leave the baby with though? I wasn't close to any of my siblings. My parents wouldn't do it. They were way too old.

Maybe I could try to make Christopher and I work. I couldn't raise a baby on the road. With Christopher, I had a home. He wanted kids, he would be happy. Ethan would freak if I told him. He didn't want kids. I curled into a ball and tried not to cry.

Ethan suddenly opened the curtains and came to lay with me. He climbed behind me so he could wrap his arms around me. I tried to pull away, but he held on tightly.

After a few moments of remaining stiff against him, I relaxed into his arms. I would miss this, I thought. I really would.

"You're not coming with me," his voice hollow. I tried to stop the tears. It was easier to talk while facing away from him. I shook my head slowly.

"This was one of the best summers I have ever had," I told him truthfully. I smiled and laughed a little through the tears. He squeezed me tighter. I think he knew that I needed him to right now.

"Mine too," he paused. "Cleo, I..." he started but I couldn't take it. I couldn't stop the sobs. Pulling away I stood up and held up my hand for him to stay as I tore open the curtains and left quickly.

I was so stupid. I loved Ethan and was leaving him to go back to a man I despised. A man I didn't even know anymore. I curled up inside my bunk and let myself cry.

I had no idea how I was going to do this. I was walking away from a great guy. I used to see a future with him, but that future didn't have babies and hard drugs in it. I cried until I could barely breathe. Soon I was heaving and sure enough my nausea returned, which turned into me leaping to the bathroom to vomit.

I couldn't choose. It was too hard. Ethan meant so much to me. Either go with him and ruin his life or leave and break both of our hearts. Could I really do that to him? I was such an awful person. He was trying to tell me he was in love with me, and I ran. Again. I climbed back into my bunk. Closing my eyes tight I tried not to think about what I was giving up.

Finally, sometime in the middle of the night, I pulled out my phone and text Chris. Telling him when and where to pick me up. I was going home. This kid better appreciate the sacrifices I was already making. He or she would have a good life, even if I was settling. They would only know happiness. Never want for anything. I would make sure of that.

Chapter Nine

WHERE WE WENT WRONG

Five years later

I celebrated my 26th birthday alone. Opening up a bottle of pink moscato, I poured myself a glass as I sat in my little home studio trying to work out some kinks our newest song had. There were a lot of them.

Adrian called to wish me a happy birthday. He wanted to be here, but he couldn't get away from whatever he was doing this week. Christopher didn't like the guys, so they stayed away most of the time now.

Mark and Derek called too. Mark was on vacation with his new wife Renee. Derek only called to make sure I would be okay alone. They all moved to California, while I stayed in Michigan. We were over 2,000 miles apart now. I spent most nights like this, so one more night wouldn't make much of a difference. As I poured myself another glass I thought about how I got here.

I told Christopher I was pregnant the night I returned home from the tour. At first he was in shock, but then he grinned, hugged me, and then promptly called his mother. She was getting worse and could use some good news, he told me.

He promised me the world. He screwed up before, but he was going to change. He swore up and down. I wanted to believe his stories, so I did.

Of course, all the promises he made that night in the diner were all lies. There was no pool, and the remodeled bathroom meant he had someone add different wallpaper. Those things didn't bother me as much as how gullible I had been.

When I came home, we had a long talk about his affair. He confessed to everything. It started off innocent enough, but long nights doing paperwork and prepping for cases together things started to get flirty.

"You were always gone. I felt lost, neglected, I liked feeling like someone cared," he said. That stung a little. Before I discovered them together, I used to call every night. I truly cared for him. He swore that he let her go and would no longer have any contact with her. I believed him, because I needed to. I was desperate to feel that he still loved me.

I pretended it was the pregnancy hormones making me crazy when he came home smelling of different perfume. He told me it was mine, and that my senses were just going wacky. I struggled to remember just when I bought the lacy bra that was way too big for me. Chris explained that he ordered it for me for when my breasts enlarged. I even went as far as to believe he happened to meet Holly at his hotel during a conference because she had a list of potential nannies for us. I was stupid and miserable, while Chris was on top of the world. But I remembered Adrian's words to me that day on the bus. I had made a choice, and I couldn't take it back.

Halfway through my pregnancy we went for an ultrasound. We were going to discover the gender. I wanted a little boy. A little Ethan. He wanted a girl to name after his mother, Clara

Sue. If it was a boy, he wanted Christopher Junior. I wasn't too keen on either name, but I went along with it to appease him.

I lay on the table with my t-shirt pushed up, staring at the monitor. The lady doing the procedure had an odd look on her face as she started furiously moving the wand around.

Chris had been standing off to the side, bored. Finally he turned to her and saw the same look on her face.

"Is there something wrong?" He asked, his voice carried an air of authority that normally frightened me. Today it was comforting. I knew that if something was wrong he would fix it. The woman shook her head and then smiled.

"No sir. I was just trying to confirm something we had apparently missed before."

Chris leaned towards the screen and squinted. I couldn't really tell much. I saw a tiny head and a bunch of other lines that were confusing.

"Well, what is it?" He demanded. The woman smiled again and moved the wand around until we saw two giant balls which I could tell were only one thing.

"Twins?" I whispered in shock.

"Twins," she answered me excitedly. There was a moment where we all stared at the screen, watching the two babies wiggle around each other. Christopher broke the silence.

"Well how about that? On our first try! Can you see what they are?" He asked her, happy for the first time in a while. After a more thorough examination she was able to tell us that I was having one boy and one girl.

That night just like most nights since I returned home, Chris drove off to tell the news to his "mother", while I sat at home and tried to figure out how to make the best of the situation. Twins. Leaving now would be that much harder. He was excited, and I was depressed. I had been so naive.

Five months later, I drove myself to the hospital. I had called him and told him I was in labor and needed him, but he was busy and would come when he could. I couldn't wait forever though, and him showing up with Holly made my water break right then and there. I gave birth two hours later to my son Dallas, and my daughter Jimmy, not giving a damn about what he wanted to name them.

After finishing a second glass of wine I stood up and left my studio. There wasn't any music being made tonight. I walked through my house, thinking about all the false hope I had for this place. I was going to turn this house into a home. We were going to be a happy family. I would still be able to make music, and Chris would continue climbing the political ladder. Only one of those dreams ended coming true, and they certainly weren't any of mine. Holding tight to my glass, I sat down on the couch and turned the TV on. I began flipping through the channels and settled on a music channel. There was a block of music videos. Many of the people on the screen, I had met and used to know personally. It only depressed me more. I was just about to switch the channel when the music videos ended and a familiar news anchor came into view. I remembered, after every show this channel liked to have her do five minutes of music related news.

I was mildly interested in the news, but suddenly a familiar band logo appeared in a small box in the top right corner of the screen. Cruel Distraction. I took a gulp of my wine and sat up a little straighter. What was going on with them these days? The woman replied to my unspoken question.

"In other news, the popular alternative rock band Cruel Distraction is taking a break from touring. Their last album, Typical Tease, went platinum breaking three different records. After their show last night the band reportedly were partying in a local hotel. A call was made to 911 saying that Ethan Andrews had overdosed."

My heart began pounding out of my chest as his face came

on the screen. In the corner was a photo of him, while a video of the band played on the screen. Overdose?

"The heartthrob vocalist has struggled with drug addiction for almost six years now. The band's manager and Ethan's proxy admitted him to a rehabilitation facility this morning after he was released from the local hospital. He is now resting and will be undergoing treatment until further notice. We were able to catch up with Spencer Darwish, the bands bassist who spoke to us about the band's future."

Spencer appeared on the screen, visibly annoyed at being pestered by whoever was behind the camera. "We aren't really thinking about what will happen to the band right now. We just want our friend to get better and we plan to be there for support."

"We wish Ethan the best and hope this isn't the end for a band that has already achieved so much success with their previous albums." They cut back to the newswoman who smoothly changed subjects.

"Does anybody remember the one hit wonder "When in Rome"? Well the group Badgers is back with a new song..." She continued but I lost interest. I sat back, setting the glass down, I took in the information.

My heart still ached for him. Just seeing his face made it react fiercely. I usually tried not to think about the decision I had made. It was for the best, I had told myself at the time. He could still have his career, and not worry about me. I thought I had been helping him. But, as it turned out, I had just made it worse.

Overdose. I repeated it again. I was having trouble absorbing the fact that he wasn't okay. Something inside me twisted, making me sad again. I longed for him. I longed for the life I could have had with him. Traveling, making music. His face popped back into my mind and I chocked back a sob. I let my head fall back onto the cushion. I guess life really wasn't greener on the other side. I had given up my freedom to give Ethan his, and he didn't want it. He'd rather throw everything away.

As I drifted off to sleep on the couch, my last thoughts were that we were both paying for our bad decisions. The only difference was that now he was working on getting himself out of that hole, and I felt like I was just burying myself deeper. The question that lingered at the edge of my mind as sleep finally overtook me was, would either of us really escape?

Chapter Ten

BLACK INK REVENGE

*F*our years had passed since my twins were born. My relationship with my husband had been filled with its ups and downs, like any marriage. On more than one occasion I almost broke my promise to myself. To stay in this house, until I knew our future was secure. However, spending my birthday alone finally prompted me to move into the guest room. I couldn't take sleeping in that big empty bed anymore. That was almost three months ago, and he hadn't even mentioned it. It didn't even phase him.

Today was one of no real importance. It was just like any other morning. Chris was just coming in, smelling of bourbon. His antics had only gotten worse since his mother had passed last April. His two-day business trips had turned into week long disappearances. Late at the office meant he wasn't coming home at all.

Chris came into the kitchen to sit with the twins. Even though he absolutely hated their names, especially Jimmy's; he cared for them. He smiled through his hangover and placed two boxes in front of them. They squealed with glee. Their tiny fingers reaching over their blueberry pancakes to open the presents. That was his answer to everything. Showering the children with gifts made up for his absence.

"Thank you, Daddy!" Jimmy told him, hugging her new doll to her tiny chest. Dallas smiled at him and thanked him more quietly for his red sports car. He loved the color red. Christopher snatched Jimmy up from her seat and squeezed her tight.

"You're very welcome sweetie. Now what are we doing today?" He asked, more at me than her. I ignored him as I continued making pancakes. He would no doubt want some too.

"Music class. Are you coming Daddy?" Jimmy asked. Despite Christopher never being around when it counted, he still tried when he was here. She loved him and he adored her. Dallas was more perceptive. He was hesitant with hugs and kisses when Chris was around. I think he noticed more than we gave them credit for.

"Oh no sweetie. I have some work to do at home. But I'm sure Mommy will take lots of pictures for me," he assured her and then turned to me.

"What are they playing again?" He demanded, turning towards me. His gray eyes cold, uncaring.

"Dallas is learning the guitar and Jimmy is on the drums," I told him for the thousandth time. They had been taking lessons for a year. He snorted. He wasn't happy about me enrolling them in music classes. He wanted Jimmy in ballet and Dallas in sports, but honestly, I didn't care what he wanted. I wanted a husband who wasn't cheating on me. A husband who loved me.

"Why don't you go ahead and order instruments for home. If you plan on going through with this, they might as well do it well," he told me, but all I heard was "This could be bad for my image, so if they get really good then I can show them off and boost my ratings." Always the politician.

I ignored his comment and set down his plate in front of

him. He put on his charming smile and tried to kiss my cheek. I leaned away and he frowned.

"Mommy is upset. Why is Mommy upset?" He asked, as if this surprised him.

"Mommy was in her studio last night. She was sad," Jimmy told him. Christopher turned his cold gray eyes to me.

"Talk to me," he sighed.

"Chris, you've been gone for a week," I said.

"Maribel, let me explain." I cringed at the use of that name. I hated it. He knew I hated it. He insisted that my other name was childish. Cleo was a dumb name, he decided. I had been using the name since I was ten. When I first met the guys, I told them my name was Cleo. I thought the guys would make fun of my real name. Once they found out, they laughed for a few minutes but decided I looked more like a Cleo than a Maribel so I kept it.

Chris changed that as soon as I returned. He needed a wife that was dedicated to his career. Cleo De La Rosa was my stage name, he insisted. When he first requested I start using my real name, I went along with it. He said it was our way to get a fresh start. A life away from crazy Cleo and Ethan obsessed fans. Considering what I was hiding from him, I didn't find his request that unreasonable. Now it felt like it was a leash he could pull whenever he chose. Only my bandmates and his brother called me Cleo now.

"We haven't been happy with each other for a long time now."

"So what, you think we should divorce? You think you're better off without me? How are you supposed to pay for the twins' things? Without me, you wouldn't be able to support them," he smirked. I hesitated. He was right. Since I stopped touring, the money wasn't coming in like it used to. I still got royalty checks from music sales or merchandise. They still sold our shirts at the mall. Other than that, I had no income. I had nowhere to go. I left my career behind to raise the twins and stand next to him at functions. I was a full-time mother and wife now.

I sighed, looking at him with exhausted eyes. "What are we doing Chris?" I asked. He came over to me, eyes pleading.

"We can make this work. I'll go to counseling again. I'll stay home more, go to the damn music class. Just don't leave. Not yet. Give us a chance," he begged. "It was what my mother wanted. It won't be good for my campaign." I looked at him blankly. Screw his stupid campaign. Screw his image.

I turned around and went to my studio. I closed the door, grabbing my guitar. When we stopped touring, I found I had more time to learn new things. Like the guitar. I started to play one of the newer songs I had written. I hoped one day to make another album. We couldn't really do anything without all of us, and it wasn't often we could make that happen these days. So instead, I played alone. It was my escape.

Closing my eyes, I got lost in the music. Only when the song was over and my guitar down did I notice the little boy near the door. "Dallas, baby come in," I told him and he scooted his little feet along the carpet towards me.

"Mommy, can we go to class now? I want my guitar," he told me. I nodded and took his hand to go find his sister. Chris was with her in the living room reading a book. This was what he always did. For the next few days he would be a model husband. Home at five, playing with the kids. After about night three he would come to my bedroom. I would turn down his advances. He would grow angry, frustrated, and leave.

He looked up from the book. "Queer eye called." I grabbed my cell phone off the coffee table and called Adrian back.

He was absolutely furious when I chose to name the girl twin after my best friend instead of his mother. Adrian James. We had picked it out together one night when Chris was off on a trip to New York.

The phone rang twice before he answered. "Hey you! What are you guys up to today?" Adrian greeted warmly. Oh how I missed him. After years of begging, I finally convinced him to come back to Michigan. He acted like it was such an inconvenience, but I knew he missed me just as much as I missed him. He had been in town for a little under a month.

"The twins have class in an hour. After that we're free. Why? What's up?"

"I have a surprise for them. Can you come over at about one? Don't be late," he ordered. I laughed. The kids loved their Uncle Adrian.

"Alright, we'll be there. I'll see you soon," I told him and hung up to face Chris' wrath.

"What does he want now?" He demanded. Out of my three friends, he hated Adrian the most.

"Nothing, he just wants to hang out. Why do you care?" I snapped as I helped the twins with their winter coats. It was November. Snow was already covering the ground, I hated it. I prayed it would melt early this winter. Chris had left the room rather than help me. He didn't even bother to say goodbye when we left.

Jimmy and Dallas loved music class. The class lasted roughly an hour and a half. The first 15 minutes, they let them explore the main room. Letting all of the children meet each other and try out any instrument that struck their fancy. After that they were then taken to rooms for their specific instruments.

Jimmy was the only girl who played the drums. She was in a class with two boys a year older, but she held her own. Her instructor Dominique loved having her in class.

Dallas' class had six other children. I didn't want to brag but although he was the youngest, he could already play just as well as the others. They shared my love for music. I was so proud of both of them.

The only thing I hated was that I couldn't watch them both.

I would have to wait for the monthly recital for the parents. Until now, I realized. Chris said to buy them instruments for home. That will be fun. I'll take Adrian with me, he'll know exactly what to get. My husband wasn't all bad, I thought. Without his successful career, the twins wouldn't be able to have music lessons, let alone instruments.

I waved goodbye to Jimmy as she ran to her friends and I followed Dallas into his classroom. I would spend today with him. I took turns, one day at hers, the next at his. That way I wasn't interrupting either class by coming and going.

As I sat watching my son attempting to play a new song for the recital, I thought about their future. I hoped they would keep on with music. I prayed that no matter what happened with Christopher and I, they knew how much I loved them.

I listened attentively, clapping at the appropriate times. When he finished I took his hand and we hurried to grab his sister. Jimmy was waiting at her door impatiently.

"Are we going to see Uncle Adrian now?" Dallas asked excitedly. I nodded, pulling them towards the door. Glancing at the clock I saw that we would have to hurry to not be late.

I called ahead, letting Adrian know we were on our way. As we drove I listened to my twins argue with each other in the back. Dallas told his sister red was better than blue.

"No one likes red Dallas. It looks like blood!" Jimmy screamed. He swatted his hand at her, trying to grab her hair.

"No one likes blue Jimmy! You got blue eyes and you look stupid!"

"Daddy said my eyes are gray. I don't look stupid, you look stupid!" They stopped forming sentences and just started trying to hit each other. I stifled back a laugh. Soon we pulled into Adrian's apartment complex. He was waiting for us outside.

"Look guys, its Uncle Adrian!" I called back. They stopped hitting each other to look out the window. They spotted him instantly and began calling his name, although the windows were closed. I hurried to get them out of their carseats. Adrian came to get Dallas out on his side, while I let Jimmy out of her straps.

"Hey twins! I missed you!" He told them, extending his arms out for a hug. They ran to him and snuggled close to the one man I could really count on. Over the past five years Adrian hadn't changed much. He was still muscular and tan. He kept his blond hair, only now he cut it shorter. The only real difference was like me, he had mellowed out. He wasn't drinking and smoking as much as we all once had.

He didn't party hard anymore. He stopped sleeping with everybody he could. Actually, last time I heard he was casually dating a woman named Cristina. Even though he was a gentler, calmer version of Adrian; he was still the Adrian I knew and loved.

"Uncle Adrian can we get ice cream?" Jimmy asked, recalling our last visit. He told them no and they started to whine.

"I have something better. I have four tickets to go see Murphy's Friends today! Who's coming with me?" He asked and for a moment the two toddlers didn't understand. A second later they erupted in screams and leapt into his arms.

I smiled warmly. Murphy's Friends was the twin's favorite TV show. The show was about Murphy, this guy in an obnoxiously big red and purple sweater who had a giant magical library. Every book you opened would take you to a far off land to interact with the characters.

For example, yesterday he opened Peter Pan. He was immediately transported to Neverland to play with pirates and the lost boys. The only part watchable was that every episode they had a celebrity of some kind as a book character and at the end of the episode they would do a musical number. I had met quite a few of the guests. It was amusing seeing these bad asses dressed like princesses or cowboys. Murphy's was the "IT" show right now. You weren't truly big until Murphy's friends asked you to come on the show.

As much as I hated to see this show any more than I had to, I couldn't say no to those matching pair of big eyes and pouty lips. So we piled into my car and drove to the stadium it was being held in.

The place was packed full of parents with toddlers waiting to see Murphy. It was so loud inside I could barely hear myself think. Kids were screaming and parents were loudly chatting. Music from the show was being blasted through speakers as we found our seats. I was ready for it to be over already. I asked Adrian if he knew any specifics about the show. He said they didn't have celebrity guests for the live shows. Adrian had gotten seats in the very front. He really went all out on this one.

"How did you manage this?" I called over the squeals of all the excited kids. He smiled wide.

"That chick Cristina I was seeing. Remember, I told you about her. Well turns out Murphy is her ex. She called in some favors when I mentioned the twins loved the show." I thanked him again as we placed the wiggly children in between us.

The lights dimmed, and the music lowered. Murphy ran out with his friends and the show started. I watched my little boy and girl light up like they were seeing the real Santa Claus. I bobbed my head to a few songs and tried my hardest to forget about my argument this morning with Chris. It was easy in situations like this. With Adrian, I felt normal again. Like we were back on the road, and this was just a pit stop. I made a mental note to call Mark and Derek. I missed them so much.

Halfway through the show I saw Adrian check his phone. He frowned. I nudged him with my hand, giving him a questioning look. He smiled weakly and shook his head. Hm, I wondered if he was having trouble with Cristina. He pushed a few buttons, typing out a text. Shoving it back in his pocket quickly, he turned back to watch this guy in the ugly sweater sing about dinosaurs.

The show ended with Murphy singing the crowd goodbye. My two were long asleep. The show had run through their regular nap time. We gathered the sleeping four-year olds and headed home to get them into their beds.

"Thanks Adrian," I told him as I drove back to town.

"I really needed this. Chris was... being Chris." Adrian was checking his phone again. It was annoying. Finally, he put it away and looked up at me.

"Cleo, what is keeping you from leaving exactly? The kids are still little. They won't even remember." I sighed. Of course I had thought about this a million times. What was keeping me from leaving? I found myself making excuses for him again.

"His mom just died. That and he's running for senate. He doesn't want a scandal. I'm waiting for her will to be read. He'll get the money to pay for the campaign and he won't have to worry about sponsors," I explained. "After that, I'm divorcing him. I don't think he'd dare contest it. He will want to keep it all hush hush. So, hopefully we can leave without a fight."

"You think it'll be that easy?" Adrian smirked, he had heard my excuses a million times.

"I'm hoping. Maybe we'll head out to California with you guys. I've got some money saved."

"Did she leave him a lot?" I shrugged, not really knowing the answer.

"I'm assuming she did. Well Chris is sure that she left him almost everything."

"Maybe his mom left the twins some money. Did she like them?"

"Oh, she adored them," I told him. "They were her only grandchildren. She spoiled them. I did consider that. His brother did hint at the possibility, but no one has actually seen her will so we won't know for sure for a few more months."

"I didn't know he had a brother. I can't imagine two of them," he grimaced.

"They are nothing alike. Eric is way nicer. They don't get along. It's gotten even worse between them since she died. Rumors are flying over what she put in it."

"That's probably why he wanted kids so bad. To give him leverage when it came time to divvy out the money," he smirked. These were all theories I had already thought about. He pulled out his phone again.

"Hey, I have something I need to do tonight, can you drop me off as soon as we get into town?" He asked. Something was up.

"Are you ditching me to go get laid?" He laughed nervously.

"No, nothing like that. Cristina and I ended things." My mouth dropped. I really thought they were good together.

"You broke up with her and she still gave you tickets to that show?"

"She dumped me. This was her parting gift." I didn't say much after that. He kept his eyes glued to his phone. I was tempted to throw it out the window. I noted that he never said what he was doing tonight. When I dropped him off, he stood at the closed car door looking at me with guilty eyes.

"What?" I snapped. I never wanted him to think I couldn't handle things. I didn't want anybody's pity.

"You know I love you, right?" He said.

"Of course, Adrian. I love you too. What is this? Are you breaking up with me again?" I joked but he didn't smile.

"Just remember that okay. Don't hate me."

"For what? What's going on?" I was growing worried. He shook his head, not answering. Adrian smacked the car door and pushed off to go into his building. I wanted to call after him, but something held me back.

I went to my empty home feeling more alone than ever. I

couldn't shake the feeling that something awful was going to happen. I went to bed dreading the morning.

Sunday afternoons were reserved for visiting Christopher's brother. He had moved into their mother's house after her passing. Christopher liked to go to make sure his brother wasn't trying to do something sneaky with his inheritance. I thought it was ridiculous paranoia but went anyways just to shut him up.

I dressed Dallas in a blue dress shirt and Jimmy in a dress of the same color. His mother had loved that color on them. She had always been sweet and kind to me and the twins. Chris must have gotten his personality from a different relative.

As a family, we drove in Chris's suburban to her mansion. Her family came from what she called old money. The daughter of a wealthy oil man, she brought her money with her when she married. She was frugal, but never had a problem spending it on the twins. The caretaker, Grant, greeted us at the door.

"Mr. Thomas is in the tea room," he told us, taking our coats. I was dressed outside of my personal style. I traded my ripped jeans and t-shirts for a white blouse and dress pants. I also curled my hair into soft waves and my makeup was softer, with very little eye liner. Like a politician's wife.

Eric Thomas stood at the window, facing away from the door. He turned when Grant announced us. The twins ran to offer him hugs and kisses. He smiled kindly and motioned for us to sit.

I liked Eric, he took after his mother; unlike his brother. He was tall and handsome, like Christopher. With the same curly blond hair and stunning gray eyes. A lawyer who, again like his brother, had an air about him. When he spoke, everyone listened. He was strong and confident. That's where the similarities ended. His comments weren't backhanded, and he didn't have a passive aggressive way of speaking to people. The only exception was when he spoke to Christopher. He was blunt, but never rude. Exactly as his mother had been.

The brothers hated each other. They were only born a year apart, but it was as if it had been ten. This was the only good part about Sundays. Eric enjoyed taunting Chris. He didn't suck up to him like everyone else. He called him on his crap every week.

"Cleo, Christopher! You look lovely. Your black eye has healed I see," he commented. I smiled, glancing over at my husband, who was already irritated.

"It was an accident. Maribel is fine. She's a klutz." He tried to toss the blame off of himself but Eric stared him down until he looked away guiltily. We all sat down. The twins found the toy box in the corner and were quickly pulling everything out. His maid, Michelle, came by to ask if we were ready for coffee. Once she left the room, Eric smiled at us again.

"Your new haircut suits you," I told him, being honest. It was shorter than usual and made him look more dashing. He thanked me and asked Christopher how the campaign was going.

"The campaign takes up most of my time these days, but I always find time for my family. It will be worth it when I win," he said, taking my hand. I flinched. Eric looked bored. We were all tired of hearing about the campaign. He did, however, glance at our hands when I flinched. He stayed silent but took note of it.

Michelle brought in the coffee while we talked. For the twins, she brought milk and peanut butter and jelly sandwiches.

When there was a lull in conversation Christopher brought up the twin's music lessons. "The twins have been learning to play instruments. They have recitals every month and they are some of the best in their classes," he told him matter of factly. I almost laughed. He had never been to a recital, how did he know?

"Oh? I would rather enjoy watching them play. I'm sure they received their musical talent from you, Cleo. Mother tried for years to get Christopher to learn the piano, but he never figured it out." I smiled kindly. Of course they got that from me. I prayed they never picked up a single mannerism or trait from Chris.

"I play the drums, Uncle Eric!" Jimmy told him from across the room.

"I have a guitar!" Dallas added. He chuckled.

"Just like your mother," he murmured, tilting his head. "Do they inherit anything from you at all Chris?" He smiled; a twinkle in his eye. It was said as a fun jab, but it didn't feel that way. Did he know? A shiver ran through me. Chris laughed and said something smart I didn't hear.

"What are your plans for the holidays? Thanksgiving is coming up," Eric mentioned. Christopher perked up, a smug smile on his face.

"Well actually, I was invited to the senators annual Christmas Eve ball. So we will be attending that," he boasted. Eric nodded approvingly.

"And Thanksgiving?" He repeated. Chris frowned, glancing my way.

"I have business that weekend. I will be gone most of that week." I pressed my lips together. Of course, he did. Smirking, Eric turned to me.

"Well, since Christopher will be so busy with his mistress… the campaign," Eric paused for his comment to sink in. Christopher began huffing. I looked over, his face was red. He was fuming.

"Why don't you come here for dinner? Invite Adrian if you'd like. Or anyone else for that matter, just let me know sometime this week how many will be attending with you and the twins. I would be honored to host this year," he said. His smile was genuine, but his eyes were sparkling with excitement that only came from getting to his brother.

We spent another hour chatting while the twins played. When we finally got up to go, Eric saw us to the door.

"I saw your commercial, Chris. Looks like you're going to be the next senator," he said. Chris looked at his brother proudly.

"That's right. Polls are looking good. Soon I'll be Senator Thomas."

"You can't let things go, can you?" Eric said cryptically before we left. What did he mean by that? Was I missing something? Christopher glared daggers at him but said nothing else. What was that about? His comment made no sense to me. We left quickly, each holding a twin's hand.

Only when we were all settled in for the ride home did Chris speak again. We were stopped at a red light when he reached out and slapped me hard! I screamed and tried to shield my face. "What was that for?" I cried. He snarled.

"I saw you eying his new butler. Am I that repulsive you want the help now?" I covered my cheek in shock.

"Grant? Chris he's a kid! Why would I…" He slapped me again, harder this time. My face stung as tears began to fall down my cheeks. I couldn't control it.

I stopped talking and let the tears pour out. Why did I even bother? He mumbled about how I flirted with him when we were leaving. I was just thankful the twins were asleep.

I carried them together to their room, placing them in bed as softly as I could. Without acknowledging him, I went straight to my studio and turned everything on. I avoided the mirror on the far wall. I could already feel a bruise forming, I didn't need to see it.

I plugged in my guitar and began playing an old song. I just wanted to run away. Leave and never come back to this house. I dreamt of the day I could take the twins and get on a plane to California. Mark and Derek would be waiting for us at the airport. Then we'd go back to making music and touring and all would be great again.

I pretended I was on stage, playing for sold out shows again. I played for hours until I fell down in exhaustion. Eventually I went to the kitchen for something to drink. I stopped heavy liquor when I discovered I was pregnant. Now, I mostly drank wine.

Chris was sitting at the table, a single light was on. I could smell the alcohol right away. His tie was undone, his blond hair disheveled. I ignored him when he called my name. I grabbed a glass and a bottle of red out of the fridge. I poured it, leaning against the counter.

He wanted me to go to him, to apologize for flirting with the barely 18 butler his brother employed. I thought back to Eric's comment before we left. It had pissed Chris off. He was just using me to let out his frustrations. I was his punching bag.

"I'm sorry. Maribel, I am so sorry!" He choked. This was what he always did. He would lash out, then cry and apologize. I said nothing. I listened to him cry. He dropped his head to the table with a thump.

"You can have anything you want. The money, the house, the kids. Just wait. I've been stressed at work. I'll get better," he promised. I finished my drink, washed the glass calmly and went to my room. Leaving him to wallow in his self-pity.

Bringing my fingers to my sore cheek, I wondered if I could make it to the will reading. It was months away. I didn't want to be here anymore.

Eric's little remark about getting any traits from Chris this afternoon returned to me. He was always kind to me. Would he tell me if he knew? I stood up and locked my door. Changing into my pajamas quickly, I laid in bed trying to figure my next move. I had no one. I was just a statistic now. An uneducated, battered wife.

California. That's where I needed to go. I knew Adrian missed Mark and Derek too. If it wasn't for me, he would have stayed. California; I repeated over and over until I was almost asleep.

Chris came to my door, knocked and when I didn't answer fell to the floor where he continued to sob. Then the pounding started. He went on to tell me how worthless I was. That I was never famous, and that I couldn't sing. He was the only reason I wasn't on the streets. He had seen my bank account and knew I was broke. I was nothing without him. I was stupid for naming the twins ridiculous names. On and on it went until he started crying again. He passed out leaning against my door.

He was gone by morning. Somehow he managed to wake up in time for work. He left a note saying he was going on a business trip. He would be back in a week. What a surprise, I thought bitterly. I wondered if he treated her the same way, or if it was just me he hated.

Chapter Eleven

MAKE BELIEVE

*L*ife was tense in the Thomas house, but that was nothing new. Chris came and went as he pleased. There were no major arguments, we simply coexisted.

Thanksgiving at Eric's was lovely. He insisted the entire band come, since they had flown back to see their families. Mark brought Renee, who was a doll.

Eric to my surprise had his own guests. I was unaware he had a girlfriend. Debra was a stunning, elegant woman. With a supermodel body, olive skin and a flawless face, I was shy at first. However, she was just like her boyfriend; beautiful yet kind.

We ate, drank and talked long into the night. It was a night filled with no stress from Christopher. It was the first night in a long time I had really enjoyed myself.

After Thanksgiving, came Christmas. The plans were to join him at the Senators Christmas Eve ball. Chris was so excited. He had picked out his suit and I was going to look for a gown to match later that week.

However, one night he came home unexpectedly. Storming in, he slammed the door shut so hard the windows rattled. I ran to see what had him so angry. "What's going on? I thought you were in Detroit?" I questioned. He threw his suitcase and jacket down.

"The Senator's assistant just called. The ball is canceled. First time in over a decade," he spat. I didn't respond. Why did this make him so angry?

"Did they say why?" I asked hesitantly, following him into the den. He went to the bar, grabbing a tumbler and quickly pouring himself three fingers of bourbon.

"Some family emergency. He hopes we understand." His voice dripped in sarcasm. I went over to him and put my arms around his shoulder. His body was stiff but after a moment he softened.

"That means you can be here with us. The twins will like that." My tone was desperate. Please, stay. I didn't want to spend Christmas alone; I silently begged.

He pondered it, then took my hand and squeezed it. His touch was gentle for once. I only flinched a little.

"Sure. That sounds great honey. We can get pictures taken. Perhaps send out Christmas cards." His mood shifting from fury to the old Chris.

He spent most of December with us. We baked cookies, went sledding, watched Christmas movies. He treated us like we were his world. It reminded me of when we had first gotten married. This was how it was supposed to be. It was perfect. We even made love on Christmas. I had my husband back.

Christopher sent cards to everyone. Our pictures were plastered all over the local news and papers. The picture perfect family. According to Christopher's campaign managers, he was now leading the race by a landslide. The other man, Michael Ross, was barely keeping up.

We had plans to spend New Years Eve at home together, but Chris was so thrilled about the numbers that he couldn't stay still. His friends invited us out, but it was too late to arrange a sitter, so I stayed home. He truly seemed sorry about it. He was too excited to stay at home. He wanted to celebrate, and I understood that. I let him go with the promise that he would be home around two or three am. He didn't come home until evening the next day.

With barely a full month under our belt, my dream deflated, life returning to status quo. He began taking long business trips again, while I pretended to not care that my heart was broken.

The new year had started and with that came the depressing, reoccurring thoughts that I was going nowhere. This was all my life was now, and I just had to accept it. I told this to Adrian, who had come over for dinner to celebrate Valentine's Day with me. We were both solo for the holiday, so we figured we might as well spend it together. I saw him more than I did my husband these days.

He was just about to scold me and tell me to leave Chris again when his phone went off. He quickly pulled it out, looked at the message, typed a reply and shoved it back in his pocket. I gave him a knowing smile.

"Ooh, who was that?" He rolled his eyes.

"It's a secret." I raised an eyebrow and he shifted away from me.

"I didn't know we kept secrets from each other," I accused playfully, but Adrian didn't catch my tone. He shot back quickly.

"Really, so how exactly did you get that bruise?" He poked my arm where four small, purple circles were clear on my skin. From where Christopher had grabbed me the last time he was here. I had wanted to visit my parents, and that had started an argument that led to him grabbing me to stop me from walking away. I pulled my sleeve down and glared at him.

"I was just kidding. Calm down. Keep your secrets," I told

him and turned back to the television. His phone went off again and he shot back another response. I was officially annoyed now. He suddenly stood up.

"Hey, I've got to go. I'll see you later," he said. I got up with him and walked him to the door, confused.

"Did I do something? What's wrong with you tonight?" He shook his head, fumbling with his keys.

"No, I've just got a lot on my mind. Promise me you won't hate me?" He said, reaching for the door handle.

"For leaving? I mean, I'm a little bummed but it's whatever. They'll be more weekends. Go get laid," I joked. He shook his head.

"No, it's not like that," he hesitated, as if he wanted to say more. I stared at him impatiently.

"Just remember that I love you, alright?"

"Why do you keep saying that? I'm starting to think you really do have a secret," I said, but he just stared blankly at me. After a moment I nodded and he kissed my forehead as we hugged goodbye.

The snow was lightly falling the next morning. I stepped out of my room with the desire and plans to spend the Saturday on the couch with hot chocolate and a book.

The twins were their usual chipper selves. They wanted cheesy eggs for breakfast, but as soon as they were placed in front of them they wanted French toast. I sighed as I sat down to make sure they ate. If I didn't, they would revolt against me and make a mess on the floor.

We spent the rest of the morning playing cars and restaurant. I stepped away to start preparing lunch and when I peeked back in, they were both asleep on the carpet.

Placing them in their respective beds upstairs, only then did

I sit in my recliner to continue the book I had been working on since January. I let out a breath of relief, enjoying the silence I knew would only last a few hours at best.

However, as soon as I reached for my book there was a knock on the door. I sighed, looking down at myself. I was in worn, baggy sweatpants and a dirty black shirt with a giant bleach stain on it. My hair was a big bundle of mess on top of my head. Great, I thought. I went to the door and unlocked it, opening it quickly before completely freezing. My breathing stopped completely as I stared into familiar blue eyes. There in the flesh, for the first time in almost five years, was Ethan Andrews.

I panicked. He had his simple, shy smile on his face. The one I fell for so long ago. It took me well over a minute before I snapped back to reality. Stepping forward, I closed the door softly behind me.

We stared at each other for a long time. It felt like an hour. He was still just as handsome, if not more than before. Ethan looked healthy. His eyes weren't as gaunt and his posture was different. He was wearing a black jacket with tight jeans. His jet black hair was longer now on all sides of his head. He tossed it back with quick movement of his hand. He was still so ridiculously good looking. Sticking his hands in his pockets, he rocked slightly on the heels of his black boots.

"Hi." Ethan finally broke the silence. I still couldn't say anything. I didn't know what to say. I never thought he would show up on my doorstep. It was so quiet I felt like we both could hear my heart trying to thump right out of my chest.

"Hi. Uh, how… why… what are you doing here?" I stumbled. His cheeks turned a slight shade of pink. He didn't say anything for a moment.

"Part of my program is to apologize to people I have wronged. You were on my list," he told me.

"Why? I left you, remember. I should be the one apologizing

Ethan," I told him, crossing my arms. I remained against the door. He shrugged, looking more and more uncomfortable.

"Look, either way I just wanted to see you and show you that I'm clean now. Six months. I'm not the same person I was before. I lost the one good thing in my life because of it and I was hoping I could take you to coffee or something." I was too stunned to speak. Coffee? How did he even find me? I was Maribel Thomas now. I had buried Cleo deep inside me. Suddenly I realized how he had found me. Adrian.

My blood ran cold. Did he tell him? He wouldn't. Would he? I closed my eyes. This is what Adrian was talking about after that Murphy concert, and then again last night, about not hating him. That's who he was on the phone with. It hadn't even occurred to me that Ethan was probably out of rehab at that time, and that Adrian would be talking to him. Why would he do that?

"You spoke to Adrian," I said, not asking. I already knew. He shook his head and smiled shyly.

"Kind of. I tried calling your friends for a long time after the tour, but they wouldn't give me anything. After my overdose, Spencer called Adrian. Then when I got out of the center, Adrian called me. We've been talking off and on the last few months. I mentioned that I was in Michigan to see my folks for the holidays, and he invited me to his place to catch up," he paused, clearly nervous. I just stood there, listening to all the puzzle pieces fall into place. That was why Adrian had left so suddenly last night.

"I got into town last night. Spent the night over at his place. We talked a while and then he gave me your address. Once I looked it up I realized why I couldn't find you, Maribel." My name rolled out of his mouth, smoothly. I snapped my eyes shut. That was the point, I thought. This couldn't be happening. Not now.

"What exactly did he tell you?" I asked, keeping my eyes

closed, I pinched the space between them. I wasn't prepared for this.

"About you? Not much, just the address. I didn't know you were living under a different name. Your real name. I called him from the road to ask about it, but he said if I wanted to know how you were then I needed to ask you myself. He said you might have some things of mine."

Adrian thought he was so funny. Oh boy, he was probably laughing his ass off right now. I stood there, a mix of thoughts and emotions bubbling up inside me. Suddenly laughter erupted from my mouth. Dry, harsh laughter. This could not be happening. Damn him! Why would he do this? This was not the time to do this. Not now! Not ever!

"I wanted to see if we could have coffee. Maybe dinner. Just to talk. No funny business," he swore, holding his hands up in innocence. His eyes grew desperate, afraid I would dismiss him. When I finally stopped laughing, I tried to process what was happening. Everything about this was wrong.

"Fine. I can't right now. How about tonight?" I offered. He smiled wide, I blushed. I missed his face.

"Yeah, of course. How about I pick you up at eight?" I nodded and he stood there awkwardly before I told him goodbye and went back inside. As soon as his car was gone, I called Adrian. He answered on the first ring. He had been waiting. Adrian knew he would be here today. Hate filled me, how could he? He knew how I felt about this. He promised me. I felt so betrayed.

"What do you think you're doing?" I snapped at him, before he could say hello.

"Whoa, whoa, whoa. What are you talking about?" He asked innocently. I wasn't in the mood for his crap right now.

"You know exactly what I'm talking about. You need to be here at six. You'll be watching the twins tonight." Adrian laughed, which made me more angry.

"This isn't funny Adrian! What are we supposed to talk about?"

"Well I don't know. How about hey Ethan that jacket wasn't the only thing I..." I interrupted him, not wanting to hear the rest of the sentence.

"Stop! So help you Adrian, if you tell him about Jimmy and Dallas I will kill you."

"Yeah, yeah, alright I'll be there. Is hubby's bar locked?" I hung up, furious. How could he get ahold of Ethan? He promised not to say anything if the situation came up. It's been five years, why would he choose to call Ethan now? It made no sense.

I stormed up the stairs to the bathroom to look at myself. I was a mess. It had been so long since we had been face to face. He was still so handsome. No, even more so now. I on the other hand wasn't what I once was.

I worked hard to get my body back after the twins. My hips were a little wider, but my waist was still slim. I had hoped Chris would want me again and leave her finally. What a laugh. I rubbed my face. I could use some makeup, I thought. My hair and face needed washed. I looked tired and my cheek was bruised from Christopher's hand. I sighed and after checking on the twins, I jumped in the shower to prepare for a night I prayed would never happen.

Adrian showed up at five carrying two large grocery bags. I left the twins in the living room playing with Dallas' train set to follow him into the kitchen.

He plopped the bags down and started unloading them. Cheese puffs, pop, chocolate cupcakes, potato chips. I sighed, thinking about the sugar high I would be returning to. Licorice, chili in a can, frosting. What the hell was he making?

"I'll make dinner. You need all the time you can get to get presentable," he teased. I put my hand on my hip, looking at the table full of garbage.

"Is that so? What do you plan on making? Frosting covered cheese balls?"

"This is for me," he said as he continued unloading.

"Well if you have control down here then I'm going back upstairs to, oh I don't know, be away from you. I am still mad at you," I reminded him. He turned to me with arms full of candy.

"Okay, okay. You'll thank me later. Just go and brood somewhere away from us," he said just as the twins ran into the kitchen to see what Uncle Adrian was doing.

As I sat in my bedroom I pulled out my old photo album. I was never one for scrapbooking, so it was just pictures of us from when we were kids and clippings from magazines and newspapers. It felt like I was looking at a stranger's past. Was this really me once? I was so badass, and now I'm just a deflated balloon of a person. Chris had inhaled my happiness, only to grow bored quickly, tossing me away. The party was over.

I stared at the very last page. It only had one picture. It was of the four of us. Mark, Derek, Me, and Adrian. We were sixteen. We were so happy, and so goofy looking. I smiled, looking at my younger self. My hair was short, my lips black. Adrian had just started bleaching his hair. Mark was going through a phase where he straightened his hair, and Derek was wearing pants with chains and straps. I started to chuckle. God, I missed them so much.

I hadn't realized I was crying until a tear fell onto the page. It was like taking a step through time. Back to when we were happy. I wanted to feel that again. Closing the book, I knew that this was right.

As much as I was dreading it, I was a tiny bit excited. I didn't want to admit it, but I missed him. I wanted to see him one more time. To feel young again. I wanted to talk to someone who wouldn't ask me constant questions about what it was like raising twins. In fact, he wouldn't even mention it, because he had no idea they existed. That was how I intended to keep it. One free night away from Chris, the twins, my failed music career.

Looking at the clock I saw it was 7:30. I leapt up and started rummaging through my closet. What was I supposed to wear? We never specified where we were going. Was I supposed to dress nice, or just my normal self? Finally, I gave up and called Adrian upstairs.

"I have no idea where we are going. What am I supposed to wear?" I asked him and he grinned devilishly.

"You're nervous about seeing him. I knew you'd forgive me. Here let me see what you have. You need to start wearing skirts again, Mom," he teased. These days I stuck mostly to jeans and hoodies. I glared at him.

"Well, you don't want to look... like that. So, none of these," he told me, pushing half of my closet away in disgust. "The nicest place in town is a sports bar, so you shouldn't wear something formal. What about this?" He held up my old leather jacket. Tossing it on the bed he grabbed a black and white striped tank top alongside my last good pair of skinny jeans.

"You still have those black boots?" I pointed him to the back of the closet as I pulled off my sweats. He handed them to me as I finished getting dressed.

"Alright, this isn't bad. Now, your face. When was the last time you put on makeup?" He scowled. I shrugged, it had been awhile. "You're on your own. Just because I like men sometimes doesn't mean I can do makeup and hair." I smiled. Ethan probably could, I thought. Remembering our night at the drag show.

Adrian looked me up and down and kissed my forehead. "This is a long time coming. You need this," he whispered to me. I smiled, he was probably right. "We probably shouldn't leave the twins downstairs by themselves. They're eating spaghetti," he said, turning towards the door.

"You gave them spaghetti and left them alone! Adrian I'm going to kill you!" I swatted him as he hurried downstairs to the mess I knew awaited him. The twins absolutely loved to play around with the noodles.

I sat in front of my vanity playing with my hair and makeup. I settled on a classic, and easy look. Thick black eyeliner, smoky eyes, and a dark wine-colored lipstick. Smiling a few times at my reflection I felt ready for this.

I heard Adrian struggling up the stairs with the twins. "Are you staying the night with Mommy?" I heard Dallas' tiny voice ask.

"I don't know. Does she have your other uncles stay the night?" He asked loudly, knowing I could hear him. He chuckled. If he didn't have my children in tow I would have pushed him down the stairs. Although, I couldn't stop the smile.

"What uncles? We went to Uncle Eric's," Dallas replied. That started an argument with his sister over where his Uncle Eric was. Jimmy told her brother that he was at work, while Dallas argued that he was at the doctors. I was so happy that Adrian was here to listen to them tonight. All they did was argue. People say that twins are close and loving but these two did nothing but bicker.

"I'll bite you!" Dallas yelled, which prompted Jimmy to scream like she was being murdered. Adrian was trying to calm them down, but I could tell he was struggling. I debated going in there and ending the fight now. Instead, I took the stairs two at a time. Adrian deserved this, most definitely.

I paced around the living room waiting for Adrian to come down. Finally the upstairs grew quiet and he slowly came down. He glared at me. "I hate you and your devil spawn," he said, sinking down into the recliner.

"You get used to it I guess," I lied pushing my hair behind my ear. I sat down and turned to him.

"Why does he want to see me? It's been years. I don't get it," I said. I played with the bottom of my jacket. I had changed too much. I wasn't the crazy carefree girl I once was.

He would realize that right away. Adrian leaned forward to look at me.

"Cleo, you crushed him. I never told you but for months he was constantly texting me and calling. Asking me why you took off. Why you went back to Chris. Was there something wrong with him? I finally told him to stop calling. He never got over you."

"What made you open your mouth this time?" I snapped. He shrugged.

"Spencer pleaded his case. I felt guilty. I mean, come on, how long are you going to pretend you don't know?" He asked me pointedly and I tossed a throw pillow at him.

"I just don't know what to do. I really don't," I moaned. He rolled his eyes.

"You could always ditch your idiot husband. Take him for everything he's got. You and the twins would be fine. Between me, Mark and Derek we would make sure you were okay."

I grew quiet. He wasn't telling me anything I hadn't already heard before. It wasn't that simple. Chris had connections. He wouldn't just let me leave. He would make me pay for any embarrassment he would suffer. It wasn't money keeping me here. It was fear.

I saw headlights through the window, and my stomach flipped. Was I really ready for this?

"He's here. Okay go upstairs or something. He'll wonder why you're here." I pulled myself and him up. We hugged and he kissed my cheek.

"Hey, I never thought to ask but what if Chris comes home? What am I supposed to tell him?" I snorted.

"He's been gone on a trip to New York for three days now. He's supposed to be another four days which translates to seven to ten. You don't have to worry." He raised his eyebrows and shook his head in disbelief.

"Okay. I swear if he shows up and beats the crap out of me

I'm going to be seriously irritated," he joked. I cracked a smile and rolled my eyes. He always knew what to say to help me. I was a little calmer now.

"Got it. Now go!" I pushed him towards the stairs.

"Okay, okay. Do you have like a puzzle or something for me to do?" He whined.

"Go!" The doorbell rang and I flinched, cursing Ethan for possibly waking the kids up. Of course, he couldn't have known though.

I took a deep breath and went to the door. It rang again so I opened it with a forced smile. It instantly turned into a real one. Ethan was holding roses. He thrust them at me and I stumbled back with a laugh. I saw him gulp. Was he nervous?

"I missed Valentine's Day. I thought maybe we could start over," he said. I wanted to, oh how I wanted to.

"I thought you said no funny business." I told him after I returned from putting the flowers in the house.

"I lied." He said with a grin. Something in his smile made my stomach flip. He opened the car door for me and I was even further impressed. He was driving a sleek black Cadillac. I commented on it and he shrugged.

"It's just a rental. I flew out here." Once I snapped my seat-belt, he pulled away quickly and we started going towards downtown.

"Where are we going?" I asked, breaking the silence. He brightened immediately and glanced at me.

"What are you in the mood for?" I thought for a moment. It had been a long time since I got to pick where I ate. We started driving through town. I pointed to a small restaurant that I loved but Chris hated. It was locally owned. Blue collar ate there, he told me once. We only ate at the highest starred places.

Ethan pulled into the parking lot and helped me out. He read the sign out loud. "Uncle Remus'. Sounds good." I nodded excitedly.

"They have the best fries. They use a special seasoning," I told him.

The restaurant was small, but full of customers. It was an old-fashioned burger joint. They had seats at the bar, and tables and booths scattered around. Everything was red or a crisp white. The smell of frying beef and fries filled the air.

"I didn't realize I was starving," Ethan said as he inhaled deeply. A waitress came over and directed us to a booth. She gave us menus and told us her name was Chelsea. I waited until she left, then I leaned over to say quietly.

"Chelsea Sometimes?" He laughed loudly.

"It's gotta be."

When Chelsea returned, we ordered our burgers and fries. I ordered water, but Ethan insisted on sharing a strawberry shake with me. I grimaced but agreed. Keeping my weight in check now that I didn't really exercise was difficult. Chris always noticed if I gained weight.

Ethan put his hands on the table and gave me a smile. "You look great. Different, but great." I blushed.

"Thanks, you too. You look healthy." He smirked. Chelsea brought our drinks. He took a giant gulp of his shake.

"I feel healthy. I guess. Sobriety is different. I'm still getting used to it, but I like it."

"That's good to hear Ethan," I told him. He waved it away and smiled.

"Enough about me. How about you, what have you been up to?" He asked. Where to start?

"Not much, Chris is running for senator. That keeps me busy," I told him lamely. He raised his eyebrows.

"Ah, so you're a politician's wife now? Look at you, all domesticated," he teased. I relaxed again. He wasn't going to give me crap or dive deeper into things.

"You don't miss touring?" Oh, you had no idea. I looked away. I missed it more than anything.

"A little. I still write music, it's just for me though." He shook his head.

"You need to get out to Cali. You'd love it there." Yeah, I probably would. We talked about lighter subjects while we waited for our food. When she finally brought our burgers, we stopped chatting and dove in. I almost moaned with how good the burger was.

"You weren't kidding. These fries are killer," he said, dipping one in ketchup and popping it into his mouth. "How's this winter been treating you? It's been awhile since I've seen snow on Christmas," he laughed. I looked up from my plate.

"You were here in December? How long have you been in Michigan?" He shrugged. "I flew back right after Thanksgiving. Went to visit my mom. Part of my program. We had a lot of things to get out in the open."

"Oh. Well that's good. Did it help?" I felt uncomfortable now. I didn't want to pry.

"Yeah, I think it did. We'll never be as close as we were, but I think we'll be okay. I told her i'd come back soon."

There was little talking while we finished our food. When we were done Ethan paid the bill and we left. Disappointment came when we got into his car. I wasn't ready to return home. I had missed him, missed being Cleo.

"That was nice. We should hang out more often," he said, pulling onto the road. I knew what he was doing but I had to shut it down. As much as I wanted to spend more time with him, we couldn't.

"You live out west," I pointed out.

"Actually, I'm staying with Adrian right now," he revealed. I whipped my head around. He didn't turn, his eyes glued to the road.

"What? Since when?"

"A few days ago. We've been talking and when he heard I was in Michigan he invited me down and then offered his spare room." Oh, I was going to kill him. I didn't say anything for a while. I was stunned into silence. What was Adrian doing?

"Ethan, this was great, but I'm married. My life is different now. I'm not the girl I once was. I don't live that life anymore," I told him flatly. It was the truth, and I hated it.

"Was it because of Chris? Cleo, I don't mean to be that guy, but you shouldn't change for anyone. You're a great performer. People still talk about the band. What happened? You guys just kind of dropped off the face of the earth." I stayed silent. He was prying. Getting too close to what I intended on keeping a secret.

"There were some things I couldn't get away from. We still get together, but aren't working on anything solid right now."

"You should, it would be fun catching a show of yours. Or we could always collaborate on something again. That video never was continued. Everyone always asks about it," he said. I didn't respond. After an awkward silence he moved on to talk about his own successful music career. I was so jealous.

When we pulled into the driveway my stomach dropped when I saw that Adrian had turned some lights on. He had pulled his car to the back so Ethan wouldn't have seen, but the lights were obvious. They hadn't been on when he had picked me up. Ethan stiffened. "Is he home?"

"No, he'll be gone all week. It's Adrian," I told him and he didn't question it. He parked his car and walked me to the door. I knew he was hoping I would invite him in, but that was out of the question. The twins could wake up and see him.

"Thanks for coming out tonight, Cleo. It was hard for me when you left. I fell, bad. But I wanted to show you I was better now. I appreciate you giving me that chance." I hugged him and kissed his cheek.

"Sure. I had fun. I'm glad we did this," I said lamely, knowing there was so much more I wanted to say. His eyes told me he knew it too.

"Can I see you again?" He pleaded. I had to turn away before he saw me cry. I would never forget you Ethan, I thought. How could I?

"I'll see you around, Ethan. Maybe you shouldn't stay with Adrian," I told him before going inside quickly. Leaving him at the foot of the stairs.

Adrian was sitting in my bedroom going through my things when I came in. He took one look at me and I burst into tears. I needed my best friend more than ever right now. He took my shoes and jacket off and started rubbing my back.

"Shhh, calm down and talk to me. It's okay," he repeated until I was able to speak without my voice cracking. I told him everything. He nodded the entire time as if he knew this would happen. I hated him for it. Why did he talk to him? Why was he letting him stay with him?

"Cleo, I love you. I really do. I only did it because you needed to see him. Now you have some kind of closure. You had your chance and you decided not to take it. That's alright." I nodded, too tired to argue. There would never be closure with Ethan. I scooted over and turned the light off. Adrian moved to spoon with me as we fell asleep moments later.

In the morning I woke up, leaving Adrian in my bed. The kids were up early and being their normal terrible four-year-old selves. It was setting up to be a great morning, I thought sarcastically. I felt like Cinderella returning back to her house after the ball. The only thing is, I wouldn't be trying on any glass slippers. This was my life now. I had to forget about last night. It would be like it never happened.

Adrian came down shortly, dressed and grabbing his coat. "I have some things to do today but I'll be free later tonight if you need me. I'll call you later." He came over kissed my forehead and then hugged and kissed the twins before running out. I glared at him.

"Tell him to leave," I demanded. Adrian glanced at me and muttered

"Okay, sure," before quickly leaving.

I was cleaning the kitchen from the twin's lunch mess when there was a knock on the door. Perfect timing, I groaned as I picked up a screaming Dallas. Jimmy jumped up to follow us to the front of the house. She held tight to my t-shirt yelling that whatever she did wasn't her fault. The knock came again, so I called that I'd be right there.

It was probably some important papers from his various business partners. We got packages constantly and someone had to sign for them. I ripped the door open, irritated already by the sudden interruption of our afternoon. I was ready for the twin's nap more than they were. I looked up and nearly dropped Dallas. My blood ran cold as I stared at Ethan.

His mouth was agape looking at Dallas. He took a step back in shock. He shook his head slowly, eyes bulging out of his skull. He stared hard at the little boy in my arms. As if trying to count the similarities.

He saw what I saw. What Adrian, Mark, and Derek all saw but refused to say aloud. He saw the raven black hair, porcelain skin, and baby blue eyes.

Chapter Twelve

TOO LATE

I didn't know what to do. I wanted to run inside and pretend this wasn't happening, but he knew. He knew. I stayed silent, letting him take in the sight. My pulse was hammering in my ears. Time had stopped.

Finally he cleared his throat, his voice cracked as he asked me the question I didn't want to answer. "How old?" He croaked, his voice breaking like a teenage boy. He held another bouquet of flowers in one hand. I only noticed because I saw that his hands were shaking. Petals fell to the porch. Ethan turned around, looking towards his car. He was starting to panic.

"I have to get him inside. I'll be back," I told him quickly. I tried to shut the door but as I was backing up Jimmy called out from behind me.

"Mommy, it's snowing, I need my mittens! Don't leave me!" Ethan's eyes jerked to look at the little girl hiding inside. He opened his mouth and then shut it quickly. His face was white as a ghost. I sighed and closed the door on Ethan.

I climbed the stairs, rushing to get the kids down. Dallas fell asleep almost instantly, while Jimmy wanted water and a bed full of animals before she would take her nap. Grabbing the monitor, I went back downstairs. I found Ethan sitting on my steps, his shoulders collapsed into him, his head in his hands. The flowers lay next to him crushed and wet, like Ethan. He was shivering. I didn't know if it was from the cold, or if he was crying. I was tempted to run back inside. I never planned on having this conversation. He wasn't supposed to find out.

It was snowing, as Jimmy had pointed out. The snow was light, barely a dusting. Before I walked outside I quickly put on boots and a jacket. Shivering, I went to sit with him. I didn't say anything. He felt my presence but didn't look up.

"Which one is mine?" He demanded harshly. I smirked.

"Both." Ethan's head whipped up to glare at me. Tears in his eyes. His face was contorted in confusion and pain.

"Both? They're twins? They're…" I nodded. Shaking his head, he began to laugh. It was a dry and humorless.

"What's so funny?" I asked.

"I'm a twin. My brother was 27 minutes older than me." He shook his head again and put his forearms on his knees. I had no idea. Why had I never known that? "So what, are they five?"

"In April. Ethan, I need to explain."

"No, I get it. It makes sense now. Everything. You knew. When I asked you to come with me, you knew you were pregnant. That's why you ran. I was in bad shape. I didn't mean to get that way in front of you." He turned his sad eyes to me. "That's why no one would tell me anything about you. Good thing too. I would have brought you down. I only got worse before I finally went to rehab. You didn't need to see that." I touched his hand and he flinched, pulling away quickly like I was on fire.

"The only thing I can't figure out is why you are still with him. This could have been your way out. Not saying you had to come with me, pregnant and all. But why would he want to raise…" His voice trailed off with the realization. His eyes grew wide again, turning to anger.

"He doesn't know, Ethan. That's why I stayed. He wouldn't just let me go knowing I was pregnant. All he ever wanted was a family, I couldn't leave," I lied. I could have, but I was too scared to do it alone.

"How could that be? You came home pregnant. How could he think they would be his if he… oh God." He leapt up. His eyes bulging, realizing everything then. His hands went to his face. He pulled on his cheeks in frustration.

"That night. When you came back and we… against the bus. Jesus Cleo! You fucked us both? Fuck!" He let out a cry of anguish as he started pacing again. He kept sideways glancing at me, his eyes were blazing with fury. The look on his face was pure disgust. He made me feel like trash. It wasn't my proudest night. My silence wasn't helping.

"Ethan. You said yourself you were in no shape to raise a child, let alone two. I had to make a choice. It hurt me too! The only difference is you didn't have two constant reminders of me staring at you. For the last four years I have had to look at them and see my biggest mistake. I should have told you yes, but what would you have done? You were just getting big and I couldn't take that from you. I was the one that screwed up. You didn't deserve to have your future stolen from you for this!" I motioned to the house.

"You didn't give me the choice!" He shouted back at me. I flinched.

"What choice, Ethan? Would you really have dropped everything to do this with me?" I asked him. His eyes were wild with anger and disbelief.

"Cleo those are my damn kids! I have every right to be there." I stopped him.

"No. No you don't. You were about to kill someone when

you didn't have your fix. You were in no shape to be a dad. How could you help me when you couldn't help yourself?"

"So, what? You dropped your career and became the house-wife he always wanted you to be?" He accused. Tears welled in my eyes over the truth. My lips trembled. I tried to stop, but I couldn't. This was not how I wanted this to happen.

He stopped talking and just gazed at me. Pain shone in his eyes. We stared at each other unsure of what to say. Suddenly we both turned to the baby monitor which Dallas' voice was coming out of.

"Jimmy, are you awake? I want to play trucks." We turned back to each other and he gulped nervously. His hands on his arms, rubbing them nervously.

"Could I... can I meet them?" He asked, almost pleading. I felt sorry for him in that moment. He was asking to meet his children. I nodded and motioned for him to follow me inside. It was perfect timing, because the snow was starting to fall faster.

"Stay here, I'll go get them." I pointed to the couch. He looked around my home curiously, and then took a seat on the furniture.

Dallas was standing next to his sister's bed with one of his cars. He had his little arms raised above his head, preparing to smash the truck down onto her tiny, matching body.

"No!" I whispered as I ran into the room and snatched him up. I scolded him as quietly as I could and led him out of the room. He began to whine that she wasn't up yet.

"Let her be. You have plenty of time to play. Let's go down-stairs. Mommy has a friend waiting to meet you," I told him. He crossed his arms and although not happy about it, followed me down the stairs with no fight.

Ethan stood up when he saw us. I smiled reassuringly to him. Dallas looked at Ethan curiously, then went forward to give him the truck in his hand. Ethan grinned ear to ear and took it. "Thank you. I'm uh…" He looked at me to answer for him but I had nothing.

I panicked and blurted out, "Uncle!". He nodded, his jaw tightening as he focused back on his son.

"I'm Uncle Ethan. What is your name?" Dallas stood up straight and put his hands behind his back as I taught him.

"Dallas Edgar Thomas. It's nice to meet you." He recited and then extended his hand. Ethan stared at it. He took it and shook it gently. He didn't say anything else, but Dallas ran to grab more cars.

There was movement on the stairs. We turned to see little Jimmy coming down holding a book. Ethan didn't take his eyes off her. It was a mix of shock and awe. My eyes started to water. I went to her and took her hand, helping her the rest of the way down. Ethan stood back up, Dallas stared at him from the floor, curious.

"Jimmy! Uncle Ethan is here. Come play," he shouted. She glared at him. Jimmy always took longer to wake up. She rubbed her eyes and yawned. She moved to where Ethan was and handed him the book. He took it and kneeled down to see her better. She sighed.

"Can you read this to me?" She asked. He smiled so wide I thought it would permanently stick. She climbed onto his lap and he read her the story of the rain babies. Her favorite book.

She fell back asleep before the book was over. The sound of the snow and wind outside must have been soothing for her. He looked content watching Dallas play on the floor. I sat down in the recliner watching them. I smiled at my daughter. She was always so comfortable with new people. She didn't care who you were, just as long as you did as she wanted you to.

It was an odd feeling, but this felt right. Chris made things uncomfortable when he was home. He was always angry or depressed. The kids were always so much worse when he was around. Like they had some kind of extra sense. They knew that our relationship was strained. Sometimes they even seemed to forget about him when he was gone. He could never just spend time with them, with us. Ethan on the other hand looked content. I wondered about his own family. What was it like for him growing up with a twin? Why didn't he tell me? The thought actually hurt my feelings a bit.

Ethan adjusted her and turned to look at me. "What is her name?" He whispered, and I smiled. This could go either way. The only ones who liked her name was Adrian and her grandmother, Clara Sue.

"Jimmy Paige." He smiled softly and squeezed her a bit tighter.

"I like it. Jimmy and Dallas. Who came first?"

"Dallas, seven minutes." He looked down on the floor where my son, our son, was laying down, starting to nod off. It grew quiet in the house with only the wind to tell me I hadn't gone deaf.

"I want to be here. Involved. Somehow. Is that possible?" He looked at me, desperate. I was hesitant. The twins deserved to know their father, and Ethan had a right to know them as well. But would Chris connect the dots if he saw him coming around? Honestly, he was so self-centered there was a good chance he wouldn't. He hadn't figured it out yet. His ego was too big. No one would ever dare choose another man when they had Christopher Thomas as an option.

Reluctantly I said, "We'll see." He nodded understanding my hesitance. He mumbled a bit, looking at his sleeping daughter. He ran his empty hand through her thick raven hair.

"I can do this. I can do this right?"

He was talking to himself more than to me. Like he was trying to convince himself that he was strong enough to handle all this new stuff. One moment he was just a guy trying to right some wrongs and the next he was a father of two. He chuckled.

"I never thought... my brother died before he had any. It's

weird. I always thought it would end with me," he told me. I nodded, it was weird thinking about the past. Who knew this is where I'd be at 26?

"Why did he…" I started, but quickly shut my mouth. I realized that Ethan not only never told me he was a twin, he never said really anything about him at all. Instant regret filled me. That wasn't something you asked someone.

He looked away from Dallas and gave me an odd look. Maybe remembering an old conversation or something about his brother. "My mother told him he was dead to her if he was going to keep being who he was. So he decided to make it come true."

I didn't know what to say so I didn't say anything at all. We sat, watching the twins sleep, not saying anything else. We didn't need to.

Once the shock started to wear off I asked Ethan why he had showed up on my doorstep in the first place today. I told him rather rudely, to go away last night. He looked at me oddly and then laughed.

"Adrian came home and said that you had some things of mine. That I should come over. I thought you knew, he told me you said it was alright. I was going to try to ask you out again." I shook my head. Of course, it was Adrian.

It was evening now. The twins were playing with Jimmy's play kitchen while I was in the real one getting dinner around. Ethan sat at the table watching me. "Is he a good dad?" He asked suddenly. I kept my back turned, afraid of what my face would reveal.

"He is when he wants to be. He likes to think that presents solve everything," I sighed.

"I always hated my stepdad. Mom said once that she

thought my real dad would have been a shitty one. Maybe I was better off," he revealed. It was odd hearing Ethan talk about his family. In all the time we had spent together, he had only briefly mentioned them. I wanted to keep him talking.

"Where do they live?" He stared at me with a blank expression.

"My mom and Bob still live in Lansing. He's a..."

We stopped talking when we heard the front door open and close. Panic shot through me. Was Chris here? Ethan looked at me and I shook my head. Neither of us moved. We heard footsteps, then suddenly Adrian popped his head in from the living room. I let out the breath I had been holding. He was grinning and carrying a large brown bag.

"Hey! I brought ice cream!" He said brightly. Ethan and I both glared at him.

"I can't believe you," I told him as he came in, setting the bag on the table.

"Yeah, I know. I thought I'd pop over and make sure no one had killed the other." The mood in the room switched from anger to excitement when Jimmy walked in and saw Adrian. She screamed and ran to him. I saw Ethan frown. Dallas came in slower and instead of running to Adrian, he chose to climb onto Ethan's lap.

Ethan smiled and ruffled the little boy's hair. Dallas touched his arms, looking at his tattoos. He was always so curious.

"Uncle Adrian has ice cream Dallas!" Jimmy screamed. Dallas perked up but Adrian told them they had to wait until after dinner. He squirmed out of Ethan's lap and asked him to come play. Jimmy moved away from Adrian to join her brother. Ethan's eyes lit up and let them lead him out into the living room.

"You can wash dishes," Jimmy told him as they left. She had a way of making anyone she met want to move the earth for her.

I know she was my daughter, so I was a little biased, but she really was a beautiful, stunning little girl.

Her eyes were so blue, like the sky on a cold winter's day. They contrasted so harshly against her jet black hair and fair skin. Her brother had the exact same features. It was no real surprise Ethan realized the truth within a few moments of looking at them. They were the spitting image of him; except for one small detail. While Ethan's hair was straight, mine and the twins had natural soft curls. Everyone always complimented on how beautiful they were, and it was true.

I peaked at them from the other room. When Ethan came and sat down with her she quickly changed her tone of voice. When asking for help, originally she asked very politely. Now she demanded Ethan get started on the dishes while she cooked dinner. "Aye, Aye, Captain," he told her and went to work in the small sink. I turned back to Adrian, who was opening a bottle of beer.

"What is your problem?" I stormed over to him and grabbed the bottle. He protested.

"What? The Ethan thing? Come on, it's not like you could have kept it a secret forever."

"Adrian, that's not the point. You shouldn't have meddled. Chris is their dad," I reminded him. He rolled his eyes.

"Is he? It's after five, where is he? If the twins really mattered to him, he'd be here."

"Stop. I'm not talking about this tonight," I finished and left the kitchen. Dallas was pulling on Ethan's arm.

"Come play cars," he said. Ethan stood up to go but Jimmy threw her arms over him.

"No Dallas, he's eating!" She cried. Ethan jumped a little, startled by the volume that came out of her little body.

"Eating is boring. Kitchen is boring, Jimmy! I want to play cars!" He matched her shrill voice with his own. Ethan looked up at me with wide eyes. Shock on his face. I tried hard not to laugh. This was my life. Everyday.

I stepped in to explain to Jimmy that they had to take turns. She crossed her arms but stalked over to the cars and picked one out to play with. Ethan gave me a grateful smile. I winked at him.

After a while they grew bored of playing with him and decided they wanted to play alone. He went back into the kitchen with Adrian and I. We chatted at the table, although now it felt awkward. When Adrian's phone rang, he excused himself. I felt myself relax.

Ethan wanted to know everything about the twins. Everything they liked, they hated. What mannerisms they picked up, what weird twin things they did. I was mildly annoyed by the amount of questions but, considering I had kept their existence from him for five years it was the least I could do. When dinner was done I brought the kids to the table and began serving. Adrian was still in my studio on the phone.

"So, do you think he's ever thought about it? I mean, I realized it right away," he asked as he helped me feed the twins. I fed Jimmy while Ethan fought with Dallas over the food. The twins were oblivious to us. They were arguing about who was the better Batman.

"I'm Batman, Dallas! ME! You're Robin!" She told him. He smacked her hand and told her that no, he was in fact Batman. Moving their seats further apart, I turned back to Ethan and rolled my eyes.

"No, not ever. He's too cocky. Why would I look somewhere else when I have such a gem at home." He smirked, but said nothing. When Adrian came back from his phone call the conversation turned lighter. We laughed and talked about our old touring days. I think it was the first pleasant meal ever served in this house.

After dinner I started getting the kids ready for bed. Ethan followed me around, watching me. We went through our nightly routine of baths, pajamas, stories and then finally, sleep. He helped wherever he could.

Once they were in bed, I went back downstairs to where Adrian and Ethan were sitting. Adrian had turned the TV on, they were watching a movie. Ethan stood up as I entered the room and smiled nervously, stuffing his hands in his pockets.

"I think I'm going to head out," he said, his voice hesitant. I wanted to say something, but with Adrian five feet away it was hard to talk. He pulled out his car keys and I walked outside with him. I saw Adrian raise his eyebrows suggestively before I closed it.

"Thanks for letting me stay today," he said.

"Yeah, sure. Look I don't know how to say…" He put his hand up to stop me.

"It can't be changed. I understand, kind of. I wasn't in a good place. But I'm sober now and I can't go back. I can't pretend they don't exist." I gulped, nodding. He stepped off the porch and turned back to smile at me. "So I will see you in the morning," he said, leaving before I could argue.

Adrian stayed over again. Claiming he wanted to give Ethan space to process everything, but I felt like he was hiding something. I didn't have the energy to argue, so we watched movies until we fell asleep on the couch together.

I awoke to Adrian already gone and the twins coming down the stairs. I went straight to the kitchen to start the coffee. Just as I was pouring my cup, there was a knock on the door.

The twins ran to the door. I let Jimmy open it. As soon as they saw Ethan carrying donuts they bombarded him. He laughed, handing me the box so he could hug them. I tried not to smile but I couldn't help it. His smile wasn't forced like Christopher's always were. He really wanted to be here.

I snuck the box into the kitchen hoping the kids wouldn't

remember he had brought them, which they didn't. I wasn't going to deal with that sugar rush this early.

He came into the kitchen after he set them down in the living room. I looked at him and shook my head. Ethan was the poster boy for bad boys. He had his leather jacket on with black, worn doc martin boots. I think he even put some eyeliner on today. He flushed red when I asked about it.

"I feel weird without the eyeliner sometimes. I'm so used to it." He opened the box and proceeded to shove a donut into his mouth.

"What are you guys doing today?" He asked me with his mouth full. I sipped my coffee and thought about our schedule.

"The twins have music class today. While they are at preschool I have a few errands to run. Their birthday is coming up, so I need to start getting stuff around." He perked up at music class.

"They are into music? What do they play? Is it serious? How good are they?" He asked eagerly. I smiled, I should have realized he would be pumped for this. Adrian was just as excited when I told him. I took another sip and continued.

"Dallas plays guitar. Jimmy plays the drums, and yes, they are very good. We have instruments here for them. Maybe if you ask they'll play for you." He was almost bouncing in excitement.

I followed him as he went to ask. They looked at him like he was crazy. He looked like an excited puppy. Dallas looked at Jimmy and she turned back to him; silently communicating to each other. They did this often. I loved it. It was pretty much the only twin thing they did. Ethan noticed it too, because he stood back up and his face changed to a more serious one. His smile faded, eyes growing dark.

Jimmy stood up and helped her brother up. "Uncle Ethan, come on!" She took his hand and pulled him forward, down to the basement where my studio was.

"Oh, uh it's just Ethan, Jimmy," I told her. She paused, her and Ethan looked up at me. Jimmy's face showed understanding. Ethan's showed surprise. I smiled at him and he smiled back weakly. Jimmy pulled on his hand again, ushering him forward.

Dallas and I followed behind. When we stepped inside Jimmy dropped Ethan's hand and hurried over to her drum set. I had instruments here for when the band came to town, but out of courtesy to the guys I ordered the twins their own.

I had been so excited when they finally came in. I had them customized. Jimmy's kit was her favorite shade of blue, and Dallas' guitar was a bright cherry red. Each had their names painted on them. Ethan stood near the door in shock of what he was witnessing. I set Dallas down and he hurried to his guitar. I helped him plug it into his amp. Then I gave him a pick from the little box I had on a table along with his headphones to save his precious little ears. I gave Jimmy hers as well. I was excited and proud to be showing them off. We had been working a lot together.

Drumsticks in hand, Jimmy began doing some practice beats, just trying to get her rhythm down. Dallas did the same, playing a few chords. I glanced at Ethan whose eyes were huge, not taking his eyes off them.

"Mommy are you going to sing?" Dallas asked me. I smiled at him, quickly grabbing my microphone and turning it on. I turned back to Jimmy and gave her my thumbs up. She took her music very seriously, so she didn't smile back. She did however give me a thumbs up. She remained focused while warming up.

After a few minutes Jimmy called to Dallas. They gave each other another look and then she clicked her sticks together and counted down. They started playing a song I had taught them. Well, Adrian and I. I had to call him to help with the drums. He had also picked up another instrument during our off time.

Dallas started playing first. It was a full-size instrument so he still struggled a bit at first, but he adjusted quickly to it.

Ethan started to smile and looked at me with incredulous eyes. I looked back at him and tightened my grip on my mic. I opened my mouth and started singing the words. His jaw dropped.

"You taught them Queen? Holy shi… cow! How?" He said after a second. He was using his hands rather excitedly. I just laughed and stopped singing for a second.

"It was hard, but we have a lot of time on our hands. Can you play bass?" He nodded and I moved further into the room to pull out Derek's guitar. Taking it, he set himself up and waited for a spot to join us. Once he started playing I grabbed for my microphone again and continued singing Queens 'Now I'm here'. I turned to watch my children's reactions. Jimmy looked confused but kept playing. It had thrown her off, understandably.

We were used to just having the three of us in here. If Dallas noticed, it didn't phase him. He was always so focused and it was like he had found his happy place in playing. When the song was done Jimmy hopped off and went to Ethan with her hands on her hips. Dallas kept playing, moving with ease to another song we had been working on. One of my own band's songs.

Jimmy's face was scrunched up. "That's Uncle Derek's guitar. You're not supposed to touch it," she told him. He put his hands up, quickly removing the strap from his back and handed me the guitar.

"He said it was okay. I called him. Did you like Ethan playing with you?" I asked after she calmed down, thinking for a moment. Dallas finally put his instrument down and came to stand with us.

"I did! Mommy you sang the words great!" Dallas exclaimed. I nodded and hugged him.

"When me and your Uncles come in here I always sing with them. I can sing with you more if you'd like." I offered.

"Okay, but Ethan will come too," Jimmy demanded. I

agreed, then took their hands to lead them out. They weren't allowed to wander around in here. There was too much expensive equipment to let them explore without supervision.

Looking at the clock I saw we had just enough time to get ready for school. Having Ethan to help me get them dressed was nice. Chris, in the four years since they were born, never once helped me with any of this. He would leave the room, pretending he didn't notice I was struggling to wrangle both of them. With Ethan, we got out of the house in almost half the time. It helped that they were finally potty trained. We didn't have to wrestle with them to put diapers on.

Ethan joined me in my errands while we waited for preschool to be over. As soon as they were done we drove over to the music school. He was almost as eager as they were to go inside. I introduced Ethan to the instructors. Many of them recognized him immediately. They were so excited and bashfully asked for autographs. Without hesitation he took their pens and signed everything they asked. He even offered to help with the guitar class.

"I can take a picture with everyone if you want," he offered and they jumped to find a camera. I laughed and nudged him in the ribs. He feigned innocence. "What? I'm just trying to be friendly," he said with a smile. I rolled my eyes and took the camera from the shy piano teacher.

They set the kids in the front, the staff in the back standing up and they had Ethan in the middle of the picture. They organized the kids by classes so the twins were far apart. I saw Ethan look for them, and his face fell when he saw they weren't closer to him. I felt a twinge of guilt as I was a little relieved. It would look bad if the picture leaked to the media. People would ask questions.

When the kids were sent to their individual classes Ethan asked me if he could go with Dallas. Of course he could! That meant that for the first time since I started classes both of my kids would have someone there for them.

As I was sitting in the corner watching Jimmy practice for the recital, I imagined a life where me and Ethan were parents together. A life without Christopher. My life could have been so different. Could Ethan be the dad I always imagined them having? I told myself that it was better this way, but only after two days I was already reconsidering.

If I took the twins and left, revealing the truth, they would for sure lose whatever inheritance they were going to get. Christopher would probably try to take what little savings I had, or any rights to the band. He would get his revenge. I would be completely broke by the end of it all. That meant that I would have to figure out a way to support us quickly. I had no job and no high school diploma. The thought of being homeless was terrifying.

I could go back to music, but it wasn't as easy and glamorous as people thought. It would be awhile before I was making enough money to support me and the twins. It wasn't possible.

On the other hand, Ethan's music career was still on the rise. He wasn't a millionaire, but could still be some security for their future. If I left, I could also begin touring again, something I craved every day. I could get a nanny and we could tour together. Or even on and off, taking turns. I realized as the class ended that these were all pipe dreams. My music career was long over.

That night, after the twins were asleep, Ethan and I sat at the table. There was cold silence between us. "We can't tell anybody. Chris can't know," I reminded him.

"Okay. I can deal with that. Just let me be involved. I never had that. It was just us and my mom for a long time. Then when she married Bob it wasn't what we thought. He wasn't much of a dad. I want to be the one I never had, even if they can't know it," he said, his desperate words hanging in the air. I wanted that more than anything.

"I think we can figure something out," I assured him, taking his hand in mine and squeezing. He raised his eyes to mine, they were filled with tears struggling not to fall. He left before they did.

"So he actually wants to help raise the twins?" Adrian asked me as he moved to sit on the couch with his glass of rum and coke. I had called him as soon as Ethan left. I tried to explain on the phone, but he told me he would just come over. I nodded, drinking my own. I sighed with pleasure. Adrian always made the best mixed drinks. Rum and coke was a pretty easy recipe, but he did something different I swore. I flipped the TV on and turned it to an old rerun.

"Yes, and I want him to be involved too but if this leaks... I'm afraid of what will happen if Chris finds out the truth. It could screw up whatever is in that will and if he loses money because of this he will flip. Or worse, his campaign," I explained. He nodded and looked at me thoughtfully.

"And no one knows what she put in the will?" He asked.

"I don't think so. Christopher for sure has no clue. He's the one that explained it to me. I think he's actually afraid that she left it all to them, and none to him. I have a feeling he plans on trying to control whatever money they get."

"Okay, okay I get it. So that means that no one can officially know that the twins aren't his." I nodded.

"But now that Ethan knows, he wants to be a part of their lives. Like a huge part," I added sadly. I shouldn't be sad that their father wants to be around, but it made everything so much harder.

"When is the will read?" I shrugged.

"Hell if I know. She died last April. Most wills take at least a year, and the more money they have the longer it takes."

"Well next time you go to Eric's get him alone and ask him. Don't let Chris know you're curious. We don't want you tripping on the stairs again," he snorted. I punched him and handed him my empty glass. He stood up to refill both glasses.

When he returned he continued, "So how has it been with Ethan? Like besides all the kid stuff? Is there still that crazy sexual tension between you two like before?" I shook my head as I gulped down my drink.

"Oh no. I'm pretty sure he hates me. Ethan and I as a couple are officially done," I mourned, the alcohol making me dizzy and emotional.

"But what about you? Do you still have feelings for him? If he asked, would you run off with him? Or whatever you guys do? You know I had no clue what was going on? Like before the tattoos. Me! Your best friend. How come you never told me? I'm still hurt over that." He frowned, his eyes big and sad. I shrugged, it was weird with Ethan.

"Maybe it was because whenever I got a boyfriend you guys turned him against me. It always turned into one long joke on Cleo. I needed someone who wasn't just one of the guys. I wanted someone that was just mine," I explained. I started to think back to our relationship before everything, when we were teenagers. We were only able to meet when the bands crossed paths on the way to gigs.

"So, you diddled him for a while, then get his name tattooed on the side of your neck, then drop him for Mr. President?" He asked. I could tell he was getting braver from the alcohol too.

"I wanted it to be just some fun we had when we got together. He wanted more. I was afraid," I said, my voice dripping with regret.

"What? Did he ask you to marry him?" Adrian laughed and

when I didn't say anything he turned his entire body towards me. "No! He proposed to you and you turned him down, and then married this guy?" I put up my hands to calm him down.

"No, not quite. He found out that Chris had proposed. He was upset. He wanted more. I didn't. So, instead we decided to get completely hammered. When I woke up, I had this." I pointed to the side of my head where my hair covered his name.

"Then the whole world saw his about a month later in that magazine. Everyone was trying to figure out who I was," I laughed. Adrian stared at me with his drunken, non-blinking gaze. He then started to laugh as he finished his drink.

"So you have no memory of getting it done?" I told him no.

"You think I would soberly do something that stupid? That was kind of why I left. If we convinced each other to get tattoo's together; what was stopping us from doing something even more stupid?"

He shook his head. I know, I left an amazing guy because I was afraid to commit. Instead I eloped with a complete jerk I barely knew. Suddenly I hiccuped and the tears started. I sniffled but I couldn't stop myself. I covered my face with my hands and let go. What did I do? I was so stupid! I thought being with Ethan would be a mistake, but it turned out that Chris was the mistake.

Adrian leaned over and pulled my hands away from my face, wiping my tears away. I sniffled, trying to get myself to stop crying. After a few minutes I was calm enough that my cries were just hiccups now. He put his arm over my shoulder, rocking me calmly. He was always there for me. I loved him so much, he had no idea. I would never be able to repay him for loving me for the mess I was.

"It's okay love. In the end, it'll all work out. We'll have our house with the picket fence," he promised.

Chapter Thirteen

BE STRONG

*E*than came by every day that week. The kids loved him. They always wanted to take him into my studio to play. It made me happy because they happily spent hours in there working on new songs. He came along to the classes, alternating twins. Now both of them had someone in class supporting them, although he enjoyed watching Dallas play more, but only because that is what he played. He never complained.

Saturday came too quickly, and I knew Christopher was supposed to be home tonight. Now whether or not he did was a different story, but I had to prepare for it just in case. I had worked out what I was going to tell him as to why Ethan was around. I just hoped he accepted it and didn't lash out.

I sent Ethan home early, explaining that I needed to do this alone. Sure enough he showed up drunk and out of his mind. I was reading a book in the living room, waiting up for him. I didn't want him pounding on my bedroom door. One of these days it would end up breaking.

He stormed in, dropping his suitcase on the floor with a thump. I looked up and then went right back to my book. My initial reaction was to play the dutiful housewife. Smile, offer him dinner. On second thought, I realized he would know I was up to something. So instead, I didn't get up when he entered the house.

He grabbed the book out of my hands and tossed it across the room. I flinched. I should have been nice. He pulled me up and tried to push his lips against mine. I turned my head in time for him to press them to my cheek, leaving my face sopping wet. I couldn't breathe, the smell of her perfume and the alcohol was making me sick.

"I've been gone a week and you can't get up to kiss me hello?" He demanded, squeezing my shoulders. I winced, but stayed standing. I needed to stick up for myself. I couldn't keep living in fear of his hands. Ripping myself away, I glared at him.

"How was your business trip? Did you have enough condoms, or did you have to go to the store? I tried to pack you enough for the week," I spit out. He stood there, eyes bulging, trying to take in what I had just said to him. I regretted it immediately. Why would I bait him like that? I should have kept my mouth shut.

"What did you say to me?" He demanded, and I started backing away towards the stairs. I just had to make it to my room. Once I was inside I could lock the door.

"Don't you dare. I know what you're doing. You think you're so funny with your little remarks. She told me you'd do this. Just because you're bitter. I don't see how. I'm giving you everything Maribel!" He bellowed, storming towards me. I turned and ran towards the stairs. I had made it up two steps before he caught my leg and pulled me down, hard. My entire body slammed into the stairs as my face bounced off each step as he dragged me down. I screamed out. He snatched me up, covering my mouth. I tried to bite him, but I was already feeling weak.

"Shut up you stupid woman. You think you're better than me? You wouldn't have anything without me!" He screamed but

I was already going in and out of conscience. The force of my head hitting the stairs had me feeling sick.

He dropped me on the carpet. Stepping over me, he walked to the stairs. My entire body was throbbing, I stood up dizzily and made it to the couch before I closed my eyes and prayed for sleep.

Jimmy woke me up by tapping on my bruised face. I groaned, opening my eyes. "Mommy, Daddy's home. He said get up. We're going to Uncle Eric's."

I sat up slowly and let out a yelp. My entire body was bruised. I looked at my arm where I had landed. Purple. I lifted my pant leg up a bit and sure enough, purple.

I didn't know what to do. I was afraid to look at my face. It felt swollen, and my eye hurt to open. Instead of going to the bathroom I went to the kitchen where Christopher sat reading the newspaper while the twins ate bananas. I shook my head. Really, you couldn't even fix them a bowl of cereal? My thoughts went to Ethan. He would have. Hell, he would have fixed them eggs and bacon.

"Are you going to get ready? I don't have time for your laziness today. Eric expects us in an hour. Oh, and put some makeup on. I think it's time to get you some heavy duty cover up. You look ridiculous with all those tattoos. How am I supposed to take you out in public looking like trash? I want you to start covering them, you need to look presentable. Maybe we'll even get you some of those invisible braces. Close that gap," he told me. I turned to him, holding the empty coffee pot. I imagined swinging it at his head, his skull cracking on the tile. Instead, I sat it down and left the kitchen to get ready.

Just as I had suspected, my entire face was black and blue. I gasped, holding in the sobs when I saw my reflection. I must have hit the stairs harder than I thought. With a sigh I took a quick shower, then began attempting to cover it up with concealer. I used an obnoxious amount but finally there was only a hint of yesterday's fight. I took some medicine to reduce the swelling in hopes that as long as someone wasn't looking hard they wouldn't notice. I wasn't going to cover my tattoos. Screw him. I certainly wasn't going to get rid of my gap. It made me who I am.

Of course, after I was ready, I had to struggle with the twins. The entire time I was getting them washed and dressed Christopher sat on the couch looking at his phone. Finally, we were all ready and loaded into his car headed for his brothers. Christopher was all smiles as he drove.

"Alright. I don't want to see you flirting with that damn butler again. I'll fire him. We don't need people like that taking care of my mother's house," he snarled. I didn't say anything. Glancing at him, I saw his face twitch.

"I don't know why you are so upset with me. I came home on time, just like I said. The boys wanted to go for a drink after the trip, but I told them you wanted me home," he lied. I wanted to laugh. He had used that line a dozen times already.

"We got a significant amount of work done for the campaign. Hopefully I won't have to go away for a while. Running for office is hard Maribel. Once I win I'll have more time for you." Again, I ignored him, turning to look out the window.

"You know, your constant moping around doesn't help me. I'm gone night and day for this family and…" He started yelling and I snapped. I whipped my head around and glared.

"Don't lie to me Chris. I know damn well where you go. Why bother hiding it? There's no point when I see her at the store. She smiles, grabs the wine you like, food you like and condoms. She likes to get in the same checkout lane as me, thinks it's hilarious as she pulls out your credit card. Stop lying!" I shrieked, and Christopher slammed on the breaks, forcing me forward. I hit the dash with my head.

The twins cried out, but more out of shock. I started to cry, not meaning to. I was in so much pain already, now my chest hurt from the seatbelt. I was getting a headache. He sighed and started driving again.

"You must be mistaken. It was someone else in line with you," he said, finishing the conversation. We drove in silence the rest of the way. When we arrived he went to the door, leaving me with the task of getting the twins out alone. I was so sore I felt like I was eighty years old with how slow my movements were. When I went to Dallas' door he looked like he was going to cry. I wiped my own tears away and forced a smile.

"What's wrong baby? Don't cry. We're at Uncle Eric's. We'll have some peanut butter sandwiches," I promised but he shook his head. I wanted to cry again, my sweet boy. He always knew more than I gave him credit for. I kissed his forehead and set him on the ground to take his sisters hand as we hurried inside.

Grant answered and refused to look directly at me. He had gotten talked to as well. "Both of the men are waiting in the tea room," he said, taking our coats. I thanked him and he gasped as he saw some of my bare arm as I shimmied out of the jacket. I ignored it and followed him with the twins.

Eric was sitting down cooly while Chris was standing up yelling. He stood when we entered. Opening and closing his mouth, he saw my bad cover up job immediately. He motioned for us to sit. I did so silently.

Chris stormed over to the window and looked out, not acknowledging our arrival. The twins hurried to see their uncle and he presented them with two boxes. They looked at him in awe. He smiled and helped them untie the red and blue ribbons on each gift.

Dallas's box was tiny while Jimmy's was long and slim.

"Your mother told me that you two played instruments. I got you an early birthday present," he told them as they held up their new guitar strap and drum sticks. Jimmy's had her name burned into the ends while the strap had been embroidered with

Dallas' name. I had them thank him and they hurried to put them aside for the sandwiches that were brought in. I thanked him myself and we began chatting about very basic, safe things. The weather, local news. Still, my husband stood by the window.

Suddenly, after about twenty minutes he pivoted, saying he needed to make a phone call and left quickly. Eric laughed but didn't speak until we heard a door slam from the second floor. I smiled, wincing at the pain. "What did you say to him?" I asked and he chuckled again, shaking his head.

"I just made a comment that I had information about the will. It is going to be a very interesting afternoon." He nodded in agreement with himself and ordered Grant, who was at the door, to get him a scotch. This was it. I grew excited. This was the opportunity I needed. I leaned forward and dropped my voice, even though I knew Chris was still upstairs.

"You know what's in it?" I asked and he smiled.

"Her lawyer has been getting it around to finalize it and he mentioned some things. I worked for him for a year after college. We touch base every so often."

"So, Chris is pissed," I said, matter of factly.

Eric was downright giddy. "Just wait. He really has no clue. I only gave him the tip of the iceberg."

"What did you say exactly?" I had to know, afraid of what he would do to me in his anger. Grant returned with his drink. Standing up to stretch his legs Eric took a long swig. He looked at it, then back at me with a smirk.

"I let him know that Mother knew about his mistress. Even naming her specifically; and she was not happy. No sir, not at all." I was stunned. I didn't know whether to laugh or freak. Did that mean that Eric inherited everything? We heard the door slam. Chris started down the stairs.

"One more thing, before he comes back. She knew. About the twins. She loved them regardless. But you need to find a way to tell Chris before that will is read. If he finds out that way, you are going to be a lot worse than you are now," he warned me. My eyes bulged. His dark eyes changed quickly. He smiled kindly at me.

"I don't pretend to understand your motivations for anything, but I don't blame you," he said, swiftly changing subjects as Chris came into the room.

Chris declared that we were leaving. Not even saying goodbye to Eric, but being a good host he followed us to the door anyways. Kissing the twins goodbye, he smiled once more at me kindly. I was still trying to comprehend what he had revealed. I smiled back, but it was forced.

I didn't ask questions in the car. I didn't want to anger the beast. He gripped the steering wheel tightly, still fuming. As soon as we got home, he went to his office, slamming the door shut. I went to work preparing dinner. Nothing fancy, just baked chicken. I was never much of a cook, just the basics. My mother was too old when I was born. She didn't want to teach me, which was just as well. I didn't want to learn. I wanted to play in a band.

It was deadly quiet throughout the house. Even the twins sensed his mood and kept their voices low. They played silently. It was eery. They used their eyes and hands to communicate with each other.

When dinner was ready, he came out in a better mood. He smiled at the kids and tried to chit chat. I forced a smile and talked to him. I decided this was the best time to talk to him about Ethan.

"I want to get back into music," I started. He stared blankly at me. If it wasn't about him, he didn't care. "Adrian called an old friend who had some time on his hands. He flew out here to record some songs with us. He was here all week. The rest of guys plan to come soon. He's staying with Adrian until we have a full album done." He smirked.

" Did he get bored and ship his boyfriend here already? What's it been, like six months?" He commented and I just sighed. God forbid he take me seriously.

"It's been nice catching up with old friends. I can't wait to see Derek and Mark." Chris set his fork and knife down with a loud clink. I recoiled when he glared at me.

"Why do you keep up with this? I thought we discussed this being just a hobby. We don't have time for this." Tears welled in my eyes, but I pushed for them not to fall.

"I love music. You can't take that from me. I just thought you'd like to hear what I've been up to." He snorted and cleared his plate. Getting up quickly, he went back to his office. I finished my glass of wine. Well at least I told him. Now he can't say I was hiding it from him, I thought bitterly as I began to clean up the twins. Sure enough, as I was just finished with the evening dishes he came in with his suitcase.

I turned to see his bloodshot eyes and disheveled hair. He had been crying. "I have to go. I have no idea when I'll be back. A week, maybe two. Don't give me shit for this Cleo. I don't want to hear it." He left quickly before I could retort. His car quickly sped away.

I sat down at the table and called Adrian. When he answered, I started to cry. He didn't say anything as I sobbed into the phone. When I stopped he told me to stay put. "Ethan's coming to watch the kids. We'll be there in 15."

Ethan took one look at me when I opened the door and dropped the box he was holding to embrace me. I had washed the makeup off hours ago. The medicine I had taken to reduce the swelling hadn't worked even a little.

Ethan held me as I started to cry again. Adrian honked the horn twice and I pulled away. "I have to go. Chris knows about you. I told him what we had talked about. If he comes back, just tell him I had to go grab something for the kids. I don't know. I have to go." Giving him one last look I turned, running to the car. As soon as I was in, he backed up and we drove for a while in silence.

"I called Mark and Derek. They are already on flights. They are going to stay awhile," he promised. I broke down again. I had the best friends. They were my lifeline.

From California to Michigan was a four-hour flight. Adrian said they already boarded so we had about three and a half hours to wait.

We drove to the airport and waited for my oldest friends to arrive. While we waited, I told Adrian what happened last night. He held me while I cried. He kissed my head and rubbed my back.

"It's okay. You'll be okay," he murmured over and over until my sobs turned into sniffles. He held my hand the entire time.

I was elated when Mark and Derek walked out from the gate and towards us. I started to cry again as I ran to them, hugging them both tightly. It had been too long. I pulled back and Mark, seeing my bruised face, gasped. Derek looked at me and I could see tears forming. I put my hands up.

"I'm okay. I'm just glad you're here," I said and took their hands, pulling them out of the airport and into Adrian's car. They never let me go the entire way. I felt so loved.

Once Adrian started driving, I told them the truth. I had lied about everything. For the last few years I told them I was fine. I was happy. I didn't want them to worry. But I couldn't really lie now. When I finished my story, the car fell silent.

Finally, Adrian stopped the car. Looking out the window I saw we were parked outside of an apartment complex. "Where are we?" I asked. Adrian cleared his throat. We all got out and leaned against his car.

"This is Holly's apartment. Look." He pointed and I followed his finger. My blood ran cold, Chris' car was parked about twenty feet in front of us.

"When I was looking for a place, I saw them. I overheard them talking, he's paying for this place."

The air was suddenly heavy. My lips started to tremble, tears started welling up. I hated that I was still hurt by him. I looked up at the lit windows, wondering which one they were in.

"Cleo, I knew Chris was cheating on you before you got married. I saw them. Chris told me not to say anything. He said you would hate me if I told you and that it would accomplish nothing. I chose the cowards way out. I am so sorry." Mark's voice cracked. I turned and embraced him. Assuring him this wasn't his fault. It was no one's fault but my own.

It was a beautiful scene. All of us together, just us, for the first time in years. I missed these guys so much it hurt. I needed them more than I needed anybody else. They surrounded me, embracing me as I cried. Not for my failed marriage, but for my best friends. I had put them through so much, and yet they still came. In that moment, I knew that they would always come. I was never truly alone.

I walked into my house as quietly as I could an hour later. The house was silent. I checked on the twins, who were sound asleep dreaming of Batman and Murphy. Going back downstairs I saw the light from the oven on, throwing a dim yellow light on parts of the kitchen. I paused and heard the clink of glass so I went in to see Ethan at the table, staring at a bottle of Christopher's good bourbon. His face grim, unwavering. He didn't even glance up at me when I came in. There was an empty tumbler in his hand, just waiting to be filled.

We didn't speak for minutes. Finally, I chose to say something. "Thank you for watching them. I needed some time to clear my head." His face was grim.

"How long has he been doing this? Has he ever hurt them?" He demanded. His calm face quickly replaced with anger. I shook my head, this was not what I wanted to be talking about right now. I didn't want to be talking at all really, but I really, really didn't want to talk about Chris.

"No, it's just me. He would never hurt them. Ethan, it's not a big deal." I tried to explain but he shook his head.

"I may be a drug addict, but I would never hurt you like he has. Physically or emotionally. And it really sucks that this guy was chosen over me. This arrogant bastard literally beats you until you're black and blue and you still wanted him to be the father of your children over me. Why are you still here? Are you still sleeping with him?" He accused.

"Of course not! Ethan, it's not easy. I don't have any money. I can't leave," I tried to explain but he smirked.

"It always comes down to money. You remind me so much of my mother it's unreal," he spat.

"I'm sorry." Was all I could say. He stood up, hands in the air. I flinched away without thinking, immediately regretting it. I couldn't help it anymore. I had become so used to Chris' hands. So harsh and hateful. His jaw tightened and eyes welled up.

"Those kids look exactly like me Cleo. You can't deny that. I don't want them living with him. Right now it's just you, but what happens when they're older and he decides to start taking his anger out on them?" He began to get shrill. I backed away from him, which only seemed to upset him more and make his case. I forced myself to stop moving and stand up straight. I looked him square in the eyes before talking again.

"Oh so what, you're going to take them from me? You really think if you took me to court they would give you custody? You've known of their existence about a week and now you want to play dad. It doesn't work like that, Ethan!" I said, my voice harsh. He shook his head, letting out an incredulous laugh.

"You can't get mad at me for that. Cleo, you can't stay here with the kids. Do something before I do," he said and then turned away, leaving me in the kitchen to cry. I heard the front door shut quietly. He was right. I couldn't keep living like this. Christopher was growing more and more violent by the day. I wiped the tears from my face and decided it was time to get my life back.

After a hot shower, I sat down at the kitchen table and began to figure out a plan. In the morning, I was calling a divorce lawyer. I would use my personal bank account, so he didn't see when I hired them. Chris said he'd be gone a week. Normally that meant at least two to three weeks. I had two months until the will was to be read. I would hold off on filing and serving him with the divorce papers until then. That way he can get his money and leave me alone.

I decided I didn't want the house. It held no good memories. I was going to move out to California with the guys. If I had to, I would get a place with Adrian until I could find a home for just me and the twins. The only thing I had to do for the time being was make sure Chris didn't get suspicious of anything. He had to think things were normal.

Ethan didn't show up in the morning. The house felt empty without him. Even the twins asked about him. They never asked about Chris. I called the guys for lunch. They all were so happy and more than eager to help me in any way they could. I told them right now all I needed was moral support.

Mark and Derek decided to stay with Adrian until I was able to come with. They weren't doing much out in California without me and Adrian anyways. He was less than enthused, but got over it quickly. However, Mark did mention that since he was staying, Renee was joining them soon. I told him I couldn't wait to see her. She was so nice. They really were perfect for each other.

It had been two days since I had fought with Ethan. Adrian had told me that he got an apartment close by, signed a month to month lease. It was getting crowded at Adrian's place. I hadn't heard from him since that night. He didn't call or text me. So instead, I called him. He answered after about five rings.

"Hello," he said, his voice tight and distant.

"Uh, Hi. I haven't heard from you in a few days. I wanted to talk and explain some things," I started. He was silent.

"I called a lawyer. I'm going to wait until their birthday. It gives me time to figure out some things. I'm leaving," I revealed.

"You deserve better. So do the twins," he said. My stomach flipped.

"They miss you. They've been asking about you." There was a heavy pause. "I miss you," I whispered into the phone.

There was silence on the other end. A knock on the door made me pause. I crept to the door, slowly opening it. I almost cried when Ethan was on the other side of the door, holding his phone to his ear.

He was trying so hard not to smile, but when he saw me he slipped. I hugged him and after a moment he hugged me back.

"I missed you too," he told me.

Chapter Fourteen

WHEN YOU'RE GONE

The twins were so happy to see him and he was happy to be there. Jimmy even asked him to never leave. He kissed her forehead but didn't reply. When they were in bed for the night, we went downstairs. I plopped down on the couch exhausted.

He sat down with me, but his posture was tense. I sat up slightly to gaze at him. My heart began to race when he looked at me. "I won't be around for a week or so. I'm going to visit my mother," he said finally. I sat up, pushing my hair back.

"Oh, okay. Well, when you get back call me. The kids will have driven me nuts by then, I'll need your help," I teased. He smiled and stood up. I followed him to the door. He hesitated with the handle.

"Cleo, I'm sorry. For a lot of things," he started, but I interrupted him by reaching up and pushing my bruised lips to his soft ones. It took him by surprise, but then he kissed me back. It was tender and loving.

"I really hate that I'm always missing you," he whispered. My mood fell. It was true. It felt like Ethan and I's relationship was just a bunch of missed connections. Nothing ever lining up for us. I gave him another kiss and then pulled away.

"Have a good trip," I told him before he left.

Chris came home later that week in a terrific mood. "Robert called. He invited us to brunch Saturday." I wasn't interested in the slightest.

"That's great. Sounds fun," I told him, trying to keep the peace.

"Yes, it will be. You need some new clothes. Something with long sleeves. Maybe a pantsuit. Wear your hair down," he ordered. I didn't say anything. I didn't have to.

When Saturday came, I put the children in their Sunday best and waited for Chris to pull into the driveway. As usual, he showed up an hour late and rushed us into the car. He was cheery and full of energy. He talked the entire way about all the good things in his life. His polls were looking good, work was going great. He couldn't wait to see Robert. He noted that his opponent hadn't been invited to his house. I listened silently.

An hour later we pulled into the large metal gates of the senators home. I looked up at the huge house. It was practically a mansion. Tall and white, complete with pillars and a huge staircase. I felt nervous already. I wasn't exactly the picture perfect senators wife.

Chris had been here before, so he knew where to park. He grabbed my wrist as I went for my seatbelt. He squeezed and I gasped in pain. "Don't embarrass me Maribel. There are very important men here. I don't need you getting sloppy drunk and acting a fool," he told me in a low harsh voice. I nodded quickly and he let go. I rubbed my skin, already feeling the bruises forming.

We each got a kid out of the car and then held hands on the way up to the door. I was already regretting agreeing to come. The door swung open and we were greeted by an older Asian woman. She was dressed in rose colored scrubs.

"Hello, you must be here for brunch. Let me take your coats," she said, leading us through the house. "Mr. Pierce is in his office if you'd like to join him," she offered. Christopher nodded and departed the group quickly. I looked towards the housekeeper.

"Mrs. Pierce is in the library, I'll take you that way." The twins and I followed her down the long hall and took the last turn on the right.

She opened the massive double doors with a flourish, stepping back to let us enter. The room was surprisingly huge. The walls were completely lined with books, floor to ceiling. Despite the size, the room felt cozy. I noticed I could smell a hint of fresh flowers. Roses.

I didn't see anyone at first, but I heard the distinct sound of a croquet mallet on a ball and swung my head to the left. That's when I saw him.

Ethan was standing in the very back of the room in his standard skinny jeans and black shirt. Holding his mallet, he looked up when we entered. We were both deer in headlights. My shock was interrupted by a woman's laugh. I looked around for the source of the noise.

"Ethan, I swear if you break something you will never be allowed back in here," the voice teased. My eyes finally found the source of the laughter. Near the window, on the other side of the room was a woman standing in front of an easel, painting. She turned to us and took off her apron and set her brush down.

She was wearing a blue dress with three quarter sleeves, it was tight at the waist and was very stepford wives. Her black hair was styled in a short bob. The woman smiled at me kindly. After a moment's hesitation, my feet started to move towards them. "What are you doing here?" Ethan asked, a confused smile on his face.

"Um, I am here with Christopher. The senator invited us," I whispered. The woman moved closer.

"Well, hello. Did I hear you say you came with Christopher? You must be Maribel Thomas. Do you two know each other?" She looked between us. I stepped further away from him. Ethan turned red and coughed.

"Mom, this is Cleo. Cleo this is my mother, Charlotte." She nodded, although clearly confused. I smiled politely, already feeling the heat rising to my face.

"Cleo, the young woman you told me about?" She asked hesitantly. He nodded. She frowned. Her eyes darted down to the twins at my feet. They grew huge with realization. Ethan gulped.

"Ethan! Where have you been?" Jimmy piped up. He pursed his lips. His mother looked like she was going to faint. He squatted down and the twins ran to hug him.

"What have you two been up to?"

"Ethan, are those," Charlotte started but couldn't finish her sentence. He stood back up and took a deep breath.

"Mom, this is Jimmy Paige and Dallas Edgar. Yes, they are," he told her. Her eyes were bulging out of her skull. She didn't speak for a long moment. After a few deep breaths she composed herself.

Besides the hair color, her and Ethan shared many other similar features I noticed. Only his eyes were different. He must have gotten the blue from his father because hers were darker.

"Hello. Ethan has told me so much about you." I could sense the uneasiness in her voice. I smiled and told her her home was lovely. She thanked me and motioned for us to move towards some couches in the room, where the housekeeper had just brought coffee and snacks. The twins saw the cookies on the coffee table and lunged.

"They are beautiful. Dallas reminds me of you as a baby. Spitting image," she told him with a small smile. She glanced at me and a tear fell. I had to look away so I didn't start crying too. Jimmy and Dallas sat on either side of their grandmother as they ate. She looked so happy. She asked them all sorts of questions. What did they like? What instruments did they play? What was their favorite food?

Ethan didn't stay sitting long. He stood up and went over to her painting. I couldn't see the details, but it looked like she had been painting four girls playing croquet. He stood near the canvas, but didn't seem to be really looking at it. I think he just didn't want to be at the table anymore. His mother glanced over at him and her face fell slightly, revealing her age.

I forced myself to stay smiling and upbeat, although me and Charlotte both had stuff we wanted to say to each other without Ethan present. Finally he excused himself to go to the bathroom. Only when she was sure he was out of earshot did she speak.

"What is going on? I thought your name was Maribel. Aren't you married to Christopher Thomas?" She demanded. Her eyes were hard. I flinched, guilt rushing over me.

"Maribel is my real name. Only Christopher calls me that. I can explain. Kind of. Please don't tell my husband. I can't. Not yet."

"Who is the father of these children?" She hissed. I smiled uneasily.

"Ethan is." She instantly relaxed and put her hand to her head.

"And Christopher has no idea," she stated, more than asked. I nodded.

"Please, he can't know. Not yet. I plan on telling him, I just need to get some things in order," I explained quickly. She paused but then nodded.

"My son is madly in love with you." I looked down, barely hiding my smile.

"He didn't tell me you were married. Now I do rather like Christopher, he is a fine young man. But seeing my son so happy is wonderful. I just ask that you give him a chance. He wants the life you already have. Perhaps it's something to consider," she finished, taking a sip of her coffee just as Ethan returned to sit with us. I leaned over the table and hugged her. She was stiff at first but then hugged me back. Ethan looked at the two of us and his face relaxed.

We returned to happy chatter. This time it felt genuine. After another hour or so, there was a friendly knock on the library door. The three of us turned and my heart stopped. A handsome older man and Christopher stood there smiling. That must be the senator, Robert, I realized. Charlotte stood up and hurried over to him. He hugged her and they came towards us.

"Chris, this is my stepson, Ethan. I see you two have been keeping Maribel company." Charlotte smiled tightly. Chris glowered at Ethan. Ethan glared right back. Chris recognized him. I gulped.

"Yes, I believe we've met before," he said, extending his hand. Ethan shook it quickly and sat back down. Robert cleared his throat.

"Well Dear, I'm afraid we aren't staying. I came out to let you know Chris and I are heading to an early business dinner with some great potential sponsors. Are you okay keeping Maribel entertained for a few more hours?"

"Of course, It's been a wonderful day. Go ahead. I'll see you later this evening. Bring me some dessert," she told him sweetly. He looked at her with love and kissed her quickly.

"Sure thing. We'll be back in a bit," he promised. I let out a deep breath when they finally left. I did not want Christopher and Ethan in the same room ever again. I relaxed once I knew they had left the house.

It was fun listening to Charlotte tell me about Ethan as a little boy. He was always getting into trouble, she laughed. She began telling me about the time she had smelled smoke coming from his room, so she tried to catch him but he opened his window and climbed out onto the roof.

"I hurried outside with my broom and began to swat at him. He was trying so hard not to make any noise because he knew he was gonna get it when I caught him. But after a few swipes of the broom, I finally hit something and I hear a scream and there he comes rolling down off the roof. He falls, cigarette still in hand. So of course, I drop my broom and hurry to see if he's okay. He's screaming bloody murder like he's broken something. I'm yelling for someone to call an ambulance, but then he stands up and is holding his hand over his eye. I finally convince him to show me. He pulls his hand away and I see that he burned his eyebrow off! He was so mad at me because I couldn't stop laughing. I decided that him having to walk around like that was punishment enough." Our laughter was interrupted by Ethan who snorted and whipped around from where he had been reading a book to Jimmy, pretending not to listen. His eyes were dark, and angry.

"That wasn't me. That was Evan. Or did you forget about him entirely now?" He said with a snarl. I glanced at Charlotte. She looked away, her face quickly turning red.

"Oh, of course it was. I'm terribly sorry. My memory isn't what it used to be," she started to explain but stood up and stalked back over to us.

"Oh, don't try to act like you accidentally forgot it was him. Do you not remember that I had been hiding behind him and was laughing so hard that I fell off the roof too, breaking my arm? Why are you doing this?" He raised his voice. She cringed and her eyes filled with tears.

"Tell me, why is it that all through the house there is a ton of pictures of you, Bob, and his kids? I didn't see any of us, not even just you and me. I know Evan didn't fit into Robert's picture perfect family, but am I a big embarrassment too now? Why did I even come here? You're still lying about everything."

He was shouting now. The room was silent. I glanced towards the twins. They seemed completely oblivious to Ethan's meltdown. I couldn't react to anything, frozen to the spot and unsure of what was happening.

"I don't know why I came. This was pointless. I can't. Just being here in this place, it's too much," he mumbled. Charlotte stood up and left the room. She returned quickly with a light blue bag. She rummaged inside until she found a small wallet. Opening it, she pulled out something and went over to Ethan and handed it to him. He gripped it tightly, his hands shaking. He looked down at it, still not speaking.

"Don't ever assume that I stopped loving you. I think about you and Evan every single day. Pictures are not around because I was tired of seeing the pity in everyone's eyes. I grew sick of the questions. I don't need to justify anything to you, Ethan," she said sharply to him. Looking at them, I knew I needed to give them privacy.

Hurrying over to the twins, I ushered them out of the library. We walked back to the main area of the house. The housekeeper spotted us and took us into the kitchen. She offered the twins ice cream. I made small talk with her while we waited out the storm. After another twenty minutes, both of them appeared in the doorway. Both of them had red, swollen eyes. I gave him a reassuring smile and he returned it. Something in his eyes shifted when he looked at the twins.

"Mom, can you watch the twins? Cover for us for a bit," he asked. She nodded and wiped her eyes with a handkerchief.

"Sure. Robert usually stays out late," she assured us. Ethan extended his hand for me to take. Leaving the kitchen, we grabbed our coats and headed towards the door.

"Cleo?" Charlotte said, her voice barely audible. Ethan was already outside. I turned back to her. "Please, wait a moment," she said. To my surprise she gave me a big hug.

"Ethan needs this. You. The children. I always wished his father had been able to be around. I was never meant to be a mother. I was so young. I took the easy way out when I met

Robert. I lost both of my sons trying to give them a better life. I could never see that they didn't need fancy things. They just needed me," she told me.

"Ethan has his flaws. I know better than anyone that my son is damaged. He's been hurt too many times," she confessed quickly. My eyes wide, barely breathing. She took a deep breath and held onto my shoulders.

"But I see the light in his eyes when he talks about the children. He was so happy when he told me. I know he's only just met them, but he adores those twins. If you let him, he will be a great father to them. I know you have a husband, but please don't shut him out because of it. He can be a great man, he just needs a woman like you," she finished. I gulped and forced back tears. She had no idea how much I wanted that same thing. Pulling away I nodded and thanked her.

Dallas appeared from behind her and tugged at the hem of her dress. Charlotte blinked a few times and pulled away from me. She was holding back her own tears. I smiled one more time before I hurried out to the car.

We drove in silence for a while. I was still in shock over the afternoon's events. After about twenty minutes, I watched the pain melt off his face. "I'm sorry for fighting in front of you. All those pictures on the walls. There were tons of her, her husband and his kids. So happy and perfect. Only one of me, and Evan was just completely forgotten about."

"I understand. That would upset me too," I told him. I thought back to my own parent's home. There weren't many pictures of me either, but that was my fault. I left as soon as I could. Ethan didn't have a choice. He smiled weakly and took one hand off the wheel to take mine. He lifted it to his lips and kissed me softly. My heart picked up the pace.

"Where are we going?" I asked as we drove. He didn't answer me. It was only a few more minutes before we were driving through cemetery gates. I realized quickly where he was taking me.

"We won't stay long," he assured me as he began weaving through the thin roads between tombstones. We went to the way back, past the military plots before finally stopping. The sun had officially set, making this place way creepier than it had been five minutes before.

"It's not far. Just over there," he told me, pointing about thirty feet away. He went into the trunk and rummaged through a duffel bag until he pulled out something that made me laugh. The red boa I had given him years ago. I glanced over and he was grinning ear to ear, which was contagious.

I looked for the moon, but it was behind clouds. It was warm for March, but still chilly. We reached a tombstone that was very simple. It was a dark, onyx color. The clouds parted a tiny bit so we could read the epitaph.

Evan Daniel Andrews

1992-2009

Beloved friend and brother

I stared at it for a long while. Ethan stood alongside me in silence. Finally, he stepped forward and draped the red boa across the stone. "Do you have a pen or marker or something?" He asked me. I frowned.

"Maybe some lipstick in my purse?" His face lit up.

"Perfect."

I hurried to go get it and return back. He uncapped the lipstick, turning towards me.

"Does your cell phone have a flashlight?" I quickly dug it out of my pocket and flashed it onto the slick marble. Ethan smiled devilishly and quickly started writing. When he was finished, he stood up and stepped back to admire his work. Right over his name he had written

Penelope Felony

"That was his drag name," he explained, although he didn't really need to, I remembered. The tombstone looked much better this way, I assured him.

"Tell me about him." He thought for a moment and then spoke.

"Well he was damn sexy. Best looking guy I've ever seen," he started. Letting out an involuntary giggle I jabbed him in the ribs with my elbow.

"Ow! Anyways, he was funny. He loved making people laugh. That and he was always the one in charge. I was basically his shadow. All the bad stuff we did was all his idea. Every time!" He was laughing. Genuinely laughing. This was new.

"He wasn't shy. I wouldn't have ever taken the stage without his push. We both learned how to play guitar, but he wanted to do the drag scene. He pretty much found my bandmates for me," he added.

"So, his name was Penelope Felony. I'm trying to envision this," I said to him. Ethan had tears in his eyes but was still smiling. "Did he have a certain song that was just his?" I asked and he laughed.

"Yep. He did actually. 'Hot Child In The City'." I burst into laughter and took his hand. He held it tightly. I leaned my head against his shoulder.

"He sounds like he was an amazing person. I wish I could have met him."

"Me too," he sighed and then we turned to walk back to the car, leaving the boa and the lipstick.

"Have you ever thought about doing something for him? Like in his honor." I suggested once we were nice and warm and back on the road. He glanced at me curiously but said nothing.

"You were really upset when you thought your mother had forgotten him. You could do something to make sure no one forgets him. Show the world what an amazing guy he was," I explained. Ethan continued to stare at the road, but didn't say anything.

"Maybe. I don't know," he mumbled. He held tightly to my hand until suddenly he pulled over into a fast food parking lot and parked. I turned to him but before I could speak he leaned over and kissed me. It was long and tender. He pulled his face away but I leaned forward and kissed him back.

No matter how much time would pass, something about Ethan Andrews pulled at my heart. I loved him just as much as I had years ago in that hotel room on Christmas. On stage, when I heard him sing our song. And that last night on tour, when I left him. He continued to hold our kiss. I think we were both afraid that if we stopped we'd never kiss again.

Finally he pulled away and pressed his forehead to mine. It was dark, but I could still see his smile, or feel it rather. Everything about this felt right.

"Thank you for coming with me today. For everything. I really needed it," he told me as he put the car back into drive and started towards his mothers.

When we returned Chris and Robert were still gone. Ethan dropped my hand when we exited the car. Jimmy and Dallas were fast asleep on the couch. Charlotte was in an armchair reading a book. She smiled at us as we stepped into the room. Ethan kissed my forehead and said goodnight. He headed down the hallway and disappeared from the room.

Barely five minutes later our husbands returned, and seeing the twins asleep Chris decided it was time to leave. I said goodbye to Charlotte one last time. She hugged me tightly and when I pulled away she winked at me.

I spent the next hour in the car watching the cars fly by. Wondering if after all was said and done, if her and Ethan would be able to work things out. To be able to be a family again. Would Ethan and I be able to be a family too? For the first time since I had laid eyes on him so many years ago, I wanted to commit to him. Was this finally our time?

Chris was so satisfied with his dinner that he had all but forgotten about Ethan. He spent the drive home bragging about it. A wave of relief washed over me as I went to my room with no argument from him that night. When I woke up, he was gone again.

I called in the morning to confirm some things for the twin's birthday. It was now less than a month away. I rented the hall, and ordered a cake. It would be April so it needed to be inside. April in Michigan was kind of a gamble. It would either be ridiculously warm, or still snowing.

As far as entertainment, I was at a loss. I was afraid a clown might scare them, and Jimmy wasn't really into princesses so I wasn't going to call for one. After too much thought and nowhere closer to having something I changed my thoughts to food instead and started calling pizza places to get estimates and see what they offered.

Ethan showed up in the afternoon to my surprise. He made the kids lunch for me and took them to the studio to practice. I loved seeing his face light up when they played. After another hour of searching the phone book for children's entertainment I gave up and went to join them. It was still three weeks away. I had time.

They all looked like they were having so much fun. Jimmy looked so happy, while Dallas was jamming hard on his guitar. Ethan was just following their lead as they played together. This was how things were meant to be, I thought.

Later in the afternoon I called Adrian to ask if him and the guys wanted to come for dinner. Derek yelled into the phone.

"Cleo can I come live with you? I can't get any sleep here," he complained. I heard Adrians deep sigh.

"Why not?" I asked and I could hear Derek imitating the sound of bed springs squeaking in the background.

"Adrian James. What are you hiding?" I teased. He chuckled.

"I've been seeing someone. It's nothing serious… yet." This was odd of Adrian. He was never shy with talking about his love life, especially with me.

"Oh, okay. Well, I can't wait to meet them," I said lamely.

"Yeah, maybe soon. She's shy," he explained.

After dinner we got the kids around for bed. When they finally grew quiet I turned to Ethan who was sitting uneasily in my armchair.

"Hey are you okay?"

"I just hate that I missed so much already. I come here and see family pictures of you, Chris and the twins." He turned back to me. His fists were clenched like his jaw. I tried to look away, but I couldn't. The guilt was too much.

"I should be the one in those pictures, Cleo!" He said in a hushed voice, not wanting to wake the twins. Standing, he moved towards the front door. Pulling a cigarette out of the case in his pocket he glared at me as he went outside. I followed him out. Ethan was inhaling his cigarette deeply, then glanced at me, fury in his eyes.

"Those are my kids Cleo! Mine! And you were never going to tell me. You never even told the man raising them, for that matter. He thinks that those two perfect little people in there are his. How is this supposed to work? I can't just know that I'm their dad and never tell them. I kept you a secret from everyone forever, but I can't. Cleo, I can't deny those two," he choked, his voice cracking. He was right. All of this wasn't fair. He dropped his cigarette, crushing it with his foot. He rushed over to me and took my hands. I looked up into his pleading eyes, those gorgeous baby blues that made my heart speed up every time they looked at me.

"Cleo, I want you. I want the twins. We should be a family. Leave. Please. We can start a new life out in Cali. This isn't right. Chris doesn't deserve you and the kids. I can make you happy," he pleaded. I didn't say anything back. I wanted that more than anything, but I needed to know that whatever I did, my children would be taken care of. It wasn't as easy as just leaving. I was married. I needed to get divorced. I would have to fight over everything. Chris was going to make my life hell.

"This is so unfair. I'm sitting here with you, planning a birthday party for our kids. Hanging around, playing with them, helping you with them. I make breakfast, drive them to school, help them get to bed every night, and I get to be called Uncle Ethan, while he gets to be dad. Chris gets to claim them in public, to show them off. He is the one who has it all, but doesn't appreciate it, doesn't deserve it!" He yelled. I opened my mouth and closed it quickly. What was I supposed to say?

"Ethan this is too much. It's too fast."

"Why? Am I getting too ahead of myself? It's not like we are going to run off together and have kids and all that. Oh, wait," he said sarcastically. He began pacing around the porch.

I was so sick of him always making snide remarks about me keeping them a secret. I knew I screwed up. I knew this, so he didn't have to keep bringing it up every chance he got. Something in me snapped. I couldn't have him constantly throwing it in my face.

"Ethan, you are thinking too much into this! You're living in this dream world where there's no issues and everything is so easy but it's not! Please just stop. The kids still don't even know anything. I'm not ready for all this!" I cried.

He stopped pacing and faced me again. His eyes were wild with incredulity. "Yes. We don't want the kids to know the truth, ever. God forbid they find out that their constantly MIA daddy isn't actually their father, but the guy who is actually trying his hardest to make up for the five years he's missed. The one who is here more than he is, no he isn't allowed to reveal himself." I stopped moving, my tears betraying me.

"Cleo, I bet you I love those kids more in the one month that I've known of their existence than Chris has their whole lives. They deserve to know the truth," he said.

"You aren't the only one suffering Ethan. How do you think I felt getting to see them every day, knowing the truth? I couldn't say anything in fear. Yes, I will tell them. But for now, please just let me breathe."

"Fine. You got it." He stormed off the porch. Climbing into his car he slammed the door, quickly driving off. I didn't run after him like I should have. I let him go. There was nothing more to be said that hadn't already been said. I let the tears slip down my face freely. No one would see them anyways. In the end, I was always left alone.

Chapter Fifteen

SURRENDER

*E*than stayed away the next few days. I knew he needed to cool off. I managed to get the kids to school with little issues. Although, I realized it was much harder doing it alone again. Chris still wasn't home, which was such a relief. I didn't need him here on top of everything. One evening after the kids were asleep, I got a call from Eric.

"Hello?" I answered, hesitantly.

"Hey Cleo, how are you?" He replied brightly.

"I'm okay. You?" I asked.

"Great! I have a surprise for their birthday. I have the entertainment covered."

"Oh. Okay, what is it?"

"I'd like to keep it a surprise," he said.

"Alright, well thanks. I appreciate it."

"It's my pleasure. I love those little guys," he said. I thanked him again and hung up.

A few days turned into a week, and a week turned into two, with no sign of Ethan. The twins party was now only a week away. I had invited all of my siblings and their families. My parents sent their love but wouldn't be attending. They were well into their seventies now. They were about two hours away and didn't like the drive. My siblings also made excuses as to why they couldn't come. I wasn't too upset. I kind of expected that. It only mattered that my true family came. The guys and their new significant others. Renee of course would be there and I think Adrian was going to let us meet his new girlfriend, but he made no promises. I couldn't get much out of him, but he did mention her name was Dita. I told him I couldn't wait to meet her.

The night before the party I had Adrian watch the twins while I went to the hall to decorate. No sooner had I parked my car did I see a familiar figure waiting next to a black Cadillac. I recognized both immediately. My heart thumped hard inside my chest.

Ethan stepped away from his car and came to open my door. I climbed out and met his gaze. He didn't say anything. Silently, he helped me get the boxes from the car into the building.

We went to work hanging balloons and streamers. Still we hadn't said much of anything to each other. When we were finally done with everything, I turned to him. He looked away, shoving his hands in his pockets. "I should probably get going. I'll come around in a few days to give them their presents."

"Come to the party," I blurted. He blinked a few times, surprised.

"What?"

"Come to the party. I don't care anymore. You should be there. If he finds out, oh well." He came towards me and our mouths met quickly. I don't know what was coming over me but I was sick of hiding. I had been keeping secrets from everyone for so long I had gotten used to it, but I didn't want to anymore.

"Okay. I will," he promised.

Eric showed up before everyone else to greet the entertainment with me. We stood outside, enjoying the fresh air while we waited. "You are going to love me," he said, beaming.

"Are you going to tell me yet?" And before he could answer I saw the bus and I screamed. I literally screamed like a little girl. Well, like I imagined the twins would be screaming when they saw it. He started laughing.

"You got Murphy? Is this for real?" I gasped as the bus pulled up in front of us and the door opened. Eric moved forward and directed the driver to the back.

"You love me yet?" He asked me. I threw my arms around him.

"How did you manage this?" I said after I pulled away.

"Money talks," he said simply. I smiled and we went inside to greet Murphy and his friends.

Murphy was actually named Paul and he was really chill. It was weird seeing him in his Murphy clothes but talking in his normal, adult voice. He recognized me and we traded autographs.

"Man, can I get a picture? I had no idea you had kids, this is awesome!" He exclaimed. I laughed and he ripped off his sweater to reveal a black band shirt and tattoos covering his arms.

"I don't want a picture with my Murphy crap on," he laughed.

"Just wait. The rest of the guys will be here soon," I told him. He put his sweater back on, and with reluctance started to get ready for the party.

I tried to hide my anxiety when everyone began to show up and Ethan was nowhere to be found. I kept calling but it just rang and rang. My mood plummeted even more when Chris showed up. Seeing him made my stomach lurch. Just seeing him brought a shiver of fear through my body. But then he walked around the car to the passengers side, and opened the door, letting Holly out. I almost choked. He brought her? I couldn't believe it.

They walked in separately. I glared at him when he came over to me. He held up his hands to explain.

"Maribel, she's working at the firm and had some time off. I was leaving work to come and she didn't have anything left to do. Don't make this into something it's not. Not today. No drama," he said and hurried over to talk to Robert and Charlotte, who had just arrived as well.

I checked my phone one more time for Ethan before the twins arrived. Adrian pulled up with the twins and I hurried out to see them.

Dallas had gotten a haircut. It was similar to Ethan's hair a few years back; short on the side and long in the middle that flopped over. He looked so handsome. I told him so and he blushed and thanked me softly.

Adrian set Jimmy down next to her brother and I snatched her up in a hug. Her hair had been put in a bright red bow and she had been dressed in a big poofy black dress with a red ribbon around the waist. They looked adorable.

Out of the corner of my eye I spotted a woman next to Adrian. I stood up and smiled politely. She did the same and waved fast. She looked nervous.

Adrian took Jimmy's hand and I took Dallas'. We entered the building and everyone cheered and yelled "Happy Birthday!" Dallas almost started to cry but Jimmy got so excited seeing all the balloons and her friends from school. She took her brothers hand and pulled him over to the other kids.

After about thirty minutes of attempting games with them, Murphy's theme song started playing through the speakers. All the kids stopped playing and began looking around, I couldn't contain my excitement. Adrian came over and whispered in my ear.

"Is that who I think it is?" He asked. I nodded excitedly as he laughed and rolled his eyes.

A moment later Murphy came out through the back door followed by all his friends in full costume. Every kid in the room started screaming. He quickly launched into his show, which gave me time to socialize.

I talked with the parents and chatted with Robert and Charlotte. She was smiling wide the entire time. Robert looked happy too, but I had a feeling he had no idea why his wife was so happy. I did talk to Chris a bit; but stayed clear of Holly. It was bad enough he brought her. I refused to be cordial and act like I had no idea what she was doing with my husband.

I glanced at my phone again but there was nothing to see. I didn't want to show how upset I was so I went over to where my bandmates and their ladies sat watching the show.

I sat down next to Adrian's friend Dita and offered my hand to shake. She smiled and took it. Now that I had some time I took a good look at her. Dita was strikingly pretty. Her dirty blond hair hung all the way down her back. She had bright, hazel eyes and a kind smile. Her nose and septum were pierced. She was dressed in a cute jersey and designer jeans. When I looked at Adrian he was looking at her, beaming. That alone made me so happy.

We chatted for a while. I noticed that everyone refrained from asking about where Ethan was. But I knew they all noticed. After Murphy's performance, we had cake. Murphy approached the bands table and they offered him a seat. I laughed at how excited he was. It was nice to know we still had fans.

Right before the cake I saw someone come through the front door out of the corner of my eye. Flipping my head around my heart sped up. He showed. He was late, but he showed.

Ethan looked around and when he saw me, brightened and

came over to me. I stood up straight and before I could say hello he pulled me into him and kissed me straight on the lips. My eyes flew open in shock, horror, and at the same time excitement. I pulled away and scanned the room. All adult eyes were on us.

Adrian, Mark and Derek were smiling. Charlotte and Robert looked uncomfortable. Parents looked confused. Eric was laughing. When my eyes finally found Chris and Holly I was prepared to run for my life. Holly had a smug look on her face. Her arms were crossed and her lips pursed. Chris on the other hand was furious. His fists were tight, his jaw clenched. I could see the muscles in his neck bulging. I gulped and looked away quickly. Suddenly Renee appeared by my side to help me with the cake and ice cream.

After cake came presents. Then finally time to clean up. Everyone said their goodbyes and love you's and soon there were only a few of us left. I was purposely avoiding being near Ethan or Christopher. I didn't want to anger Chris more. I was regretting telling Ethan to come. If looks could kill, I'd have been brutally murdered a while ago. I had never seen Chris so silently furious.

Mark and Renee came over and offered to take the twins back to Adrian's. They knew that I would have to face Chris eventually, and the twins shouldn't be around for it. I thanked them and reassured the rest of the band I'd be okay. Soon it was only the four of us. Ethan, Chris, Holly and I.

I tried busying myself with cleaning up tables, but when Ethan came to help me Chris erupted. "Who the hell do you think you are?" Chris demanded, storming towards us. Ethan backed up, with his hands in the air.

"Whoa man, look…" Ethan started but Chris was past angry. He ignored him and came straight towards me. Chris picked me up by my shirt and lifted me off the ground, then slammed me into the wall. My body collided with it with a thud, knocking the wind out of me. I couldn't breathe. I could barely move.

"Don't touch her!" I heard Ethan shout, but I wasn't seeing well. Chris took his other hand and grabbed my face, forcing me to look at him.

"After working like a dog for you, giving you everything, I find out you're cheating on me with some whiny musician," he snarled. I tried to focus on him but was having trouble. His hand slipped down to hold onto my neck tightly. He began to squeeze. My eyes rolled into the back of my head. Suddenly Chris was ripped away from me.

Falling to the floor in a heap I tried to sit up. I struggled to breathe as I watched Ethan punch Chris square in the jaw. Chris stumbled and fell into a table, but he caught himself with his arms behind his back. I was frozen in shock and fear. I had seen firsthand what Chris could do. This was going to end badly. We heard a scream and turned towards the other side of the room, where Holly was running towards us.

"Stop you monster!" She cried out. No one spoke. It worked. Both men stopped fighting to look at her. Chris stood up and looked up at me embarrassed.

"Honey, you should go to the car like we talked about," he murmured to her. I could hear him clearly. Holly crossed her arms across her ample chest and glared at me. She was dressed up, in a cheetah print, tight dress and six-inch heels. With her hair and makeup, she really was gorgeous. Especially when compared to me, dressed in a t-shirt and ripped jeans. My face bare and bruised with my rat's nest of hair flying everywhere. No wonder he never loved me. She should be on the cover of a fashion magazine, while all I ever could manage was being one of the boys.

"No. I'm not doing this anymore." She turned to look at me. "He's leaving you. He loves me. Always has. I'm pregnant.

He doesn't need you anymore," she taunted, her face scrunched up in triumph.

I really didn't know what to say. But for some reason this is what broke me. Finally shattered the illusion I had been under. It was over. She was pregnant. He could never give me a single gentle touch, but he got her pregnant. I started to cry. Ethan didn't move forward. He was confused about what was going on. Chris turned back to me and started stumbling over his words.

"Cleo, it was an accident. A one-time accident. I was going to tell you after the party. Holls, Get in the car NOW!" He yelled at her. She shrunk a bit and did as she was told, but she smiled back at me one more time before leaving.

"Ignore her, she's just hormonal." He came to me, attempting to put his arms around me. I shrugged him away. I never wanted him to touch me again.

"Cleo, come on. It will work out. Even if you were cheating on me. We can go to a counselor and talk through it all. I forgive you already. It's just me and you baby," he said, trying to soothe me. My crying stopped. I looked up at him, and the look I gave him must have been a good one because his smile fell of his face.

"What are you upset about? Holly? Don't worry about it. So I'll pay some child support. No big deal. I make more than enough money. We won't even miss it," he said. Wow. He. Forgives. Me. I struggled, but I stood up from where I had fallen before. I rose up from everything I had been put through for so long. I was seeing red. I started to laugh. Chris looked at me with raised eyebrows.

"You forgive me? Christopher Thomas forgives me? Oh, thank God. I was worried. But you're right. I'm not going to worry about Holly. Or you, because we're done." He snorted and glanced over at Ethan who was staring at me, his mouth agape.

"For this guy? Come on, Cleo. He's a coward. He didn't even have the balls to come around when I was here. You guys snuck around behind my back. Even you can do better than that," he told me. I ignored him.

"I'm not leaving because of Ethan. I'm leaving because you are the worst person I have ever met in my entire life." I turned my back to him.

"So what? Have you been screwing around this whole time on me? Cleo don't you turn away from me!" He shouted as he grabbed the back of my shirt and spun me around. I screamed out and Ethan lurched forward.

"Get your hands off her," he told Chris and shoved him away from me. Chris stumbled and then spit at our feet.

"You think you can just run off together? I'll take everything from you. The house, the cars. I'll make sure the judge gives me the twins. You won't ever see them again! You're trash. I'll make your life a living hell," Chris threatened me. Ethan started laughing. The sound stopped us all cold. We looked towards his crazy, maniacal laughter. He was holding his gut and hunching over.

"What's so Goddamn funny?" Chris snarled. Ethan stood up and wiped tears from his eyes.

"Take the house, take everything you want. But you can't take kids that aren't yours."

I let out a small shriek and my hands flew to my mouth to stop myself. Chris took a moment to let that sink in. He blinked a few times and swiveled back to me. Before anyone could react, he lifted his hand and swung his fist at my face. His knuckles collided with my cheek and then nose. I fell to the ground. He kicked me in the gut. One, two, three times! The entire time screaming.

"You bitch. You fucking bitch! I'll kill you!" I heard a piercing scream from Holly and then everything went black.

I awoke in the hospital surrounded by my bandmates. Once I was coherent enough they explained everything.

Holly called the police on Ethan. By the time they showed up, Ethan was trying to pull Christopher off of me. I was already unconscious. My face was swollen and almost completely purple and bruised.

He had managed to crack some ribs. Nothing too serious, but it was still extremely painful. Chris was immediately arrested. Ethan rode with me in the ambulance and stayed with me until the guys·came. They all were taking turns watching me and the twins.

However, I hadn't seen him since I had woken up; and no one was answering me when I asked about it. Finally, Derek confessed that he hadn't shown up for his turn in a few days and they couldn't get ahold of him.

After a four-day hospital stay, I was allowed to leave. I told Adrian I didn't want to go home alone, even if Chris wouldn't be there. He promised me I wouldn't have to.

I stayed with him the first night. The next day the guys came with me and we packed up all of mine and the twin's things and put them in a storage unit. I left the key in the mailbox. I wouldn't be needing it.

That second evening at Adrian's seemed more depressing, even though I was surrounded by friends. I had just laid down on the couch for sleep when there was a knock on the door. Groaning I struggled to get up. I was still moving slowly, so Mark ended up coming out of his room to answer the door.

Ethan fell into the apartment, face first. I gasped, wincing at the pain of it. Mark nudged him with his foot and he rolled over. I could tell right away that Ethan was drunk. Oh no. He had fallen off the wagon. That's why he'd been missing, I realized.

Mark got him up and pulled him onto the other couch. He was mumbling an apology to me over and over in his drunken stupor. Mark shut the door and asked me if he was okay sleeping it off there. Looking back at Ethan I saw he was already passed out. I nodded and instead took my blanket and snuck into Adrian's bed. He grumbled but moved over to give me room. I fell asleep worried and disappointed.

"What are you going to do?" Adrian asked me in the morning.

"Ugh, I don't know," I mumbled lamely.

"You know when he wakes up he's going to come looking for you," he told me. I sighed, of course he was.

"Tell him to go away. I can't deal with this," I moaned.

Sure enough around noon he was knocking furiously at the door. Adrian gave me one last look and after sighing went to the door.

"Where is she? Adrian, I need to talk to her. I need to explain," he said quickly. His voice was frantic.

"I don't think that's a good idea. Dude, go back to rehab. You can't be doing this. The twins don't need to see you like this."

"But the rehab center is in California, I can't go that far away. Please just let me talk to Cleo. Just one time and I'll leave." I gulped and stepped into view.

Ethan was a mess. His hair greasy, his face still shiny with sweat. Adrian looked at me, waiting to see what I wanted to do. I gave him a half smile and followed Ethan out the door.

"I'm going to take a walk. I'll be back," I told him. Adrian rubbed his cheeks but said nothing.

We didn't speak until we were outside and a distance away from the apartment building. "Cleo, I know I fucked up. I don't know what I was thinking. I was pissed and stressed and so upset. It's hard to say no when it's all in front of you," he said quickly. I whirled around to look him in the eyes.

"Please don't make me leave. I won't do this again. I'll be there. Every step of the way. I don't care if I'm just Uncle Ethan, but please don't do this. I want to be here, with you. With them," he begged me. Stepping in front of me, he fell to the ground. I stopped and stared down at him. I didn't know what to do anymore.

"Ethan, you need to go back to rehab," I sighed. He shook his head.

"It's in California, I can't go without you," he protested. He grabbed my hands and squeezed them softly. He looked up at me with his big beautiful blue eyes and my cold heart started to melt.

"How about I make you a deal? If you leave today and get enrolled back into the rehab center full time, I will tell Dallas and Jimmy the truth."

Ethan's eyes hardened. He got on his phone without answering me. Standing up, he put the phone to his ear and held my gaze as he talked to what I could only assume was an assistant, or maybe his manager.

"Kyle, I need to go back to Three Rivers. Oh and a plane ticket back. Tonight," he told him and then quickly hung up.

"Done. I'll do anything. Whatever I need to do." He took my hands again. "Cleo I am so sorry I put you through this. I am trying." His eyes shone. I pulled away but stayed close. I needed to stay clear headed and being this close to him made it hard. We walked back to the apartment in silence. As the building came back into view he stopped me with a gentle tug on my arm.

"You're going to tell them, right?" He asked, his voice desperate. I thought for a moment.

"Wait here," I ordered. He stood there as I walked slowly back to the apartment. Adrian was at the door ready and waiting. He must have been watching us. Soon I was walking out the door with a twin on each side. We stepped outside and began walking towards Ethan. His face lit up in surprise and both of the twins dropped my hands and ran to him.

He got down and let them run into his arms. I wanted to cry. He really did love them, and they loved him.

"Ethan, I had a birthday!" Jimmy told him. He smiled wide.

"Is that right? What about you Dallas?"

"I got a new truck, and a Murphy book! Will you read it?" He asked him. Ethan pursed his lips and I saw his eyes go glassy with tears. He forced a smile and shook his head.

"Not today guys. I have to go on a trip. But when I come back I would love to read that book with you," he told Dallas.

"Where are you going?" Dallas asked.

"I want to go!" Jimmy demanded. Watching this play out was breaking my heart. I wanted to look away. I wanted to tell him he could stay forever. But he needed help. Otherwise he wouldn't really be here for them the way they needed him to be.

"Not this time. But I'll be back," he promised. "Oh, I almost forgot. I have presents for you." They began to get jittery and excited. He pulled out a little blue box and told Jimmy this was for her. She peered closer and tried to take it but instead Ethan opened it for her. Inside, laying softly on top of tissue paper, was a thin gold chain. My heart stopped. He didn't even glance at me. He unfolded it to reveal a necklace. There was a tiny letter E that hung from it. I recognized it immediately. He had given it to me the night we got drunk and got our tattoos. I left it behind when I ran. He had kept it. All these years.

"I gave this to your mommy once, but I think it would look good on you Jimmy Paige," he told her. She looked entranced.

"It's so pretty!" She said, and Ethan put it around her neck and adjusted it to fit her. The little E hung right under her tiny neck. It looked lovely.

"And for you, Dallas, I have something I think you'll find pretty cool." With a swift movement he pulled a ring from his pocket and gave it to him.

"This is for you. It's my favorite ring, very important stuff okay? My daddy gave it to my mommy. She gave it to me, and now I'm giving it to you." Dallas took it in his palm and closed it shut. He looked at Ethan like he fully understood. Dallas always seemed so much older than he was. The twins thanked him again and he pulled them in for another hug. When they pulled away he sighed and put his head in his hands. This was hard for him. He didn't want to leave, but he knew I was right.

He looked up at me and gulped. He shook his head and raised his shoulders. I realized he was trying to tell me he had no idea how to explain what he wanted them to know. I didn't know either. I couldn't help him. He had to do this his own way.

"Do you know who that is?" He asked them and pointed to me, standing a few feet away.

"That's my mommy silly!" Jimmy said.

"Her real name is Cleo if we get lost," Dallas explained. Ethan smiled and nodded. He was so close to cracking I felt my own tears forming. I looked away towards the apartments. I couldn't watch this. A tear slid down my cheek and I wiped it away quickly. I couldn't break.

"That's right. Her real name is Cleo, but you call her mommy."

"What's your real name?" Jimmy asked him. Ethan hugged her tightly.

"My real name is Ethan. But you know what you can call me?" his voice cracked completely. Tears rolled down his cheeks as his son and daughter stood there transfixed on his every word.

"What?" Dallas asked.

"You can call me Daddy," he said slowly.

"Daddy?" Jimmy whispered. Ethan nodded and she moved to hug him.

"Don't cry Daddy. Why are you sad?" She asked.

"Where is my other daddy?" Dallas asked me. I froze, unsure of what to say.

"His real name is Christopher. We call him Chris. He is going away." I stepped forward, unable to bend down without pain I reached for their hands.

"Dallas, Jimmy, this is your daddy. Daddy is going away for a while. But we will call him on the phone and write him letters okay?"

"Are you coming to my birthday?" Jimmy asked. Ethan was letting the tears fall off his chin onto his shirt. He smiled through them and nodded.

"Of course. But I have to go now. So I will see you soon, okay. I love you," he told them as he stood up.

"Okay guys, tell Daddy goodbye." They paused at the word. Still confused but hugged him anyways. I stepped forward and hugged him one last time.

"Get better," I said. I also added that I would work on trying to get them to understand. He thanked me again and hugged me.

"I am so sorry, Cleo. I'll get clean," he swore before I pulled away, urging the kids back towards the apartment. Once again, leaving Ethan alone with his heart broken. This time it wasn't me breaking it.

Chapter Sixteen

REVENGE IS SWEETER

I filed for divorce the same day Eric stopped by with a copy of his mother's will. Given the circumstances, Eric thought it was best there wasn't a formal reading. He held a large, tan envelope in his hands as I invited him in. He sat it next to him as he took the cup of coffee I offered him.

"We're having a meeting with the lawyer this afternoon for my brother and I," he told me.

"You haven't read it yet?" I asked and he smirked.

"Oh, I have. I'll let you see for yourself, but I will say that instant karma is the best. How are you doing, by the way?" I shrugged, trying to seem stronger than I felt. The last two weeks since the party had been physically and emotionally draining.

"I'll be okay. Chris was served with divorce papers about an hour ago," I said, and he grinned ear to ear and leaned forward. Putting his drink down he grabbed the envelope and passed it to me.

"That's why I'm here. I wanted to congratulate you."

"Why?"

"You're free."

Eric wanted me to read the will with him present, just to see the shock on my face when I discovered that Clara Sue's money was split between Eric, the twins, and me.

Eric was given half of her money, her house, cars, and other small things. The twins were given forty percent of her wealth, divided into two trust funds. The money would be available upon their 18th birthdays. Even though they were not her biological grandchildren, she loved them just the same.

I paused in reading the will to ask Eric how she knew. He looked at me with incredulous eyes. "Cleo, Chris was the only one who didn't see it. My mother noticed your tattoo one day and did some digging. When she saw a photo of Ethan, she knew. There's no denying it. She just didn't care. She understood. Chris is…" he smirked and tossed my last words to Christopher back at me.

"The worst person I have ever met."

I blushed, not knowing how he knew what I had said, but I didn't argue. It was true.

Continuing with the will I realized why Eric had waited to let me see what the will said. I inherited ten percent of her wealth, under the condition that I was either divorced or in the process of being divorced from Christopher by the time the will was read. If he had brought me this before, I would have gotten nothing. I had just inherited 1 million dollars.

Everything went so quickly after that day. Because of the DNA tests we had done and Chris being in jail for domestic assault, the judge didn't hesitate to revoke all rights he had to the twins.

Christopher didn't argue anything, although there really

wasn't much he could say at this point. He tried to apologize, but I was finally done. I didn't even go to his trial for the assault. Although I did hear that Holly went and sobbed loudly the entire time. I stuck around just long enough to say goodbye to Eric and leave him an address so we could keep in contact.

As soon as the money was deposited into my bank account, we left. The money Clara Sue gave me was enough to get me started out in California. I could find a house, a car, and while the band worked on new music, we would have our bills paid. It was the greatest gift anyone would ever give me.

Adrian and I moved into an apartment we had found for rent. I wasn't going to blow through the money. I had a plan, and I was sticking to it. The apartment was small but fine for now. I finally felt like I was making the right choices in my life. All members of the band were in the same state. We were talking about music again. I felt safe and happy for the first time in years.

The first thing I did when I arrived in California was legally change my name to Cleo De La Rosa. I would never be called Maribel again. I also changed the twins from Thomas to Andrews. We were finally free.

We soon developed a routine. The twins had their music lessons, then preschool. During that time, I worked with the band on new material. I got to show off my guitar skills, which compared to them, wasn't great. In the evenings Adrian and I would hang out with the twins. Life was good again.

I tried to contact Ethan, but the rehab center refused to release any patient information. However, about three months after he checked in I received a phone call.

He was finally able to talk to people. His program had very strict rules and he was determined to stay sober this time. He planned on staying for a few more months and once he was out he'd come visit. I told him we couldn't wait.

I never broke my promise to him. Every night before we went to bed I would tell the twins goodnight and we would look at the framed photo of Ethan holding the twins. I don't remember when it was taken, but it was a great photo. They were all smiling and facing the camera. Every night we made sure to look at the picture and say goodnight to Daddy.

Eric called only once, to tell me about Christopher. He was given one year in jail despite me not being present for the trial. There was no contact with me or the twins. He agreed to sign the divorce papers in jail once he received them. He had also lost his election. It was over.

Very rarely did I feel sad now. Although, when I looked at pictures of Ethan I did feel a little lonely. I tried not to think about him, but some days he was the only thing on my mind. The only thing that helped was knowing that soon he would be out and ready to see us.

I had been so worried about the twins being confused about the situation, but I think it worked out as best as it could. It was September now, and the last time they had seen Chris was in April at their party. They never asked for him. Where he was, or why he wasn't around. To be fair, they never asked before either when we were living with him. I think him continuing his affair all these years worked out in our favor.

They called Ethan daddy now. I think they may have forgotten his name to be honest. Ethan will be so happy when they see him and start running towards him. I could see it all in my head now. He would open his arms and engulf them in a giant hug, remembering that this is why he gave all that junk up. To have them.

I spent the next few weeks giving as much of myself as I could into the band. Since I had always been the primary song-writer it was easy to step back into that role. I wrote songs about my abusive relationship with Christopher. I wrote songs about leaving, and I wrote songs about moving forward. My bandmates listened to every single one with such respect. I felt truly cared for. They loved them.

We started recording. Soon a few songs turned into a full album. In the following month, we finished our fifth studio album 'Conquering Fears'. We released the album the day my divorce was finalized. Right off the bat reviews began flooding in, most of them positive. Our fans had missed us. They loved my songs and welcomed a comeback. Eric was right, instant karma was the best. Chris always told me that music was a stupid career, and now, the album about him had more sales than any other album before it. We were breaking records. Topping the charts. Everywhere we went, my voice was blasting through a radio, TV, or cell phone, singing about how awful he was.

We played a few local shows, testing the waters. I didn't realize how much I had missed the stage until I stepped up there and saw the screaming crowd. I felt alive again.

Time flew out here. We had barely released the album when Sam wanted to discuss touring. It was all a little overwhelming. Everyone else was good to go, but my situation was the only thing that held us back from signing a deal. I couldn't just leave my kids.

One day in October when we were all over at Mark's place having pizza and hanging out, Renee came over to me. We were watching Derek and Adrian play pool.

"Hey, can I talk to you for a minute?" She asked me. I smiled as we took a step away from the guys.

"Sure, what's up?" I asked. She smiled brightly. I hadn't really gotten the chance to know her very well yet. I liked her well enough, and she made Mark very happy.

Renee was short and dyed her short tight curls a deep purple framing her head. She wore thick black framed glasses and her lips were always a bright red. She was a huge bookworm and kind to everyone. I could easily see why Mark had fallen for her.

She smiled, and I noticed she was wringing her hands nervously.

"Well Mark brought up the other day that you guys were wanting to tour again now that your album is out."

"Yeah, it's been talked about, but nothing is set in stone yet. Don't worry. It's not as bad as you think. He'll call all the time and you can come hang out on the bus when you can," I assured her but she shook her head.

"No, it's not that. Mark told me that the only thing holding you guys back was the twins. I want to help. I could tour with you guys and be their nanny. I've always wanted kids, but Mark and I aren't ready yet. I would love to help. Mark said the busses have twelve beds so there is room. I haven't talked to Mark about it yet, but I think he would love the idea," she said quickly.

I was silent for a long moment stunned. This was the nicest thing anyone has ever done for me. I hurled my body towards hers for a giant hug and thanked her.

"The twins would love that! They love their Aunt Nay Nay! I don't know about them staying on the bus, or even coming with, but having you as their nanny totally works. Even if you guys stayed here I would be able to go without worrying so much. This is perfect. Thank you." She was beaming. The guys stopped what they were doing to look at us.

"We're going on tour!" I announced and everyone cheered. I walked back over to tell them what Renee had offered. Of course, we'd work out the details later, but this just made everything just a little easier.

With my mind focused on the band, I had little time to dwell on Ethan. He called once a week to update us. Whenever I asked him when he would be out he avoided the question or would talk about something else. My mind started to run wild with paranoia. I thought maybe he was never coming back. That maybe he was just telling me what I wanted to hear. Every phone call that came I became more and more sure that he was hiding something.

Then one morning I woke up before the twins and went into the kitchen for some coffee. I told Adrian good morning with a loud yawn. He was in the living room and shushed me loudly. He had the TV on and it was blaring what sounded like the news. I poured my cup and went into the living room to see what had him so transfixed.

There was a blond woman on the screen sitting at a news desk with an older man. The banner under them that was always moving had the words in all caps "EMILE DAHL, LEAD SINGER OF ACCEPTED PERVERSION FOUND SAFE AND SOUND" I gasped and moved to sit next to him on the couch.

Emile Dahl had gone missing about three years ago, just out of the blue. There was no note or any trace left behind. It was the biggest news in music for a long time. I had only met Emile once in passing. He reminded me quite a bit of Ethan. Handsome, funny, a great performer, and of course, he was also into drugs. Most people assumed he had gotten in with the wrong people, or possibly overdosed and someone covered it up. Apparently we were all wrong.

We sat for the next hour listening to various people talk about him. Pictures and videos flooded in of him. Before and after pics. He didn't look much different really. He had a different haircut. When he had disappeared it was kind of long, now it was similar to Ethan's preferred cut, but a dark brown instead of Ethan's raven black.

No one had been able to speak to him yet. From what people were saying, he just appeared out of nowhere last night. Everyone was waiting to hear something from one of his bandmates or PR rep. Something legit and not just rumors. The twins woke up and reluctantly I got them breakfast. Quickly I returned to the living room. This was huge.

Everyone thought he was dead. Adrian still hadn't left the couch.

Finally, around 11 a.m. they had a guy coming to talk to some news station. The guy was named Tom something. He told the cameras that Emile has returned home. He is safe and of sound mind. He was in Europe, getting his degree in English literature. At the time, he no longer wanted to be Emile Dahl. But now that he has his diploma in hand he is ready to resume his life and continue writing music. He is truly sorry to all the fans and friends who worried about him during the last three years and he hopes the music and other ventures he has planned can make it all up to everyone," he recited.

Sounded like a bunch of crap to me. "Maybe he was in rehab." I told Adrian, who agreed with me. The whole thing was weird. But it took my mind off my own worries for a few days, which was nice.

About a week later, Mark and Renee came over one afternoon practically jumping around with excitement. "What?" I asked, their smiles contagious.

Mark was holding an envelope that was already opened. "Accepted Perversion is back. They are having a huge bash. A welcome home party for Emile. We got invitations," he said excitedly, handing Adrian the invite. What? For real?

"How did they come up with this so fast? How did we manage to get on that guest list? You're kidding me," I said as I read the invite myself. I was stunned silent. It was true, the invitation had all of our names on it.

"Does Derek know? Who else got invites?" I asked quickly. Mark began listing off some other people we knew. All musicians. I understood why they all got the invites, but we had been off the grid for a while. Our album was still new. We just recently started playing live again. This was too crazy.

Mark and Adrian were busy on their phones talking to

others who were going. I looked at Renee who seemed just as shocked as I was. "This is crazy, right?" I asked and she laughed.

"Your guy's entire lifestyle is crazy to me. I've talked to people who married musicians and it's not really real until you go through it, you know?" I laughed and nodded. It could be overwhelming at times.

"What are you going to wear?" I changed topics and she brightened again, telling me about this green dress she had that she was considering. The guys came back to where we were and confirmed that this was the real thing. Mark kissed Renee and bumped Adrian on the shoulder.

"We gotta go, we need to get suits." He told us.

"Renee, you coming?" He asked her. She looked at me nervously and I smiled.

"We're having a girl's day. I need to get a dress too," I told her and she beamed. I asked Adrian if he wanted me to call Dita too and he loved that idea.

When Adrian moved back to Cali, Dita stayed in Michigan and they tried to make the long-distance thing work. One day I walked in to find him fighting on the phone with her. She hung up on him and he swore up a storm and didn't want to talk about it. The next day there was a knock on the door. Apparently she was tired of fighting on the phone and decided to pack up her stuff and move out here to be with him. It was all so romantic.

After calling Dita, I called my babysitter and soon enough we were on our way to pick her up and start shopping.

We were in the second store when a lady who was assisting us asked us what our dates would be wearing. Dita and Renee quickly shot their men a text, while I stood there uncomfortable and mildly embarrassed. I would be flying solo.

Renee bought a burgundy V-neck dress with a high waist. I made her buy shoes to match. Mark had plenty of money, I joked with her. Dita had decided on a short silver halter with a low back. She totally rocked it. Moving from store to store I soon became the only one without a dress. Finally, I found something. It was black, with no back but a high front and long sleeves. It was bedazzled with different gold things all along my chest. It was edgy and feminine. I loved it. I bought a pair of black booties to match and I was set.

The next few days just flew by. All topics of conversation were about the party. It was starting to drive me nuts, but I couldn't help but be excited too. Getting invited to something like this made me feel like we were really back. It was about the band again and not just me.

Derek offered to be my date, as long as I put out afterwards. He teased me at one of our recording sessions for some b-sides. I tossed my water bottle at him and we all laughed. "I am not that desperate," I told him.

"Yeah, yeah, yeah. Let's get on with this. My wife's waiting at home with dinner on the table and only an apron on. Come on!" Mark yelled and with that we finished up for the day.

That night, once the twins were asleep, me and Adrian sat up drinking rum and cokes and watching a movie together. He could sense that something was on my mind, so he set his drink down and grabbed a throw pillow, putting it on his lap.

"Alright patient. The doctor is ready." I eagerly moved from his side and put my head in his lap, looking up at him. He stroked my hair a bit and sighed. "Shoot."

"Party is tomorrow," I started.

"That it is. Are you rethinking Derek's offer?" He asked me in his terrible British accent. I giggled. The rum was already settling in a bit.

"Yeah, and I already have my appointment at the clinic for the next day," I retorted. "It just sucks. I want to be excited, but I can't stop thinking about him. He won't tell me when he's getting out."

"Do you think he's avoiding you?" Adrian asked. I hadn't

thought of that one. Perhaps. Maybe two kids is too much for him to handle right now.

"Am I putting too much pressure on him?" I asked and he snorted. I burst into laughter and when we both calmed back down he shook his head.

"No, hell no. He loves those kids. I just think he knows he needs to do it right this time."

"Do what right?" I looked up at Adrian and his eyes grew wide.

"Nothing. Just staying clean. You know, I'm a little hurt that Derek was your first pick for a date Saturday," he changed the subject quickly. I laughed again.

"Yeah, I know. I swear you and Mark were my first choices, but I don't want Dita and Renee to think we're too close or make them jealous." Adrian's eyes darkened. He shook his head.

"Don't ever think that. They both know how important you are to all of us. Cleo, why do you think it took me so long to introduce you to Dita? I told her right off the bat that you always came first and if she had a problem we wouldn't work. She was terrified of you," he laughed. I smacked him.

"She was not!" He put his hands up.

"I kid you not. So was Renee. Mark told me. I guess we talk so much about you it was hard to want to meet you. They were afraid if you didn't like them that we would kick them to the curb." I laughed at how ridiculous that was.

"We all know that's not true." I said, and he shrugged. "To an extent. If you had a good reason why you didn't like her or vice versa sure. But there's been plenty of girls and guys that you didn't like."

"Oh my God. Remember Mickey! That backup singer!" I burst into a fit of laughter just remembering him. Adrian rolled his eyes and pushed me off of him gently.

"Ah yes, Mickey. I still have his solo album somewhere," he told me as got off the couch to go find it.

The day of the party was finally here. The girls all had an appointment to get our hair done. I felt guilty when the babysitter arrived to watch the twins. They had spent a lot of time with her this week. I kissed them both and told them I loved them. Jimmy was playing with her necklace and Dallas was clutching the ring that I had strung onto a chain for him that hung around his own neck.

My stomach was in knots all day. I tried to be happy and giddy with the other girls but I couldn't get into it. I missed Ethan.

Dita had the stylist give her a blowout and Renee had her color freshened. When it was my turn to get my hair styled I was stuck on what to have her do. I didn't want to color it, not right now at least. She threw out some suggestions but Dita and Renee would shake their heads no. Finally she sighed heavily and begged me to let her cut my hair. My hair was long. It touched the top of my pants. I hesitated but the girls urging me to let her finally made me give in.

"Fine. Do whatever you want. Dye it, perm it, cut it. I'm closing my eyes and not opening them until you're done," I said dramatically and the salon cheered. Not really, but everyone was relieved I picked something, sort of.

Closing my eyes, I attempted to relax and let her go to work. After washing my hair I could smell the chemicals she was mixing up. I opened one eye and she chastised me. Laughing, I quickly shut it and let her apply the color to my hair. After I relaxed I was able to joke with the girls and ended up having a good time. I noticed that they were getting close to each other. A twinge of longing crept up in me. It made sense really; that they would become better friends than me and either of them. I had never had a girlfriend. Just the guys. With me and the band always busy, of course they would turn to each other to cure their boredom.

Too soon she rinsed my hair and picked up her scissors. I cringed when she began chopping off my locks. She took the hairdryer to my head and then a curling iron and tons of hairspray. After she emptied the entire can on my hair, she announced I could open my eyes.

I gasped. I was blond. She had bleached my black hair, so it was yellow. She then had given me thick straight bangs across my forehead and cut my hair a few inches past my shoulders. She threw in soft curls and pinned some back for the party. I was in love. I was stunned. I looked amazing. I actually hugged her when I stood up.

"Just wait until you put on your dress and get your makeup on," Dita added when we left the salon. I was actually getting excited for the party.

My bandmates seemed to like it, as much as guy friends could, I guess. When we got back to mine and Adrian's apartment, we took over the place and finished our makeup and getting dressed.

Sooner than what I was ready for, we were headed to the party. It was being held at Accepted Perversion's bassist Davis Waters house. When we got there I saw that it wasn't just a house, it was a mansion. I wasn't surprised. Back in the day, before Emile left, they were the biggest band out there. They sold out arenas all over the world in minutes. It was pretty impressive. I'm sure they still made tons of money during his absence with merchandise and stuff.

When we arrived, it was already pretty packed. The music was loud and the air was alive with excitement. Everyone looked so nice, in sleek suits and expensive cocktail dresses. I nodded and said hi to a few people I had met on my own career path. It was so funny seeing so many musicians, many of which usually were dressed pretty rough, dressed so nicely. I could tell many of the guys were uncomfortable.

Plenty of people were already drunk. Dozens of servers were walking around with trays of alcohol. I noticed to one side of the backyard that there had been a bar set up. I was so nervous I decided I needed a drink. I had been latched onto the arm of Adrian, while Dita was on his other side. I pulled away and smiled.

"I'm going to order myself a drink," I told them. He eyed me warily but nodded. Derek came to stand with him. He saw where I was heading and offered to join me. I rolled my eyes but didn't protest. Their intentions were sweet, but I wasn't in the witness protection program. I didn't need to be protected at all costs. I was a big girl.

The bar was open, so I ordered four shots of tequila for me and Derek. We downed our two each quickly and fist bumped each other. I needed the courage today.

I was nervous. I hadn't been to any sort of thing like this in years. I knew lots of people would either want to talk about my absence, or my new divorce. A magazine recently wanted to write an article on the new album. So the whole band did an interview and somehow they found out about my ugly divorce and put it in the article. That, paired with the lyrics in our songs, made people quickly form rumors about my marriage. Most of which were true, but not something I longed to talk about with strangers.

Soon Mark and Renee came to join us sitting by the bar. I ordered more shots and I heard Derek groan.

"I love you Cleo, but I am not doing shots with you all night." I laughed and took the glasses quickly, shoving them in front of everyone.

"Stop whining and take your shot!" I demanded. He rolled his eyes but took it anyways, this time using lime and salt. I took mine straight.

"If this is how tonight is going to be, I need a break. When I see Adrian and Dita I'll send them your way," he told me. Mark and Renee laughed with me and took two more shots each. I was quickly getting a nice buzz. If I didn't pace myself, I would be drunk soon. We moved from the bar to a table, so others could order drinks.

We sat around the table drinking and eating the snacks that were being passed around. A few people from other bands came by and hung out with us. We were quickly becoming the 'it' table. People were surrounding us.

The party as a whole was growing louder and louder the longer it went on. The backyard was now packed with people all wanting to get a peak of the strange and unusual Emile Dahl.

After an hour or two, someone went to the stage and interrupted the music. Turning that way I recognized the man. It was Davis Waters, our host for the evening. He thanked everyone for coming.

"Hey everyone, having a good time?" Everyone cheered. "Great, Great. I'll let you all go back to the party after this, but I just wanted to say something. We are all here to welcome back Emile. One of my best friends and brother for life. It took you a few years, but you finally decided to answer my phone calls," he joked. The spotlight turned towards where Emile was standing. He smiled and waved. But his smile was definitely forced. He looked like he really didn't want to be here. Man, he really was hot. Even with a scowl on his face, I could see why he drove girls wild. He drew people to him, even if he didn't mean to.

"But I'm not here to cry about it. I'm just glad you're back buddy and can't wait to get back to where we left off. So a toast. Everyone, to Dahl. Welcome back asshole!" He yelled with a big smile. Everyone lifted their glasses and yelled back "Welcome back asshole!" Emile laughed and took a sip of his beer, nodding and lifting the bottle to us all. Davis left the stage and the music began to play again. A small wave of nausea hit me as everyone clapped. Oh no. It was time to switch to water and eat some food. I didn't want to be the person to get sick and ruin a good time.

Davis came to our table a little while later. "I keep hearing this is where the real party is?" He shouted over all of us. I called for another shot and a server brought us a few more for the table. Davis took his quickly and sat down to chat for a while. His wife Angie came and joined us for a bit too. It was really shaping up to be a good time. Davis and Derek talked about our new album while I chatted with Angie about their new house. They had just bought this place and were excited to host something.

Eventually they took their leave and new people took their place. It was getting hot so Adrian decided to take a walk with me around the yard. I had switched to water a while ago, but the walk would help to sober me up more.

"How are you feeling?" He asked me. I smiled and leaned into him a bit.

"I'm okay. I'm having a good time." He laughed and took my hand.

"I love you," he told me and I told him the same.

"I have to pee. Are you good on your own?"

I rolled my eyes. "I'm fine. I'll be around," I replied as he left me to socialize alone. I went and ordered myself another glass of water.

I stood by a fountain, drinking my water when I heard "Cleo? Cleo De La Rosa?" I turned around to see a handsome man that I recognized but couldn't remember from where. He was tall and slim, with long dirty blond hair that fell just above his shoulders. His eyes were dark blue and he had a dimple on his chin. He was scruffy and the more I stared the cuter he got. He was dressed in a black suit. Even with all the layers I could tell he worked out daily. He was built.

Well hello. Where did I know him from? "Yes, that's me. Do I know you?" I asked, trying to be polite. He turned red.

"Uh, yeah. It's been awhile. I play guitar for Cast Offs. We toured with you like seven years ago. Patrick Eger," he chuckled a bit. Suddenly I remembered!

"Oh my god! Patty! Blast from the past!" I exclaimed and leaned in to hug him. He seemed relieved that I recognized him.

"How've you been?" I asked him when I pulled away. He shrugged and smiled. He was really handsome.

"Good. We actually just finished the tour for our last album. We just got back into town a few weeks ago. What about you? I've been listening to your new stuff. It's pretty great," he told me. I beamed.

"Thanks, I think so too." We laughed and I invited him to come hang out with the rest of us, which he eagerly did.

We spent the next hour laughing and joking around with everyone. Patty asked me to dance. Mark groaned that he was making him look bad, so he took Renee out to the dance floor too. Dita then pulled Adrian up to join us.

"I'm really glad I saw you tonight, Cleo. I felt kind of like a fish out of water," he told me as we danced.

"Oh, me too. I'm surprised we made the list, since we haven't really been doing much until recently." I said. His face grew serious.

"You should let me take you out sometime."

I smiled in pleasant surprise. "Yeah, maybe. If you can catch me between getting ready for the tour and all," I said.

He laughed. "So that's a never? I know how that goes."

"No, I didn't say that. I would like a date. It's just hard sometimes." He nodded.

"Well can we consider tonight the first date?" I pulled away and punched his arm playfully.

"Nuh uh. You have to take me to dinner and movies. I want the whole nine yards," I teased.

"Me too," he said, pulling me close to kiss me. His lips were warm and inviting. It was a quick, simple, no strings attached kiss. Suddenly I felt the atmosphere around me shift. I stiffened and saw Mark staring past me. Before I could respond there was a light tap on my shoulder. I turned around and froze.

"Do you mind if I cut in?"

Chapter Seventeen

JUST ANOTHER GIRL

*M*y eyes were frozen on the man in front of me. When I finally broke my gaze I turned back towards Patrick. His mood instantly deflated. "Yeah, sure. Hey, I have to get going. I get my daughter tomorrow, so I need to get a good night's sleep." I smiled wide at him.

"You have a daughter? I have twins! How old?"

He grinned. "Beverly is four. How about yours?"

"They turned five in April."

"Maybe one of these days we'll do a play date," he offered, giving me another charming smile. Ethan cleared his throat loudly and Patrick gave me a hug and told me goodnight, kissing my cheek. I thanked him and he disappeared into the crowd.

"I guess I missed my chance again, huh."

I spun around and stared at him. Ethan Andrews, in the flesh. He looked dashing. His hair cut and styled, was slicked back. He was wearing a black suit with black dress shirt and tie. I had never been so attracted to a man in a suit before in my life.

"What are you doing here?" I hissed as he extended his arms

for a dance. Looking around I saw people watching, so I took his hands and began to dance.

"I was invited. Why else would I be here? I just wanted to see my friend who I haven't seen in a while," he said innocently.

"Yeah, who is that again Ethan?" I hissed. He shrugged.

"I like your hair like that. It's no cotton candy pink, but it looks good," he flashed that smile I loved and hated at the same time. He extended his arm and gently rubbed his thumb over his name on my neck.

"I always assumed you'd get rid of it eventually," he said. I could hear the snark in his voice. I glanced at his own neck where my name lay. A twinge of sadness pushed through the armor I had put around my heart. There were murmurs around us, but I ignored them, as did he. He never took his eyes off me. We danced in silence for a minute or two. I refused to look at him. I chose to focus on the tables behind him as we danced in lazy circles.

Finally I gave in and raised my chestnut eyes to meet his baby blues. I still loved him. After all the hurt and betrayal between us, after all the lies and secrets, I still loved him.

"Are you going to yell at me yet?" He asked, cracking a small smile. I glared, wiping the smirk off his face.

"Why didn't you tell me you got out? Why didn't you try to get in contact with anybody? You could have called Adrian." I was trying to keep my voice down, but I was still slightly tipsy so I had no idea how loud I was.

I tried to pull away but he squeezed my hands just slightly tighter to keep me close to him. I flinched, a flash of the million times Chris did that passed in front of me. Ethan saw it in my eyes because he let go instantly.

I shook my head and put my arms around him to continue dancing. It was a slower song, so he placed his hands on my hips and leaned his head down to whisper into my ear. He told me he was sorry for everything. We embraced each other for a moment before I moved to talk to him directly.

"I have been working on something. Something big. I didn't want to overload myself."

"Overload yourself with your kids? That's what parenting is. Grow up!" I said, ripping myself away from him. Pushing past him, I got lost in the thick crowd of people. Turning back, I couldn't see him anywhere. I leaned against a stone pillar, closing my eyes. I wasn't ready to see him apparently.

"Wow, you found a way to weasel your way in here too," I heard a familiar females voice say. Opening my eyes I saw Duchess holding a drink, eyebrows raised in annoyance.

"What do you want Duchess?" I asked, not in the mood for her crap. She looked gorgeous as usual. Dressed in a skin-tight silk dress, six inch heels to match. I looked massively inferior to her. Her hair was dark brown, her makeup reminded me of an old Hollywood starlet.

"Nothing. I just saw you dancing with our boy and then running away. Figured I'd see if you were okay." She flashed a fake smile at me. My jaw tightened.

"He's not our boy," I snarled. She shrugged.

"Yeah, I guess not. He won't even return my calls anymore," she pouted. I rolled my eyes. Poor her. She pounded the rest of her drink, pulling a little case out of her bra she popped a pill into her mouth.

"I didn't think you'd be back. You know, after you changed your name and all, Maribel," she said to me after she swallowed. I stared at her in shock and disgust. She crossed her arms and looked towards the dance floor. Ethan was making his way through it, searching for me.

"I thought about telling him when you first had them. But I knew if I said anything he'd do exactly what he always does. Run to you and give up everything."

I backed away from her, surprised and a little scared. "You knew I was pregnant?" I asked.

"I knew you had two kids nine months after you spent the summer screwing my boyfriend," she glared at me, daring me to look away first. I did.

"Yeah, I knew. Figured I wouldn't tell if you didn't," she said, disappearing into the crowd just as Ethan spotted me.

I didn't know how to react. I was frozen to the spot. I was disgusted. What a vile woman.

When he reached me he tried apologizing again. I shook my head and told him to leave me alone. I needed space.

"Cleo, come on. I really need to explain," he said. I ignored him and began pushing back to my table.

When I got there I was surprised to find Duchess chatting with Renee and Dita. They were laughing and smiling brightly at the celebrity. I saw red. Mark and Adrian were nowhere to be seen.

"I would love to do a song with your husband's band. They were so much fun when we did the video together," I heard her say to Renee. Duchess saw me and raised an eyebrow. What was I going to do, cause a scene? Adrian and Mark returned with drinks.

"Oh wow, okay." Mark said, causing everyone to turn. Mark and Adrian looked confused, unsure of how to react. Ethan came up behind me and swore. She flashed her fakest smile at him and I lost it.

"She knew. The whole time. She knew about the twins and didn't tell you," I blurted. I watched the blood drain from her face. The entire table stopped talking. Mark and Adrian grabbed their dates and pulled them away. I turned to Ethan. He was furious. The veins in his neck were bulging. His jaw was so tight I thought he was going to break a tooth. He didn't take his eyes off her. She looked panicked. Standing up, she tried to go to him, but he moved away.

"Don't touch me. Stay the hell out of mine and my kid's lives," he snarled. She shrunk away before Ethan could react any further. He closed his eyes, trying to calm himself. Everyone returned to the table, but the conversation was quiet.

Finally Ethan opened his eyes and turned to me. "Can we go now?"

I nodded quickly, wanting to leave before Duchess found a way to get her revenge.

We said our goodbyes and Ethan took my hand gently. The valet quickly pulled up his slick, very new, black Cadillac Escalade. I raised my eyebrows at him and he grinned. "I've been hard at work," he said, not revealing anything more.

Ethan quickly had me in his car and was speeding off towards the highway.

"I'm sorry. I shouldn't have said anything. I was just so mad," I tried to apologize but he put his hand up to stop me.

"I'm not mad at you. You didn't tell me about the twins because you didn't want to burden me. You sacrificed your freedom to give me mine. She didn't tell me because she needed a bump buddy. I'm over it. I finally see her for what she is." His words were meant to be reassuring, but guilt still clung to my gut.

I closed my eyes. The blur of the road was making me sick. "Where are we going?" I groaned.

"I want to show you something," he replied. There was silence while we drove. I was so mad at him for everything. I wasn't in the mood for small talk.

"How long have you been out?" I shot.

"Month and a half," he said quickly.

"I hate you," I told him. He nodded and looked like he was pondering my words.

"I get that. It was a dick move."

"So, how have you been? You like Cali?" He asked me as we turned onto the highway. I glared out the window.

"I listened to your new album. It's good. Really good," he continued attempting small talk.

"Thanks," I said flatly.

"So that guy. Is that a new thing or have you two been seeing each other?" He asked me casually.

"Why do you care? Who I date is none of your business." I whipped my head around to look at him. His eyes stayed focused on the road. His jaw was tight, his eyes angry.

"It is when they are around my kids," he said sharply. I shook my head in disbelief.

"Your kids? The ones you haven't even tried to see in months? How are they your kids, Ethan?" I snapped. His face twisted into pain.

"I couldn't. I had a good reason, Cleo. Do you think this is what I wanted?"

"Well you could have fooled me. It's okay. I don't need you. I can take care of Dallas and Jimmy by myself. I don't need anybody!" I cried. Ethan was fuming. He laid his foot on the gas, speeding up.

"Screw this. Ethan, just let me out. I'll walk home," I said and started to unbuckle my seatbelt. He took one hand off the wheel and reached across to hold tight to the belt. He clicked it back in place and let off the gas.

"How am I supposed to know what is going on if you don't talk to me?" I asked. Without warning he put his hazard lights on and pulled over to the side of the highway and turned off the car. Unbuckling himself he turned his body to face me, brushing the few strands of hair that had fallen down out of his face.

"I know I didn't handle the situation in the best way. I got out and had something that I needed to do. A few things. If you let me, I'd like to show you," he said, his face was tired. I softened.

"Okay. Sure. Let's see it," I said, and he smiled back at me.

He put his seatbelt back on and started the car again, turning his hazards off.

"So what is this thing you have to show me?" I asked, trying to keep my tone light. He didn't say anything, but continued driving. He took my hand, squeezing it softly once and let go quickly. I closed my eyes and let him drive us towards his surprise. I must have dozed off because I was startled awake by Ethan nudging my shoulder.

"Unbuckle and come out with me," he said, his face lighting up. I tried to look out the windows but didn't really see anything exciting. I did as he asked and he came around to take my hand.

We were standing in the driveway of a huge building. It was old, but you could tell that there had been some extensive work on it. Was it a hotel? Maybe an old library or museum. It was a two story, brick building. A dozen stairs led up to the giant red doors. I looked around for a sign or some lettering on the front but didn't see anything.

"Where are we? What is this?" I asked, turning to face him. He was beaming. His megawatt smile was almost lighting up the dark building.

"This is Evan's. That's what I'm calling it. For now, anyways. I'm hoping to come up with a better name," he said, still remaining coy.

"Did you buy this? How? When? I'm so confused," I told him and he laughed again. It was refreshing, his laughter. Was this a new Ethan? A sober, actually happy Ethan? He moved closer to me so we could stare up at the building together.

"When we visited my brother, you told me I should do something to keep his memory alive. This is how I'm going to do it," he explained.

"What are you doing with it now exactly?" I asked as we stared up at the huge building.

"It's a boarding house for abandoned and disowned teens

and young adults. More specifically, for homosexual, transgender, or even just kids in drag. A warm bed, warm meal and help getting on their feet."

I was in shock. This was amazing. Ethan was amazing. He cared so much about his brother and now he was finally able to channel his pain into something good. I was at a loss for words. Instead I turned and hugged him tightly. He was stiff at first but then accepted it and wrapped his arms around me.

"What do you think?" He asked and I laughed through my tears.

"You are going to help so many people," I told him and he beamed. His eyes grew a little watery but the tears stayed put.

"I really, really hope so," he said and we turned our backs on the building to go back to his car.

"So, I've got to ask. Where did you get the money for all of this?" I said once we were driving away. He laughed.

"Bob mostly. He regrets what he did to Evan. He wanted to be my first major donor. He also is helping me get it all organized and set up to be a legit charity. That way it will run on sponsors and none of the people we help will ever have to pay to stay here.

Bob gave me quite a bit. It's guilt money but I don't care. It's going to good use. The second donor was Evan," He paused and then continued.

"Turns out my biological dad's dad, my grandfather, ran a rather successful construction business. He helped my mom get on her feet when we were first born and as it turns out, left everything to us. He died when we were just kids and my mom never told us.

Since we were underage, she was in charge of the money. She split it down the middle and put them in accounts for us, for when we went to college. Well, Evan didn't make it to graduation and I left before she could tell me. So, she let it sit and collect interest. Her name was still connected with the accounts.

After making sure I was okay with it, we took all the money and added it to Bob's to start the charity," he finished. I was once again stunned. This was insane and awesome at the same time.

"I didn't know your brother, but I think he would have loved that idea," I told him. He smiled again and when I looked over I saw that a tear had sprung loose and was running down his cheek. He brushed it away.

"Yeah, I think so too."

The rest of the way back to my apartment he gushed about the details of the house. What he had learned and had been doing all this time. He was almost a different person than the one that left us for rehab only a few months before.

When we got to my place I asked him if he wanted to come in. He hesitated. I smirked and pulled him inside.

"Are the twins here?" He asked immediately. I shook my head and kicked off my boots. Instant relief flooded me. They had been tight on my feet all night.

"No, I hired a sitter for the night. They'll be back in the morning. Are you ready to see them?" I asked, hesitantly. I didn't want to pressure him. He looked uncomfortable. He wouldn't meet my gaze.

"Yeah. I miss them. I really do. I'm sorry I stayed away. I wanted to make sure I was ready to be a good dad before I came back into their lives. You know?" I nodded. Moving to the kitchen I opened a cupboard.

"Want a drink?" I offered and he rolled his eyes. It took me a second before it dawned on me. I felt my face get hot.

"Oh crap. I'm sorry. I totally blanked. How about some water?" I started rambling but he smirked, shrugging his shoulders.

"All good. I'm used to it. Water sounds great," he said. I got two glasses and went into the living room. I grabbed the remote, turning the stereo on. It played one of mine and Adrian's favorite stations. I turned the volume down so we could still talk. I plopped down onto the couch and pulled my legs up to fit under me. My dress was short but it covered up what it needed to. He stood there awkwardly before he stiffly sat down on the other side of the couch.

I stared at him. He looked uncomfortable in his suit. We glanced at each other and after a moment we both burst into light laughter. "This is weird, right?" I asked and he nodded.

"Yeah a bit. A bit." He relaxed and turned towards me.

"Tell me about your new life as the divorced rock star mom of twins," he said and I chuckled.

"Well, you've heard the album. Things are pretty good, actually. The twins adjusted pretty fast. They like it here. The guys definitely like having me here. It feels right. I missed making music. I was never meant to be the stepford wife," I laughed. He smiled and raised his glass.

"Yeah, I never saw it. I didn't have the heart to tell you before, but your cooking is horrible," he told me, flinching away when I jokingly punched his shoulder. We joked and laughed some more, rehashing old memories.

"Now that you're out here for good we can finally start writing that sequel," he said after a while. I got up to refill our glasses. I offered him coffee. When he accepted I prepared the pot and started brewing some. Turning back to him I shrugged.

"Sure. I don't really know what we'd write about this time around." He thought for a minute and then shrugged himself.

"Yeah me either, but I'm sure we'll figure it out," he said and silence suddenly surrounded us. The weight of his words hung there. Now that Chris was gone and I was here in Cali we could finally stop hiding everything.

"You know you can start coming around, if you want," I said rather awkwardly. I turned back towards the coffee still brewing. I knew my face was probably red.

"I'd like that. I really do miss them. I want to be a big part of their lives," he told me. I nodded. That made me happy. They missed him too.

I heard him stand and turned back to see he had come to the kitchen. He took a few steps towards me. "What about us?" He asked, his voice low. I looked into his eyes. That intense blue I would never get enough of.

"What about us?" I repeated his question back at him. He took a step closer and put his hands around my hips. I gently pushed my body into his. He groaned.

"Cleo, I can't do it. I can't keep seeing you with all these other guys. I feel like I keep missing my chance," he murmured into my hair.

"Here's your chance," I groaned, closing my eyes. "Don't miss it."

"I wouldn't dare."

Ethan kissed me. It was a gentle, pure, no secrets kiss. This was the first kiss we had ever had that wasn't dangerous. This kiss couldn't break someone's heart. It couldn't ruin a career. We weren't doing anything wrong with this kiss. Someone could walk in and we didn't have to move away from each other to hide it. We had never kissed like this before.

He kissed me harder. The first kiss demanded a reply. Then again, another kiss. He kissed me until I kissed him back. One kiss from me and he pulled away, pressing his forehead to mine. I looked up into his eyes but paused at his soft lips. They were turned up into a beautiful, crooked grin.

"This is different," he chuckled. He felt it too. The freedom.

"Good different or bad different?" I asked, and he smiled.

"Good different," he said before kissing me again, harder this time. This kiss was demanding. Everything we kept hidden for so long was in this kiss. The sound of coffee pouring into the pot stopped. Taking a step away from Ethan and the counter I took his hand and gently pulled him towards my bedroom.

He closed the door softly. There was no one home, but the mood called for quiet. I moved into his arms again and kissed him once more. This had never felt more right. Ethan brushed my hair behind me and touched my neck with his thumb. He rubbed his name and pulled me close again.

Slowly, like we were new to all of this, he took off his jacket. I loosened his tie and unbuttoned his shirt just a bit. I paused when he grabbed my hand and kissed my knuckles. I opened his shirt and leaned forward to place my lips on his exposed skin. He inhaled a sharp breath. His hands were on my hips but steadily moving higher. He reached my breasts. He cupped one and then moved the other hand to my hair.

I let him unzip my dress and it fell to the floor. I watched him as he took his shirt and tie off. He kicked off his shoes, leaving him in just his pants. I was only in bra and panties.

I smiled and pushed him backwards towards my bed. He chuckled and then stopped short as I began kissing his chest and lowering my body as I did so. I undid his pants and slipped them down. He lifted his hand to my face to stop me going any lower. I paused and looked up at him. He smiled down at me with those gorgeous blue eyes. Even in the dark they shone bright. He took the hand off my chin and ever so softly pushed me onto my back.

I fell onto my pillows, my hair covering my eyes and mouth. Ethan crawled over me and pushed the hair away from my face. He kissed me. Just as gently as that first kiss in the kitchen. I kissed him back with as much passion as I could muster. I needed to show him how I truly felt about him. His hands moved slowly from my hips up to my breasts. His mouth moved slowly from my lips down to my neck, down to my collarbone, down to my breasts.

I gasped as he moved the fabric of my bra away to reveal my naked chest. For the first time in my life, I truly felt loved. It wasn't rushed. We weren't moving quickly to not be caught. It was pure.

Once my bra was completely gone, Ethan moved lower. Kissing my belly. Reflex made me try to cover my soft stretch marks with my hands, but he pushed them away with his nose.

"I don't care. I like them," he told me. I relaxed once more as he kissed them. His hands went to my panties. He pulled them down and I lifted my legs to slip them off. I gasped with surprise when his lips moved between my legs to my most sensitive spot, teasing me. I moaned with pleasure. He chuckled and came back up to kiss my neck and then my lips again. I realized then that somewhere along the way he had removed his boxers.

We made love that night. For the first time, in all the years I had known Ethan, we made love. It felt right. I was used to sex feeling dirty and wrong and for a while that worked for us. For me. I had never experienced anything like what I was feeling right here, right now with Ethan.

He took me into his arms and loved me like I deserved to be loved. I had let every relationship I had ever been in tear me down. I thought no one would want me, but here I was. Being wanted.

He was gentle, and slow. He didn't push for anything more than I was ready to give him. Finally my body surprised me with a rush of pleasure I hadn't felt in years. I let out a cry and soon Ethan joined me in ecstasy.

He embraced me afterwards. He was warm and his body felt soft and inviting. I didn't want to let him go. I fell asleep knowing that I was loved.

I awoke the next morning alone and confused. Sitting up I looked around. His clothes were gone. As were his shoes. It was as if I had dreamed Ethan being here. The only sign that I wasn't insane was a glass of water on my nightstand paired with two aspirin and a folded piece of paper. I took the pills and opened the note.

Thank you for last night.

I will never forget the way you looked at me like I really mattered.

I'm still broken, I still have feelings I'm unsure of and until I can figure them out I need to take a step back. From US. Not the twins, not you, just US.

I'm sorry. It's complicated.

Call me,

E

I sat on the bed, staring at his note, trying not to cry. What did this mean? It made no sense. I crumpled the paper up and threw it across the room. I wouldn't let myself dwell on it. I was done letting a man control any part of me. Even if it was just my thoughts.

Getting out of bed I tossed one of Derek's oversized shirts on along with some underwear and went out for some coffee. I groaned as I realized we had left that full, fresh pot out last night.

"Yeah, I had to clean it out this morning. Thanks," Adrian said as I walked into the kitchen. He read my mind.

"I would be a lot more pissed if I hadn't walked in as Ethan was sneaking out." My head whipped up from the coffee pot I was staring too hard at.

"What time was that?" I asked and he shrugged.

"About six," he replied. I looked at the digital numbers on the machine. It was ten.

"How are you awake right now?" I asked incredulously, turning around to talk to him. He shook his head and smirked.

"No, you are not asking the questions this morning. It's my turn." I groaned but knew that I had it coming. I sat down at the little island we had across from Adrian. He had a smile plastered on his face. It was his "I can't wait to tell everyone what I know" face.

"So, Ethan came over. Even stayed the night," he started. I eyed him, not making any sudden movements.

"Yeah, and he left at six am," I countered back.

Adrian shrugged. "He looked like a deer in headlights when I flicked the light on as he was walking out of your room. Scared the crap out of him."

"Did he say anything?"

"Just to make you call him. He said he knew you will refuse to, but he really wants to see the kids and to talk to you about some stuff. So call him." I rolled my eyes.

"You know I hate all of you right."

Adrian had that grin on again. "Oh we know. Call him."

"I don't have his number."

"It's in your phone. He programmed it in before he left; and then gave it to me in case you deleted it." I swore. That was actually exactly what I was going to do.

"Cleo. I don't know what you guys are fighting about, but that doesn't mean that he doesn't care about you. Call him. At least for the twins. They miss him. You miss him," he argued, and he knew he had me.

As much as I didn't want to see him, the twins deserved to. I glared at Adrian as I left to get showered and start my day.

I waited until the next day to call. I wanted to let him know I was angry, but still reasonable. The phone call was awkward and full of uncomfortable silences. We agreed on him coming over later in the afternoon to see the twins and talk.

The twins were over the moon excited when he walked through the door. Unlike Christopher, Ethan didn't come bearing gifts of forgiveness. It melted some of my anger towards him.

He embraced them tightly and told them he missed them.

They couldn't stop squealing and talking to him, updating Ethan on everything of importance in their lives.

"I got a new school now, Daddy. My teacher is Miss Emily," Jimmy told him.

"We live with Uncle Adrian now. He's so funny," Dallas told him. Ethan smiled and looked up at me. His eyes told me that he had forgotten how overwhelming they could be sometimes.

"That's awesome guys. What are your plans for today? Can I join you?" He asked Jimmy. She shrugged, irritated that he interrupted her.

"Sure. When mommy goes to work, we go with Aunt Renee. Sometimes she takes us to the park."

"Mommy, can we go to the park?" Dallas asked, his eyes hopeful. I laughed at their excitement.

"Sure. Let's get our shoes on and we'll walk."

We got to the park and Ethan ran around with them while I sat on the bench watching. I thought about joining them but felt like Ethan really needed this time with them.

After about half an hour of running Ethan was huffing and struggling to catch his breath. He said something to them and they went off to keep playing while he came to sit with me.

He plopped down beside me to steady his breathing. Once he was okay he gave me a halfhearted grin.

"Picking up smoking at 16 was a genius idea," he said sarcastically. I smiled but didn't reply. I was still confused and hurt. "Can we talk?" He asked and I looked away from the kids for a moment.

"About what?" I asked him, knowing exactly what he wanted to talk about. He sighed deeply.

"Look, I'm just unsure of a lot of things right now. Until I figure it all out can we still be friends?" He asked me. It hurt, hearing those words. Like a punch to the gut. After the wonderfully tender night we had, he wanted to be friends.

"Sure. I get it. I just want you to be here for the twins. They love you," I told him. Trying not to let my voice reveal my pain. I didn't want to ruin his relationship with them over his relationship with me. He sighed with relief and smiled back at me.

"I love them too. I really do, Cleo. They are so awesome. I don't want to miss any more of their lives. I want to have visitations. I'll make the time. A few times a week, the weekends. Whatever you're okay with."

"I'm sure we can work something out. Probably no overnights until I get back from the tour,, but you can definitely see them as much as you want. While I'm gone you'll have to get with Renee and figure out some sort of schedule that will work for you guys," I told him and he gave me a confused look.

"You're going on tour? When?" He looked upset. His face contorted to confusion and then irritation.

"In about two months. After the new year. We're top billed. No fighting this time," I joked. His face still showed surprise.

"What? I got it figured out. The twins are staying with Mark's wife Renee and will come see us when they can. It's really no big deal." He seemed to relax, but barely.

"It was hell, leaving them with you in Michigan when I flew back here. And I had only known them a short time. I can only imagine how hard it will be for you," he finally said. I nodded, looking back to them. We were the only ones at the park today. It was nice.

"Yeah. We actually weren't going to tour until Renee offered to take them while we were gone," I explained.

"Well I can help too. I want to." I smiled and took his hand in mine as we watched our children play.

"I want that too."

Chapter Eighteen

IT HAD TO BE YOU

*E*than kept true to his word. He saw the twins about three times during the week and at least once on the weekends. Every night he called to tell them goodnight. He hadn't missed a night yet.

After that day at the park, things became less awkward and it actually worked for us. Somewhere down the line our relationship shifted from one of lovers to good friends.

Sometimes after the kids went to bed he would stay and hang out with Adrian and I, or whoever else was at the house. He was another unofficial member of the group. It seemed like it was always expanding these days.

The weeks leading up to the tour was filled with tons of promotions, interviews, practices, and anything else Sam or the record label could come up with us to do. They even had us shoot two music videos. One would premier before the tour to hype it up. The second was going to be released about a month into it. Keeping it up.

I was always busy. I barely had time to eat or sleep. Thanksgiving came and went. It was just about our only day off. I was exhausted trying to plan Christmas and work. Having Ethan around was a life saver.

About two weeks before the tour was set to start I was making a quick coffee run before heading to the studio to knock out some more b sides. I placed my long order and moved to the side to wait. I was nibbling on a cookie when someone tapped my shoulder. I turned around and smiled with pleasant surprise. "Patty!" I exclaimed. We hugged quickly.

"What's up? How've you been?" I asked. Patrick was looking handsome as ever, this time in relaxed jeans and a tight shirt that outlined all his muscles in all the right places. I couldn't help but check him out. He was looking good.

"Great. Same old, same old. I forgot to get your number at the party," he said. The barista called my name and I hurried to grab the cup holder full of coffee. Patrick scurried to help me. His order was called. He grabbed his single cup and offered to walk with me.

On the walk to the studio we had a pleasant conversation. He was fun to be around. He made me laugh. It was over way too soon. We stepped into the studio. I set the coffee down and thanked him.

"I'd stay and chat, but I really have to get to work. Everybody's waiting for me."

He flashed a perfect movie star smile. "All good. I know how that goes. You should let me take you out to dinner."

I laughed at his bluntness. It was refreshing. "I barely have time for coffee." He wiggled his eyebrows and I relented. I really wanted to have dinner with him. After all, it was time to start moving on.

"Sure. Okay. Here, take my number. How about late dinner. Maybe nine? Tonight?" I suggested.

"Awesome. I can't wait. I'll see you at nine," he said, taking my number. I hurried back to my waiting bandmates.

When I told the guys about Patrick they all frowned.

"What? It's just a date. You know Patrick. He's nice," I defended. They shrugged and didn't say much. It was really annoying. As soon as we were done with work Adrian and I went home to find Renee and Ethan hanging out at the apartment with the twins. We had ran so late I barely had time to shower and change; and even that would be rushed.

I hugged the twins who were getting ready for bed. I felt so guilty that I wasn't the one getting them to sleep. I would miss them while I was on tour.

After my shower, I practically ran into my bedroom and started flinging clothes around trying to find something to wear. There was a knock on the open door. I looked up to see Ethan. I paused to look at him. God he was so damn hot. He was wearing a leather jacket, tight, worn jeans and black boots. Even when he was just doing everyday stuff he was sexy. I turned away. I couldn't think like that anymore. Things were different, I reminded myself.

"You going somewhere? Maybe want some company?" He asked me. I shook my head. Ethan was the last one I wanted to talk to about my date with Patrick.

"Just grabbing some dinner. You don't have to stay Ethan. Adrian can watch the twins," I told him. Trying politely to hint for him to leave.

"Dinner? I could go for some food. I know a burger joint I think you'd like," he pushed, coming further into the room. I was still in just a towel, my hair soaking wet.

I sighed, grabbing some underwear and a bra and slipping them on. I didn't really have time for modesty. Looking at the clock I saw Patrick would be here in twenty minutes.

"I saw a flyer for this outdoor concert, about fifteen minutes away if you were interested," he offered. I thanked him but moved past him as I pulled on my nicest jeans. They flattered my curves well. I found a nice black top and grabbed my olive jacket.

"I can't tonight. Maybe tomorrow." I gave him a quick smile but turned to my vanity to fix my hair and throw on some eyeliner.

"Oh, I gotcha. Girls night?" He asked, he stuffed his hands in his pocket. I looked up at him from the mirror. His reflection showed nervousness. He was digging. Was I really going to have this conversation with him? Right now?

I turned around to face him. I didn't really know how to approach the situation.

"Ethan, I'm going on a date," I said, deciding being honest and upfront was probably best. He straightened and pulled his hands out of his pockets.

"Oh. I didn't realize you were... sorry. I'll get out of your hair. I... sorry," he mumbled and quickly left the room.

Before I could react, I heard a knock on the front door. I swore as I heard Adrian greet Patrick. I didn't expect him to be right on time.

I hurried over to my mirror and tossed my hair into a messy bun and put on some lipstick real quick. There was another knock and I turned to see Ethan again. His face was flustered. He looked uncomfortable. "Uh, your date's here."

I thanked him and he practically fled my room. I stepped out and went to the living room to see Adrian, Ethan, and Patrick all standing around chatting. Well, Adrian and Patrick anyways. Glancing at Ethan I realized that he was just staring at Patrick, his eyes narrowed.

With the two of them standing next to each other it was hard not to compare them. They were total opposites. Patrick was tall and very muscular. Ethan was more lanky. His muscles weren't as bulging, but I liked that. The memory of laying my head on his chest returned but I quickly shoved it away.

Ethan was dressed like he was going to a rock concert, while Patrick was more casual. He had on a white button shirt with clean jeans and nice shoes. Ethan, even on his off days still had makeup on and styled his hair. Patrick looked like he probably just brushed his naturally blond mess. They were polar opposites, but I was still attracted to both.

All three men turned when I came into the room. "Hey you. You look great." Patrick spoke first. Ethan shot a dirty look at him. I don't think he realized I saw. Adrian noticed it too. I thanked him, and a very large silence fell over the room.

"Alright. I had a long day. You two go so I can get down to my boxers and watch porn on the big screen," Adrian said suddenly, practically pushing us out the door. Ethan didn't say anything.

Patrick laughed and grabbed my hand, leading me out. His hand was huge and warm. Once we were in the privacy of his car he spoke.

"That was Ethan Andrews, right? From Cruel Distraction," he asked. I sighed. Okay, I kind of figured eventually he would come up. I just didn't want to talk about it right now.

"Yep. That's the one," I said flatly and tried to change the subject. He wasn't ready to. My excitement over the date was already fading. This was a bad idea.

"I don't mean to push, but I remember the song and then your tattoos. I'm sorry. I know this is weird. I just didn't expect to see him at your place."

"No, it's okay. I didn't expect him to be there either. He was watching the twins while I was at work."

"Oh," was all he said. There was uncomfortable silence.

"He's their father." It was very weird saying it aloud. He visibly relaxed.

"Oh, okay. That makes sense I guess. And you guys are just cool now? Me and my ex are on pretty good terms now too. You kind of have to be at some point. I don't know what I'd do without Beverly." I sighed with relief when he dropped the subject and we returned to the happy banter from this morning.

Patrick took me for Chinese. He offered a few different

places but I really wanted some beef and broccoli. After dinner we decided to take a walk to ease the pressure on our bulging bellies. I swore I ate my weight in rice.

"There's this mini festival going on not too far away if you're interested. We could sit on the roof of my car and listen to some shitty bands play their shitty music." He flashed a gorgeous smile. I frowned. That was probably the one Ethan wanted to go to. It would feel weird going with someone else now.

"What about a movie?" I asked instead. He shrugged and hand in hand we headed back to his car to go find a theatre. I let him choose the movie. He picked some thriller about a detective and an underground vampire clan. It had the typical guy stuff. Lots of action, blood, and swearing. He held my hand during it, but as much as I tried to stay interested in the movie and in Patrick I found my thoughts returning to Ethan.

Why was he so bothered by me going out? Was it because I should be home with the twins? Once again that mommy guilt came back. I really should be spending as much time as I could with them. If Ethan could make time in between making music and starting a whole charity, I could find time too. I understood why he'd be so upset at me.

When the movie was over, Patrick asked if I wanted ice cream. I thanked him but told him I was tired and should probably head home. I had another busy day ahead of me. I thanked him for a wonderful night and gave him a long hug. I felt his muscles under his shirt and almost groaned. He was so hot.

He even walked me to my door. He was such a gentleman. I couldn't help but lean in for a small, light kiss before I unlocked the door and stepped inside, telling him goodnight. I shut the door and leaned against it, disappointed and exhausted. As charming and handsome as that man was, it wasn't a love connection.

A moment later Adrian walked into the room from the hallway. He was in his boxers, like he said he would be. He ground sleep from his eyes, even though it was barely after midnight. Usually he was up until early morning.

"Hey, you're back," he yawned. I tossed my purse on the couch and kicked off my shoes.

"Yeah. We went to dinner and saw a movie." He smirked. "Real romantic that one." I rolled my eyes. I wasn't in the mood to be judged on my choices in men tonight.

"He's really nice. I had a good time," I lied. Well, half lied. Patrick was wonderful. If I had been able to stop thinking about Ethan for even a second then I'm sure I would have had a great night.

"So, is there a second date when we get back?" He asked me, heading into the kitchen. I followed him in as he got a glass of water. Scratching his head he yawned again and looked my way.

"You're tired. You okay?" I asked him, trying to change subjects. He shrugged, taking a drink.

"Yeah, just Dita. If I'm not doing band stuff she wants all my extra time. I mean, I get it. Since she isn't going to follow us. I really like her, but I am kind of excited to get on the bus and have some time away," he chuckled. Poor him, someone loved him. I told him that and he gave me an exaggerated eye roll and sigh.

"I know, it's awful!" He said and we both got a good laugh.

"When did Ethan end up taking off?" I asked as I slipped off my jacket. He moved to the couch with me and pulled down the small blanket he kept on the back of the couch and wrapped himself in it. He then flipped on the TV and we started mindlessly watching a rerun of some comedy he liked.

"I don't know. Dita stopped over for a bit before work. He left when she got here."

"Did he say anything when I left?" I pushed. He darted his eyes over to me for just a second.

"I don't know. Don't think he liked Pat. Stop asking me questions. My show is on," he complained, and ended my line of questioning. He had just lied to me. I knew that look anywhere. I stood up, telling him goodnight. He offered a mumbling of something similar. He was already falling back to sleep.

After the date with Patrick, I decided it was best to just work on the band and my relationship with the twins. I had such limited time right now, and those were my priorities.

He did text me a few days later. I thanked him again for the night out, but when he asked about a possible second date I told him I wasn't ready to start dating again. Which was true. I was still finding myself. Even though the reason I gave him was an honest one, I still felt guilty. It was an excuse and a lame one at that.

With only a few days left, Adrian and I were busy moving the twins things and cleaning everything. Ethan came and helped when he could. However, since my date with Patrick I noticed he was spending less time with us. He didn't ask about it, but seemed bothered whenever we were alone. I could tell he was holding something back, but I didn't have the energy these days to get into an argument so I let it be. He claimed that he was working a lot more with the charity, but I sensed that it was just an excuse. As long as he was still here for the kids I was happy.

We celebrated Christmas at Mark and Renee's. Our place was all packed up and Derek had somehow turned into their rent-free tenant. The twins were overloaded with gifts. I noticed that even Eric had sent some things. The holidays were fun, but they came and went. It was weird celebrating them with no snow.

After that the time just flew. We were all ready to move out in two days. Everything was packed and all of our ducks were neatly in rows. We could just relax and enjoy the rest of our time with our loved ones.

Mark and Renee never stopped holding hands wherever they

went. It was adorable. I knew she was going to miss him terribly, but she understood this was our life. What we were meant to do.

Dita, was less accepting. I noticed her and Adrian's relationship was very love and hate. The more I got to know her, the more I realized that she was the female version of Adrian. Which meant that she also was used to always having her way; and just like Adrian, if something wasn't going the way she liked, there was hell to pay. It was actually quite funny to watch Adrian have to deal with someone who was exactly like him.

"I don't want you to go," she pouted. He smirked as she tried her best to keep a straight face. "I demand you stay here. We can skype you playing when the rest of the band is on stage. It will be like you're really there," she insisted. He pretended to think about it for a minute, then kissed her nose quickly. She giggled and he kissed her lips.

"Anything for you babe," he said. They were absolutely smitten with each other. This was the first time he was going on the road and he had someone waiting for him at home.

"It's nice, I'm not going to lie," he confessed while she was in the bathroom. I was so happy he found someone.

"Do you see a future with her?" I asked.

"I'd like to think so. I don't know about the 2.5 kids and picket fence, but something sure," he said. I smiled, thinking only for a moment about my predicament. The craziness that was my life. That kind of future wasn't in the cards for me either. Maybe I was never meant to have that.

Seeing both couples made my heart warm. I was so happy that the most important men in my life were finding people to love. Derek on the other hand, was still finding himself. I asked him about it and he just shrugged.

"Haven't met anyone worth looking twice at. Haven't really been looking either. I'm still having fun," he said, innuendo heavy in his voice.

"And man, am I going to have fun on this tour," he joked. I smirked but let him be. One day he'd find someone, I was sure of it.

"What about you? What is going on with you and Andrews?" Derek asked me. I frowned.

"What do you mean? Nothing. We're just friends," I said. He raised an eyebrow in doubt.

"Really? Then why aren't you going back out with Patty?" I looked away quickly, taking a long gulp of my drink.

"It just wasn't right. I don't want to commit to something right before I leave," I argued. "Plus I need to be focusing on the kids right now, not my love life."

"So, it had nothing to do with Ethan pouting about it?" He accused. I shook my head.

"He was the one who wanted to be friends. Not me. I wanted to be with him and he shot me down."

"Yeah, but he was just out of rehab, still figuring stuff out. He's changed. You're telling me that there's nothing there?" I nodded.

"Positive. We're in a good place right now and it's best we stay this way. He was done a while ago, and I'm done now," I swore. Derek kept his small smile and shook his head.

"I wouldn't rule him out yet," he murmured and left me alone watching Renee's crackling fireplace.

The next morning was our final full day before we left for the tour. The gang had plans to spend it all together. To have a true family day. I woke up to the smell of bacon.

Heading downstairs, I saw Renee at the stove while the twins sat with Dita and Adrian eating pancakes. My stomach churned for food, but I needed something to drink first. I think my nerves were kicking in.

"What's the plan for today beautiful?" Mark came into the room, moving to kiss his wife. I poured myself a tall glass of water and then turned towards the table. Derek had shuffled in behind Mark. He had sat down and almost immediately started shoveling bacon into his mouth. I had to look away, it grossed me out.

"Well, after breakfast I figured we could all get ready. Maybe take some pictures. Relax a little, lunch at the park, and then after dinner could all go see…. Murphy's!" She exclaimed, pulling a stack of tickets out of the back pocket of her jeans.

"It's a live show, but it's going to be televised. We might end up on TV!" She told us excitedly. The twins started screaming. I smiled, as her intentions were good; but I was really starting to hate that guy. I glanced at the adults around the table. They each gave each other looks but no one said anything. Dita put her hands up in mock excitement and everyone followed suit with their own positive comments.

"Sure. Sounds fun. I'm going to get ready." I left quickly. I couldn't take Derek's noises as he inhaled his food any longer. I took a long shower, knowing that I would miss this on the road. When I finally stepped out and back into my room, I found Adrian and Dita rummaging through my things.

"What the hell! Get out!" I threw my hair brush at Adrian. He dodged it and went to my suitcase.

"I was thinking maybe that black jacket, those jeans and boots. Ooh and maybe this hat. He pulled out a big floppy black hat. Did you pack any of that? Here's that jacket."

"What about a dress? Does she have any?" Dita asked him. They talked about me like I wasn't there. I glared at them through my mirror as I brushed my hair. I saw them lay clothes out and give each other satisfied looks. They instructed me to wear them.

"Fine, just get out!" I shouted and they left quickly, after making a mess of course. I could hear the rest of the guys downstairs as I got ready. Renee knocked and asked how I was doing.

"Good, but I'd get ready faster if everyone left me alone," I growled. She apologized and tried to back out, but I felt bad and told her to stay. She brightened.

"I like that outfit," she told me. I smiled, although I felt too dressed up for a day out with the kids.

"Thanks. Adrian and Dita picked it out," I admired myself in the mirror. I looked at my abdomen and tightened the shirt a bit, sighing. This wasn't going to work. I needed a new wardrobe.

"Where are the twins?" I asked, and she giggled.

"Mark was going to try to curl Jimmy's hair by himself. He has never done it before. I made him leave the bathroom while I did it." I turned away from the mirror.

"You're curling her hair? I thought we were just going to a Murphy thing," I questioned. Renee's eyes grew big for a split second and then she smiled brightly.

"Yeah, we are. But I was going to try to get family pictures of all of us before you leave. That's why I want everyone to look great," she explained. She really was the sweetest woman ever. Mark needed her. He was a lucky man. I thanked her and hugged her hard.

"I'm glad you're here. None of this would be happening without you," I told her. She sniffled and thanked me. We were supposed to be relaxing all day but Renee had us on a tight schedule shuffling us from place to place. At dinner everyone was super energized and excited for the show. I just wanted to go home.

"Who plays a kids concert this late anyways? Where are all the signs?" I groaned but no one answered as we drove into the parking lot.

"Stop complaining and just come on," Mark said when we started walking towards the venue. We got inside and found it already crowded. I told Renee to hold on to Dallas tightly. I had Jimmy on my side. We didn't want to lose them.

Seating was general so we found a spot that fit us all and sat down. The band currently on stage was some hippy dippy thing that didn't interest me at all. I chatted with Mark about some video he saw online and sent to me last night. But I stopped short when I caught a bit of the conversation the people in front of us were having. There were two girls, barely eighteen I decided. They were holding their phones and talking loudly.

"You really think they are going to be here?"

"Duh, why do you think all those camera crew are here. Not for these bands. Everyone here is here for them."

"I heard he's the MC. Like the host. For the whole thing. I guess he was the one who set it all up."

"My roommate is Seth's girlfriend's sister. She swore that they'd be playing. He's out of rehab now. All that hosting stuff is just rumored."

"Yeah, but why didn't they advertise it? Why wouldn't they want people to know who was playing?"

"Because he's Ethan Andrews. He can do what he wants. If he wants to be the secret host of some charity thing then he can."

"So then maybe it's all a rumor." The girl conceded and frowned. The other girl shrugged, not seeming to care either way.

"Probably. Honestly I think Beth got it wrong. Why else would the tickets for this be so cheap?"

I turned slowly to look at Mark who looked so guilty it wasn't even funny. Everyone in our row had stopped talking to listen to the girls in front of me. Their faces all looked identically guilty.

"Is Cruel Distraction playing?" I asked loudly, not caring who answered. Girl one turned around. She didn't look friendly but answered anyways.

"Supposedly. I guess they got added to the list last minute. Who knows if it's true though," she said.

"I thought this was a Murphy concert. For kids," I said,

looking at the girl in front but saying it loud enough for my friends to hear.

"No. Well kind of. That guy is here. He's in a punk band, like on the side. Nothing great, but him playing on that show helps with publicity. I think he may be an opener."

"I need some air," I said and hurried away before anyone could stop me. I was furious. Why didn't anyone tell me? I knew they were hiding something, but refused to say anything. Why wouldn't Ethan tell me he was working on music again? I knew it shouldn't be a big deal, but everything about this felt fishy. Like I was the only one not in on a secret. I didn't like it.

No sooner had I started out of the theater a member of security told me the show was starting. Sighing, I headed back in. I barely had a minute to stew. I debated going to sit with my friends, but I was too mad to be around them right now.

I stood in the back and brooded while I watched some local bands play. Some were good, some weren't. I did see Paul, who played Murphy. He was the singer of some band called Blue Hail. They weren't great, but not awful either. After they finished their small set the atmosphere changed completely. I looked down at my watch and realized an hour and a half had passed. Based on what I was seeing the crew doing, they were preparing for the headliner. The cameras were turned on, the reporters started their intros. Stage crews flew around getting instruments ready. I looked back at my family. Family.

It just hit me. They were looking back at me, all smiles. Waving for me to come back. They were my family. They loved me for the mess I was and vice versa. Whatever reason they had for hiding this from me, they had the best intentions.

I joined them and tried to enjoy the show. I looked around. Adrian had his arm thrown over Dita, who was snuggling close. On my other side, Mark and Renee had the twins in between them. I caught them looking at each other with love in their eyes and then down at the twins. I smiled. I couldn't wait until they decided to have a baby. Just like my kids, that baby will be showered with love.

Suddenly everyone around us stood up and cheered for the band that had just walked on stage, all dressed in suits and ties. I gulped and my heart skipped a beat as I saw Ethan looking just as handsome as ever.

He wore a suit that highlighted his toned muscles but still trim figure. His hair was freshly cut and styled. It reminded me of when we were younger, short on the sides, longer in the front and flopping in his face. I think this was the best look for him yet.

"Hello Los Angeles!" Ethan called. I looked to make sure the twins still had their noise canceling headphones on.

Jimmy looked at me with wide eyes. "Is that Daddy?" Pressing my lips together, I nodded. The music grew quiet. Ethan put the microphone back on the stand and turned to his bandmates. He made a motion with his hand, queuing them. They started playing one of their songs. They played low, as to not overshadow Ethan.

"First off, I want to thank everyone who came out tonight to help support a great cause. I will get to that later. We will be playing soon don't worry. So let me hear some noise!" The crowd went berserk again. I had to cover my ears. When it died down he continued.

"So as many of you know. I'm newly sober. Nine months," he said shyly. "Now I did a lot of thinking in rehab. Where I had gone wrong and all the things I ruined in my life because of my addiction. Blah, blah, blah, you know the routine." He flashed a small smile to the crowd and they chuckled. God that smile always made me melt.

"They wanted me to talk. To open up. What was I trying to bury inside of me? What was making me want to torture myself so much? Well finally, after losing literally everything I cared about, I decided it was time to tell my story." Continuing to face the crowd he took a step to the side. His band mates left their instruments and came to embrace him. They each hugged him tight and quickly left the stage. The entire venue was almost deathly quiet now. Suddenly a white curtain unfurled behind the instruments and a picture was projected onto it. I gasped with realization of who we were looking at.

"This is Evan. My twin brother." He paused as the crowd erupted in shock and confusion. They were looking at a picture of Ethan it would seem. Another picture replaced the first one. It was of both of them with their arms wrapped around each other's shoulders. This was the first time I had ever seen them together. A tear escaped my eyes.

Only when put side by side could you see the difference in the two young boys. Evan was smiling wide, his hair cut shorter than Ethan's. Ethan's hair hung over his face and seemed to be embarrassed to be taking the picture. While Ethan wore the standard black t-shirt and skinny jeans every kid wore back then, Evan was wearing a bright yellow shirt and khakis. But despite their contrasting clothing choices, they still had the same gorgeous face.

With a huge sigh Ethan continued. "Evan was gay. From the time we were about six he knew he was different. But we didn't care. No one held it against him. It was just us and my mom at home and we embraced it. Evan was who Evan was." He looked back at the photo of them together and kept talking.

"But then a day came when someone did care. Someone who had become very important in our life. I never cared for the asshole but my mom did so I dealt with it. I was told to cut my hair, wear different clothes, to stop wearing face paint and to put down my guitar. Those were requests that every now and again I could adhere to. Because clothes don't define me. I was still the same Ethan inside. My mother knew that and she loved me for who I was."

A third photo flashed on the screen. It was a family photo of

Ethan, his mother, Evan, and Robert. Both twins looked identical now, with sharp, short haircuts and sharp blue suits. It was a very formal picture. No one was smiling in it.

"The requests made upon Evan went a little deeper than changing a t-shirt. My stepfather wanted a normal family. He refused to accept the truth about Evan's sexuality. It was blown up into a huge deal when before no one ever cared." The picture changed again to a one of Evan in a wig, face full of makeup and a dress. He was on stage at "What's The Password". I pursed my lips, trying not to cry. He was doing it. Finally. I was so proud of him.

"My mother didn't care when Evan strode around our tiny little house dressed as Penelope Felony. She didn't care that the police were constantly being called because I was playing my guitar too loud and that her other son was a fag!" He screamed to the crowd. They grew quiet again. He began pacing the stage. His anger was rising. I saw his fists were clenched tight.

"But someone did. That person made my brother feel like less of a human being for three years. He threw it in his face that he would never be accepted. He treated him less than dirt. He made Evan miserable." He stopped talking as another photo came onto the screen.

It was Ethan, in a cap and gown. Diploma in hand, but what should have been a happy moment, was more somber. Ethan wasn't smiling in the picture. His hair was a mess and he was wearing dark eyeliner. He was rebelling against them, I realized.

"This is me on my graduation day. Alone." His voice held no emotion. "Evan killed himself before this picture was taken. We weren't even eighteen." He paused for a long moment to let the crowd take in his words. Glancing around I saw shock and pain in people's eyes. Many were crying right along with me.

"See, Evan couldn't live in a world without acceptance. He didn't want to be hated. He loved everyone with all of his heart but the people that should have been there for him refused to be. Evan decided that his life wasn't worth living if he couldn't be Evan." Ethan pinched the bridge of his nose, taking a deep breath to steady himself.

"A huge part of me died that same day. He was my twin. He came into this world with me. We were ride or die. He wasn't supposed to leave me! He never even told me what was going on. Sure, he hated it and complained but so did I. Evan had felt so low that he couldn't even tell me what was going on in his head."

The picture was cut off the screen abruptly. Lights that had been dimmed brightened again and Ethan began to smile. He was so handsome when he smiled. My heart fluttered. He was finally telling his story.

"A good friend of mine told me not too long ago that maybe I should use his story, his life for something good. Tell the world. I was hesitant at first, of course. Honestly she was the first person I had ever told about what happened to my brother. Hell, most of the world didn't even know I had one, let alone one with my matching face.

But sitting in that rehab facility, I started to give her words some real thought. Maybe I should use his story to help others. I could do some real good in this world. I didn't want him to be forgotten and here I was covering him up all these years." He began to pace again. Every eye was on him, no one dared even to cough.

"When I got out of rehab I decided to get to work on something that I knew could help the world. Help people like Evan. The world has too much hate. The world has too many young kids who are afraid of who they are, afraid to be themselves and too many of them can't live with that. There are too many Evan's out there.

With the help of too many people to call off right now, I want to announce that I have founded a charity in Penelope

Felony's honor. We made a safe house for teens and young adults who are gay, trans, drag, whatever. So no more kids will have to become homeless, unloved, or dead. I present to you Evan's Place.

The very last picture appeared. It was the building that he had shown me that night of the party. Although, this picture had been taken in the daylight. I noticed that they had added a sign in the front. EVAN'S PLACE was in giant letters, with FOR PENELOPE FELONY right under it, in a smaller print. Tears fell freely now. The crowd was silent for a very long moment but then suddenly erupted into screams and cheers. Everyone stood up and applauded Ethan for his courage.

Ethan smiled, but I could tell it was forced. He had said what he wanted to. He was drained. I wanted to go to him, but it didn't feel right anymore. We really were just strangers now. Friends, I guess. Our relationship wasn't what it used to be. I hated that. I missed the way we were.

When the screams died down Ethan clapped his hands and the rest of the band returned to the stage. I watched crew run across the stage to grab guitars, amps and anything else taking up space. What were they doing? Ethan walked towards the microphone stand. His bandmates stood in a row behind him. Their hands in front of them. I noticed the picture of the house fade and the white curtain was rolled up.

They were on to something else now. After a moment he began talking again. Music from a sound system started playing. What was that song? It buzzed lightly in my ears. I could not for the life of me figure out that familiar tune.

"One of the parts of the program I'm in is admitting all the bad shit I've done and apologizing for them. Now usually I skip that part. But I really need this to work this time. So, for everyone here. I have one last story for you. I promise I'm almost done. I'll try to make this one quick." He winked and in unison Cruel Distraction took off their jackets and loosened their ties. The crowd went wild. Unbuttoning their shirts, they tossed them into the crowd. Then, about two dozen drag queens walked onto the stage from both sides. They surrounded the men.

People gasped and screamed as four of them handed the band feather boas. Three black and one single red boa. That's when I realized what song was playing. I cupped my hands over my mouth to stop from screaming. Ethan set the microphone into its holder and held onto the stand tightly, waving it around as he paced. Everyone else stood perfectly still.

"I fell in love with a girl. But I was so high all the time she left. Broke my heart. But then I overdosed. They revived me and I realized I needed to make some amends. I looked her up and a friend told me that she had some things of mine that I might be interested in. For nostalgia's sake, I went for a visit."

My heart stopped pumping. My eyes widened. What was he doing? Oh my God. It was all happening in slow motion. This was not the time Ethan. Not after that emotional outpouring. I could feel my head shaking. No, Ethan. Not now.

"That same friend that helped me get ahold of her then, helped me today. I want to show everyone the reason I am going to stay sober this time." Everyone in my row stood up. Jimmy and Dallas were bouncing out of their seats wanting to go see him. Then just like that Mark picked up Jimmy and put her on top of his shoulders, while Derek grabbed Dallas and did the same. Adrian jumped out of the row and began getting people to move out of their way so they could get down to the stage.

People grew quiet. The whole place was buzzing with excited whispers. Security helped the twins up to Ethan, who was waiting with open arms. The three of them stood wrapped in a big hug, surrounded by half naked men and twenty drag queens. The crowd cheered and Ethan pulled away. Holding onto them tightly he faced the crowd.

"Everyone, I'd like you to meet Jimmy and Dallas. My kids."

The crowd erupted. Ethan hugged the twins closer as they stared out into the crowd in wonder. He kissed them once more before Mark and Derek came to take them back. They left the stage, waving to the crowd. It was adorable. I stopped wiping my tears away. I let them run down my face, ruining my makeup. Renee and Dita moved closer to hug me. Ethan grabbed his microphone again. He was facing the crowd, eyes moving over us all. He was looking for me.

"But what I really came here today for was to apologize to someone else. So Cleo, I have waited way too long to say this. Please don't leave me hanging. I hate this. I'm crazy about you."

Suddenly the group behind them started moving, as if getting into position. He gulped, pursed his lips and took a deep breath. Then, someone pushed through the group of queens and grabbed the mic from him. My eyes almost fell out of my head. It was Chelsea Sometimes.

"Cleopatra, darling. What Ethan here is not telling you, is that he paid for all of us to fly here. He made deals with his bandmates to get them to dance for you. It's always been you. All those songs. I've listened to his albums. They were all about you. Good or bad. I swear if you break his heart one more time, we are all coming for you!" She waved her finger and the song grew louder. The crowd laughed and cheered for Chelsea. Ethan was beet red. He laughed too, shaking his head as she gave the mic back.

The moment he started singing I couldn't hold back a laugh. It was Sin with Sebastian's 'Shut up'. The song he sang at the drag show. I cupped my hands over my face and peeked at him through my fingers. He was putting everything into this performance. He walked around the stage just like that night. Everyone was his backup. I saw that he was looking for me. He hadn't spotted me yet. My heart was racing.

He picked the perfect song. Ethan and I were special. Regular words and phrases weren't right. This was our secret, special song. The lyrics were so inappropriate for this setting, but it was the perfect choice. It wouldn't make sense to anyone but us. I watched him from my spot, stunned. Dita and Renee nudged and pushed me towards the aisles. The crowd was going crazy.

I started towards the stage slowly, almost in a daze. I was confused yet so excited. What was happening? I caught my best friends before I was helped onto the stage. Each one gave me a quick kiss before I climbed up. Mark, Derek, and finally Adrian. I paused when I reached him. He smiled at me, eyes wet with happiness. I could only imagine how bad I looked. He wiped my cheeks before leaning in to whisper in my ear.

"Go get your picket fence." I kissed him one more time and thanked him for everything. I climbed up on stage quickly before I broke down again.

The twins wanted back up, so I helped them too. We went over to Ethan who had stopped singing. The dancers slowed to watch us. Music continued to play as Ethan reached out for Dallas.

"Dallas my boy, can you help me out?" He asked. I smiled at Ethan in confusion. He just winked and wiped sweat from his face. Dallas looked at him blankly, but Jimmy nudged her brother.

"He wants his box back Dallas!" She yelled. I frowned but my little boy's face lit up. He produced a little black box out of his tiny coat pocket. "Open it Dallas!" She demanded, and he struggled but finally got it. Opening it he revealed a beautiful diamond ring. He tried to give it to Ethan but he laughed and shook his head.

"No son, that's for Mommy. What do you say babe? Marry me, babe?" He asked me, leaning down on one knee. He wasn't even looking at the crowd or his friends anymore. It was just me, him, and our beautiful children. I cupped my hands to my mouth, covering my surprise. Was this really happening?

I nodded and immediately began crying again. He was amazing.

Ethan leapt up to embrace me. He had his head in my neck. He pulled away and placed a huge kiss on my lips. The room erupted in cheers. I had almost forgotten about them. I waved to the crowd. Ethan laughed at me as he kissed me again.

"I love you Cleo. I'm sorry for being cold. But somewhere along the way I realized if I didn't do it right I'd miss you again," he said into my ear. We kissed again.

I moved to glance back at my friends who were beaming and clapping with the rest of the crowd. Turning back to Ethan I saw he was talking to the twins. He stood back up and I moved to whisper something of my own in his ear. He stood up straighter and his eyes grew big. He turned to look at me face to face.

"Really?" He mouthed, and I nodded. He started to laugh and snatched the mic again.

"Well good thing I finally asked because we've got baby number three on its way!" He shouted into the microphone.

I looked at my friends who were shocked but still smiling. Adrian was the only one not surprised. He knew before I did. Our eyes met and I couldn't stop smiling as he rolled his eyes slowly. He was trying so hard not to smile, but soon enough it broke free. I loved him so much. I couldn't do it without him, without any of my guys.

Ethan rubbed my stomach, bringing me back to him. I laughed as he kissed my neck one more time. Turning to face away from the crowd I took his head in my hands so for just a moment it was just me and him.

"You are crazy."

He grinned sheepishly. "I know." He pressed his forehead to mine.

"Can we not fuck it up this time?" He grinned, giving me

one final, long, swooping kiss. I looked into those baby blues and nodded.

"I am not missing you again."

Turn the page for a sneak peek of book two,
Promising You, Promising Me

Promising You, Promising Me

PROLOGUE

She was beautiful. I stood up at the altar and watched as she walked slowly down the aisle.

Dressed in white, her lacy gown flowed out around her. It trailed behind her slowly, swaying back and forth as she walked. Her lace veil covered her face, but that didn't stop my heart from racing. She was stunning.

Her father held her close as they took small steps to reach the stairs. He was in his 70's now, but he still flew to California to be here. As they finally reached the altar they paused, turning to each other. With tears overflowing his old eyes, he lifted her veil, planting a light kiss on her cheek.

He whispered in her ear, "Te amo, *Cleo,*" before moving to sit down next to her mother. I was almost sure that was the first time he had used her new name. Her real name. She turned to face the stairs and my breathing stopped. She was stunning. Absolutely gorgeous. I had never seen anyone as beautiful as she was right now.

With one hand holding a bouquet of red roses, she lifted her dress with the other to step up. Our eyes met once she got to the top. I smiled at her and she pressed her lips together tightly. I could tell she was moments away from a complete breakdown. So was I. I lifted my hand to take hers, briefly squeezing it. I winked at her, to let her know that she could do this. I knew she understood.

With one last look she turned around and I watched with a forced smile as she married Ethan Andrews.

For a further sneak peak turn the page for chapter one of Promising You, Promising Me.

Promising You, Promising Me

SNEAK PEEK OF BOOK 2

Chapter One
The Fourth Drink Instinct

I'm sound asleep in my bunk and all of a sudden I'm jolted awake by someone slapping me across the face with a pillow!" I started my story for the hundredth time. Everyone loved hearing it. It was the most interesting thing to happen to me recently. It was all over the internet.

"I jump up and look around, but its dark and I'm still half drunk from the night before. I get hit again and she starts screaming. She's all like "you're a bastard, you cheated on me. How could you?" And I'm beyond confused. I look around and there is this chick I had been dating for maybe a month if that." I waved my arms around emphatically. All eyes were glued to me.

"I leap out of the bunk and book it out of there. I'm in my boxers trying to cover my balls while she's following behind me throwing anything she can reach. I jump out of the bus, and just

312

run. I don't know where we're at or who I cheated on her with, but I was too tipsy to think straight." Everyone around erupted in laughter. I paused to take a drink of my champagne.

"That's the picture everyone's been seeing then?" Sam, a guy working with Ethan at his Charity house asked me. I nodded, chuckling.

"Yep, that's the one. Me in my skivvies being hit in the back of the head with a giant book. Girl was a fast runner and had good aim." I shook my head, remembering that night. She was a great rebound after Dita and I broke up, but there was nothing there but sex. Apparently, she thought otherwise.

"When she finally stopped hitting me I was able to ask her who exactly I cheated on her with and she tells me it's Derek." I finish my story, letting everyone laugh at my expense. It was all good. I found it hilarious. I'm just glad I was wearing clean underwear.

Derek happened to pass right at the climax of my story. He stopped and rolled his eyes at my cluster of friends. "We kissed a few times on stage. Just kissing. It's not like we were blowing each other on the bus or anything. Chick was nuts," he said, making them laugh harder. I finished my drink, and before I could add more to the story I was being pulled away.

Turning, I saw Mark, one of my best friends and our bands drummer. He was dressed in a black suit with a red rose boutonniere, just like Derek and I. Cleo had made us her bride's men. She didn't really have many options. Renee was there sure, but she had the kids. I'm sure she would have asked Dita if that hadn't ended with as big a blow up as it did. Somehow I didn't find it as funny being cheated on as I did cheating. It was months ago, but I still never found out who the guy was. He was one lucky guy, she was a catch.

I looked at Mark expectantly, waiting for him to speak. "What's up?" I asked him.

He brushed his inky hair back, "Cleo wants to take a few

more pictures before the sitter takes the kids home. They're getting antsy," he said. We grabbed Derek, our bassist, and went towards the cake where the happy couple stood.

We were a crazy line up. Ethan's bandmates made up his wedding party, so it was seven men and Cleo. Cleo originally tried to make us all walk down the aisle together but that was where we drew the line. We all loved our girl, but sometimes it was good to say no.

Once the wedding party was all together Renee, Mark's wife, ran up with the twins, Dallas and Jimmy. She put them in front of their parents. Behind Renee came a taller, more demure woman. She was dressed in a classy blue cocktail dress, and her black hair was styled up. Coming forward, everyone made room as she walked, carrying a tiny little blue bundle in her arms.

My eyes jetted back to Ethan and Cleo. Cleo was watching Charlotte, her new mother in law, waiting for her to bring their new baby boy to her. Ethan, I noticed, clutched his wife closer. He was looking down at her with such love in his eyes. Jealousy flashed over me, but it passed an instant later.

I guess I always kind of thought it would be me marrying Cleo. In some absurd scenario where I didn't break her heart and she wasn't head over heels with Ethan. I couldn't be too upset over it though. They were way more in love than Cleo and I ever were. They were meant for each other.

Charlotte placed the baby in his mother's arms and the photographer started moving quickly, trying to get those perfect shots. Once they had all that they needed of me and the guys, we stepped aside and let him get pictures of just the family. They looked so perfect.

Despite Cleo being Latino like myself, all three of her children looked just like Ethan. Instead of her dark hair, chocolate eyes, and slightly tanned skin, all three of their children were pale, with the darkest black hair, and the bluest eyes you ever saw. I still never understood how Chris never figured it out.

Seeing Ethan standing with them, it was obvious he was their father.

The photographer finally announced they were done and Cleo looked towards Renee to take the twins. She hurried forward and took each kid by the hand, while Mark himself took the sleeping infant out of Cleo's hands. Renee turned and promised they'd be back as soon as the kids were settled in with the sitter.

Renee adored them. I remembered when we first were considering touring again. She had surprised us all by stepping up and offering to be the twin's nanny. It was perfect, we had someone we could trust and still travel. She loved it. Mark had told me that she was considering doing it full time.

It was great because now Cleo could focus on both the band and the kids. Those years with her in Michigan sucked. Mark, Derek, and I didn't do shit. We had to take on side gigs while we waited. Well, hoped and prayed it was only waiting. There were times when we didn't think she was coming back to the band.

After the photos came cake and then the first dance. I was asked to dance with a girl I didn't know. Her name was Lexi, and she was a cousin of one of the groomsmen. I was polite, and accepted, but my mind was elsewhere. When I spun her around I caught sight of the newlyweds. Ethan glanced up and we caught eyes for a split second. He smiled gratefully, and I just nodded. This was getting annoying.

As soon as he could get away, Ethan stepped over to me to thank me one last time. "Adrian, I just wanted to tell you..." I put up my hand to stop him. This was nothing I hadn't heard before.

"Look, Ethan, it's cool. You two were meant for each other. Stop thanking me," I sighed. He frowned, furrowing his brow. He had been thanking me for the last year for helping him reconnect with her. I got the message after the first month or so, he was very grateful,

"Well, I owe you one. I'm serious. You name it, whenever, whatever." He turned his head to look back at his new wife, his eyes were filled with adoration. "It's still hard to believe. Look at me, I'm a family man now!" We laughed and I patted his shoulder.

"I'll hold on to that favor for now, but go have fun. Enjoy it. Now, if you'll excuse me, I'm going to find someone to spend your wedding night with," I winked, and turned towards the open bar.

I ordered an old-fashioned, and scanned the room. There were lots of familiar faces. Most of them were music artists like us The ones I didn't recognize were usually their spouses. Other than Cleo and Ethan's kids staying for pictures, it was an adult only reception. The bartender handed me my drink and I sipped to that. I loved her kids, don't get me wrong, but if I never went to another Murphy's party ever again it would be too soon. Speaking of Murphy, I spotted Paul in the crowd. The man behind the sweater.

I tipped the bartender and sauntered over to him. He was carrying on a conversation with a group of musicians. I recognized them but couldn't remember their band name. Something with lizards, I thought. They welcomed me in and we discussed some of the newest trends in the music industry.

"Have you guys started working on new music?" Jeff, their drummer asked me directly. I shook my head.

"No, we just got off our extended tour right before Cleo had the baby. We all need a break." Everyone nodded in understanding.

"Yeah, I was shocked you guys kept touring for as long as you did. She was huge!" He exclaimed. I agreed with him fully. She was a trooper, I'd give her that.

"We went back and forth with it forever. We all wanted to

cut it short, but she insisted she could still perform. We had chairs and plenty of water for her. She pulled it off. Her last trimester was some of our biggest shows we've ever performed. Of course, having Ol' Blue Eyes at every one probably helped," I smirked.

Ethan threw a fit when he found out Cleo wanted to keep touring until the baby came. He had stayed behind to help Renee and work on his charity. When she told him, they had a screaming match over the phone and Cleo actually hung up on him. I thought it was funny at the time until he showed up at the show the next night.

His arms were crossed over his chest and he glared at her from across the room. For a split moment I thought it was going to be a Chris situation again. He says jump and she jumps, but he surprised us all.

"If you insist on doing this, we're coming along. I'm not missing you having this baby," he told her. Then he revealed he had rented a small bus and driver for him and the kids. We finished the tour as one giant family.

"It was impressive regardless. She's a bad-ass. Ethan landed a good one." Looking around, I found her wrapped in his arms on the dance floor.

"Yeah, yeah he did," I said, just as Mark and Derek showed up to pull me away.

"You ready?" Mark asked, his breathing heavy. I gave him a questioning look, but he waved his hand. "I just got back, I know I'm a little late. My bad." I followed them towards the band they had hired for the reception. The singer looked down at us and smiled. We had given him a fat tip to help us out tonight.

"Ladies and Gentlemen. If you would turn your attention to the stage for a moment," he said as the three of us climbed onto the stage. The band stepped aside to let us take their places. "The bride's men have a gift for the happy couple." He finished his introduction just as I put the guitar over my shoulder. He placed the microphone on its stand and stepped off the stage, letting me take the center.

I searched the crowd for them. They had stopped dancing. Ethan looked curious, and Cleo was trying to look angry, but her smile was showing. She hated when we kept secrets from her. Her first husband had really done some lasting damage.

I gulped and leaned into the microphone. "Hello everyone. Are we having a good night? I won't bore you all with some sappy speech about how much we love our girl. One of them can later," I pointed back towards Derek and Mark. The crowd chuckled. "Anyways, a few weeks ago we realized that we needed to give them a gift. Since none of us really have any sort of skills other than music, we decided to take the easy way out on this one," I paused for light laughter. Cleo's face softened. "No, but we actually had to rehearse quite a bit for this. Ol' Blue Eyes ain't the only one who can serenade," I said, looking at Ethan and then Cleo, winking. I tilted my head towards the guys and they began playing the song we picked. I started playing my guitar and leaned into the microphone to croon 'I wish you love'.

It was the perfect choice for me to sing to her. Cleo and I had the closest relationship of the group. Opening my eyes, I looked around and saw her dancing with Ethan's stepfather.

When we finished our song and stepped away from the instruments, all of us meeting in the middle, Mark took the microphone off the stand.

"Well, I'm not used to being center stage. There's not much for me to say. Really happy for you guys. This wedding should have happened like eight years ago, but better late than never! We always knew in the end you guys would find your way back to each other. Can we get a cheer for these two?" He shouted and as the guests erupted into applause and various shouts as he gave the mic to Derek.

"Alright, looks like they left me to do the cheesy, emotional speech. Cleo, we've been friends since the fifth grade. At first we thought you were going to be a drag, but our moms insisted we ask you to play. You were starting to depress everyone playing in the yard by yourself all the time," he smirked. "None of us thought that it would turn into this amazing friendship. We've been through everything together. I'm not gonna get into the nitty gritty details, that will get us all in trouble. We've been together since the beginning and we'll be there 'til the end." The crowd erupted in claps and cheers.

"And Ethan. Welcome to the family, man." He finished his speech and we leapt off the stage to let the hired band get back to playing. I wiped the sweat off my brow and saw Cleo rushing over to us. With huge grins on our faces we picked her up and held her sideways. Mark held her head, Derek had her feet, and I held up her midsection. She squealed with surprise as we smiled for the cameras. We each took a turn giving her a hug and kiss. She thanked us individually. I was last in line. By the time she reached me tears were sliding down her face.

"That was the perfect song," she whispered into my ear when we embraced. I kissed the top of her head. The band they hired resumed playing.

"Can I have this dance?" I asked. She grinned and took a step back to let me put my hand on her waist. We moved to the dance floor and moved in slow circles. We laughed at some of the guests. I guess some were shocked that we were the ones to stand with her at the ceremony.

"I was so nervous. There were so many people! I was worried that I would trip or that Duchess was going to burst through the door or something ridiculous!" She exclaimed. I scowled.

"This is a happy day. Don't think about her. Or him, for that matter," I murmured low. Her face fell slightly, knowing who I was referring to. I pulled her closer to hug her as we swayed.

"Do you think people are judging me?" She asked me, her voice barely audible.

"Screw 'em if they are," I said quickly and she scowled. I sighed, "If there are people like that, they aren't here. Look around." Her head turned side to side, gazing out at the two hundred plus guests, all smiling. She looked back to me.

"All these people came today to see you get married to the love of your life. They are happy for you. It's a happy day. No one else matters," I assured her. I saw Ethan moving through the crowd towards us. I kissed her forehead and pulled away just as her husband made it to us.

"Can I steal her away?" He asked. I let her go and bowed out.

"Just remember what we said. We were here first," I teased and left them on the dance floor.

I grabbed another drink from the bar and cruised the floor. I decided I needed someone to share a bed with tonight. Three more drinks in and I was there. I had been dancing with a hot brunette named Allie. She came with her roommate Jamie, one of Ethan's friends.

For a wedding she was dressed rather slutty. It was black and backless. The front dipped low. It did pass her knees though, so maybe that was her justification for wearing it. I didn't care, as long as she let me take it off her.

We paused in our dancing to get another drink. I glanced at my watch. It was after midnight. The party was still in full swing, the guests hadn't thinned out at all. Cleo wouldn't miss me, I bet.

"So, Allie, you wanna get out of here?" I asked, pushing her hair back behind her ear. She raised an eyebrow suggestively and nodded.

"I'll grab a ride," she said. I told her I had to say goodnight to the happy couple. I kissed Cleo one more time and shook

Ethan's hand, congratulating him again, hurrying out before I lost any of my buzz.

Allie had a car waiting to take us back to her place. As soon as the car took off she pounced on me. I had to push her away so I could unbutton my shirt. She was intent on getting me naked as soon as she could. Thankfully the ride was short.

Stumbling up to her building, we took the elevator up to her floor. Her hands were down my pants tugging at me. I closed my eyes and let out a groan. Oh, I missed this. I haven't had sex in months.

As soon as we were in her apartment, I picked her up and she directed me to her bedroom where I promptly banged her brains out.

Acknowledgments

This book started with a scene from a dream. (Cheesy I know) A young man and young woman were in a parking lot at night fighting over the fact that he was helping her plan a birthday party for their kids, even though he couldn't even claim them as his own. He kept asking where the supposedly great dad was, but she couldn't give him a good answer.

I don't remember how the rest of this book came to be, but that dream always stayed with me and still to this day is one of my favorite scenes in the book because it started it all.

Now to get a little more real, I do have some people to thank. Steph Hightree, without you I wouldn't have found my editor. Kristin Downer, my editor, you were the first one to read my book to completion and stuck with it despite the lack of commas or the ones placed in, weird, places, where they, shouldn't be. My Beta readers, when I asked, you said yes before I could finish my sentence. I needed that support. Mae, my critique partner, you read some of my most intimate scenes first and helped me make sure they were just right. FrinaArt for the perfect cover, happened upon by pure chance. Caroline Andrus for making my book look pretty, and last but not least, Celina Saucedo, for taking a chance on me and my book by agreeing to narrate it. You will give Cleo a voice, and you are going to rock it.

About the Author

With her dark eyeliner, My Chemical Romance tattoo, and the Twilight series still proudly displayed on her bookshelf, Tylor Paige is punk rock kid. A sucker for a good love triangle and second chances, she knew the wonderful world of romance writing was where she was meant to be.

When she's not writing, Tylor enjoys watching cult films, procrastinating on twitter, and searching for the next book to add to her ever growing collection. She writes for the readers who love, obsess, and collect, like her. Her ultimate dream is for people to write fanfiction about her stories and characters. Perhaps she'll inspire someone to write their own book boyfriend.

Find her on:
Tylorpaigebooks.com

facebook.com/tylorpaigeauthor
twitter.com/TylorPaige

CPSIA information can be obtained
at www.ICGtesting.com
Printed in the USA
FFHW020400120119
50104981-54970FF